BEAUTY'S CURSED PRINCE

A CINDERELLA FAIRYTALE RETELLING

THE CURSED BEAUTY SERIES
BOOK THREE

MARY E. TWOMEY

MARY E. TWOMEY, LLC

BEAUTY'S CURSED PRINCE

A Cursed Beauty Novel
Book Three

By

Mary E. Twomey

COPYRIGHT

Copyright © 2018 Mary E. Twomey, LLC
Cover Art by Shayne Leighton
of Parliament House Book Designs

For information:
http://www.maryetwomey.com

DEDICATION

For Maybee

Forever my princess who conquers whole kingdoms with her gentleness.

HENRY AND HENRY

Henry stared at his phone, his face a wash of indignation. Since he had no audience, he spoke to his phone as if it was his best friend's stubborn face. "The nerve! You can't hang up on me just because I check in on you, Rory. You married a man whose Pulse had to be taken away, it was so deadly. I'm not overreacting."

Henry wanted to say more, but slid his phone into his pocket. He tried not to let the frustration affect him, but that seemed to be a losing battle.

Rory Johnstone had married a Lethal, which meant Henry felt no shame in calling her more often than usual. He'd felt a mild pang of chagrin when he interrupted her honeymoon, and even permitted her new husband, Cordray, to chew him out for a good five minutes before he'd agreed to back off. That, of course, meant only one phone call per day, as opposed to nearly a dozen. As her best friend, Henry felt it was his duty to make sure Rory was, at the very least, alive.

Henry ran his hand through his blond hair, glancing around the foyer of the palace before his eyes landed on his father's raised eyebrows. "Oh, I didn't see you there."

The King of Avondale was known and beloved for many things, and rarely spoke out of turn. He closed the leather-bound day-planner he was holding and tucked it under his arm, adjusting his tie. "How is our dear Rory doing? Settling into married life well, I hope?"

Henry took in a long breath through his nose before he answered. "She's fine. I'm fine. We're fine. I'm glad she's happy and all; I just didn't expect her to settle down with a Lethal. I'm worrying more than I was expecting to."

The king smoothed his hand over the buttons on his pressed shirt, looking every bit the part of the professional. Since they were on the main floor of the palace, important officials were permitted to walk through with the escort of a guard. King Hubert's hair, angular jaw, high cheekbones and easy smile matched his son's perfectly. The only difference was that the king had a few wrinkles around the corners of his pale blue eyes, and his chest was slightly less barreled than the late-twenties prince. "Cordray is still on the pill, yes? His magic is muted?"

Henry nodded. "He can't hurt Rory by accidentally Pulsing his deadly electricity into her with a stray touch. I get that." He shook his head at himself, his shoulders slumping. "The whole thing is throwing me, is all."

"Did you wish your betrothal to Rory had held? Is that what's really bothering you?"

Henry's eyes widened as he leaned back against the closed front double doors, glancing up at the elaborate crystal chandelier. He recalled running around the palace with Rory and Adam when they were children. They'd chosen the ornately tiled circle under this chandelier as the safety zone when playing tag.

How he wished for a safety zone now, one where he could tell his oldest friend anything, and she'd truly hear his heart. Henry studied the golden loops and twists above, wondering where things had fallen so far off the track that he couldn't make himself understood to the one woman who'd always known his mind. "No, I don't want to marry Rory. She's like a sister to me. It's that she just barely woke from her coma, and now she's diving headfirst into what could be a dangerous situation."

The king nodded sagely. "Ah. The papers are still printing pictures of the kingdom's Sleeping Beauty. Her wedding was months ago, Henry. Perhaps you should let her go a bit."

Henry snorted at the name the press had given her. Before, they'd called her "the Chancellor's daughter," or the snarkier papers, "the Chancellor's shamed Deadpulse daughter." When true love's kiss had woken her from her coma, Rory's magic was finally awakened. She could perform all the spells she'd failed at before, and finally won the respect that should've been hers all along.

When her father passes away someday, she would sit in the Chancellor's chair as head of the council. When Henry's father passes someday, he would rule Avondale. The two got along better than most President and Vice President pairings did.

Henry shoved his hands into the pockets of his khakis. "What if Cordray forgets to take his pill? What if he rolls over in bed one night and electrocutes her by accident? I like him and all, but this whole thing is going to give me an ulcer."

The king chuckled at his son's consternation, letting his folder go and floating it in the air at his side, so he could reach down and tug at his sock that had slipped to discomfort. "I guess I know how you'll be voting on Proposition 7," the king said as he stood. He looked every bit like his son, only with brushes of silver lining his temples. While his glory days playing rugby were far behind him, he was still almost as imposing as his tall, broad-shouldered son, especially when he went head-to-head with members of the council who occasionally got out of hand.

Henry shrugged. "I had my opinions before, but now I don't know. I keep going back and forth."

"Forfeiting all of one's magic to mute one's Lethal abilities is a steep price to pay, but that's the only option I can offer them. The pill has its shortcomings, but it took so long to get it where it is now. It's a viable option if you want to keep your loved ones safe when your Pulse is deadly. I've invested all I care to in the project. The Baron thinks privately-funded companies might be able to take the pill to the next level—muting the deadlier aspects, while still allowing Lethals to perform perfunctory magic."

"And what do you think?"

The king met his son's gaze with a tight smile. "Henry, it's the Baron's idea. When have I ever not trusted the Baron?"

The two shared a loaded chuckle. The Baron was a snide, sniveling weasel who was always vying for more power. It had been the Chancellor's seat he'd had his eyes on for too long, but now it seemed the Baron had moved on to wanting control over the pill. "Fair point. So you're saying I shouldn't vote yes on Proposal 7?"

The king shrugged, a wizened look softening his eyes, making them crinkle around the edges. "I'm saying I have faith in your decision-making process. I know you'll steer the country well someday." He glanced at the watch on his wrist. "The guests will be arriving soon. Remind me again why I host these dinners?"

Henry gripped his father's shoulders, looking him in the eye as if he were a football coach. "Dinners for the Elite are important rituals for the council and other officials to get together in a non-political setting. They're supposed to use the opportunity to make friends with people who have opposing views, and not talk politics, so we have a more unified nation, even when we disagree."

"Right. That sounds exactly like something I'd say—wise but taxing. Tell me that each day only holds twenty-four hours, and this one won't drag on beyond it."

"This evening will feel like an eternity, but it's worthwhile. This is a good thing you're doing—encouraging the leaders to see beyond their own agendas."

"Yes, I'm very smart. One day when the throne is yours, I hope you have a son of your own who can talk you through each of the brilliant ideas you hate." King Hubert and Henry shared a smirk as Henry slapped his father hard on the shoulder twice. The king checked his watch. "See that you make it to the dining hall before the Baron, otherwise I'll be forced to sit next to him. He's been taking garlic pills." He shuddered, and then grabbed his folder out of the air and tucked it back under his arm, kissing his son's cheek before leaving for his study.

Henry deflated against the doors the moment his father left. He always hated when his father made comments like that, bringing to attention that the adored king might not always be around. Many people in Henry's position would be happy to inch closer to the crown, but that would only mean his father wouldn't be there—a concept that sat heavy in his stomach. He knew that when the time came, he would rise to the occasion. But no one seemed to realize that the day he put on the crown would mean that his father was no more.

Henry couldn't think of a worse thing.

His secondary cell phone buzzed with a text from his date last night. He thumbed the nude photo she sent him to entice him into another night out, at which he merely chuckled. That was far beyond his level of commitment. No matter how much fun they'd had during their night together, a second date felt like a marriage, which made him itch to delete her from his contacts.

His primary cell phone rang, and he answered immediately. Only his family, the palace staff and his small circle of true friends had his real cell phone number. "I'm sorry, Rory. I was overbearing."

Rory's gentle voice came out in a rush. "I don't like it when we fight. Let's be sorry and forgiving, and forget it ever happened."

A lazy grin swept over Henry's handsome face. "Darling, telling the kingdom I'm amazing in bed means never having to say you're sorry."

Rory giggled through her nose at the innocuous flirtation. They'd never slept together, though the tabloids had entertained the masses with many stories countering the truth. "I'll be careful. Cordray doesn't have a problem taking the pill. We both have alarms set to make sure we don't forget."

"For what day? I'll set one, too. Then you'll only get a territorial overprotective phone call from me once a month."

"I can't imagine you'll show that much restraint."

Henry could hear the smile in Rory's voice. "First of the month. But if you're not barking at me about things I'm already on top of, then I'll miss out on all of your fantastic apologies. I'm not sure it's worth the trade-off."

"I miss you," Henry admitted. "Tell me you're almost here."

"I am. Be nice to Cord."

"Fine. I'll offer to make out with him first, and then you second, so he'll feel all important."

"What a gentlemanly proposition."

"Pass!" Henry heard Cordray shout in the background.

Henry sighed as he walked through the walls of the palace that were outlined with gold-painted wainscoting and baseboards. He passed the portrait of his deceased mother on the wall and blew her a kiss, as he always did whenever he happened by it.

"That was our longest fight yet," he commented. "I didn't care for it. In fact, I wrote whole oceans of sappy poetry in the two minutes we were at odds. Would you like to hear some of it?"

Rory groaned good-naturedly. "Not even if it's in song form."

"Of course it's in song. How else does one apologize to a fine lady like yourself?"

"You're too much," Rory chuckled.

"You're exactly the right amount of everything. Tell your husband the second he drops the ball, I'll be marking my territory, peeing all over you to tell the world you're mine."

Cordray sounded bored, if not mildly irritated when he chimed in. "You realize I can hear you, right?"

"Oh, Cord. Don't be jealous. I can pee on you, as well. I had no idea you were so fond of such things." Making Rory laugh was easy enough for him to accomplish but it was satisfying every time. "See you soon, sweetheart. You too, Rory."

"Please don't pee on me when you do," she requested through her laughter.

"I make no promises." Henry ended the call and moved into the kitchen, pinching Carlotta's pudgy waist just to make her jump and shriek with indignation. She'd burped him as a baby, but didn't hesitate to get out the dish towel and whap at the prince's caddish grin.

"Henry, I swear! I'm putting the finishing touches on the rolls. What if I'd messed up the Baron's?"

"Which one is the Baron's? I'll rub it under my armpits for good luck."

Carlotta narrowed her eyes, her flour-covered hands on her generous hips. "I swear, you make me crazy some days." The doorbell rang, and her eyes widened. "They're already arriving! Move out of the way. I have to get these in the oven."

"You have to relax, otherwise people are going to think we run too tight a ship around here. Dinner will be served when it's ready. You're looking at this all wrong. The stuffy officials don't hold the power; you do."

"Said the stuffy official himself."

Henry scoffed, his hand over his heart. "Dad and I adore you. Dinner is served when you get to it, and we're grateful every time."

Carlotta shoved the rolls in the oven and sighed. "I know. I love you, too, you sweet boy. It's not you; it's the others. The Baron's date has called three times with different specifications on how her meal is to be served. I'm half-tempted to rub her portion in the dirt."

Henry's eyes danced with mischief. "Which one is hers? Come on, let me mess with it."

Carlotta's round face was red with sweat, but she grinned for the boy she'd always adored. "You can mess with her all you like, but not her food. That will come back and bite me, for certain."

"Did you make me a pre-meal snack?"

"Only because I know you'll dig into the meal early if I don't. Top shelf of the fridge, sweet pea. But if the guests are arriving, you should go out and greet them with your father."

"I will, I will. But a growing boy needs nourishment."

Carlotta blew a raspberry and waved her hand at the jar of preserves, so it screwed itself on without her having to touch it while she busied herself in the cupboard. "You're nearly thirty! The only way you're going to grow is wider if you keep eating two dinners."

Henry rubbed his toned abdomen as he pulled down a bowl of cut-up fruit and tossed the lid into the sink. "Just more of me to love. From Avondale's sexiest bachelor, to Avondale's sexiest Santa. The tabloids will eat up every glorious ounce of me."

Carlotta tossed her dish rag in his face, shaking her head at him with a smile as the cloth fell to the counter. "At least take that food out back. Don't eat it in front of your father's guests."

"Alright, alright." Though the air had the chill of fall to it, Henry didn't bother with a jacket if it meant he could put off the stuffy formalities for a few more minutes. It had been his father's idea to get the notable officials together every other month to have social niceties, so every interaction wasn't always about furthering an agenda. It was a good system, but Henry grew tired of the many occasions that required him to be on his best behavior.

The kitchen door on the side of the palace led to a small gazebo that was visible from the long, winding driveway. Henry didn't mind if the chauffeurs saw him, and sat and ate his bowl of berries while he waited for Rory's driver.

His phone buzzed with a text from Adam, his other best friend. The three had been inseparable from childhood, but recently Rory and Adam endured a falling out, in which she'd needed Adam, and he'd remained a hermit, stalwart in his resolve to seclude himself while the world still turned, often in need of his intervention.

"What have you done to me? You've stuck me with a cyborg. This woman you hired never sleeps. I swear, I got up this morning, and she'd shined all my shoes in the night. What am I supposed to do with that?"

Henry chuckled and typed in his response. *"Why yes, I believe I did see some wires sticking out from her hair. She's working out alright?"*

Henry loved his friends as they were, but every now and then, he found that they needed a little push. Rory had needed a push with Cordray in the beginning, and Adam needed someone to make sure...

Henry swallowed hard, the strawberries losing all flavor. He didn't like thinking of one of his best friends holed up alone in his castle, secluded from the world. The nurse and housekeeper Henry had hired to look after Adam seemed capable of handling Adam's prickly nature, which, Henry reasoned, perhaps did make her part-cyborg.

He could hear Adam's acerbic nature coming out in his text. *"Belle's fine, I guess. The next time you go hiring someone to work for me, make sure I actually need the help, which I don't. I can shine my own shoes."*

But you won't, Henry thought, pain twisting his handsome features. He summoned up his courage and spoke the truth to his friend. *"You haven't showered or gotten dressed in who knows how long. You wear that bathrobe like it's a uniform. Belle stays."*

Adam wasn't labeled "the beast" by the media for no

reason. He'd been cursed by Malaura nearly ten years prior. On his next birthday, Adam was destined to turn into a wolf and go off to join the Lupine. The curse deformed him and made fur sprout all over. Adam didn't go out of the castle much anymore—only when Henry and Rory forced him outside.

Henry knew Adam wouldn't respond to the hard truth, so he tucked his phone back in his pocket.

His attention was drawn from Adam's predicament when a car backfired up on the winding driveway. He didn't think much of it until smoke started spilling out of the hood. While most of the vehicles were sleek and waxed town cars, this sedan was a bit older, though not decrepit just yet. Henry put down his bowl of fruit on the bench in the gazebo and trotted up the embankment toward the car. "Can I help you out? That didn't sound all that great."

He expected a suited man in his fifties to come out of the driver's side, since that was the norm for these types of events. Henry's eyebrows rose when a flash of golden curls caught his eye, a look of determination pinching her button nose as she emerged. "I've got it. Thanks. Stupid carburetor. Does this all the time."

Henry was fascinated with her preoccupation, utterly transfixed by her frown. Usually women got within ten feet of him and lost their minds with the excitement of stardom. Her informal attire made him wonder whose driver she was. It seemed none of the more notable officials' staff got out of bed in anything short of a full business suit.

None of the other drivers offered to help until they saw the stunning woman in jeans and a white button-down inspecting the contents of the engine. Then suddenly everyone was a car expert, getting out of their vehicles to lend a hand.

Henry waved them off. "I think we've got it, gentlemen. As you were." Then to the woman, he offered a smile through the autumn chill that stung the nape of his neck. "I take it you're in need of a mechanic?"

She peered into the mess of wires as if frustrated with the puzzle she knew how to fix, but somehow couldn't. "Actually, just a wrench would do the trick for now." Her eyes closed in frustration. "But my tools are at home."

"You can use ours. Though, I confess, I don't know much about fixing carburetors."

"Thank you." She glanced around to the line of town cars, and waved them to pull around, mildly embarrassed. "Is it okay if I leave the car here like this while we go get some tools?"

Henry smirked at her, though she hadn't even looked up at him yet. "I'd wager we don't have much choice. The garage is just over there." He proffered his elbow to her, but she didn't take it.

Instead, she held up her hands and finally met his eyes with a sheepish note of apology. "I don't want to stain your shirt. But thanks for the gentlemanly escort."

She was stunning in a way that made him wish he could study her features for far too long. Her deep blue eyes were more vibrant than his. Her heart-shaped face was utterly captivating – complete with naturally pink and plump lips, rosy cheeks and a sweetness to her smile that made him want to lean a little closer.

Henry walked beside her, shoving his hands in his pockets to keep from fidgeting. "I'm Henry."

"Nice to meet you. Do you get many cars breaking down in the driveaway of the royal palace, or am I just the luckiest of all the girls?" She grinned over at him, revealing deep dimples that didn't disappear when her smile faded to a pleasant expression.

"The fortune's all mine." Henry blanched the moment the words hit the air. He'd wanted to come across as his usual charming self, but he sounded like some stuffy royal. He wanted to say something funny just so he could see her smile again, but he was coming up empty. "That sounded stupid. My name's Henry."

The woman sniggered, but covered her mouth out of politeness. "You said that already."

He cringed. "This would be the part where you tell me your name."

"My name is also Henry," she deadpanned, her hands in her pockets.

He narrowed his left eye at her. Most women were too nervous around him to poke fun, or they came onto him like cats in heat. "Hilarious."

"That's what they call me. Hilarious Henry who can't go on the freeway without overworking her carburetor." Her smile drifted away, but the wells in her cheeks remained, transfixing Henry as they walked. He wanted to touch them, but guessed that wouldn't be appropriate. "I'm not a fan of unreliable cars, but that seems to be the way of things."

"To be fair, you're relying on one that's probably more than half your age."

When they reached the garage, Henry cursed himself for not spending more time learning how to fix cars. He'd had a driver since he was born. Though he had his license and drove himself occasionally, he didn't know the first thing about vehicle maintenance.

He cast around for a toolbox, relieved when he opened the third tall white cabinet on the side of the sixteen-car garage and found one. "Here you are, Henry," he said with that same squinty eye.

"Why, thank you, Henry." When she glanced up at him, he was treated to a fresh view of her loveliness. Her blonde waves were swept back, fashioned with two crossed pencils that allowed a handful of ringlets to escape and tickle the nape of her neck. "You're the prince, then?" She shot him a look that bore a small bit of hesitance, as if needing it confirmed how far out of her world he was.

Henry flashed a bright smile that always dazzled his dates. "It seems a little showy to introduce myself with my title." He reached into his pocket. "Let me call Maximus. He services our cars, and he can give yours a look."

The woman waved her hand, gripping the toolbox with the other. "No need. Unless he's got a new carburetor up his sleeve, I can handle it." When Henry's face fell at not having a reason to stick around her, a small smile pulled her mouth to the side. "Feel like learning how to do a poor man's fix on an old engine? Being that we've got the same name and all, I figure you'd be good with your hands. All Henrys are."

The prince's face lit up at her slight teasing. "Only if I can carry the toolbox. It'll make it more believable when I tell my dad I helped fix a car with my bare hands."

The two chuckled together as they walked back up the embankment. With every step they took, Henry realized when he bantered with her, the fall breeze wasn't quite so chilly anymore.

2

BAD BOY HENRY

"You're ridiculous," Henry commented, turning the bolt as per her instructions. "There. Is that right, then?"

"You're holding back. She's an old one, so the bolts come loose at the slightest bump or rattle. Crank it until she won't turn for you anymore."

Henry complied, letting out a small grunt as he gave it his all. "Why does everything you say sound so filthy?"

"It's a gift." Then she looked down at his wrist and grimaced. "Oh, no! Your sleeve is dirty. I told you I should be the one with my hands in her."

"See? Absolutely raunchy."

She sniggered, shaking her head at him. "Seriously, Henry. Your sleeve has an oil stain on it. If you've got some club soda, I can get that out, and no one will know."

Henry quirked his eyebrow at her, tilting his head to

the side at her fretting. "Wow. Who do you work for that runs such a tight ship? We're not nearly so strict around here."

"Lady Tremaine," she replied with a closed expression that chased away all the lightness from her features.

"Who?"

"Exactly." Then, as if catching herself being sassy, she straightened, looking over her shoulder. "That was rude. I didn't mean that. I just meant that this is her first time at one of your events. She was invited by the Baron. She's very excited to be here; I shouldn't have been so rude."

"Ah," Henry replied with a knowing nod. "Carlotta mentioned the Baron's date was a bit of a pain."

She giggled, but then caught herself in the scandalous act. She stepped back and fiddled with her sleeve, and Henry could practically see the guilt washing over her in waves at speaking her true mind. "Lady Tremaine is particular. Lots of very successful and amazing people have a keen eye for detail."

Henry turned to her, confused at her sudden shift. "I guess that's true. You alright?"

She shook her head, biting down on her lower lip. "I don't like to gossip. It makes me feel dirty to say mean things about other people, even if they're true."

Henry studied her slight movements as if she were a strange bug he couldn't help but be endeared to. His social life was peppered with, and surrounded by, gossip. It's what made the tabloid world go 'round. "Then you'll have to forgive me while I try to catch up. If I leave the house without a tie on, the rumors start to spread that I'm on the brink of losing my title and my fortune. A citizen who doesn't appreciate gossip? I think you just might be the first." He tossed the wrench back into the box, and then watched while she straightened it, hooking it inside the tin lid on a small loop he hadn't thought to look for. "I wonder what you might say if you gave in to such tawdries as gossip. You look like you have oceans inside of you, just begging to burst out."

Her eyes darted around, noting that all the other drivers were in their cars, waiting out the event with their noses buried in books or tablets. Still, she lowered her voice. "I might say that Lady Tremaine could find the flaw in anything—create a smudge on a pure canvas with her imagination, and then blame the world for not being as sparkly as everyone else sees it."

Henry leaned in, utterly captivated by her response, and felt privileged that he'd been the lucky one to coax the truth out of her. "You can't confess your true thoughts to me and still keep your name a secret. We're old friends now. You can't be 'Henry' to me anymore."

She shook her head, a bashful smile playing on her lips. "I'm no one you'll see after today. Let's just let this be a fun memory."

Henry's lips pursed at her secretive nature. "I'm just going to ask Lady Tremaine who her beautiful driver is."

All the play fled from her face as her eyes grew wide in

earnest. "Don't. Please. She doesn't like when people notice me. It'll get me into trouble."

Henry's brows pushed together as he frowned. "I hardly think it's possible not to notice you. I mean, look at you." He motioned to her face and then her form, but then straightened awkwardly, hoping he hadn't been inappropriate. She had a trim waist, a sweet curve to her hips, and sizeable breasts he tried not to glance at. "Sorry. But have you seen the other drivers? You're a diamond in a sea of trolls."

Her chin lowered as if to savor the compliment. When her eyes lifted again to meet his, true appreciation shone there, bathing him with the full force of her beauty. "See? You can't be doing that. You just went and said the perfect thing. How's a girl supposed to resist charm like that?"

He crossed his arms over his chest. "I think I should get your name for my good behavior."

She opened her mouth, but closed it again when her stomach rumbled. "You should go back to your party. I'm keeping you from the fun."

"Come on inside. I'll get you something to eat."

For the first time in their exchange, she looked scared. Her gaze shifted toward the palace, and she visibly backed away. "No. I mean, no thank you. I'm not hungry." As if on cue, her stomach growled again. "Ignore that. It makes that sound sometimes."

"When you're hungry?" he asked, perplexed. "Funny, that." When she didn't concede, he motioned to the gazebo in the backyard. "How about the outdoors? Are you allowed to eat with me there?"

She met his eyes with a look that told him something was burning to burst out of her, but her lips kept whatever confession she had tucked tight inside. "I think that would be okay. So long as no one sees us."

Henry craned his neck back to look at her from a slightly different angle. "Is this... Is this what it feels like when someone's ashamed to be seen with a person? I'll admit, that's a first for me."

She shook her head apologetically. "No! No, it's not that. Who would be ashamed to be seen with you? You're perfectly nice. It's just that Lady Tremaine wouldn't approve. When she gets cross, she's... unpleasant to live with." She covered her mouth and let out a bleat of frustration. "You're a bad influence on me! I never gossiped this much before I met you."

Henry's cocky smile crept back onto his features. "That's what they call me. Bad Boy Henry."

She sniggered at him and picked up the toolbox. "They call you Prince Charming, and they're not wrong." She walked with him to the gazebo, sitting down a respectable distance from him. Her dodgy glances didn't stop until Henry offered her the bowl of strawberries he'd left on the bench, and her eyes zoomed in on the goodness.

"Have some," Henry said when it was clear she wasn't presumptuous enough to take what she wanted.

"Are you sure?"

She was so adorable, but Henry couldn't enjoy the sight of her cuteness. There was something sad about a woman who was astonished over a bowl of fruit being shared with her. As if she didn't deserve nice things such as... food. "Help yourself. I can get you an extra dinner from the kitchen, too."

"No, no. Don't go to any trouble. This is plenty." She bit into a berry, moaning at the luxury. "Oh, these are amazing. Have you tasted them? They're so fresh."

Henry chewed on his lower lip, reminding himself to be a gentleman. Watching her eat was positively erotic, her lips wrapping around each berry, savoring every bite. He draped his arm across the back of the bench behind her, loving that he could fulfill a need she had.

"I'm being rude," she said apologetically, and then offered him the bowl. "I'm sorry, I'm plowing through more than my half. Here."

He could've watched her eat forever, but at her insistence, he opened his mouth and moved his chin a little nearer, wondering if he could tempt her closer.

Her cheeks heated as she glanced around, confirming that they were alone. "Bad Boy Henry, indeed." She smirked as she fed him a berry, wetting her lips when she brushed her fingertips across the curve of his mouth. Then she pulled back, caution flaring in her eyes. "We can't do that," she whispered, offering him the bowl.

"Can't do what? My arm is broken. In fact, it's fallen clean off. I'm utterly helpless. Are you the kind of person who turns her back on the wounded?" He feigned a pitiful sniffle and gave her a clear shot of his puppy dog eyes. "If it helps, I served a term in the army, so technically I'm a war vet."

She shook her head at him. "You are absolutely incorrigible." Despite her scolding, she pressed another berry to his lips, letting him kiss her fingertips this time. Her breathing grew uneven at the slow tease, taking in Henry's hungry eyes with unconcealed longing.

And yet, she continued. Another strawberry, and another—each one brought the two inching closer until he could smell the sweetness of her breath.

Henry wanted to pounce, to devour her lower lip that seemed to call to him and erase all higher brain functions. Though he still didn't know her name, he was desperate to kiss her. Through her hesitance she leaned in, and Henry knew this was the green light he was yearning for. No one captured his attention like she had. No one made him wonder as much as her.

The moment he leaned in, Carlotta's voice broke through the grounds. "Henry! Son, are you out there? Your father's looking for you."

Henry was crestfallen when she jumped up and shoved the bowl of berries at him. "I have to go! I'm sorry. I shouldn't have... I wasn't thinking!"

"Wait! It's just Carlotta. She doesn't care."

"I'm supposed to be waiting in the car. You never saw me out here!"

Henry wanted to grab her and demand she tell him her name, birthday, address, shoe size, favorite color, and a million other things. He wanted so much more, but she was already scurrying off the gazebo and running away. Henry stood, his fist clenched in frustration with himself. He'd never cared much who occupied the seat next to him —there was always someone to take it. But now that he finally had an opinion about who sat there, he couldn't keep her in one place long enough to understand her.

What's more, she'd only eaten a handful of fruit, and he wondered if she needed more.

"Henry, don't you make me come out there."

"Coming, Carlotta." He clutched the bowl, wanting to follow after her, but knowing he had to tend to his duties. His entire body tightened with regret as she trotted up the embankment toward the driveway, disappearing into her car as she locked herself inside.

3

A LETHAL AMONG THEM

*H*enry cringed at the grating laugh from across the table. It sounded like a mix between a cartoon character and breaking glass. He'd never paid attention to who the Baron brought to these dinners, but tonight he was tuned in to every move made by Lady Tremaine. She was tall with a long neck, reminding Henry of a gangly ostrich. She had black hair that was pulled too tight into a bun at the top of her head, wreathed with golden combs. Her low-cut dress stood out, since all of the other women at the dinner were either in professional office wear or tasteful dresses befitting a refined dinner at the palace. Lady Tremaine's freckled and wrinkled breasts were on display for the Baron, pushed up garishly and demanding attention.

"I mean, his butler had never heard of a ceramic burr grinder. Can you imagine?" Again, the tinkling laugh tumbled out of her, and she placed her hand on the Baron's forearm.

Henry blanched, but tried to keep his displeasure from view. The Baron's hooked nose was constantly wet, and his greasy slicked-back hair made him look as slippery as his motives. He chortled at Lady Tremaine's quipping, his eyes slipping to her cleavage none too subtly.

Rory touched her fork to Henry's knife. "Hey, mister. You look about five seconds from jumping across the table to throttle the Baron."

"I've got a solid ten seconds in me before anything like that happens." Henry tore his eyes from the odd couple and brushed his shoulder to his best friend's. She'd always been placed at his table because of their betrothal. Their constant companionship was also due to her father being the Chancellor, which meant he was second only to the king. They'd kept each other company through too many of these dinners over the years, and now they had Cordray to share in their private asides. The dining hall was filled with almost a hundred notable officials, but when they were together, the whole world felt simpler and manageable.

Cordray cut a portion of his steak, a smirk playing on his ebony features. "Imagine if I hadn't asked you to marry me. You could've ended up with the Baron as your father-in-law if you'd given into his son's offer. Then your new mother-in-law could dress you."

Rory narrowed her eyes at her husband, keeping her

voice down. The table was long and wide, and the chatter around them was loud, so their conversation managed to stay semi-private. "Hilarious. Even if you hadn't proposed, I never would've married Calvin."

"Now, now. Don't say that. Calvin could've given you a good life, filled with leering, posturing and backstabbing."

"Every little girl's dream," she simpered, reaching over to lace her pale fingers through her husband's. A few diners nearby caught the scandal and hissed their disapproval. Rory's chin raised in defiance, her grip on her husband tightening to declare to the elite that her love for Cordray wouldn't be hidden or shamed to make the meal more palatable for those who felt her love life was their business.

Henry noted with relief that Cordray was wearing black driving gloves. Though Cordray was on the pill to mute his Lethal abilities, it was widely known that the Chancellor's daughter had been saved from her coma, only to marry a man that might one day accidentally murder her with an errant touch. Everyone was a little wary around Cord who, aside from his deadly Pulse, Henry had no issues with.

As the meal went on, course after course was served to the sound of polite, thinly-veiled political posturing. Henry's father, the Chancellor, and the Chancellor's wife were having hushed conversations about the many ramifications of Proposal 7, and what could be done to soften the blow for anyone who fell on the losing side of their vote when the ballots were cast.

Henry usually did his part to be the son of the greatest ruler their kingdom had seen in decades. His great-great-grandfather had been a horror to his people, taxing them beyond reason. His great-grandmother had been dubbed the "Wicked Queen" for going after Snow White, who next took the throne. Then of course, after Queen Snow came Malaura, his aunt, who'd been killed by Cordray upon his escape from her clutches.

Henry sighed as he glanced at his father, wishing his mother were alive to see him handling the throne so regally. Henry knew it was not without much effort or upset, but King Hubert loved his people. Henry only hoped that one day when it was his turn, he would rule with the same level head and generosity of spirit.

He wanted to wolf down his dinner and slip out so he could spend more time with... He still wasn't sure what her name was, but the woman waiting just outside in his driveway had drawn him in so thoroughly that he barely tasted his dinner.

"Prince Henry, your pictures in Lady Aurora's wedding were simply adorable," Lady Tremaine said, leaning forward so she could give the prince a clear shot of her bosom. She was a few seats down and across from them, but lifted her voice so she could be heard by him and several others. "I can't believe she had you declared her Maid of Honor. You two must have a special bond—to have been betrothed, and then be given up for an outsider."

Rory stiffened, but her smile remained firmly in place while she chewed. Henry touched his foot to hers, as they often did in solidarity when one of them was challenged. He imagined that when he became king and she was the Chancellor, they would have each other's backs much the same way.

"Indeed, we do." Henry donned a light smile, making sure not to glance down at Lady Tremaine's breasts, as it was clear she wanted him to do every time she leaned forward with a faux-coy smile.

The Baron elbowed his date and pointed with his knife at Cord. "Cordray isn't just an outsider; he's a Lethal, as well."

Henry met the tightening of Cordray's gaze with a silent warning to breathe through the public needling. This was part of the gig; but losing one's temper when pushed was not. Cordray's shoulders remained taut with tension, but the affront smoothed from his face at Henry's nod of solidarity.

Lady Tremaine feigned surprise with wide eyes and a hand across her chest. "My! You know, I think I did hear something about that. I just assumed it was all rumors. To think that the Chancellor would allow his daughter to take up with someone who could murder her if left unchecked! But then again, perhaps that's why Chancellor Stefan has held onto his seat for so long when it's clear retirement should be in the cards. He knows not to pass his power down the bloodline when his daughter's in such a precarious position." Then she laughed at the absurdity. "Smookie-poo, could you pass me the gravy? My potatoes are a little dry."

King Hubert placed his hand on his son's knee under the table. "Steady, son. Let Stefan handle it." There was the weighty command to stay in place, since Henry didn't take kindly to complaints about Rory, Cordray, or the food. Henry was viciously protective of his best friend, and by proxy, Cordray. Carlotta had been his surrogate mother growing up, so a slight on the meal was a slap across her face, as far as he was concerned.

The Chancellor's tone was light as he placed his napkin on the table. "Forgive me, what is your name, ma'am?"

"Lady Tremaine," she said with a saccharine smile. She had thin lips that revealed her wide, bubbly gums when she grinned. "I'm so pleased to be eating at the same table as the great Chancellor and the King of Avondale."

"Pleasure. My daughter was only in danger from Malaura, whom Cordray was instrumental in taking down. We trust our new son with our daughter's life, and don't lose a moment of sleep about it."

Rory's Uncle Remus, the sharp-dressed Chancellor's brother, chimed in from his brother's left. "Cordray is my nephew now. He's part of the ruling families. Lethal or not, it's not a person's Pulse that decides who they are, but what they do with the power they have—whether it be great or very, very small." Remus said the last few words like a dig, making sure Lady Tremaine knew her sugar-coated slights would not be tolerated. Remus exchanged a look of familial loyalty with Rory, and then with Cordray.

Henry had always loved Remus, and tonight was a perfect reminder why.

The Baron's smile always looked like a grimace, unless he was gleeful over something terrible happening, in which case the expression came more naturally to him. "Now, now. There's no need to worry, my sweet. Cordray is on the pill, so he's no harm to you." He fawned over Lady Tremaine, touching her face as if he was preening her. Though she was easily four inches taller than him, he acted as if she was a wilting flower, and she played the part of the delicate damsel to appease him. The Baron's eyes cut to Cord. "Isn't that right, Cordray? Assure my date that she's in no danger of being murdered in cold blood by a Lethal. Tell her you're on the pill, and she has no need to fear you."

Cord's jaw was tight. His eyes were on his food, but he opened his mouth to comply with the public needling he found himself subject to at random. "I..."

Remus was quick to cut off Cordray. "I can't imagine how that's any of your business. We aren't asking you about what medications you're on over your supper. You can see he's wearing gloves, so of course he's no danger to anyone here." Remus ran his hand over his tie, changing it from canary yellow, to pink, and finally settling on blue. It was a subconscious habit he did when he was in deep thought.

Rory put down her fork and glared at the Baron. "My husband is a great man. You'll do well to remember who defeated Malaura. It's gratitude you should be giving him, not a subtle inquiry." She turned her chin to address her uncle. "And you don't need to ask the Baron what sort of medicine he takes. It's clear he swallowed an entire bottle of garlic pills before he came here."

Henry choked on his lambchop, his eyes watering. He took the glass of water Rory offered him and washed his mouthful down, wishing he could jump in on the subtle digs.

The Baron chuckled, as if Rory had said something funny. "Now that you've finally found your Pulse, you've got something to say. Good for you, Aurora. Tell me, have you learned to levitate a teacup yet?"

King Hubert picked up his fork and tapped it twice to his crystal goblet, clanging it gently to rein everyone in. That was all it took for the table to fall silent. The other tables in the dining hall also ceased their chatter, respecting the king as he stood.

"It seems there's some confusion over whether or not the pill is mandatory, and whether or not it's anyone's business what another person's Pulse is." King Hubert didn't raise his voice, but it carried effortlessly through the room.

The king's expression was pleasant enough, but there was a firm command in his eyes that warned the world he would not be trifled with. "Let me be perfectly clear: it is not. Just as we don't expect you to report if you own a knife in your home to protect yourself with, we don't expect Lethals to register themselves or wear some sort of sign to declare to the public that they should be feared and treated as lepers. The only reason they come to us is for help to make sure their loved ones are safe from errant mishaps, and we are glad to assist." He looked out at the elite and raised his glass. "We will not have division amongst ourselves over a simple flip of genetics. We will be unified, or we will be nothing."

Then the king glanced down at Cordray, who sat taller in his chair. "I don't know about you, but I don't want to be nothing. I don't prefer a legacy of simple and petty nothing. To us," he said, and everyone toasted the king's words, making them their own.

Henry always loved his father, but that night he was reminded anew of how much he respected the man who saw through the fight of the moment to a brighter outcome for his people. Henry nurtured a deep respect for the relationship between his father and the Chancellor. They didn't always agree on every single issue, but they found a way to hold tight to their friendship through the years. Henry only hoped he would have the same tight bond with Rory forever, taking on her causes and shielding her when the public threw stones, as they inevitably did.

When King Hubert was about to sit, it was clear Rory decided she couldn't take it anymore. She rose from her seat and moved past Henry to his father. She wrapped her arms around him, raising up on her toes like a ballerina. "Thank you," she said to him. "I would have been proud to call you my father-in-law, had that been my destiny."

"And you are always the daughter I'm most proud of. Cordray is a good man." King Hubert embraced the girl he'd known from birth, and had hoped would one day marry his own son. Though fate had other plans, he never stopped looking at Rory as the daughter he'd always wanted.

Henry loved his father for that, as well.

When the whispered fawning over the king's kindness finally died down, Rory moved to her own parents, kissing them both on the cheek, and then to her uncle, whom she high-fived.

Henry caught Cordray's tight gaze and gave him a nod of brotherhood, which Cord returned. It would be a long time before people accepted Lethals into the community, but Henry was determined that Cord would not be the leper among them. He was the only Lethal in the entire Dinner of the Elite.

Lady Tremaine's smile was tight and forced, and the Baron's had vanished completely.

4

TWO HENRYS IN THE CAR

*H*enry knew it was foolish to try and sneak back out to see Lady Tremaine's driver again, but he found he couldn't help himself. Cocktail hour was for mingling, with everyone milling about while a string quartet played in the background. It was usually the point in the evening where he, Rory, and now Cordray, too, would sneak out and play poker in the kitchen while Carlotta made them root beer floats, like she'd done when he, Rory and Adam were children.

Henry thanked his lucky stars that Rory seemed to want to introduce as many people as possible to Cord, integrating him into her world, so they wouldn't be so very afraid of him. The prince slipped away to the kitchen, grabbed a carton of strawberries, a banana and a tin of yogurt, and shoved it all in a bag. He wondered if he should bring her more, or if he was already looking a little desperate.

If he was being honest with himself, he was feeling a longing for something real. He didn't know if he would find it waiting out in his driveway, but something inside begged him to try.

He walked through the twilight towards the oldest car in the long line, running his free hand through his hair before he rapped his knuckles on the cracked window, startling her.

She grabbed a fistful of her shirt over her heart, her eyes bouncing toward the ceiling before shooting him a look of mild scolding. "You scared me!"

"Yeah? Well, you intrigued me. It's your own fault I'm back out here when I could be in there, eating my way through a croquembouche."

Her lips pursed before they broke out into a smile. She rolled her window down halfway, her big blue eyes soaking him in. "You are ridiculous. And you're going to get me into trouble."

"What trouble? Are you supposed to stay inside the car all evening? Were those your specific instructions?"

"I'm supposed to stay out of sight."

Henry leaned his forearm on the window, his expression growing serious. "Okay, level with me. Are you a spy?"

She paused, and then laughed airily through her nose. She unlocked the doors and motioned for him to come around to the other side. "Get in. Then I'm not breaking the rules."

Henry kept his head down as he walked to the passenger's side and slipped in. "For you. The prettiest Henry I've ever seen. Except for the one who greets me with a kiss in the mirror every morning. He's ravishing."

"Indeed. What is it?" She opened the bag and gasped. "For me?" The sun was setting, painting the sky in hues of orange and pink. He could see her tender expression as she looked over the contents with gratitude that surpassed her pride. "Thank you, Prince Henry."

He cut the flat of his hand in the air between them. "Just Henry. If you get to pick your name, then I get to choose mine. It's only fair."

"You didn't have to do this. I'm really fine."

"I ate most of the strawberries earlier. You looked like you could use a few more."

She took out the yogurt and peeled back the lid, smelling the contents with pure happiness before she dug in. "You didn't have to leave your fancy party to come out here and bring me food. That's real sweet of you."

"It was getting a little claustrophobic in there."

"With all of your adoring fans?" Her eyebrows bobbed a few times as she ate.

"Ha, ha. No. Your boss is making things real uncomfortable, talking down to Cordray in the middle of dinner, as if he needs to be put on a leash or something."

"Ah. That makes sense. She's trying to impress the

Baron, taking on his causes and putting a megaphone to them."

"I'm sure she's succeeding. But trust me, the Baron's the only one who's impressed."

She shrugged. "Then she got what she wants. Hopefully she'll be pleased."

Henry shifted in the old, yet immaculately clean grey interior. "How long has she been seeing him?"

"A few months. She's been trying to move her way up the social ladder. He was on her list."

"List?"

"Of eligible bachelors she could date to up her status." She spoke without emotion, as if they were talking about the weather. Then she smirked and pointed at Henry with her spoon. "You were on that list for a while. So was your father."

Henry shuddered. "Tell me you're joking." Though, upon second thought, he recalled Lady Tremaine trying to draw his eye with her breasts, as if that was all it took for him to follow a woman around.

She shook her head, her gaze focusing back on her yogurt. "It's best when she gets what she wants. If she desires the Baron, then I hope it works out, I guess. People should get what they want every now and then, right?"

"And what is it you want?" he asked quietly, with a slight playfulness to his voice.

She stared out the windshield without speaking for several beats, and for a moment, Henry wondered if she hadn't heard him. When she finally answered, her voice wasn't much louder than a whisper. "Nothing I can have."

Henry turned in his seat. "You mean to tell me a cup of yogurt and some fruit didn't solve all your problems? Huh. Goods not as advertised."

She broke out of her slight melancholy to share a smirk with the prince. "I'm perfectly content. I've got a roof over my head, work enough to keep my hands busy, and now I even get to share a picnic with my new friend. This is wonderful, by the way."

"I had to get out of there. Bringing you food was selfish on my part. Seeing your smile? Almost as lovely as the Baron's grin."

She laughed at Henry's imitation of the Baron's thin-lipped grimace that passed for his smile, deepening the dimples he loved to stare at. "Wow, that was spot on. I mean, if only your nose was running, you would match him perfectly." She scooped another dollop of yogurt. "I'm sorry you weren't enjoying your evening."

Henry tilted his head as he observed her. "You really mean that, don't you."

She nodded, and tucked a stray blonde curl behind her ear. "Of course. Who would wish a bad night on you? You seem pleasant enough."

"That's what they put under my title: Prince Henry – Pleasant Enough." They shared an airy giggle, and Henry realized how very easy it was to be himself around her. She was unassuming and unabashedly sweet. "Honestly, it was a little tense. The Baron is always trying to push his agenda at these things, which is a bad idea all the way around. These dinners are for officials to have a night away from politics, so we can all learn to get along as people, rather than operating only as representations of our policies."

"I think that's a wise idea for a party. So many times we get caught up in the things that divide us. It's nice to see you're part of something that's bent on uniting, even when that seems like an uphill battle."

"The parties are my father's brainchild." Henry tucked the compliment away, savoring the notion that she admired something his father had done. "He's very good at what he does."

"I'm sorry the Baron was being difficult. I guess some people can't turn it off. He must feel very strongly about locking up the Lethals."

Henry stiffened. "Is that your take on things, as well?"

She scolded him with a smile and a slight shake of her finger. "Now, I thought these parties weren't for politics." Then she leaned back in her seat and mulled over his question. "I think you can't choose the Pulse nature grants you. That's no reason to lock anyone up, as far as I'm concerned. Everyone has to learn to be responsible with their gifts. Lethals are no different." She ate another bite of yogurt. "If they do kill someone, however, then yes, they need to be locked up and rehabilitated."

"And what's your Pulse?"

"Private," she replied without missing a beat.

Henry frowned. "Same as your name? Is that private, as well?"

"I already told you, my name is Henry. It's probably why we get along so well."

"Hmm." Henry was beginning to feel the pangs of irritation. "Is there a reason you're being so secretive?"

"If there was, I'm not sure I'd come out and tell you." She sighed, staring out the window at the bumper ahead of hers. "Working for Lady Tremaine is... difficult. Nothing I can't handle, of course, but the last guy who came to the house looking to talk to me got me in a heap of trouble."

"And you think I'll come to your home and cause trouble? Do you live on her property?"

She nodded. "She's got two daughters around my age. They're not so different from their mother. They want to marry well, so any eyes that are diverted from them toward me tend to make my life more difficult."

"So, if I invited you to the next one of these dinners, you probably wouldn't be able to come." Henry's tone was glum as he scratched his cheek.

She turned to gape at him, bereft of any sort of reply. Henry watched too many emotions flash across her lovely features as she processed the offer. For a moment, his hopes raised when she leaned toward him, but then she drew back with the knee-jerk hesitance.

"I probably wouldn't." Then she did something so precious, Henry's whole body became endeared to her.

She reached across the console and linked her little finger around his. It wasn't quite hand-holding, but something that was just theirs. "But I would want to," she admitted, holding his gaze with a hint of longing for options such as the ones he presented. "I would want to very much."

Henry stared at their joined fingers, a wistfulness clutching his heart, making him wish for simpler times. "Do you ever feel like life's grown far too complicated?"

Her brows bunched together. "Aside from me not being able to go to your party, what's got you down?"

Henry's normal reaction to questions that invited him to open up was to shut tight and keep it all inside, lest his private thoughts leak to the press. But there was something about her that he instinctively trusted. He'd had that same inkling towards Belle—the woman he'd hired on the spot to be Adam's housekeeper and in-home nurse. It hadn't been long, but so far, there hadn't been any huge implosions Adam had reported, other than her egregious need to shine his shoes, apparently.

Henry studied her short fingernails, and stretched his thumb to trace along her wrist. "You can keep what we talk about between us?"

"You sincerely overestimate the amount of friends I have. Of course, Henry. What's overcomplicated in your life these days?"

Henry's mouth went dry, but he powered through. "The whole issue of Lethals wasn't a huge deal to me when we were drafting up policies, but now that one of my closest friends is married to one... I'm not sure."

She let his words hang and crackle around them for several beats before she pulled a few out of the air to examine more closely. "What aren't you sure about?"

"All of it. I don't know. I mean, I still stand by the spirit of the policy. We're not willing to divert more funds into developing the pill to grant Lethals their normal magic while muting their deadly abilities. It's a good idea, but not one that the government can justify paying for when there are other more harrowing things that need our attention and funds. Giving them a life where they don't have to be fearful of harming their loved ones is all we should be expected to provide the public. Anything beyond that is whipped cream—nice, but not crucial. Taxes should be spent on what's crucial, not what's comfortable."

She mulled over his words, running her tongue across her teeth as if she was tasting each syllable to see how it settled. "I think that's a fantastic policy. The one problem is that 'crucial' might be subjective to some people. Being cut off from all magic might seem like a Level 10 problem, while to others, it might seem to be a luxury. It may be that your criterion is good and noble, but hasn't been clearly quantified to the public. Perhaps spelling it out in terms of life and death, using that scale, might help people see your side more clearly."

It was Henry's turn to taste and test her words, turning

them over to see how they fit with his current plans and worldview. "You're right. I haven't been clear enough."

She offered him a compassionate expression, her eyes softening around the edges. "The good thing about that is it's a fixable problem."

"This is nice." Henry took a chance and brought her hand to his chest, cradling it over his heart. "You'll tell me all the holes in my politics, but you won't tell me your name?"

"You don't need my name. You're doing well enough on your own without me."

Henry plucked a pen from his pocket and took her napkin from the bag. "You may think I don't need your name, but I know for sure that you need my number. I'm guessing you won't give me yours?"

She stared at the napkin he handed her with his digits scrawled across in neat, blue script. "You're giving me your phone number?"

"I guess I am. The thing is, it's only useful if you use it."

She finally took the napkin and folded it twice, sticking it in her pocket. "Thank you."

"Still no name?" He tilted his head at her, his mouth drawing to the side in mild frustration.

She clung to her secret, while Henry clung to her hand in the quiet of their private moment.

CHEEKS AND FEET

"Ella! My dress needs ironing. It got left on the floor last night, and now it's all wrinkled."

When Lady Tremaine installed an intercom system in the house, Ella knew it would be the end of any semblance of quiet time. Her stepsister's voice was worse than a bullhorn—nasally and demanding as it was. Ella bit her tongue, but then let it loose to the squirrels that chased each other around her bedroom in the attic. "Shocking that when Anastasia leaves something on the floor, it stays there till morning." It was the fourth irritated order in the past twenty minutes, but Ella did her best to keep her complaining confined to her bedroom, trusting the pitched ceiling of the attic to trap her negativity so it didn't carry into the wind.

The squirrels paused and shook their fists in the air at

her stepsister, swearing to avenge Ella and right all the wrongs done to her.

She smiled at the creatures as she tied an apron around her jeans and tank top. Her apron was a man's flannel that had the back and sleeves cut off, leaving the high collar and front intact, with a ribbon to secure it tight to her waist. She adored her little creations that made her feel fashionable, as opposed to existing as only a functional being.

Memories of the night she'd shared with Prince Henry a week ago filled her heart, pushing out any frustrations she might otherwise dwell on. She pulled her curls into a messy bun, and then completed her ritual of pressing her hands on her closed door, shutting her eyes and repeating the last words her father had said to her before he passed. "You're capable and kind. If you have those two things, you'll never lose me, and you'll never lose you." Her lashes always pressed more firmly together when she pledged the last part of her father's final commission to her. "In all things, have the courage to be kind."

It had been just over two years since her father's death, and she'd never failed to draw hope and solace from those three sentences. As she descended the stairs in the two-story home, she locked the mantra tight in her chest and prayed it would stay there, untouched, no matter how vexing her stepfamily became.

Anastasia's voice was lower in pitch, laced with a constant whine. "Ella, I told you I needed you to pre-cut my grapefruit. I don't understand why this is so difficult for you."

Ella moved to the fridge and pulled out the bowl marked "Anastasia". "This one's yours, hun. You dug into mine by mistake. Yours is sugared and cut, just how you like it."

Anastasia sniffed at the grapefruit in front of her and slid it over, eyeing the new bowl with equal disdain. Her thick arms were crossed over her squat frame, making her look like a spoiled toddler. "I don't like grapefruit."

"I know. But it's on the list of things Lady Tremaine approved for you to eat." Ella tapped the list on the fridge, not liking the fact that she was the one who had to enforce the diet Anastasia's doctor laid out.

Anastasia's round nose rose in the air. "You're trying to torture me! You've always been jealous of my clothes and the fact that I have friends, and you don't."

Ella kept her sigh tucked inside. "Actually, I thought we could go on the same diet together. Then you have a friend going through the pain of it all with you." Ella didn't mention that Anastasia's diet consisted of far more food than Ella was normally allowed to consume. She'd been looking forward to splurging on fresh grapefruit for breakfast, carrots with hummus for a mid-morning snack, tuna with apples for lunch, and an entire dinner of baked chicken, roasted vegetables and rice.

Anastasia rolled her eyes and scoffed, always sounding like a pig when she expressed her disdain. "Like I'd want to do anything with you. Next thing you know, you'll have me cleaning the floors with you, spending my life on my hands and knees."

"I would never ask you to clean," Ella replied, keeping her voice soft and indulgent. Anastasia was the youngest, and Ella had given up all hope that the twenty-two-year-old might actually grow up. So she treated Ana like the child she was, sighing through her tantrums and cleaning up after her. She was ordered to do so by Lady Tremaine, whose daughters could do no wrong.

Ella stood at the counter with her grapefruit, cutting into it quickly before Lady Tremaine got a mind to take it away for whatever reason served her vindictive purpose that morning. She wasn't allowed to sit at the table, so she kept a safe distance from the proper women, dining while standing, and keeping the counter between her and her stepsister to give Anastasia assurances that Ella wouldn't ruin her breakfast by getting too near. "Are you ready for your photography class final?"

"I don't know. Am I?" Ana asked, batting her eyes at Ella. Ana had short, stubby lashes that matched her mud-brown hair, framing her small, beady eyes to add only malice and feigned duress to her expressions. "You know I'm no good at photography."

Ella stabbed into her grapefruit. "I told you when you enrolled for the semester, I'm not doing your homework for you. I certainly can't take your finals for you. You do such a great job picking out your clothes in the morning.

You have a real flair for colorful things. I'm sure that's translated into your passion for photography, as well."

It was true. Anastasia had stuffed herself into hot pink leggings (her signature color), a pink-and-purple polka dotted turtle neck, with a yellow scarf to match her groaning high heels.

Ana harrumphed and licked the sugar off the top of her grapefruit, blanching. "This isn't sweet enough."

Ella pretended she hadn't heard her stepsister, knowing that any response would be the wrong one. If she gave her more sugar, Lady Tremaine would surely have something to say about it. If she refused her sugar, Ana would tackle her to the ground, sit on her and pull her hair—a punishment Ella had always hated.

She wolfed down her grapefruit and tidied up the kitchen as quick as she could while Ana huffed and complained about the lack of the pastries and thick cream she was used to.

Ella was grateful to get the kitchen in order before Lady Tremaine rose, her black hair in a tight bun that seemed to give her a miniature facelift. She was tall, but even sitting at the table, Ella felt like her stepmother towered over her. "Good morning, Lady Tremaine. Did you sleep well?"

"Yes, thank you for prying into something that's none of your business." She unfolded her emerald cloth napkin with a crack she insisted must be present, or else the napkins hadn't been starched enough. "I need the house spotless today, Ella. None of your mindless daydreaming, and keep your friends out of the house. If I see one bird, so help me, I'll snap its neck and serve it to you for your supper."

Ella's mouth tightened, but she nodded subserviently. "Yes, ma'am." She set the grapefruit down in front of Lady Tremaine, along with the coffee she'd freshly brewed in a slow-drip contraption that was "all the rage" according to Drizella. Just like that, the reliable coffee maker had been sold. A ceramic grinder, as well as a new drip funnel, had been purchased. It took three times as long for the grounds to brew, and Lady Tremaine insisted that the beans had to be roasted and ground by Ella to maintain the right flavor.

Coffee had become the constant battle in the Tremaine household. It was never hot enough, and then it was never bitter enough. Ella had grown to hate the stink of the stuff, knowing that no matter how closely she followed the instructions, Lady Tremaine would never be pleased unless a new husband was serving her the beverage in a solid gold cup.

Ella wasn't sure how her stepmother sipped the hot liquid without scalding her tongue. Her working theory was that Lady Tremaine had forfeited her taste buds long ago in pursuit of the hottest cup of joe. She leaned in slightly, waiting for either the scathing criticism or the blissful silence, which would mean she approved.

Lady Tremaine smacked her lips, took a second sip

and set the cup down. "The drip method really is the only way to go. Still, I can tell you didn't roast the beans twice. I don't know why you insist on taking shortcuts, as if you think I'm an idiot you can hoodwink."

Each word was chosen with great care to inflict the most damage, her tone acerbic and sharp. Ella had roasted the beans twice, as per the instructions, but knew better than to speak up in her defense. She made a mental note to roast the beans three times instead, and kept her feelings to herself. "Yes, ma'am. I'm sorry. I'll get it right tomorrow."

"That's what you said yesterday, and yet still I'm stuck drinking slop. If you could just get one simple thing right, my world would spin so much easier." Her bony shoulders lifted and lowered in exasperation. "Come here."

Ella balled her toes inside her shoes and moved to her stepmother's side, readying for the morning ritual of insult, and then battery.

She didn't brace herself—that never helped. She merely closed her eyes and leaned in, offering up her cheek for Lady Tremaine's hard slap. She knew her skin would sting for five minutes, but the pain would dull. Everything, it seemed, had a dulling point. The pain of her father's death had dulled slightly over the years, though the sting was still there. The slaps across the face had brought out her tears in the beginning when she'd begun living with her stepmother, but all crying had stopped two years ago. She knew it didn't help anything, and she'd never been one to dwell in a pit of sadness she had no hope of draining.

Ella looked forward to the slaps some mornings, because after Lady Tremaine got it out of her system, Ella was dismissed from her sight and could go about her day. When she didn't get slapped, there was a slow, damaging needling regarding Ella's figure, her attitude, her father, and even her Pulse that slowly wore her down.

Ella ran her tongue along the inside of her cheek as she moved quietly up the steps to Drizella's bedroom. It was her task to wake her second stepsister only after Lady Tremaine had dined, since Drizella was difficult for even her own mother to deal with. Ella made sure to walk on the sides of the wooden steps, using only the balls of her feet. Lady Tremaine didn't like reminders that Ella lived there, her temper flaring when she heard her step-daughter walking through the house.

"Rise and shine, sweetheart," Ella sang lightly, as she did every morning. Though Drizella was neither sweet, nor did she value matters of the heart, Ella still called her the precious name in hopes it would someday rub off on her stepsister, and remind her that she was capable of kindness (even if there was no evidence to support that).

"Ung-mm-pffl," Drizella spluttered, rolling around in her king-sized bed. She required seven down comforters to sleep atop, so every morning, she looked as if she was swimming on a series of cloudy waves that tangled around her long and Olive Oyl-like body.

"Get out of here!" Drizella finally managed to shout, throwing her phone at Ella's head, as she did most mornings.

Ella caught the device, grateful they didn't have to replace her phone yet again. She gently laid it on the nightstand and reminded herself to keep her shoulders rolled back. She knew that if the tiniest bit of tension crept into her body or tone of voice, the day would be shot. "Good morning, Drizella. If you don't want to be late to your internship, you need to get up and get going."

"I need my pleated skirt I wore last week. The purple one. Did you think about that? About the chores that need to be done? Or did you just talk with your birds all day long—eh, Birdbrain?" She sniggered at the nickname she'd dubbed Ella with years ago. "Birdbrain. Because no one will talk to you, except for the birds."

"In all things, have the courage to be kind," she reminded herself, quoting her father's prayer for her.

"What are you yammering about? Stop being annoying."

Ella hummed a song in her head, her hips swaying as she opened up Drizella's curtains and motioned to the laundry basket in the corner filled with folded clothes. "It's right in there, sweetheart. Let me get it for you. What top did you want to wear? I thought you looked lovely in your white sweater."

"That's because you're simple and fat. The white sweater didn't hang right. The yellow blouse. The one that shows off my boobs. I've got a date tonight, and I want it to go well."

"Gary?" Ella asked, trying to keep the dread out of her voice.

"Gary Herchon," she corrected Ella, drawing out the last name to sound exotic. "He's best friends with Calvin, the Baron's son. Can you imagine? If Mama marries the Baron, and I marry their close family friend?" Drizella tumbled out of bed, stripped her nightgown off and flung it onto the floor, narrowly missing knocking over the lamp on her nightstand. She waited like a princess in the center of the room for Ella to fetch her clothes and dress her in them. Her long nose pointed up in the air while Ella threaded her arms through the blouse and buttoned it up for her. "You can't possibly understand how big a deal this is. Gary's father is one step away from being on the council. Like, on the council! The Baron's only got to appoint him, which he plans on doing once the council is cleared of the useless lame ducks. Any day now, I'll be dating the son of a councilmember."

Ella rarely paid attention to Drizella's posturing, but there was something in her smugness that worried Ella. "Cleared how?"

Drizella's grin widened, making her look like a vindictive cat. Then she drew her thumb across her throat with a wicked gleam in her eyes, evoking a gasp from Ella. "If they don't step down, the Baron has ways of making people bend. If they won't bend, he'll break them. He already knows how he'll do it."

"How?" Ella asked, her mouth dry.

"Surely you don't think all Lethals are as reformed as Sleeping Beauty's husband. Most can't get employment anywhere. Some would do anything the Baron asked for a quick buck." Drizella's pointy nose crinkled, as if talking about a woman who was prettier than her had left a foul stench in the air.

Ella knew that if she wanted Drizella to keep talking, she would have to get her relaxed. "You work so hard. I can't believe how well you've done at Hipristine Industries. You're the best social media consultant they've ever seen, I'm sure."

"Can you believe they want me to keep a schedule? They're not even paying me, but they want me to clock in hours. Ridiculous."

"Would you like me to rub your shoulders?"

Drizella bristled with self-importance. "My feet, actually."

Ella bit down on her lower lip as she descended to her knees before Drizella's vanity chair. She waited until her stepsister was comfortable, and then rubbed a dollop of peppermint oil into her palms, gearing herself up to do one of her least favorite tasks. "Is that better?" she asked politely, swallowing hard as she ran her fingers over the foot fungus that never seemed to go away. Drizella's toes were big, hairy, scaly, and smelled like rotting onions. Still,

Ella kept her politeness around her neck like armor, offering up an unbothered expression while she massaged. The only thing that would get the stink off her hands after the task was rubbing them in the cinders from the hearth, followed by a thorough handwashing.

"I do work too hard," Drizella mumbled, her eyes closing while she slumped in the chair.

Ella eased up on the pressure, not wanting to relax Drizella too much, and impede on sharing time. "Do you really think the Baron's going to have members of the council killed by Lethals, all so he can get a few more spots for his friends?"

Drizella's eyes opened. "That's what Gary said. And why not? Lethals have to be good for something, right? We've got a dinner date set for after the meeting the Baron's holding to finalize everything."

"When would you like me to have your dress for your date ready? I mean, if the meeting's nearby, then that doesn't give you much time to prepare. I know how you like to look perfect." Ella tried her best to keep her prying evasive.

"Oh, I'll have plenty of notice. The meeting's at that stinky old cigar shop closer to the capital. That's easily forty-five minutes away."

Ella rubbed Drizella's feet for five more minutes, but all her sister wanted to talk about was how good Gary was in bed. If there was one thing Ella deemed more disgusting than Drizella's feet, it was Gary Herchon.

"One day, when you find some lowly servant to give you the time of day, you'll see what I'm talking about. Gary sure knows what he's doing between the sheets."

Ella could spot Drizella's bravado and lies a mile away, but she was barely listening anymore. Her mind was focused on the potential plot that would eliminate a sizeable chunk of the council if she didn't intervene.

6

PINPRICKS OF POSSIBILITY

*E*lla usually went to the grocery store in town to get what was needed to cook for the household, but that day she drove to the next town over to the most affluent section of Avondale—the East Village. She strolled into the upscale grocer's that mostly sold vegan health food, and made her way to the far wall, where she busied herself pretending to read the labels on the bins of loose-leaf tea.

Her palms were sweating as she tried to appear inconspicuous while she readied her Pulse. Most people could touch someone and press a feeling or idea into them. A fraction could touch death into people, or extreme harm.

Ella's father knew he had to instruct his daughter carefully when he learned of her abilities.

Instead of a Pulse, Ella had been born with the ability to send out her hearing. There was no precedent for something like that. In decades past, possessing a gift that was a variant from the norm had the potential to put you in real danger. The Wicked Queen Vanessa who'd ruled three thrones before King Hubert had made it her business to round up all the variants and exploit their gifts. Most didn't make it out of her dungeons before she'd driven them to insanity. Or perhaps the mandatory lobotomies came before.

Malaura had possessed magic at levels no one ever dreamed of. Since she'd abused her power so cruelly, having anything outside the norm was often treated with skittish glances and ostracism.

King Hubert was a fair and even-tempered ruler. Even so, Ella's father hadn't been one to put things to chance where his daughter was concerned, so he taught her to hide her gifts. Upon graduation, her Pulse was declared 'kindness,' which was a relief felt through both Ella and her father. Life was simply harder for Deadpulses. Though Ella didn't have a Pulse in the traditional sense, the proctor for her final exam felt himself growing kinder around her when she touched his arm. She didn't bother to correct him, knowing that it was simply her demeanor that had made him feel a rush of tenderness in his soul.

Ella never bothered furthering her education after that. She'd considered herself fortunate to have graduated under the radar, and did her best to keep her secrets to herself.

She leaned in and inhaled a long drag, filling her lungs

with magic she'd always been able to sense in the air from birth. The particles were far too small for most people to notice, but Ella could feel the pinpricks of possibility.

When she exhaled, she sent her hearing out, bypassing the walls, the people, the shopping carts, and any other distractions, so she could infiltrate the store next to the vegan health market.

The Baron had been bragging the last time he'd been to the house for dinner about the weekly meeting of the minds housed in the backroom of the cigar shop. Gary Herchon boasting to Drizella about how important he was to know about such things narrowed down the window for Ella, so she would be at the right place at the right time to overhear all the wrong things. Ella'd had no idea this was what they discussed during their cloak and dagger meetings. They were an unofficial clandestine men's club, and the Baron assumed telling Lady Tremaine where and when they took place wouldn't do anything to expose his secrets, since no one but the invited could get in.

However, the Baron didn't know that Ella could hear through walls.

As she continued to breathe, her lungs didn't fill with the scent of tea from the barrels before her. Instead, a heavy sting of pipe tobacco weighted her body, making her feel as if she was on the other side of the wall, smelling and hearing everything going on there. She'd never been able to send out her sight. Usually Hearing and Scent were enough to do whatever spying she needed to be part of, and today was no exception.

She pursed her lips through ten minutes of posturing and name-dropping as the important men and the hopefuls tried to impress each other. She filed every detail in her mind, but most of it was either unimportant, or clearly fabricated to win the favor of the Baron.

She'd had to scrub the kitchen and living room floors twice before Lady Tremaine was satisfied and allowed Ella to leave to complete her errands. The meeting started twenty minutes ago, but Ella was grateful it seemed she hadn't missed the most important parts.

Then finally, she heard something that made her spine stiffen.

"Caleb, Eustace and Remus need to be reckoned with. They're too comfortable in their council seats, and far too vocal."

"Why stop there?" another man said, puffing on his pipe. "If you're going for Remus, why not just go for the Chancellor himself? Remus will prove far more difficult to take out."

"Remus Johnstone doesn't scare me," Mr. Herchon said, his swagger in full swing. Ella could practically picture his pot belly that he'd passed down to his son Gary.

Ella's spine stiffened at the crack of the Baron's voice. "Then you're a fool. We'll not send out an attack on Remus. If there's one way to get us all found out, it's that.

Stay away from the Chancellor, his daughter, and Remus. They're being watched too closely by the public for anyone to get too near. There's sure to be a spotlight wherever they are for quite some time."

The Baron's snide voice always had a hiss of something sniveling to it that made Ella's skin crawl, and the others fall silent. She gathered her blue flannel tighter around herself, as if she could feel his garlic breath on her shoulders. Whenever he came over to entertain Lady Tremaine, Ella was sure to make herself scarce. She pretended not to notice the way he stared at her body, but she felt his gaze as if it had groping hands.

When he continued, she leaned in to hear everything the Baron said as clearly as she could. "The way to take down the Chancellor without drawing too much suspicion is to slowly take out his supporters on the council. The ones who always vote to pass his policies, no matter how outdated and frustrating they might be. We can't kill the Chancellor. And laying a hand on Remus would be suicide. However, we can cut off their legs by taking out their supporters on the council, and then bringing in some of you more progressive-minded individuals to take their places. That's how you collapse a beloved leader, gentlemen."

"Very well, which ones are we targeting first? I assume you intend on using Lethals to carry out the job."

"Of course. I was thinking we should start with Caleb and Eustace. Nobody cares about them. Eustace is so old, people will assume he died in his sleep if the Lethal does his job correctly. And Caleb has many enemies. It's only a matter of time before one of them came after him." The Baron chuckled, and Ella could hear the clanking of ice in a glass.

Angst over picturing the Baron too near her made her lose her grip on her Hearing, and suddenly the sounds and smells of the cigar shop next door vanished, replaced with the scent of loose tea, and the sound of a mother trying to shush her fussing baby.

Ella shoved her sweaty palms into the pockets of her light blue cardigan she wore over her flannel. She'd always loved how the delicate color complimented her eyes, making them seem brighter, almost appearing as if she could afford things like makeup to enhance her features.

Ella tried to send out her hearing again, but she was too unfocused as she worried about what she should do with the information that could shake the magical community if handled improperly, or not handled at all.

She cast around for any excuse she could find for being in this particular store, wandering down the aisle that had facial serums and hair elixirs. She found an anti-aging eye cream that had been advertised on TV, and took it to the checkout. She hoped that would be enough to explain her presence here if the Baron spotted her, and also to give her stepmother a little boost to make her feel pretty for her date that evening.

When she checked out her item, she asked the clerk if

there was a payphone nearby. Ella wasn't permitted to own a phone. Once her stepmother learned of Ella's abilities, she exchanged Ella's right to walk about freely for a lifetime of servitude. Ella reasoned that working as a servant in her father's home was better than the possibility of a government-sanctioned lobotomy.

She moved down the street and turned the corner, shivering against the chill of the light dusting of snow. She'd owned three winter jackets before, but they'd all been taken away, either as punishment for a cleaning job poorly done, or because Drizella or Anastasia had seen her thrift store jacket and wanted it for themselves. Ella shut herself in the phone booth and shuddered against the pane, grateful to the simple structure for at least shielding her from the wind and peppering of snow.

Ella had memorized the prince's scrawled phone number on the napkin before she'd burned it. She didn't want her stepsisters seeing his number lying around, and then call the man who'd been nothing but sweet to her. She tried not to overindulge her imagination with memories of his handsome features, but it was hard not to. Most people in her village looked the other way when they saw Ella coming because they knew she worked for Lady Tremaine, who wasn't known for being a blessing to society.

Ella debated several times before going through with the phone call, wishing there was any other way to handle the situation. She bit down on her lower lip, chiding herself for wanting to hear him again.

When his voice sounded on the other end, she nearly hung up the phone. "Hello?"

She waited two entire seconds before her tongue unstuck itself from the roof of her mouth. "Henry?"

"Who is this?"

This time, she waited three seconds before answering. "If I told you, then you'd know my name. My friends who bring me strawberries call me 'Henry.'"

It was Henry's turn to pause for far too long. His reply came with a twinge of hurt to it. "I gave you my number a week ago. I've never had to wait for a woman to call me. I have to admit, I don't care for this life lesson in patience."

"I'm sorry. My situation is... complicated."

"Is this your cell? I'll save you in my phone under the name 'Woman who Kept Me Waiting.'"

Ella coiled the cord around her finger. "I'm actually calling you from a payphone."

"Are you married?"

Ella's nose crinkled. "No. I'm not married."

Henry gusted out his relief. "Then what can I do for you today, Woman who Keeps Me Wondering?"

Ella loved the way he teased her. No one interacted with her like that. "I overheard something bad, and I didn't know who to tell. But it seems important, so I thought maybe you should know. Maybe you can do something to stop it."

"Stop what? The constant breaking of my heart when a woman rejects me?"

"I didn't reject you," she argued, shivering in her cardigan.

"Tell that to my lonely Friday night. I had to spend it with a married couple, I hope you know. I could've been wining and dining you, but I was stuck playing board games—emphasis on the 'bored' part."

Ella snorted. "I'm sure you're not hurting for dates."

"I was mortally wounded! But now you've come back to me, begging me to take you out and show you off. Fine, Henrietta. Fine. If you insist, I'll take you out this very night."

Ella chuckled at his dramatics. "My, my. You should've gone into theater."

"When the right person's not in the audience there's less of a reason to put on a show."

Ella leaned her elbow on the platform under the large, silver receiving box. "Who makes you put on a show, Henry? Who makes you be less you? I can't imagine anything more tragic."

The mood shifted to something slightly more honest and raw. "Only everyone."

The operator's voice chimed in, warning Ella she had half a minute to end the call, or else she'd need to put in another few coins. "Henry, the phone's about to cut out. I have to tell you something important! Like, national security important."

"Where can I meet you?" he asked in a rush.

Ella cringed, knowing his presence would only complicate her life. She wanted to spend time with him—so desperately wanted nothing but exactly that. But she'd given up on wanting and needing long ago. It only ever led to dashed dreams, and her life was already too bleak to handle more blows.

She closed her eyes and willed herself to be brave. "I'm in the East Village for the next two hours. Can you meet me here?"

"Yes!" he all but shouted into the phone. "There's a little bistro at Twelfth and Walt Main. Order yourself a coffee, and I'll meet you there in twenty minutes."

"Thank you, Henry."

He tsked, using up their last few seconds just to tease her. "Was it so very hard to admit you had feelings for me? You didn't have to go and make up threats of national security to lure me in. Conniving minx."

Ella couldn't help the lightness that spread over her, now that she would be seeing him again. "See you soon, sweet Prince."

7

TEA AND NATIONAL SECURITY

Ella didn't want to wait outside, for fear of the Baron seeing her and asking questions. Also, her cardigan was hand-knitted and lovely, but didn't provide much in the way of warmth against the snow and occasional icy gusts that kicked up around her.

The jingle overhead as she entered drew a few eyes her way, so she ducked her head and beelined for the bathroom in the back of the bistro. The café had a slate floor, stone fireplaces, and plenty of cozy nooks for polite conversations over tea and scones. It was typical of the East Village, where the more affluent people lived. Her father's colonial was nice, spacious and completely paid off, but even that would be considered a tiny house in these parts that were closer to the palace. These were citizens with old money, admired by people like her stepmother, who were trying to convince everyone she deserved a better zip code with her constant struggle to keep up the appearance of wealth.

Ella had never cared what she looked like, so long as she didn't draw too much attention. This time, however, she glanced in the mirror with dashed expectations. She had bags under her eyes, her cheeks were beaten pink from the wind, her curly blonde hair was a mess, and her clothes were... Ella knew she'd be labeled a servant anywhere she went, dressed like this in the East Village.

She squared her shoulders in the mirror, reminding herself that she was her father's daughter, and the details of her current state didn't matter as much as that one shining fact that lifted her chin. She straightened her hair as best she could, and made sure she didn't have any smudges on her skin from her morning chores.

Ella moved back out into the bistro, trying not to look as if she didn't belong. The universe had led her to this place, so she wasn't about let herself believe she wasn't welcome in it. She sat down and ordered a plain black tea (the cheapest thing on the menu), letting the steaming cup warm her hands.

"Sorry to keep you waiting, love," came a voice from behind her. "I had to make sure you came alone."

Ella turned and found Henry in a booth, a hat on and his face obscured by a newspaper. "How long have you been there?" She brought her cup to sit across from him, charmed by his covert-ops body language.

"I was only five minutes away when you called. You'd

be surprised how many women try to seduce my nickers off of me, and then attempt to capture me on film in compromising positions. I had to make sure you weren't working with one of the tabloids." He stood and motioned toward the kitchen. "Actually, we'll be dining in the break-room here. Fewer prying eyes."

Ella's mouth popped open. "I hope this is one of your bits that you think is hilarious, but goes over my head. No one's ever done that to you, have they?"

"Not this month." He opened the swinging double doors for her, ushering her into the kitchen. Ella cast the cook an apologetic look, but the portly gentleman responded by motioning toward another set of doors to the right. Henry clapped the cook on the shoulder and touched Ella's elbow, walking with her through the kitchen to the empty break room.

The dining area of the bistro was upscale and cozy. While the breakroom lacked a few of the fashionable furnishings, the slate floor, tall wrought iron tables and chairs, and ficus in the corner were no less welcoming.

Henry set down his newspaper and slid onto his chair, warming her with a companionable gaze as she took the seat across from him. "Much better. Thanks for not being afraid I'll murder you in the back alley."

"I haven't ruled it out, but I'm pretty sure I could take you if you tried anything ungentlemanly."

He took off his hat, casting her a sidelong wink. "Well, then I'll have to be on my best behavior."

"You know the owner? Nice that they let you do this."

"I own the business, actually. But yes, I do still ask permission to borrow the breakroom if I need a quiet place away from prying eyes. I've learned to be a bit more careful over the years, but every now and then, I still get caught unawares."

She closed her eyes and lowered her chin. "That is the saddest thing I've heard in days. How do you let your guard down and just enjoy your life?"

"I manage."

"Well, no one will hear about you from me."

He ran his finger along the brim of his hat as he fiddled with it atop the table. "That's one of the things that drew me toward you. You seemed even more covetous of your privacy than I am. Is there a reason for that?"

"If there was, do you think I would tell you?" she countered, squeezing the lemon wedge into her tea.

Henry sighed and straightened in his seat. "So, you're concerned about a matter of national security. Is this something I should bring in my guard for?"

Ella's mouth drew to the side. "Not while I'm here. I don't want anyone to see us together. But after I leave, yes. You should probably tell him."

Henry glanced down at his toned stomach beneath his crisp white dress shirt. "Have I gotten fat? Are you truly this embarrassed to be seen with me? I've got half a mind to take dozens of photos of us together and post them all over Royal Watch."

Ella paled, imagining how badly the beating would be if a photo of her got on the Holy Grail of gossip websites before Drizella or Anastasia ever made an appearance on there. They checked the online feed religiously, and had made it their life goal to make themselves important enough to be seen hanging with the elite. "Please don't do that. Maybe I should go."

Henry reached across the table and placed his hand atop hers. "No! I was only joking. Please, Henrietta. Stay. Tell me what's bothering you. Tell me what makes you smile. Tell me anything at all."

She settled back onto her stool, melting at the feel of his hand on hers. He left it there, and she let him, even going so far as to open her hand and invite his fingers to hold onto hers. "I overheard something, and didn't know who to turn to. It seemed important, and probably time-sensitive." She kept her voice quiet, gluing her eyes to their joined hands, savoring the image as she powered through the difficult report. "The Baron's involved in a plan to take out a few key members of the council. He wants to replace them with people who will vote for his policies, like Mr. Herchon."

Henry straightened, casting aside his playful demeanor and donning his business face. "Take them out, how?"

"By setting Lethals loose on them. Eustace and Caleb are their first targets, and after that they'll move on to the others on the council who usually vote to support the Chancellor's policies."

"You heard the Baron say this?"

"Yes, and a roomful of other men I don't really know enough to pick out just by the sound of their voices. Mr. Herchon was there, but I couldn't tell you who else. Someone suggested attacking Remus Johnstone, but the Baron pushed against that, since Remus' magic is so much more powerful than anyone else's. He didn't want anyone close to the Chancellor attacked, since they're being followed so closely by the press these days. They're playing the circuitous route, taking down the Chancellor's authority by slowly replacing his supporters on the council. Cutting his legs off so his policies have no strength to stand."

Henry swore and pulled out his phone. "Victor, yes. Put in a call to Christopher. I've just been made aware of a plot on Eustace and Caleb's lives. Also, call Benjamin and make sure Rory doesn't go anywhere. Remus, either. They're not targets, but best be safe." He answered a few more perfunctory questions before hanging up.

Ella's shoulders relaxed, now that her message had been delivered. "Thank you for believing me."

"Of course. Worse thing that happens is that nothing happens, and we upped their security for no reason. That's a regret I can live with. You were right to call me about this. Wrong to not call me for anything other than this."

He squinted one eye at her in mild scolding, but didn't press the matter any further.

Ella stirred her tea, mulling over the plot. "It's strategic. I didn't hear the rest of the plan, but if I was the Baron and I really wanted my policy to get pushed through, I wouldn't just put my people on the council; I'd make sure the Lethals I'd sent in to kill the councilmembers were caught and prosecuted for their attacks. That way he'll have even more division from the public on what to do with the Lethals. When there's dissention that's whipped up to a frenzy, more radical policies have a better chance at getting passed, even when they might not be beneficial for the public. This is perfect timing to sway people to his side for the vote on Proposition 7." She'd had to endure several evenings of the Baron droning on about his opinions on Lethals in general, and that he wanted manufacturing of the pill to be sold to the highest bidder.

Henry nodded, his brows pushed together as he pondered the impending peril. "You're right. If the Baron's smart, he'll keep his name out of the whole process. Have one of the others hire the Lethals and stay far away from the action himself." He leaned back in his chair and sighed. "I loathe stuff like this. I'm guessing you won't come forward and make a statement of all you heard?"

Ella pursed her lips and slowly shook her head. "That would make things very..."

"Complicated?" Henry guessed. "I understand. But

unless we catch him with a dagger in his hand hovered over old Eustace himself, it's not going to stop."

"One battle won gives us a clearer picture of the war."

"Have you been sneaking peeks into my journal? I feel like I had a similar entry last week. Only, I was referring to my plans to cajole Carlotta into making every Saturday pot roast day."

"That's a noble priority. A good pot roast is worth a little espionage."

Henry called his guard again, relaying the additional suspicions and hanging up. "Is that all, then?"

"I thought that was a big enough deal to warrant a phone call, but yeah, that's all."

Henry sighed and seemed to relax, his shoulders loosening. "Brilliant. Then we can put away the harrowing spy nature of our relationship, and get to the bottom of which dragon needs to be slain so that we can see each other more often."

Ella laughed through her nose. "You're persistent. I've got to be honest, though. I'm not sure you'll get what you want."

"Which is?"

"Someone you can be with. I'm not that girl."

Henry frowned at the red light. "Not that girl for me, or for anybody?"

"For anybody. Trust me. I'm caught up in a world of frustration that you don't want to be part of. I'm doing you a giant favor."

"If only you'd let me decide that for myself. I'm desperate to know anything about you."

Ella cast around the quaint breakroom, taking in the corkboard with different menu items and notices tacked up. "Um, Let's see. Something about me. I made this cardigan."

"It's very nice. I think I'd like one to match."

She took a sip of her tea and glanced at him over the top of the cup. "You would not."

"I would. And I want it in that exact same blue, to remind myself of the striking color of your eyes." His nose wrinkled. "Too cheesy? I meant it, but when I heard myself say it, I cringed."

"Well, I only prefer cringe-worthy compliments."

"Should I start everything with, 'Hey baby'? Oh, I recently heard of a brilliant one. Almost lost my lunch when a man called the girl he fancies 'tasty cakes' while leering at her."

The two blanched in unison. Ella shook her head. "Unacceptable. She should've slapped him for the sake of all women everywhere. Gross."

"If it helps lessen the offense to your feminine consciousness, she didn't warm to his advances. I actually did a fair bit of puppet mastering to get her away from him. She works for one of my best friends now. No one's crazy enough to mess with anyone on his property."

"Sounds like she's lucky you intervened. Is your friend a good guy?"

"Adam Fontaine?" Henry thought on this while he sipped his tea. "No. Not really. She's safer with him, though. Adam won't hit on her in disgusting ways." Henry met Ella's eyes. "Do you know much about Adam?"

"Only what Lady Tremaine's daughters talk about from they read on Royal Watch, and of course what everyone knows Malaura did to him almost a decade ago. I can't imagine much of what's been posted in Royal Watch is true, though."

"What if it is?" Henry kept his eyes on his coffee. "What if one of my closest friends hears things that aren't there, and sees people who are long gone? What if he's agoraphobic and surly?"

Ella watched his weighted expression as she inhaled the fragrance of her tea, relishing the beverage she hadn't had to make in a slow drip contraption after roasting it multiple times. "It sounds like Adam's very lucky to have you in his corner, puppet mastering people into his life." She took a drink, and then reached across the quaint table to trace the outside of his pointer finger all the way to the tip. Something inside of her called out to touch Henry. Though she couldn't take him home, part of her wanted to tempt herself with the tantalizing offer to let at least her finger pretend as if she could indulge in the things she wanted. "It also looks like you need a friend who's well enough to be good to you, and it's a shame that Adam might not be able to be that guy right now."

Henry's lashes swept shut as he fended off the loneliness of not having the proper friendship he needed in his isolated existence. He welcomed in Ella's words, letting her gentleness wash over the jagged edges of his psyche. "It's a relief just to say it out loud to someone. Thanks for listening."

"Thanks for talking." She tilted her head to the side. The kindness her father instilled in her from birth pushed her to measure out the sadness in his eyes, and she gauged his burdens only halfway lifted. "What else is weighing you down? Worrying about Adam bothers you, but there's more."

"Am I that obviously miserable?"

"You're that obviously caring. Caring people have a hard time accepting that the world around them might always be a little bit broken." Her fingers took a chance, pushing her forward to brush a tickle across his palm, giving him her hand to hold onto when he felt lost.

"It's Rory. I don't like that she married a Lethal—a ridiculously powerful one on top of it. Cord's a good guy, but I wouldn't have chosen for her to fall in love with someone who might accidentally roll over in bed one night and electrocute my dearest friend. But of course, I can't say anything. If I do, everyone will assume that I'm all jilted because we were betrothed and she married Cordray, but Rory and I were never like that. Rory, Adam and I are closer than siblings. I even stood up as her Maid of Honor in her wedding."

"Did you get to wear a pretty dress?"

"No," Henry pouted. "Rory wouldn't let me. Had to be predictable and wear a tux."

Ella tsked and shook her head. "Shame. You in heels? That's a sight the world would swoon for."

He sniggered at her teasing and got up to slide his stool closer to hers, keeping his hand in hers the whole time as he sat back down. "Nah. The men of the world already feel inferior to my good looks. I wouldn't want to make the women question their beauty as well."

Ella's eyes fell to their joined hands, loving the way they looked together. Though he was more polished, their hands didn't care. They clung to each other, doing what the rest of her heart was too fearful to act on. "It sounds like you're in a rough spot with Rory. You want to be honest with her so she's more careful, but you don't feel it's your place."

"Exactly! And I really do like Cordray. He's a solid guy." He let out a heavy sigh. "Not to sound petty, but would you want your sister to marry a Lethal, no matter how nice a guy he was?"

Ella ran her thumb over Henry's knuckles while she mulled over his dilemma. "Since she's married to him, there's not much you can do, other than be supportive. If you're feeling all of this, I'm sure it's nothing that hasn't crossed her mind, too. You confronting her about her dangerous choice won't do anything except make her feel all those worries she has to tuck away in order to enjoy her marriage." She bumped her shoulder to his. "Also, the more time you spend with Cordray, the less worried you'll be about the whole thing. Hopefully you'll learn that he's responsible about either wearing his gloves, or about taking his pill."

Henry glanced at her sideways. "That wasn't bad advice."

"I have my moments." She took a sip of her tea, loving the luxury of sitting for so long. "There's more to your fears than that. Something deeper. Talk to me."

Henry's chest puffed with bravado, ready to push it all off and claim that he was fine, but the sincerity in her cerulean eyes gave him pause. "How do you do that? My whole goal most days is to make jokes so I don't have to reveal anything real about myself, but one cup of tea with you, and I'm hopeless at keeping my mouth shut."

"I'm sorry you can't lean on your regular friends. With Adam being ill and Rory getting married, it's got to be hard for you to be heard at all by the people who matter."

"It is. No one gets that because I rarely have private moments, but when I do, I want to be able to be a person. You know about Adam's curse, I'm sure."

"The whole 'he'll turn into a member of the Lupine when the last rose petal falls' bit? Yeah. Malaura was terrible. What a wretched person for nature to give that much power to."

"Agreed. Adam carries around her curse like that's all he is. Rory's grown up her whole life with her curse hanging over her head, and only just beat it." Henry stared at Ella's fingers, slowly touching each of her unpolished nails while he worked out the words. "I don't know how to say this without sounding melodramatic."

"I won't judge you." Ella slid her elbow toward his, joining the outside of their forearms together, and making their huddle more intimate. "How about you stop being afraid to be yourself around me, and I'll promise to let you be yourself, no matter how melodramatic you might worry you sound."

Henry stared into her eyes, seeing the honesty there for the open invitation it was. He wanted to kiss her, to draw out her lower lip just so he could have something sweet to suck on. His body wanted to lean in and close the gap between them, but part of him knew that if she wasn't ready to give him her name, then she probably wouldn't appreciate a make-out session in the breakroom.

He cleared his throat and reminded himself of their conversation. "It feels like the people around me are perpetually cursed. Like my curse is to watch the people I love struggle for years under the weight of far too much, and there's nothing I can do to stop it."

Ella exhaled in a soft, "Oh," that was filled with sadness for his plight. "That's terrible, Henry. You must feel so helpless and lonely, like you have to be positive and strong all the time to hold everyone else up."

"That's exactly how it feels." He let out a deep-rooted exhale that had been churning in his soul for far too long.

"Who holds you up?" Ella asked, compassion welling

in her. She couldn't bear the thought of someone so sweet feeling so very alone.

"My father, sometimes. Though, he's busy with all the shifting that's happening on the political landscape, so I don't like to bother him too much."

"Bother him," Ella pushed without preamble. "He'll thank you for it. Bother him any time of the day or night. If there's one thing I regret, it's that I can't bother my father anymore, and I didn't do it enough while he was alive."

"I'm sorry. How long as he been gone?"

"Two years. Life without him is..." She shook her head at herself and settled back into her chair to feign calmness while the storm of sadness brewed in her chest. "Bother him, Henry. Tonight when you get home. Promise me you'll bother him."

Henry leaned back in his stool that was pushed up next to hers and banded his arm lightly around her shoulders. "I promise."

It was all too much. Her gentleness, the way she made him open up and fight for making his life better. He knew he couldn't kiss her lips yet, so he compromised and drew her closer to him, so she was tucked into his side. His arm felt like it belonged slung around her hips, as though it was the first time that series of muscles had ever relaxed. Both of them began to breathe easier, taking in long drags to inhale the scent of each other, and appreciate how well their bodies fit together.

He pressed his lips to her temple, letting them linger there while he spoke. "Tell me your name," he whispered.

The debate was strong inside of her, warring between her need to keep him away from her messy situation, and her desire to be closer... so much closer. "Henry," she replied, hoping the lie would suffice.

"I think we're past that."

She closed her eyes, daring herself to be brave. "Ella," she admitted in a whisper.

Henry inhaled sharply and hugged her closer, gratitude beaming out from him. "Finally! Was that truly so hard?"

"Yes," she giggled, wrapping her arm around his middle like it was the most natural thing in the world. Though they barely knew each other, their bodies understood the dance without instruction.

Henry tilted her chin up, his arm still curved around her to keep them inseparable. "Thank you, Ella. It's nice to finally meet you properly."

Ella knew she should pull back, but she couldn't bring herself to turn her chin from his tender touch. He was inviting, always inviting, and when she stared into his blue eyes, she found she couldn't remember her many reasons for resisting him. He leaned in slowly, giving her handfuls of seconds in which she could've pulled away.

But she didn't lean back from him. Instead, she angled her chin up, her lashes sweeping shut to welcome the kiss she'd been trying not to dream about.

It was the worst time for her stomach to growl, but it had been silent long enough. She jerked away and banded her arms around her midsection. "Sorry. So embarrassing."

Henry ran his hand over his face to snap himself out of the haze that overtook his desire to remain gentlemanly. "Let's get you something to eat."

"No, no. I'm fine. You fed me last time. I don't want that to be your abiding memory of me."

He drew his lips to the side at her pride. "You're saying you wouldn't eat a lunch I made for you?"

"Your chef cooking us something isn't you making a meal," Ella sassed him with a scolding smile, standing as he stood. "You don't cook."

Henry wound his arm around her hips once again, surprised to find that his body wouldn't tolerate separating from hers. "Boy, are you going to be sorry you said that. What should I make you eat first—crow or humble pie?"

"Surprise me, Chef."

"Oh, Ella. Don't you know? Meeting you was my greatest surprise."

THE DANGER OF A KISS OVER LUNCH

Ella couldn't remember the last time she'd laughed so many times in a single afternoon. Henry put on quite the show for her, taking over a station in the kitchen after the lunchtime rush. He flipped the peppers in the pan for her amusement, did a shimmy as he shook in the spices, and hummed her sweet songs while preparing a quiche for the two of them with goat cheese and shallots. He did anything and everything he could think of to coax out her smile, deepening the dimples that drew him in every time.

"If I hadn't seen it with my own two eyes, I never would've guessed you're such an accomplished cook." She picked out a green onion from the pie. "I mean, look at these delicate little cuts! This is incredible."

Henry divided the six-serving quiche in half down the middle, designating one side for himself and the other for her. Most of his dates would've balked at a cheese-heavy quiche, or picked at half a slice, but Ella barely paused between whole pieces, plowing her way through her half with the gusto of a starving woman.

"I love watching you eat," he admitted, running his tongue over his top row of teeth at the erotic show that was Ella devouring the food he'd made. Every groan of pleasure that escaped her lips was one he'd placed on her tongue. Each morsel she savored was an indulgence he'd given her. He watched her polish off her side, and then he sliced off a chunk of his half and offered it to her.

Ella covered her mouth, her cheeks coloring. "I'm sorry. I guess I was hungrier than I thought."

Henry decided to cut through the polite dodging and call out the evidence. "Lady Tremaine doesn't feed you well, does she."

Ella paused chewing, and then swallowed with great effort. She wiped her mouth on her napkin while searching for the right words. "I'm allowed two meals a day. Sometimes I get to eat what I cook the family. Other times I get toast with peanut butter."

"That's hardly a meal."

"It's not a meal at all. It's a punishment," Ella said quietly, opening herself up by the smallest of degrees. "I'm allergic to peanuts."

Henry's mouth fell open in horror. "Are you serious? She gives you food that could kill you? You should tell her you have a food allergy!"

"She knows. It's not anaphylactic. I just throw up if I eat peanuts. That's my meal when I make her angry. It's a fun little game she plays."

"No," Henry ruled, cutting his hand flat across the table. "You're done working for that woman. We'll get you a better job, easily. One where no one's trying to poison you."

Ella shook her head, eyeing the last piece of quiche on Henry's side of the pie tin. "I don't have that option. My situation is complicated, and can't be undone with a simple occupation change. In fact, that would make everything far worse for me."

"I don't understand. You're being poisoned. Poisoned and starved! You expect me to just... Well, I can't."

"You can, and you will. You think you have no one? Henry, I literally have no one. My dad was my someone, and when he died, my shelter blew away with the wind."

"I'm sitting here right now, offering to be your someone!"

Ella held his gaze, wishing she had any other answer for him. "And I'll hold that offer close to my heart. But this is what it is for me, and I'm handling it."

"Any other job would be better than this. How much does she pay you to treat you like this? Whatever it is, I'll find you something better."

Ella cozied her cardigan tighter around her, wishing she'd said nothing. "She doesn't pay me. It's complicated."

Henry's fist tightened around his fork. "What does she have on you?"

Ella's stomach screamed for the last piece of quiche, but she stood abruptly, knowing she'd indulged herself for too long. "I have to go."

"Enough with the secrecy, Ella!" He rose and stood in front of the breakroom door, filling the exit with his broad shoulders and towering frustration. "Tell me why you let her treat you like this!"

Ella banded her arms around her stomach, willing her tears not to fall as her eyes watered. It had been so long since she'd cried, and she wasn't about to lose her grip in front of the prince.

Her finger rose to point in Henry's face. "This is why I don't talk about myself! It's my business, and I'll handle my life how it makes sense for me. You don't know all the variables."

"But I want to know them! Can't you see that?"

Ella stepped backward, pinching her forearm as she struggled against her tears. "I do, and I adore you for it, but trust me when I say that I need my secrets to stay mine."

Henry leaned against the door, commanding his anger to deflate. He closed his eyes and sucked in his lower lip to keep any chastisements locked inside. "I'm yelling at you. You're being starved and poisoned, and I'm yelling at you. This is exactly the problem I have with Rory. I get scared so I end up yelling at her, and I can't remember why. I'm sorry."

Ella froze, savoring his apology for the rare gift it was. No one had apologized to her in years. Yet here was the Prince of Avondale, humbling himself for her. "It's my fault. I'm making things difficult."

Forlorn, Henry remained leaning against the door and motioned her forward, his arms open to welcome her into his embrace. It took a few beats, but he was patient with her skittish behavior, understand now that there was far more to the woman than her blue eyes and compassionate smile. There were slashes and whole bruises on her heart that he couldn't heal, but he wanted to—oh, how he wanted to keep her safe.

When Ella finally crossed the room and sank into his arms, the two began to breathe contentedly in unison, matching their hearts so that each inhale felt like one body moving. The longer they indulged, the more Henry allowed her soothing presence to calm his anger. He wasn't just frustrated with her secrecy – it was Adam's illness, and Rory's laissez-faire attitude about Cordray's deadliness. And then there were the hundreds of other things that he couldn't fix, but the world came to him with the expectation that he should, and somehow must. "I shouldn't have yelled at you."

"I shouldn't drive you to insanity like this. You're a good man. I don't want to teach you not to care about people. It's just that I'm already in the mess, and I'd rather keep you like this, with that smile you sometimes save for me, rather than lose you altogether."

"However much of yourself you'll give me, I'll take it." He slowly swayed her from side to side, loving the way she felt in his arms. He thrilled at the shiver he brought out in her when his lips brushed her ear. "I'll be gentle with you."

It was the one thing she needed most of all, and when he offered it, she found she couldn't resist him any longer. "Henry?" She pulled her cheek from his chest and stared up at him, drinking in his striking features up close.

His hand only consented to part from her waist so it could trace the edges of her face. "Anything. Tell me anything. Ask me anything. It's yours. Always and only yours."

"Kiss me," she whispered, unable to work out the words with any sort of volume. "You can't say something so perfect and expect me not to need to kiss you."

Relief washed over his features, replacing his worry with a lazy smile that had served the cameras well over the years. "When a beautiful woman asks, how can I say no?" He leaned in, loving the way her lashes swept shut when he neared.

He'd been flummoxed as to how to get in her good graces. Now that he was finally there, he relished his freedom and decided to toy with her longing, as she'd toyed with his. Instead of touching his lips on hers, he moved to her cheek, gracing the heated blush with a light kiss. His arm tightened around her hips with a note of possession that belied the gentility of his lips. He was commanding behind closed doors, and finally, she was ready to be pliable.

"Is that what you meant?" he asked, a whispered tease in her ear.

Ella's arms draped around his neck, treasuring the contact. "You know it wasn't, but I'll take it."

Henry moved to her other cheek, laying a kiss in the well of her dimple to make her rouse with need. "How about here?"

Her breath grew labored as his lips dragged down the slope of her neck, exposing too much, and still never enough. Her limbs grew weighted with a jelly-like sensation that trickled through her body at his touch. "Oh, you're driving me crazy," she rasped when his lips dragged up her throat, only to make a trail over to the juncture between her ear and her neck, where his lips parted so he could suck on her creamy skin. Fireworks blasted behind her eyes, her nerves ablaze the longer he drew out the seduction.

Without warning, her Pulse was sent out, shooting from her without her consent. The sounds of the kitchen in the background increased their volume, so it didn't sound like she was in the breakroom, but fresh in the middle of the action. Her Listening picked up even more, and she heard conversations out in the dining room as if the diners were talking directly to her from a foot away.

When Henry's lips kissed a line along her jaw, she let out a frightened bleat as yet more sounds overwhelmed her, bringing her Listening out into the street. The cars seemed to zoom right around her, though she knew she was still standing in the breakroom.

Henry's thumb dug into the dip of her hip, and suddenly she could hear not just through the walls to the businesses next to the bistro, but two, three and four businesses down the strip. Too many people spoke at once, each one as if they were standing right in front of her. The world began to spin in sickening shades of white as Henry's shirt blurred before her.

She could smell leather from the shoe store a few businesses down. There was the smack of asphalt that hit her nose, coupled with the stink of exhaust from the many cars in the throes of a traffic jam. Ella heard a man laughing as she choked on his cloying cologne.

Suddenly, it wasn't just her Listening and Scent that reached out, but now a third sense was added into the mix.

Ella gasped as Henry's shirt doubled and tripled in her vision. She whined in duress when she saw clear as day the Baron stepping out of the smoke shop. She knew that was a five-minute drive from the bistro, and couldn't reconcile how she could see him, much less how she was sending out her senses so far away. He glanced over his shoulder, taking in the men who were still in the smoke shop, talking about who knows what sort of diabolical plans. She watched while he snapped his finger at his driver, as if the man was a dog.

It wasn't until the car horn blared from several blocks away that the walls of the bistro began shaking. Henry cried out, along with the patrons in the dining room and all along the strip. The crash of several objects toppling off shelves only added to the chaos, which didn't come to a stop until Ella's knees buckled.

Henry went from holding the wanting woman in his arms, to scrambling to keep her upright. "Ella? Ella!"

She fought to stay conscious, though the noises were so disorienting that a break from it all might've been a welcome respite. "Henry?" she shouted, unable to pick out her own voice from the cacophony.

With every second that passed after the romantic tryst died down, Ella's Listening began to return to normal. The cars that were blocks away slowly faded, then the business four doors down, then three, then two, and finally, she heard only the sounds of her own heavy breathing, and Henry's worrying as he lowered her down to sit on the floor. "What happened?" He pulled out his phone as he knelt before her, cupping the back of her head so her forehead could rest on his shoulder. "I'll call a doctor."

"No. No doctors. I'm alright." She touched her temple, and finally her Pulse slowed its sickening pace. "Oh, make it stop."

"Make what stop?"

"The spinning." When she could finally focus on

Henry's face, she took in the tenor of his terror. "I scared you. I'm sorry."

"Of course I'm scared! I've never held a woman in my arms while she fainted, and I've got to tell you, I'm not a fan. What happened?"

"I didn't faint," she corrected him, slumping against the shoulder he offered to steady her. She didn't fight it when he shifted to sit beside her, and guided her head to rest on his chest, her hand fluttering to his taut pectorals.

When the breakroom door flew open, she turned her head and closed her eyes, childishly hoping the man in the black suit coming into the room wouldn't see her.

"Henry, are you alright? I don't know what that was, but maybe we should go."

Henry shielded Ella with his body as much as possible. "I'm fine, Victor. I'll come out when I'm ready. Can you do a check in the neighboring businesses to make sure everyone's okay?"

"Of course. Stay here, then, until I come back."

After Victor exited, Henry guided Ella's head to rest against his shoulder again, their backs pressed to the wall as they sat with their knees bent and leaning in to rest against each other. "What was that, Ella?"

"That happens sometimes when I get worked up."

"Explain it to me. Surely I'm not the first man to audition for a kiss from you."

"No, but it's never been like that. Usually I just get a

headache, and my Pulse goes a little wonky. This was far more intense."

Henry found the grace to snigger, combing his fingers through her curls to soothe her. "I'll take that as a compliment." He pressed a chaste kiss to her forehead to center the swimming look in her eyes. "You should see a professor for that, or a private tutor or something. You made the walls shake! Surely someone can help you."

"No one can help me," she said with palpable heartbreak. The fissure she'd long tried to spackle in with denial or a plucky can-do spirit was exposed, and she wished for a blanket the size of Avondale to cover her untold crimes. Tears built up like too many piles of dirt that meant to bury her in her shortcomings. She'd wanted to steal a moment—just a moment—where she could be a woman on a date with the man of her choosing. Ella chided herself for being greedy and pining for a kiss. She'd wanted some freedom, but she knew her life wasn't her own. It belonged to Lady Tremaine.

Henry held her like that until she calmed in his embrace, remaining beside her, no matter how long it took. For all the hiding and running from him she'd done, she was finally in one place, trusting he was strong enough to hold her while she teetered on the edge of falling apart. He pulled a handkerchief out of his pocket and dabbed at her eyes, though she hadn't permitted a single tear to fall. The gesture was clear, though: should she let herself cry, he would be there to hold her, preserve her pride, and hide her away while she struggled to keep her dignity afloat. "Please, Ella. Let me help you."

"You can't tell anyone what happened. It wasn't me. I didn't mean to make the walls shake!"

Henry was patient, but firm. "Of course it was you. But I won't rat you out. I barely understand what's going on, so there's no story to tell."

Ella heaved out a gust of relief. "Thank you. It's important that I keep my secrets."

Though he knew better than to try and kiss her, he still wanted to be as close as humanly possible. With only a noise of surprise from her, he drew her onto his lap, keeping her head resting against the firm haven of his chest. He didn't speak for several minutes, but contented himself to hold the woman he hadn't been able to shake. "I'll get you a cell phone, so you can call me when you start to get overwhelmed with your Pulse, or even your normal life."

Ella stiffened. "No. You can't buy me things."

"It's not for you. It's for me. I don't like worrying. Giving you a way to ask for help is purely selfish on my part. I want to be the first name you call if the world freezes over, and you actually admit you can't do this alone." He squeezed her bicep. "I need it."

"No," she said, resolute that she wouldn't be a burden. "What you need is people in your life who aren't cursed. You need people who can help you, not ones you have to scrape off the floor. So embarrassing."

"Ella, don't fight me on this. I don't like Lady Tremaine, and I think even less of her now that I've heard some of your stories. What I need is you, blue eyes. More of you. Always and only you."

Ella warmed to the nickname, burrowing into his arms as if that was the one place where she belonged. "Henry, I..."

"Please," he whispered.

She didn't answer him for a long time, but contented herself with the quiet that fell between them as she traced her fingers down his sternum, allowing the soft rise and fall of his chest to lull her into a state of calm. "If this is what you really want, then yes to the cell phone."

He gusted out his relief. "Thank you. Tell me it's not just me feeling this thing between us. Tell me I'm..."

Ella brushed her fingers over his cheek, savoring the feel of his skin. "Always and only you," she admitted, echoing his earlier pledge.

Henry's chest puffed as he held her tight, ignoring the bustling of the kitchen just outside the door, and the worries of the diners. The impromptu earthquake had shaken the block, but left the two of them steadier than ever.

9

WHAT THE BARON REQUIRES

Having a cell phone of her very own felt like a secret that burned in her soul and made Ella a little more brave. She'd been texting Henry every night after the household went to sleep for several weeks, and relished the thrill of something so rebellious. He still asked regularly if he could bring in a tutor to help her, but she insisted she couldn't do so without massive fallout. She confided in Henry enough to tell him that any mention of her Pulse made life very difficult for her at home, so there was no use fussing about it.

However, the small scandal of the cell phone and sneaking around with Henry gave Ella just the push she needed to step outside of the tight cage she always kept herself in. Instead of making sure her animals stayed out of sight, she allowed the birds who braided her hair that morning to sing her songs around the house while her stepsisters were out, and her stepmother was in her bedroom.

Lady Tremaine stalked out into the kitchen with an irritated scowl tugging at her bony features. "Ella, if I have to tell you to keep your creatures out of my sight, then clearly I haven't made myself someone you fear. Would you like me to remedy that?"

Ella stood up from the floor she was polishing and looked her stepmother in the eye. "You're welcome to tell them to go, but I'm not sure they'll listen to you. I know the rules. No one is to know I can talk to them. But as it's just you and me, I think they're alright to hang out here and watch me work. They've even taken to preening the knots out of Drizella's hair ribbons for her."

"Can they polish the floor? Because that's what I'm hoping happens. Can you manage that without vexing me every second of the day?"

"I'm nearly finished, Lady Tremaine." Though she could've cleaned the floor with magic—commanding the rags to work without use of her hands—Lady Tremaine preferred Ella on her hands and knees. Any hint of Ella using her abilities was a threat to the ecosystem in the house of tension.

"Good. And set another place at the table for dinner. The Baron will be joining us, so it would help if the place looked like someone actually cleaned it regularly. Bird poop on the table isn't acceptable."

"Of course, Lady Tremaine. I'll make sure the birds are

out of the house before the Baron shows up." Ella got back down on her hands and knees and continued scrubbing out a scuff on the floor. She would normally keep any conversation to the birds, but today she was feeling bold from all the private texts between her and Henry. "You know, if you like, I can ask the birds to sing you a song. Whatever song you want to hear. It might calm your nerves before the Baron shows up."

Lady Tremaine blinked down at Ella, confused at the kind offer. Several emotions vacillated across her face, and Ella prayed she would land on pleased. Oh, how she wished for anything to make Lady Tremaine truly happy. Perhaps then the superior woman wouldn't be so bent on making the world around her more miserable.

It wasn't excitement, but pure malice that played in Lady Tremaine's eyes when she finally landed on an emotion that suited her nature. "Have them sing 'My Loveliest Girl'. I haven't heard that tune in ages."

Ella's intake of breath was a mistake, but couldn't be helped. "No." It was an outright defiance, which Ella knew wouldn't go over well. Even without her newfound boldness from her secret affair with Henry, she still would've put her foot down.

Lady Tremaine's haughty eyes narrowed, and her tone lowered to the deadly one Ella knew well to fear. "What did you say to me?"

"No. That's my song, and you can't have it. They'll sing it for me when I want to hear it, which is never."

The birds chirped their agreement, knowing that Ella loved the song her father had sung her every night before bed. Since his death, she couldn't bring herself to hear it. It was the perpetual knife lodged in her chest, and she wouldn't allow Lady Tremaine to touch it. There were so many things Lady Tremaine had taken from Ella, but she would not let the song be on that list.

Ella didn't rise when Lady Tremaine neared, her heels clicking across the floor slowly to drag out the ominous pounding of Ella's heart. She didn't speak, but grabbed Ella by her ponytail and dragged her down the hall toward the utility closet.

Lady Tremaine's Pulse was Submission, and she didn't hold back as she stamped out Ella's kicking legs with a few waves of the drug nature had given her. The birds were in a frenzy, chirping and swarming around Lady Tremaine's head. When she batted one of them out of the air too roughly, they backed away when their comrade hit the wall with a sickening thud and didn't get back up.

Ella let out a terrified scream for the bird, whose only crime was singing.

Lady Tremaine shoved Ella's limp body into the closet, banging her stepdaughter's head against the wall. "You'll stay in here until I'm satisfied you've learned your lesson. That will be the last time you defy me, child. I hope you enjoyed it."

Ella couldn't even cry out when Lady Tremaine slapped her across the face after shoving her in the tight space. Lady Tremaine hefted Ella up, because the utility closet was too narrow for anyone to sit in if the door was closed. Ella's body was weary, and trembled unnaturally as the door swung shut and locked, encasing her in utter blackness. She didn't like the dark, but knew there was no mercy for such things as fear.

It wasn't until the song her father used to sing to her wafted under the door from Lady Tremaine's playlist that Ella began to panic.

The song tormented the parts of her she'd tried to tuck away and never think about. Some memories were too treasured to surface in such a grim place. Her father was precious to her, and now his beautiful song was being used as a weapon to hurt her.

Her father had never hurt her, but in the dark of the closet she felt raw and worn from too many days without him. In her imagination, she pretended the closet was her choice—that she was playing hide-and-seek with her father, as she'd done when she'd been a girl with giggles and dreams. She didn't want to be a woman without dreams.

The broom closet was too shallow to lay down and too narrow to sit. Each movement was to be indulged in with care, lest she risk the cleaning supplies toppling over onto her. The broom and mop to her right and the vacuum and solutions to her left didn't leave much room. So she stood in her shame, hungry and wanting reprieve from any number of problems she couldn't conquer.

The tears threatened to fall, but she kept them locked tight inside of her. The song tortured her worse than the throbbing in her head and the ache in her ribs from the broom's end that had been jabbed into her side when she'd been so carelessly handled. The back wall was cold but clean, since Ella knew at least a couple times a month she would land herself in here for vexing Lady Tremaine. She could hear her father's gentle cadence as he sang the song to her, tucking her in and kissing her forehead. Life had been so much simpler back then. Ella recalled crying when her doll's arm was chewed off by the neighbor's dog. She longed for the luxury of weeping over something so small and simple.

She wished anything in her life could be simple.

Too many emotions filled Ella, threatening to wring her out like a sponge filled with far too much sorrow. She wanted to weep, wishing she could have the things she needed in life. The song played on repeat all afternoon, slashing the wound open over and over again.

It was four hours before Lady Tremaine unlocked the narrow closet, jerking Ella out by her ear. Ella knew it wouldn't be all night she was forced to stand there; the Baron was coming for dinner, and Lady Tremaine's daughters were home. Someone had to make dinner and get Drizella and Anastasia out of their mother's hair.

"Now, you listen to me," Lady Tremaine seethed. "If this place is not spotless by the time the Baron arrives, you'll wish for a week in that closet to escape the beating

I'll give you. We need high class all the way. I don't want him to assume I'm a fixer-upper. The menu better be top notch. Do not disappoint me."

Ella kept her head bowed. "Yes, ma'am." Then she stumbled off toward the kitchen as her knees tried to remember how to bend. She was grateful that at last, the song had stopped playing.

Ella flew through the chores and then started in on the dinner, wondering how she was going to make a meal to impress the Baron with hardly any time to spare. She decided on Spaghetti Carbonara with roasted root vegetables on the side, and set to work to make sure everything was perfect.

The table was set with Lady Tremaine's wedding china, which was only used for fancy occasions. Ella despised the look of it. The harsh pink of the roses stood out like it had been colored in with a fuchsia highlighter, with olive green vines draping across the center. Ella and her father had joked that the vines looked like they were choking the food. She knew he'd hated these plates, but he'd given his bride what she wanted.

It wasn't until he passed away that Ella realized Lady Tremaine had used her Pulse of Submission to lure her father into a languid married life of compliance.

There was no hot water for Ella after Drizella's bath and Anastasia's twenty-five-minute shower, but she didn't mind the icy blast that snapped her to attention. If anything went wrong with the Baron, Ella knew there would be no mercy.

Ella dressed in black trousers and a white blouse, knowing that was the dress code for the help whenever important guests came over. Lady Tremaine wanted it known that she was wealthy enough to have a servant, so Ella was paraded out as many times as she wished to display her opulent lifestyle.

When Ella came out of the bathroom, her skunk was sitting on the mattress, asking her why she'd been locked in the closet again. The birds were unabashed gossips, so it didn't take long for word to spread to her only friends that she'd been locked away yet again. "It wasn't so bad. I got to do some good dreaming in there," she lied. "I think we should invent a new language just for us. That way, no one will know what we're saying to each other."

The skunk offered to spray all of Lady Tremaine's expensive dresses, but Ella turned down his reoccurring suggestion. "That's sweet of you to vindicate me, but you know that's not nice. Besides, I'm the one who has to clean everything up, so it would actually be a punishment for me. But thank you for the thought. You're the best skunk a girl could have."

Ella flitted down the steps, making sure not to let the wood creak beneath her feet. She finished cleaning up the kitchen, and busied herself fixing up Drizella's and Anastasia's hair, apologizing for not helping them sooner. The table needed setting, so she worked on that, grateful that the Baron's ego was such that he was never on time.

"The Baron's twenty minutes late, Mom," Drizella observed, needling her mother, as was her way. The three sat in the living room, with Lady Tremaine forbidding them to do anything else, so they would be ready to greet the Baron upon his untimely arrival.

"He's too important to be confined by a mere schedule. He'll arrive when he's ready, and when he does, we'll greet him with welcoming smiles. I don't think I need to stress to you girls how much we need this. Ella's trust doesn't open until she's twenty-five. Until then, we have to bring in more money if we want to stay where we are."

Ella cringed at the notion that her trust could or would be slowly drained the moment it opened. She'd already met in secret with an attorney two years ago, signing specific instructions that the money wouldn't be released, but put into another airtight account that Lady Tremaine couldn't touch.

The deed to the house was also in Ella's name after her father passed it down to her, and had been paid off long ago. She'd had a second document drawn up, making sure the house couldn't be sold or given to anyone else, no matter what. Ella had a healthy enough fear to legally safeguard herself against Lady Tremaine's Pulse.

Those two documents kept her from getting too riled up whenever Lady Tremaine spoke about a future that made Ella want to scream. Lady Tremaine had squandered enough of her father's legacy. Ella vowed long ago that the madness would stop there.

The Baron was forty-five minutes late when he finally arrived, but Lady Tremaine greeted him as if she was pleasantly surprised by his visit, after shooing Ella out of sight. "Oh, David. Do come in. I was just thinking about you."

"I can't imagine a better way to spend one's time," he simpered, offering her a smile that was every bit as fabricated as the one she beamed at him. He removed his coat and dismissed his guard to go wait out in the car for the duration of the visit. "I guess I'll just hold this, then."

Lady Tremaine's eyes flashed with venom at Ella the moment she flitted to the kitchen to fetch the girl who'd been told to stay out of the way. "Are you stupid? Come and take the Baron's coat for him."

Ella bit back her frustration at being jerked around with conflicting requests. "Yes, ma'am." She kept her head down and took the Baron's coat, offering up an apology for her tardiness.

"It's so very good to see you again, Ella. My, my, how you've grown." His words were friendly enough, but the way he said them was positively sinister. His eyes always managed to drift to her breasts, which were modestly covered. The white blouse was supposed to feel like armor against his unwanted glances, but the material felt laughably thin, now that she was so near him. She made quick work of hanging up his coat, and slipped back into the kitchen, grateful that Anastasia had gotten out her flute to entertain the Baron with her off-key tunes.

Lady Tremaine's laughter sounded like breaking glass as she fawned over every word the Baron uttered. Ella had been instructed to stay in the kitchen, but the Baron mentioned that his servants stood during the meal, watching him eat to make sure they could tend to his needs without him having to raise his voice.

It was difficult for Ella to remain invisible when Lady Tremaine snapped her fingers and ordered her to stand in the corner of the dining room, a tea towel in hand, just in case. Ella felt like a wall hanging, posted to be ignored or stared at whenever it pleased the diners. She kept her head down, but her skin burned when she felt the Baron's eyes on her form. She wanted to run away and take the hottest shower of her life to scald his icky gaze off her skin.

"I think we did a fine job of presenting your concerns to the king during the Dinner of the Elite. We make a brilliant team, if I do say so myself." Lady Tremaine touched the Baron's arm, and then shot a covert glare at Anastasia, who was chewing with her mouth open like a cow munching its cud.

"The king isn't swayed easily. Perhaps you'll accompany me to the next dinner?"

True glee lit Lady Tremaine's pinched features. "Yes! Of course, David. Whatever you need. You know you can ask me for anything."

"Can I come?" asked Drizella. "I've been reading up on

Prince Henry. I know his stances on the policies. I'm sure if I could just get ten minutes alone with him, I could make him see how dangerous the Lethals are."

The Baron took in Drizella's face with a calculating squint. "It couldn't hurt. Prince Henry is swayed only by his father, but at this point, I'll try anything. Perhaps the king can be persuaded by his son. If we try both routes, that's probably more effective."

Anastasia piped in with a mouthful of food. "Ee oo!"

The Baron looked down his nose at Anastasia's round face. Her chin was glistening with butter from her meal, but her grin found a way to shine through the grease. "I only have a seat for a plus-one, and for my son. Calvin can sit this one out. I'm sure he'll find something else to occupy his evening."

Anastasia pouted, complete with crossing her arms and huffing like the toddler she'd never stopped being. "No fair."

Ella tried not to move at all at the mention of Henry. She didn't like that they were plotting out how to manipulate him, as if he was some mindless fool who needed to be instructed how the kingdom should be run.

So focused on remaining invisible was she, that she barely noticed how deliberately the Baron's elbow bumped his water. "Oh, would you look at that? All over my pants." He cast around for a towel and snapped his fingers at Ella, as if she was his dog. "You, there. Bring your tea towel."

Ella was already on her way to his seat to offer her towel, but when she reached him, he turned in his seat and opened his knees to her, leaving his hands out to the side.

Ella dropped the towel on his lap. "I'll go get you another, sir."

"Am I expected to clean up this mess by myself? Surely Lady Tremaine pays you enough to know your job by now. Clean me up, Ella."

Ella froze, certain she'd heard him wrong. "But, sir, I... Lady Tremaine?" She looked to her stepmother in hopes that she would offer to dab at his trousers for him, but her stepmother's jaw remained tight.

"Do as you're told, Ella."

Ella met the Baron's snide gaze with anger she didn't conceal. She took the tea towel and swiped over his thighs, setting it back down in his lap. "All clean. Excuse me."

The Baron was used to being the most important man in most rooms he dined. He snapped his fingers at her again and pointed to his lap. "Until it's dry."

Ella waited for Lady Tremaine to intervene, begging her stepmother with her eyes to say something. Neither woman wanted Ella anywhere near the Baron, but Lady Tremaine played the role of the cool girlfriend who looked the other way. "Do I need to repeat myself, girl? Do as the Baron asks."

Ana's mouth was dropped open in disgust, while

Drizella's vindictive grin couldn't be tamed when the Baron ordered, "On your knees, Ella."

Ella obeyed, if only to be done with the task as soon as possible. She stuck to the tops of his thighs, scrubbing at them with the balled-up tea towel as vigorously as she could, so she could be dismissed from the horror.

Blood pumped in her ears, and without meaning to, her Listening sent itself out to the neighbor's house, cluing her into what television program the husband liked to watch while his wife tucked their child in for the night.

Ella was careful to avoid the Baron's lap, though he scooted his pelvis out a few inches, spreading his legs further to make his advances completely clear. When the towel was soaked through, she sat back on her heels.

The Baron reached down and snatched at Ella's face, cupping her chin in his bony grip. "This one needs a firm hand. My servants don't hesitate to give me what I require."

Ella gulped, trying to keep her expression neutral. She could tell that he enjoyed her fear, so she refused to give him even an ounce.

Lady Tremaine's bark came out with a slight tremble. "Ella, you're dismissed. Do not frustrate me again with your incompetence."

It was the green light Ella had been begging for, and she didn't look back as she bolted out of the room and ran outside, her heartbeat thrumming in her ears as she tried to lose herself, and all of her problems, in the woods.

10

FOUR DOZEN

It was two days after dinner with the Baron before Ella's swollen and black eye finally started to open. Just the sight of Ella pushed Lady Tremaine into a rage, knowing that the Baron preferred young blondes to the woman desperate to be on his arm. It didn't matter that Ella hadn't returned his advances; it was her mere existence that drove Lady Tremaine to the brink.

Ella hadn't returned Henry's texts since the dinner, too lost in her own despair to conjure up even a passable representation of cordial conversation. She didn't want him anywhere near that humiliation. If anything, it sealed her decision that he was best kept far away from the mess she was mired in. She missed him terribly, but knew it was for the best. He had a kingdom to think about, and shouldn't be wasting his time holding together a sinking ship. She ached to return his texts, reading them over before bed, but remained firm in her silence.

Ella kept out of sight as much as she could, making sure everything was spotless and in order, so as not to give Lady Tremaine any additional ammunition that might fuel her hatred.

When the doorbell rang that evening, neither Drizella, Anastasia or Lady Tremaine moved to answer it. Ella put her tools away from her bout with the rickety garbage disposal, dried her hands on the apron she'd made from a worn men's flannel, and moved to the front door to greet who she was certain would be a solicitor, or one of Drizella's dates.

The gasp that flew from her lips wasn't telling; anyone who opened their door to find the Prince of Avondale standing on their porch would likely have the same reaction. "No!" she whispered, pain slashing across her bruised features. She didn't want him to see her like this—so clearly in need of help she couldn't give herself.

Henry gaped at her black eye in horror, speechless.

It was the man next to him who finally spoke, introducing himself with a calm demeanor that had been bred into him from birth. "Good evening, Miss. I'm Remus Johnstone. I'm looking for Lady Tremaine. Is she available?"

Ella couldn't find the right words—or any words, for that matter. She stood in the doorway, stunned and ashamed, begging Henry with her one good eye not to give their secret relationship away.

Remus stood with perfect posture in gray slacks, a lavender shirt, and a blue tie that had a streak of canary yellow across it. His knowing gaze seemed to understand the conundrum, clapping Henry on the shoulder to remind him that he couldn't behave like a man in love. He had to conduct himself like a prince, which meant he couldn't throw Ella over his shoulder and run her far, far away from the people who tormented her.

It was Drizella who popped her head into the foyer, her penciled eyebrows raised. "Oh! Mom! Mom! It's Prince Henry!" Her comical shouts died when she remembered her mission to seduce the prince, and calmed her tone to a low, coy come-hither. "Hello, your majesty. Won't you come in? Don't mind our servant. She's slow in the head. We're very gracious to have hired someone like her."

Ella closed her eye, wishing that, of all people, Henry hadn't heard her stepsister run her down so cruelly. "Please come in."

"Go ahead, Remus. I need a minute."

Remus did Henry a solid and addressed Drizella, taking the air of authority, since he was the oldest person in earshot. Ella guessed him to be in his mid-thirties, but there was a timelessness to Remus Johnstone that made him seem boyish, and yet simultaneously ancient. His black hair was neatly fashioned, and his posture upright and polished. "The prince has a few packages in the car. Might he borrow your servant to help him carry them in?"

"I can help him!" Drizella offered eagerly, standing up on her toes with wide eyes as Anastasia came bounding in, munching on a donut.

Remus smiled, and the look was so genuine that Ella almost bought the words that flowed seamlessly from his lips. "I wouldn't dream of asking a fine lady like yourself to do something as common as unloading a car. Besides, I'm here to speak to you two and your mother, if she has a moment. It's concerning important matters having to do with Avondale's future."

Drizella thrilled at the attention, forgetting all about Ella, who slipped out onto the porch with Henry. Anastasia fetched her mother, and the three fawned over every word Remus said as they dragged him into the dining room.

Henry balked at Ella on the porch, speechless in his shock.

"Your car," she reminded him. "I'm supposed to be helping you bring in packages."

"What happened to your eye?"

"You shouldn't have come here!" she whispered at him as she walked towards his town car.

"It's been two days since I heard from you. You can't blame a guy for wanting to know why he's being blown off. Now I can see I shouldn't have waited so long. Who hit you?"

Ella sized up his clenched fists and shook her head. She didn't mean for her next words to come out like the crack of a whip, but they bit at him for getting too near her open wounds. "None of your business." She covered her mouth, instantly ashamed for being so acerbic when he was only trying to be compassionate.

Henry reared back as if she'd slapped him. "Excuse me?"

She touched her forehead, overwhelmed at the mere sight of him on her property. "If I tell you, you'll confront the person, and it'll just make things harder for me. I told you, I'm stuck in this. I don't want to take you down with me."

Henry reached out for her hand, but Ella shirked away. "She'll see!"

"Who? Lady Tremaine?"

Ella nodded and opened the back door of his car, looking around for packages, but seeing none. "She doesn't like it when men pay attention to me."

"Ella, I swear to you. Tell me who hit you, or I'll make a big scene right here, right now," Henry's voice rose ominously, "and the whole neighborhood will know how I feel about you."

Ella ducked and then looked around fearfully. "Would you keep your voice down?"

"Why? I've only been keeping our connection quiet because that's what you said had to be done. I want to call up Royal Watch and let them know I'm officially off the market. I want to bring you home to meet my father. The whole nine yards of relational bliss—I want that with you."

Ella swooned and simultaneously crashed, her face falling. Emotion caught in her throat but she refused to cry. "You can't say things like that to me!"

"Why not?"

"Because I want to hear them too badly! You're trying to make me believe things can be different, but I know that they can't. You're giving me hope, Henry. It's the nicest and cruelest thing you could do to me."

Henry popped the trunk, so they could keep their fight away from Lady Tremaine's prying eyes. He reached into the trunk when she moved to pick up the separate bouquets of four dozen white lilies, four dozen blue carnations, four dozen pink roses, and four dozen yellow daises. "I'll get those. I'm not going to make you carry in your own flowers."

Ella froze, taking in the massive bouquets with amazement and fear. "My own flowers? What do you mean?"

Henry ran his hand through his hair and blew out a nervous breath. "It's been four weeks since we met. You stopped returning my texts, so I came here to win you back." He motioned to the mass of flowers. "I didn't know which was your favorite, so I tried a variety."

Ella's mouth fell open as she took in the gesture that was too grand for words. "I... You... These are for me?"

"Always and only you." Henry grimaced, looking at the

flowers uncertainly. "Too much? Rory said it was romantic, but Remus thought it might scare you. I honestly can't tell which one you'll land on, judging by your face. Pretend I only bought you one bouquet if it's too much."

There were plenty of reasons to be afraid, but Ella opted for a moment of wonder. If it was only a moment she would be allowed before reality overtook the beauty of the petals beckoning her to stroke them, then she wouldn't waste that slice of time on anxiety.

She leaned in, filling her lungs with Henry's affection, which she was learning was always a little bit too much, but somehow exactly what she craved. "These are incredible. No man's ever bought me flowers before, except for my father. That you did this?" She inhaled again, and felt transported to a world that either hadn't existed, or might someday exist if life decided it knew how to be kind. "Henry, you're making it hard to resist you."

Henry's mouth drew to the side in dismay. "Only hard? Drat. I was trying to make it impossible for you to turn me away. They had tulips there, too, but not four dozen. Would you be completely swept if I'd thrown in some tulips?"

Ella managed the first hint of a smile she'd accessed in days. "How do you do it?"

"What?"

"Make me believe I have choices. Make me trust it won't all crumble the second I smile." Under cover of the trunk, she reached down and linked her little finger around his in the midst of the petals, brushing her knuckles to the silk that felt decadent. For the span of a secret, she willed that luxury of softness to transfer into her. She prayed it would stay with her long after Henry would have to take the flowers away. Her lashes swept shut. "You shouldn't do things like this. I nearly brought the roof down on our heads when we almost kissed."

Henry ran his thumb over the back of her hand, seducing her in the quiet privacy of the driveway. "That's the other reason I'm here, and why I brought a chaperone. Remus Johnstone is the best tutor in Avondale. He's worked with Rory both before and after she found her Pulse, and never gave up on her. He was my tutor until I graduated, and I still call him up when something's troubling me. He was Adam's tutor, too. Now he works with Cordray. Whatever is unbalanced with your Pulse, he can even it out, I'm certain."

Too many responses flicked through Ella's mind. "Lady Tremaine would never allow it. She doesn't like for me to use any magic at all. Not to mention I could never afford Remus Johnstone. And even if I could, he's on Lady Tremaine's marriage list. If he looks at me like I'm not a gob of gum on the bottom of his shoe, she'll beat me something awful!"

Henry stiffened. "So it was her who hit you?"

Ella shrank. "Remus can't show me preferential treatment, Henry. It'll cause me more damage than I can handle." She pointed to her eye, letting her secrets spill out so Henry could understand the breadth of the fallout. "This shiner was because the Baron made a pass at me in front of her. Please don't let Remus be nice to me!" She glanced at the flowers now as if they pained her with their beauty. "And you can't give me these, either. It's enough that I got to see them, but I can't have them in the house or Lady Tremaine will..." Ella gulped and shook her head frantically. "Please, Henry. This is the most beautiful thing any guy has ever done for me. Don't let it end in a broken rib!"

Henry's nostrils flared as his hand stiffened against hers, tightening into a fist. He opened his mouth to speak, but was interrupted by Drizella's high-pitched lilt that always came out a whine when she was trying to be charming. "Oh, Prince Henry! Mother sent me out to see if you needed an extra set of hands. Poor Ella's just such a klutz. Fell down the other day and conked herself in the eye with the iron! Can you believe it?"

"Always and only you. Please, Henry," Ella whispered, retracting her hand and stepping back just before Drizella rounded to greet the prince with her Cheshire-like glee.

Henry couldn't shift into prince-mode, but continued to stew, his jaw taut and ready to snap. "I'm trying to decide what I need to bring inside."

Drizella glanced in the trunk and gasped, her hand flying over her chest. "Are those for me?" she screeched, rising onto her toes. In the span of the few minutes that she'd been waiting for the prince to return, she'd braided her hair, thrown on the shortest clubbing dress she owned, and applied a fresh coat of hot pink lipstick to match her eyeshadow.

"Wait! I'll help!" Anastasia called from the front porch. She tuttled down the steps and ran to her sister's side, bumping her out of the way so she could be closer to the prince. She had exchanged her top for a neon green blouse that was two sizes too small. "Oh! Are those for me?"

Henry was still numb, and unable to come up with a lie quick enough to keep the sisters from grabbing at the bouquets.

Ella knew she should've kept quiet, but she couldn't bear the most beautiful gift she'd ever received being touted around by her wicked stepsisters. "Actually, Prince Henry was just saying that he was going to donate them to a local hospital, but he wasn't sure where the nearest one was."

Anastasia deflated. "Oh, charity work? Pass."

Drizella played the cards she'd been dealt on the fly. "Oh, I adore charity work. I give out gifts all the time. This is right up my alley. Do you need help delivering them?"

Henry finally came to himself, though his body language was stiff. "No, thank you. I need... I think I need to sit down," he admitted.

Drizella and Anastasia each took an arm and guided him into the house, fawning over him every step of the way. It was the most helpful they'd ever been, and it was all done with painfully cheery grins and hearty laughter at whatever anecdote they thought up along the way.

Ella walked behind him with her head down, trying to burn the image of her stepsisters on his arms out of her mind.

11

REMUS' OFFER

$\mathcal{E}$lla busied herself making tea for everyone, hiding in the kitchen so as not to make Lady Tremaine angry. She sent out her Listening, however, and worked to tether her Pulse to the confines of the living room without accidentally overreaching and adding her neighbors' voices to the mix. After she mastered that, she was able to send out her Sight as well—a gift she'd only just discovered the last time she'd seen Henry. She'd been working on strengthening and controlling it ever since. It wasn't perfect—the edges of everyone's hair grew a little burry, like abstract representations of real-life portraits— but Ella told herself it was just as good as being there as she mixed the batter for her mother's homemade scones.

Henry was a guest in her house, sitting on the reclining chair and putting images in her mind that would be cherished for months to come. She could picture him sitting there near the fireplace, reading the paper while she cleaned.

Ella flinched. She didn't want to be the maid in her own imagination. She shook her head as she put the scones in the oven, scolding herself for allowing her dream life to become so small. She retooled the visual as she set the tea tray.

Henry would sit near the fireplace in the recliner, reading the paper while she was curled up in his lap, helping him with the crossword. Their life was so simple and stress-free that they had buckets of time for such things like puzzles and papers and pleasantries.

Oh, how she wished for time with him.

In exercising the extension of her gift, she found her fingers naturally balled up into tight fists when her Listening was fully concentrated. Her fists began to tremble when she sent out her Sight. She watched Henry's careful body language through the wall, mourning the utter muting of the smile that had charmed her so.

Remus Johnstone, on the other hand, oozed a charisma that had an adult sort of subtlety to it. He had a short, professional haircut that kept his black hair trimmed above the collar but left the top with an inch and a half of movement. He was fit, and dressed in a tailored shirt and pressed slacks that didn't shroud his toned physique. "Lady Tremaine, your home is just impeccable. I wish I could get my housekeeper to do the wonders I've seen here. I mean, there's not a speck of dust anywhere."

Ella sucked in her breath, wishing she could warn the great Remus Johnstone that his compliments would only harm her in the end.

Lady Tremaine stiffened, though she hadn't permitted a slouch in the first place. "Yes, well, a servant does best when she's kept on her toes. Ella is acceptable."

Remus leaned forward with a breezy smile that could sweep any woman off her feet. "You misunderstand me. I was complimenting *you* on how well you run your household. I'm afraid I don't have the talent for grooming servants as well as you do. I just fired mine, actually. Do you think I could..." Then he shook his head and sat back. "Never mind. I can find someone else to throw my money at. I'm sure you wouldn't dare part with your servant a couple days a week for any price."

Sweat broke out across Ella's forehead—a side effect of using too much of magic she wasn't altogether well-practiced in. Her heartrate quickened as she caught onto what Remus was trying to do for her.

But why? Ella couldn't fathom why a perfect stranger would go to such lengths to help her.

Henry. Ella cringed at the revelation. She realized the only reason the great Remus Johnstone would be in this house talking about her was because Henry had told his mentor about her nearly bringing down the roof on his head. Remus was one of the most sought-after tutors, not to mention the fact that he was the brother of the Chancellor, who was second only to the king. If Remus knew about her abilities, Ella fretted that he would take her away, as her father predicted would happen if government officials found out about all she could do.

Then again, she thought to herself, *if Remus Johnstone wanted to bring me in and lock me up, he could just take me without the charade of paying for my work.*

Ella was shaking from head to foot, sweating and breathing through gritted teeth. Maintaining prolonged concentration while sending out two of her senses was taxing. She'd never held them steady for this long.

Still, she wanted to See more, needed to Hear more.

Lady Tremaine kept glancing toward the kitchen, as if weighing the pros and cons of raking in extra money versus having to wash her own laundry. "I might be persuaded to part with Ella a few days a week. For the right price, that is."

Remus perked up, as if not expecting any sort of compliance. He leaned in and offered her a fee that made Ella balk. He could've paid for three housekeepers with that amount, but he said it like he was hoping it would be enough.

To her credit, Lady Tremaine only reacted with a slight inhale, her expression plastered in place to appear some-what pleasant. "That sounds reasonable. For three days a week?"

Remus gave her a sheepish headshake. "I was hoping I could steal her away for four days a week. I'm ashamed to admit that I'm rather slovenly. I spend so much time working that I sometimes forget about everything else. You seem to have a keen eye for the details, Lady Tremaine. I was thinking perhaps when I drop Ella off and pick her up, you and I could chat a bit more about your political views. You brought up some fascinating points at the Dinner of the Elite that I'd love to hear more about."

Though his lie was delivered flawlessly, Ella could spot the buttering up for what it was and loved Remus for the crime. He stroked Lady Tremaine's ego so deftly that she scarcely realized he was doing it to push his own agenda.

The oven dinged, and Ella's abilities disappeared as she brought herself back to the kitchen. Her whole body felt as if she'd just done a hundred jumping jacks, but she moved quickly around the space, assembling the tea tray with the hot scones that needed no icing.

She'd never been so nervous before, but she knew she had to get the service absolutely perfect. Aside from serving Henry her mother's recipe for scones, it wouldn't do for her to drop the tray right after Remus Johnstone had gone to such lengths to praise her prowess in house-keeping skills. She couldn't imagine what he wanted her for, but she decided she could trust Henry. She was just desperate enough to jump at any chance that would allow her to go through life without nursing a black eye.

Ella moved out into the living room, keeping her head down as she set the tray on the stand in the corner. She doled out the scones and served the tea with a tremble she scolded herself for. Ella didn't watch Henry take a bite of the scone directly, but kept him in her periphery, chewing on her lower lip until he took a second bite, examining the scone as if it truly pleased him.

"Ella, you'll be leaving with Remus Johnstone to clean house for him for four days. He'll bring you back, and then you'll have your work cut out for you when you return." Lady Tremaine's thin lips tightened. "I trust you won't be a problem."

"Whatever you like, ma'am."

She snapped her fingers at Ella to dismiss her, and Henry leaned forward, opening his mouth to chastise Lady Tremaine for treating Ella like a dog.

Remus leaned over with a cordial chortle, placing his hand atop Henry's with a covert warning in his eyes for the prince to keep his cool. "Henry, be a gentleman and let Drizella and Anastasia show you the grounds. I'll bring Ella out once she's packed and ready to go."

The girls fawned over Henry, each taking an arm again and leading him out the front door in hopes the neighbors would see them in their glory. Drizella had her cell phone in hand and snapped a few selfies with the prince. Henry could only muster up a bland expression that did nothing to soften the agony in his eyes.

Ella darted up the stairs and packed four days' worth of clothes, her cell phone, and her meager toiletries atop her apron work shirt. Then she tied the bundle up so it fit under her arm like a tight bowling ball. Opening the window, she let her birds out, explaining the situation to them so they didn't worry over her absence.

Ella wanted nothing more than to run straight out the door, but she kept her pace even, so Lady Tremaine wouldn't know she was excited. Though she had no idea what life with Remus Johnstone might hold, she knew it couldn't be worse than the turmoil she dealt with near Lady Tremaine.

When Ella joined them in the living room, she stayed near the doorway, her head down, so she didn't impede on Lady Tremaine's moment with the important official.

"I look forward to our talk in four days," Remus said as he stood to take Lady Tremaine's hand and place a chivalrous kiss upon the back. He oozed just enough appeal to keep the girlish flirtation buoyant in her eyes, but not enough that he could be accused of leading a woman on. It was a fine line he danced, but he performed the tango flawlessly, his smile vanishing when his eyes fell on Ella's apron ball. "I'm sorry, did I forget to mention? You'll be gone for four days. You might want to pack a few more things."

Ella didn't open her mouth; she knew Lady Tremaine would speak for her. "Things distract a servant from their duties. That's the first lesson for you in how to keep a tidy house, Remus."

Agitation flashed in his eyes, but only Ella noticed it. He turned back to Lady Tremaine with a gracious bow. "You are filled with wisdom, Lady Tremaine. Thank you for this." Then he turned to Ella. "Though, I must apologize to you, Miss Ella. I'm afraid you won't have a moment of rest; my house is quite disastrous."

"It's no trouble, sir," Ella murmured.

Lady Tremaine moved to Ella and gripped her chin hard, tilting her head up so she could meet her stepdaughter's eyes and infuse another helping of intimidation. "You'll not embarrass our name. You'll stay out Mr. Johnstone's sight and work without complaint until he's happy with the state of his home."

"Yes, ma'am."

Remus' tone was light, but his fists clenched at his sides. "I have so much to learn from you, Lady Tremaine." Then he caught Ella's eyes with a warning that his patience was nearing its breaking point. "Shall we, Miss Ella?"

Ella lowered her chin the second Lady Tremaine released it, and shuffled out. She held the door open for Remus, and wondered if her life was about to get better, or far, far worse.

12

BIG MOUTH HENRY

To his credit, Henry waited until the town car pulled out onto the main road before he turned in his seat to yell his indignation. "What was that? This is how you've been living? This is what you've been keeping from me?"

Ella didn't respond. She wasn't sure how to handle Henry's raised voice. Shouting at her usually ended in a backhand, but she didn't think Henry would resort to hitting her.

"No secret in the world is worth living with that woman. Her daughters are disgusting! One of them licked my ear! Licked my ear, El!" He scrubbed the side of his face, looking to Ella like a little boy who was trying to wipe his grandmother's lipstick off in a petulant rage.

Ella tried not to laugh, and managed to muffle any sound down to a quiet snigger.

"You think this is funny? You have a black eye! How many days were we texting, and you didn't tell me something that important?"

Again, Ella didn't respond. She knew that even doing something as innocent as answering a direct question could result in kindling a fury she couldn't put out. She wanted to live in a world where Henry never hit her, and cherished the hope that her wishes might come true.

Remus let out a heavy sigh from the driver's seat in front of Ella. "Are you quite finished, Henry? Clearly she's got her reasons, though what they must be, I can't begin to imagine. I barely made it through the hour-long stay. A little tip on women from me to you: yelling will rarely get you what you want."

Henry's lips pursed, and then he deflated in his seat, rubbing his temples as if that might rid himself of the drama of the day. "I'm sorry, Ella. I don't understand. Tell me why."

Remus stepped in again when Ella remained silent. His voice was steady and calm, offering Ella something nonconfrontational to latch onto. "Wrong again. I seriously can't believe the papers still call you 'Prince Charming.' The 'why' doesn't matter right now. First things first. Start with, 'Love bug, you have a black eye. That must've hurt.'"

Henry shot his mentor the middle finger, but hung his head, penitent when he turned back to Ella. "I should've started with that. Forgive me. I'm all turned around. I wasn't expecting… I don't know why I thought you were being secretive for other reasons. This morning I thought my worst problem would be that I would get to your employer's home and find out that you were really married. I've been preparing myself for heartbreak all day. Seeing you bruised like this?" He shook his head and leaned forward, distraught. "It's an altogether different kind of heartbreak I wasn't prepared for."

Ella didn't speak, but offered him a sympathetic incline of her head.

Henry reached over to place his hand atop hers, but she shirked away, glancing toward the front seat to warn him that there were witnesses. Henry frowned. "You don't have to worry about Remus. He already knows how taken I am with you."

"We even sneaked away from Henry's guard because he knew you preferred privacy. Would you like some water?" Remus handed back a sealed bottle.

Ella was thirsty, but she couldn't get a proper read on Remus. He'd charmed Lady Tremaine easily enough; she didn't want to fall prey to any sort of scheme. She shook her head, keeping her mouth shut.

Remus's eyes tightened, but he didn't take offense. He set the bottle back down on the passenger's seat, and Ella could tell by his careful study of the barely-there traffic that he was trying to think up another way to bond with her. When they turned onto the freeway, he said with a lightness to his tone, "I'm sure this is all very confusing.

We didn't know what we would find when we got here. You probably have lots of questions."

Ella kept her lips pressed together, but held his gaze in the rearview mirror.

Henry cast his mentor an apologetic chin dip, and pressed the button on the back of the passenger's seat to raise the partition. "Sorry, Remus. She's scared, and she won't talk because she doesn't know you enough to trust you."

Remus fanned his fingers out in surrender, keeping his palms pressed to the steering wheel. "Fair enough. I'll be here to answer any questions when you're ready. Music?" He flicked on a classical station to drown out anything he wasn't meant to hear as the partition sealed him off from the backseat.

Ella exhaled and slumped back against the black leather interior. The car smelled new and looked pristine, which made her feel like she didn't belong in it—much less with a prince. "Thank you," she finally offered, relieved that she didn't have to try and decode Remus' motives.

In the next breath, Henry had her gathered in his arms, her knees looped over his while he kissed her face frantically. "You worried me!" he accused, his fretting coming out as anger. "I don't like being worried. Do you think I got to be this handsome by staying up half the night, staring at my phone?"

"I'm sorry! I couldn't text you like this. I wanted to see you too badly. It hurt every time I looked at your number."

The partition rolled down, and Remus' frantic voice filled the car. "Whatever it is you're doing to make her excitable, stop! The computer system in here is going mad."

Ella slinked off to her side of the backseat. "I'm sorry, sir." Then she shot Henry a wounded look. "You told him?"

Henry slid closer and lifted her hand, pressing it to his chest. "You can trust Remus. He's like family to me—the big brother Adam, Rory and I never had. I had to tell him, Ella. It scared me when you almost brought the roof down on our heads! I wanted to kiss you so badly, but I need to get to the bottom of what we're dealing with first, so we don't crumble a building by accident. Remus knows more about magic than anyone. My father even consults him on occasion. Remus studied under Malaura, and even countered her curse on Rory. If anyone can help us, it's him."

"I can be discreet," Remus promised. "Though, you don't have to believe me yet. You don't know me, and your first interaction with me was a front row seat to me deceiving your employer. In time, though, you'll see that no one else will discover your secret. Then you can start trusting me."

Henry and Remus waited for Ella to ask questions, but she'd gone back to silent mode, afraid to say the wrong thing.

Henry sighed and pressed the partition button again. "Another moment, Remus. I promise to behave myself."

"Sure, sure. I've never fallen for that one before."

The second they were alone again, Henry kissed the center of her palm, drawing out her blush. "I had to tell him. He can keep things quiet, and maybe he can even help us."

Ella kept her gaze on Henry's firm chest as he placed her hand back over his heart. "Help us how? It's already done. I'm stuck like this. He can't undo a person's basic makeup."

"He's worked with people who've had trouble getting a handle on their magic before. Rory had a terrible time controlling hers when it finally came about in her. He also works with a Lethal."

Ella's eyes climbed up to meet Henry's, unable to hold back her sadness. "It wasn't your secret to tell."

"I don't even understand what I told him! I still don't get it. All I know is that I want to be with you, and collapsing buildings seems problematic." He closed his eyes, pained as the memory of his visit tugged at his heart. "Why, Ella? Why do you work for such a horrible woman?"

Ella lowered her chin. "Because she knows my secrets, and she'll tell the authorities if I don't let her treat me as she pleases."

"What secrets are worth this?" He motioned to her

black eye with a palpable ache. "Tell me, and we'll find a way around it all."

Ella couldn't bring herself to tell him, but instead leaned forward, resting her head on the firm harbor of his shoulder, trusting that the shelter he offered wouldn't crumble at the first sign of a threat. She wrapped her arms around his middle, loving the feel of his body. "I can't tell if you've made things far worse, or if they're about to get better." She burrowed into his warmth. "Either way, it's time. If I end up with you, or locked in a facility somewhere, I can't live with Lady Tremaine any longer. Something had to give at some point. Might as well be now."

"That's the spirit?" he said like it was a question. He held her, rubbing her back to soothe them both. "It'll be alright, blue eyes. I won't let anyone lock you away. Imagine how horrible the cell phone reception would be. How would we text?"

Ella sniggered, but her smile died just as quickly as it came. She was scared, but she tried to take solace where she could get it.

13

WHO ARE YOU?

"**E**lla, we're not going to get anywhere if you won't talk to him. Remus is on our side."

Ella's gaze shifted to Henry in the quiet of the study. There was a fire built in the welcoming hearth, and an antique tall lamp next to Remus, who sat beside the flames in a large leather armchair, one leg crossed over the other. He had his elbows on the armrests and his fingers pressed together under his chin, while he studied her total motionlessness on the matching couch on the other side of the hearth.

When Remus spoke, Ella stiffened. "You don't want to talk about yourself, and I can understand that. How about we start with me? I'm the wildcard. You don't seem to mind talking to Henry to some extent. Ask me anything."

Ella's eyes flicked up to him, harboring a tinge of

mistrust. "You don't mean that. People say it, but they don't mean it."

Remus smiled, relaxing in his chair that he'd finally managed a response. "Did you know that I was lying to Lady Tremaine about my interest in her fascinating ideas about how best to deal with the Lethals?"

Ella ran her tongue along the inside of her bottom row of teeth before responding. "Not at first, but after a couple exchanges, yeah."

"Then trust yourself enough to know if I'm lying to you. If you don't want to talk about yourself, then we can talk about me. Ask away, Miss Ella."

Ella's lips twitched at the formal address. She was wearing her old housework jeans, a red flannel button-down and torn sneakers. Remus looked fresh off the cover of a magazine for the modern businessman—confident and crisply put together. "Okay. Who are you?"

Henry leaned on the hearth—the only one too anxious to sit. "This is Remus, blue eyes. I told you, he was my mentor and my tutor growing up."

Ella waited a few beats, and then asked again. "Who are you?"

Remus kept his body language lax. "I'm Remus Johnstone, tutor to the stars," he replied with a flair of playful dramatics.

Ella blinked at him and dug her heels in. "Who are you?" she asked again, unwilling to smile at his light-heartedness.

Remus tilted his head at her. "I'm the man who cares enough about Henry to help him out when he's worried. He was concerned about you, so I drove him over to pay you a little visit. Good thing he brought me along. He's usually better at thinking on his feet. I daresay your black eye confounded him."

Undeterred by his attempts at making small talk, Ella repeated herself. "Who are you?"

Remus frowned and leaned forward in his seat. "Alright." He swallowed hard as he stared at her, stripping off any charisma to get to the bare bones. "I help people with extraordinary Pulses. I teach them how to get their abilities under control, which Henry mentioned might be a problem you need help solving. Think of me as a friendly guide."

Ella lowered her voice, but didn't break eye contact. "Who are you?"

Remus stopped to think, turning her question over to examine it from all angles. He rested his elbows on his knees and turned his palms up in a subconscious gesture of surrender. "I'm someone who can help you."

Ella took in his sincerity and deemed the question answered, so she moved on to the next one. "Why?"

Remus maintained his submissive posture. "You called Henry to tip him off that there was a hit taken out on a few chairholders on the council. Because of you, we were able to take countermeasures, and Caleb and Eustace are safe. Henry needs more people in his life who care about him enough to speak up when he's near something dangerous."

Ella didn't accept this as the whole answer. "Why do you want to help me?"

Remus searched through his response, and then moved deeper into his rationale. "Because Henry needs someone good in his life. He's not easily enchanted by a woman. I had to meet you."

Ella was not satisfied, and spotted a look on his face that told her he was still holding himself back from answering the question completely. "Why do you want to help me?"

Henry shifted his weight from one foot to the other, impatient with Ella's process. "He's a good person, Ella. He's helping because I asked him for a favor."

Ella held Remus' gaze, seeing in his eyes that there was more to it all than that. She made it clear that she wasn't moving off this point until he answered it to her satisfaction.

Remus hung his head, a sudden wash of shame weighting his posture. "I want to help you because it fascinates me to study the mutations in our magic."

Ella nodded, finally understanding that the root of his motives were his curiosity. "Explain."

Remus obeyed her as if she was the instructor and he was the student who was being told to search out his motives as part of his daily lesson. "The community is afraid of anything new because we've all seen what

Queen Vanessa did when anyone stood out. She took them and broke them. She manipulated them so she could use their power, and then sold them out and labeled them dangerous. They were tried for their crimes, and in the older days, they were disposed of. Malaura wasn't much different. She didn't take them to break them, but she collected the ones with odd abilities all the same, and kept them for her purposes. Being close to Malaura broke the good in people." He paused to let his eyes plead with her, permitting his decades-old hurt shine through.

Ella kept her voice quiet. "Is the good in you broken?"

Remus' expression twisted from practiced calm to positively haunted. "I've done everything in my power to make sure that doesn't come about, but sometimes I worry."

Ella inclined her head to him. "Maybe it's that worry that's kept you from crossing over completely."

"Perhaps. But I know my curiosity for the strange and new has nothing to do with how she trained me. I want to understand because I think our magic is an ever-shifting miracle. Malaura made everyone afraid of anything different, but that's never been me. The evolution of magic is happening, whether the public wants to look at it or not. If we don't understand how the world is changing, then one day we'll wake up to find nature's progress has left us in the dust."

"Those uniquely gifted were given lobotomies in

Queen Vanessa's day," Ella stated bluntly. "You can understand why I'm not eager to jump aboard that ship."

Remus held her gaze, trying to convey that nothing could be further from his intentions. "Those didn't happen under King Hubert. He's a solid friend to me, and I know his heart. He doesn't want to stamp out the people who are different. If anything, he'd want to learn from the mutations so we can add to and strengthen our community."

"So, you want to use me for political gain."

Remus raised his palms to her. "I want to study your magic if it's as incredible as Henry claims. Nuances to our ancient magic have always fascinated me. I want to help you because that's my nature. But if you're worried about being used or called out publicly, I can offer you a promise that I won't speak of our sessions to anyone, aside from Henry."

Ella quirked her eyebrow, seeing his boyish fascination of the obscure for the hobby and obsession that it was. Finally, she felt she understood Remus Johnstone enough to talk. "Does your promise come with a contract? Something legally binding?"

"It does if you need it to." He pulled out his phone, but then frowned. "But you don't have a voice in court. Servants don't have legal representation, so they can't sign contracts or hold other people to them."

Henry hissed at the insensitive observation, but didn't argue the logic. "Don't say it like that."

"Like what? She wants assurances I can't give her, and

she's smart enough to know that. If I tried, I'd be lying to her, which is no way to start this out."

"I'm not a servant," Ella admitted, tucking her hands under her thighs to keep from fidgeting. "That house you just saw? I own the deed. It's my home."

Henry's mouth fell open. "What? Why? Why would you let Lady Tremaine treat you like that? She told us you were her servant! You told me you were her servant!"

"I fill that role, yes, but legally, I'm a landowner. Lady Tremaine treats me like that because she knows most of my secrets. If I misbehave, she'll turn me in so the government can do experiments on me."

Remus was speechless but Henry was livid. "How did you come to meet this terrible woman, and how does she have so much power over you? She just took over your home? Some random stranger can just move in and... I don't understand."

Ella shifted uncomfortably against the buttery leather of the couch. "Well, she's not some random stranger, for one. Lady Tremaine is my stepmother."

14

HEARING AND SEEING

Ella wasn't expecting the huge reaction from Henry, nor the sick look on Remus' face. She wondered how numb she had become to the horrors of her life, and if things were really as devastating as their expressions implied.

"It's... I mean... You'll have to excuse me." Remus stood but Ella protested, worried he would make a bigger mess of things for her.

"You can't say anything! She doesn't like people to know I'm her stepdaughter."

Henry ran his hand over his face. "How did... I don't... How?"

Ella answered as thoroughly as she could in hopes it might keep them from confronting Lady Tremaine. "Lady Tremaine married my father. She was a good actress in the beginning, but it didn't matter. My father died a few months into their marriage. She was living here when the deed was in my father's name. Her Pulse is Submission, but my father figured that out too late. He was in the process of trying to divorce her, but he died before it was finalized. He signed the house over to me, with the legal stipulations that it would never be sold from my bloodline. So Lady Tremaine got part of the life insurance money, but the bulk was put into a trust for me. It's safe until I turn twenty-five. I've done my best to make sure she can't get her hands on it then. She doesn't know that part, though."

Remus had his cell phone out at the same time Henry pointed at his mentor. "Lock that trust airtight, Remus. We'll get my financial team to move the money on her birthday. I mean, like, 12:01am. When's your birthday, Ella?"

She lowered her chin and rattled off the date, which was two months away. It was only when her stomach growled that Henry seemed to remember his manners. "When was the last time you ate anything?"

Ella stared at the tops of her thighs, wishing Remus wasn't watching her every move. "I had breakfast."

"It's almost dinner time." Henry's agony pulled at his features as woe took him over. "That horrible woman starves her, Remus. What time will Lionel have dinner ready?"

Remus sent out a text message. "Momentarily, I'm sure. We can move this conversation to the dining room. Ella, everyone who works for the Chancellor's family signs a privacy agreement, so whatever is said in this house stays here." He stood and extended his hand to her, but Henry was already moving toward her, helping her up as if she was an old woman, too fragile for long walks.

Though Ella was usually stalwart enough to move about without an escort, she indulged herself and leaned on Henry's proffered arm, letting him steady her rocking world as they moved to the dining room.

"I can get started cleaning in the kitchen," she offered. "I just need you to show me where it is."

Henry clutched Ella closer to his side. "You aren't a servant here. Remus doesn't have servants; he has employees that he pays. You're a guest in his home. *My* guest. That means you don't do chores."

She cast a baleful look up at him, finally allowing a little of her personality to seep through. "Hello, Remus paid for me to work in his home four days a week. I've been sitting around talking for way too long. I should probably get started."

Henry paused and turned her to face him, placing his hands on both her shoulders. "I want you to hear me very carefully. Remus is paying Lady Tremaine because I told him to do whatever it took to get you out of there. He needs time, and the fee bought us exactly that. Time is what he's paying for, and that's all. Time to teach you, get to know you, and also get to know Lady Tremaine's true intentions and just how deep all the manipulative plotting goes. I'm guessing you heard the threat on Eustace and Caleb's lives because the Baron told Lady Tremaine?"

Ella cast a guilty look over at Remus, who clasped his hands loosely to imitate patience while she decided how much she was willing to trust him. "I didn't overhear Lady Tremaine. I heard the Baron himself. He was talking about it in the Smoke Shop with Mr. Herchon and a bunch of other men I didn't know well enough to recognize by the sound of their voices."

Remus' head tilted to the side. "How did you manage that? The Smoke Shop is members only, and it's generally thought of as a boys' club."

Ella shot Henry a look of pleading. "Please don't turn me over to the state. I don't want to be like this! I can't always control it." Her shoulders slumped. "But that day, I did. I knew he was in there, so I did a little trick I'm not supposed to." She glanced at Remus to show him how guilty the whole thing made her feel. "My dad used to call it 'sending out my Listening.' I can..." She gulped, worried the words might stay stuck inside of her forever. Her father had been so adamant that she keep her abilities private, showing her pictures of lobotomies, and reading accounts of people whose only crime was being in the area at the time of an attack, and they were thrown in jail without a trial.

Henry's hands slipped up her shoulders to cup her cheeks. "Please, Ella. I need you to trust me. I can't help you if you don't tell me all that's broken."

She wondered if she truly was broken, or if she was just different. Either way, she knew she'd been carrying this burden by herself for too long.

So quiet, her voice was barely above a whisper, Ella closed her eyes and finally jumped over the edge of reason. "My Pulse isn't through touch, like everyone else's. It makes me able to hear through walls. Sometimes several walls. Sometimes blocks away." She swallowed hard and glanced tentatively at Remus, knowing it was all or nothing at this point. "When Henry and I almost kissed, I got nervous and happy and all the things you feel when you're about to be kissed, and something weird happened. I couldn't just Hear through the walls, I could See, too. That was the first time anything like that ever happened to me."

"Can you show me?" Remus requested with a stern look on his face before Henry could voice his shock.

She'd half-expected them not to believe her, but when Remus took to her nuances so readily, she nodded. "I'm not dangerous. I don't hurt people. It's just how my Pulse works. I don't touch people and Hear or See them. I push it out, and it travels for me, like a friend doing me a favor."

Remus clapped Henry on the shoulder. "Henry, go into the kitchen and ask Lionel what's for dinner. Ella, I want you to see if you can hear what he says."

Her eyebrows pulled together. "I can do farther distances than that."

"Then let's go outside. Shall we?" He proffered his arm to her like a gentleman, taking her hesitation in stride.

She glanced up at Henry, as if to silently ask him if Remus was a safe person with whom she could be alone. Henry stroked her cheek and coiled her hand around Remus' forearm. "Let's do this part, and then we can eat. Seriously, Remus. She hasn't had anything in hours."

"Forgive me this one curiosity." Remus inclined his head to her, trying not to spook the cautious creature on his arm.

Ella finally nodded her consent and moved with Remus down the hall and out into the vast expanse of the backyard after he draped Henry's coat over her shoulders and put on his own.

Just like everything with Remus, his property was immaculate and well-groomed. The icy topiaries were shaped into balls at varying heights, and the entire soccer field-sized property was hemmed in by a towering privacy fence that had barbed wire coiling the top. The entire thing was a winter haven—cold but somehow it left Ella with a touch of warmth to her insides.

Remus followed her eyeline and patted her hand. "My niece is my best student, so she comes here often for her lessons. I take her safety very seriously."

Ella pursed her lips, but decided she was in too deep now not to give trusting him a try.

Remus sat her on one of the wrought iron chairs on the deck. He took the seat opposite her at the round table that had curly legs to add a bit of delicate grace to the look of the heavy furniture.

Ella sat on her hands again, and kept her head down while she sent out her Listening.

Henry's voice was easy to pick out. "Roast duck, eh? Was it a large duck? I'm only asking because my girlfriend hasn't eaten in a while."

Ella's mouth curved into a small smile. That he thought of her as his girlfriend? She wanted so very badly to belong to him, and for him to belong to her.

"I can set out more rolls. Would that help? I made some pâté with the duck fat. Mixed it with apricots."

"Sounds good."

They spoke as if Henry was being boyish while Lionel was trying to get work done. "You would eat your shoe if it had butter on it. Remus has a more refined palate. The apricot duck pâté is more for him than for you, but your girlfriend might like it, too. It'll fill anyone up." He chuckled, and the sound was deep and lovely. "Girlfriend, eh? Never thought I'd see the day."

Ella kept her Listening active, and spoke quietly to Remus. "Roast duck, extra rolls, duck fat pâté mixed with apricots."

"Incredible!"

Ella touched her temples. "That was just my Listening. I'm still getting the hang of sending out my Sight. Give me a second." She touched her temples, feeling like a cheap psychic as she grimaced and tried to focus on the other parts of her brain she'd only recently learned to access.

"She's allergic to peanuts, you know." Henry revealed the nugget of truth as if he was lauding himself for knowing some closely-guarded secret. Though, so much was a secret to Ella that she could hardly categorize that as a big one.

"I'll make a note of it."

She watched Henry leaning on the island in the center of the kitchen, taking in the majesty of the dark marble top. The base was solid stone, and looked a strange mix of modern, yet ancient. There was a hibachi between the stove and the matching stainless-steel refrigerator, and her eyes drew to it with fascination. She wondered if she could ask the chef to show her how to cook on it. "Can you sauté asparagus on a hibachi without crisping the edges?" she asked Remus, though she couldn't see him.

"You can see my kitchen?"

"I can go farther than that, if I really concentrate." She knew she was growing more comfortable with Remus if she was willing to throw a little bravado into the mix. Her fingers started to tremble, so she tucked them under her thighs, even though she longed to wipe the quickly forming beads of sweat from her brow. She widened her scope beyond Henry, seeing the mailbox in the front of the house, and the span of the sidewalk. She followed the walkway down the street, stopping at the curb and turning, as if she was an avatar in a reality-based video game of her own making. She wanted to be able to have an aerial view, but that required more concentration than she could spare at the moment. So her Sight took on movements as if it was a person confined by gravity.

"You're pale as a sheet, and you're sweating," Remus observed, worry dampening his tone.

She shook her head, her eyebrows pulling together when she let go of her Sight and brought herself back to the view in front of them. "I'm guessing that's not good."

Remus touched his frown as he thought. "For now, let's not try to Listen or See beyond my home. Let's get the basics down before we go worrying about the larger scheme."

Ella bobbed her head, trusting Remus a little more after that nugget of wisdom. He didn't seem to want to exploit or push her abilities, but to help her hone them in. "Dinner's ready," she informed him, standing. "It doesn't feel right that I'm not in the kitchen, at least offering a helping hand."

Remus rose to his feet and twisted at the waist to give his body a little stretch. "Does it feel right that your step-mother sold you to the highest bidder? I could've been wanting you to come with me for any number of unseemly depravities, and I have the feeling she would've said yes if the price was right."

Ella balked at him and took a step back. "Why would you say that to me?" She hadn't thought of it like that, but now the horror seemed glaringly obvious. "Oh! What if you're right?"

Remus held up his hands to settle her worries. "I have no intention of letting you return to your home in its current state. The moment you say so, I'll have her removed from the premises and charged with all sorts of fun things that will stick on her record longer than she can outlive them."

Ella's face was pinched with dread. "You can't do that! I mean, I appreciate it and all, but you don't understand what she's capable of. She'll out me to the community. She'll tell everyone what I can do! They'll take me, Remus!"

Remus remained calm, controlling his tone to ease her fears. "You can't go back there, and I won't let anything happen to you here."

"I just want her to leave me alone!"

Remus shook his head slowly, kindness shining in his eyes in earnest. "I think you're destined for dreams far greater than that."

15

HOUSE RULES

Ella took a step back, touching her forehead with her eyes squinched shut. "This isn't what we agreed to!"

When Henry came out to get them, his casual lightness fell when he saw Ella's guarded body language and Remus' stern expression. "What did I miss?"

"He wants to keep me here, but if he does, Lady Tremaine will tell my secrets! I'll be studied and manipulated to fight for whichever team needs someone who can hear and see through buildings."

Henry moved slowly as he approached her, shivering at the chill in the evening air. "There are lots of ways to keep Lady Tremaine quiet, if that's even necessary. The world and the government aren't the same as they were when your father made those rules for you. My dad isn't going to take you in and experiment on you. That's exactly what kind of reputation he's trying to avoid."

"Maybe not your dad, but can you honestly tell me that the Baron is capable of seeing a new flash of magic and letting it pass by him? Maybe your dad is a good guy, but not every man in power is your father. Once my secret is public, the new magic is out there for people to protest, demanding I be locked up."

"Do you think my father would cave to social pressures so easily? Have you seen one Lethal locked up who was innocent?"

"It's a gamble, Henry. I know you love your father, and I've got nothing against him. What I've got is a lifetime of hiding who I am and what I can do because I understand how quickly the political climate could shift. Your father was a great change from Malaura, but I'm not so naïve that I don't think it could someday shift back to something darker."

When Ella shivered, Henry forgot his fight and wrapped his arms around her. "We can argue about all of that later. We have four whole days to come up with a plan. Right now, you need to eat. That's the only thing you can be worried about tonight."

Ella hesitated, but finally consented to being led inside to the dining room. She paused at the table as Henry pulled out her chair. Her eyes widened as he slid it under her thighs, wondering if this was what normal people got to do. The table was lavishly set, with a gold runner down the center of the purple tablecloth. The gold-rimmed dishes were far fancier than anything Ella had ever eaten off of. The aroma of the duck filled her senses and set her stomach screaming for just a bite.

"What's wrong? You've got that face about you."

Ella leaned toward Henry and whispered, "I'm not supposed to be here."

Henry was patient with her misgivings, and handed her the basket of rolls. "You belong wherever you put yourself, and you've put yourself next to me. So I guess you belong with me after all."

"Not that." She touched the outside of her shoe to his under the table to let him know he'd touched on her sweet spot. "At the table. I'm not supposed to eat at the table. I eat standing up in the kitchen."

Henry pursed his lips, but Remus spoke up to keep Henry from saying something acerbic that wouldn't be altogether helpful. "My guests eat wherever they please. Does it please you to eat with us? To dine with Henry?"

Ella flushed at being asked something so direct and personal. "Well, yes, of course. I just... This isn't... I feel like I'm breaking the rules. Can you tell me what the rules are to this place? I do better if I know ahead of time."

Henry was about to say something flippant, but Remus took in her concerns seriously. "The rules for the house? Clean up after yourself, not anyone else. Is that understood?"

Ella fidgeted in her seat, unsure if she could agree to

his terms. Her whole life in the past couple years had been dedicated to cleaning up after others. "I can try."

"That's good. Rule two: What you learn in our sessions should only be practiced here, until we get the hang of it. It'll do you no good to take a lesson half-learned, and go out into the world with it. That sort of courage is dangerous, and could hurt you and others."

"Yes, sir."

"Rule three: Just like you, I prefer my private life be kept private. I trust that won't be a problem?"

"No, sir. Of course."

"Good. Now that we've settled that, let's eat."

The roasted vegetables were right in front of her place setting, but her eyes darted around nervously before she ventured her trembling hand out to scoop a few Brussels sprouts, parsnips and turnips onto her plate. They were glazed with a sweetness that Ella took only the briefest of moments to savor before she shoveled in another bite, and another.

Henry and Remus discussed the next Dinner of the Elite while Ella filled her plate with duck, pâté, more vegetables, and three rolls. As with any meal, she wasn't sure when the next might come, so she ate as much as she possibly could while the food was in front of her. It wasn't until she'd finished her last roll that she realized the men were gaping at her.

"I'm sorry." She shrank in her chair, grimacing at how much she'd eaten so fast.

"Don't apologize. That was right sexy." Henry's eyes were hungry for her. He looped his foot around hers under the table, drawing her chair closer to his. "Have some more duck."

Ella shook her head. "No, no. I'm finished."

Remus waited until she glanced at him to speak. "You don't have to worry here, Ella. The chef prepares three meals every day. All guests in my home are welcome to eat as they please." Remus took in her mistrust of his declaration with a sadness he couldn't conceal from Ella. "If you're okay with a few evaluations of basic magic, just so I know what we're working with, I think that's all we should concern ourselves with tonight. Formal lessons can wait until tomorrow. You've had a long, eventful day. I think rest would do us all a world of good."

Henry wiped his mouth on his napkin as he stood. "I'll take her things to the guest room."

The space between Ella's eyebrows puckered. "You don't have to do that."

"I know I don't. I want to. You've had a long day."

"No, Henry."

Henry placed his hand on the back of his chair, pushing it in with a frown. "Why won't you let me be good to you?"

"Because you're a prince! Because it's my job to put things away, not yours."

Remus excused himself, instructing Ella to meet him in the study before she went to bed.

Henry's voice lowered, even though it was just the two of them in the room. "I need to know if you're interested in me, Ella. Tell me if I have a shot."

Ella gaped at him. "Are you serious?"

Henry's jaw stiffened. "Okay. Good. At least I have my answer."

Horrified at his assumption, Ella scrambled to undo the damage. "You wondering if you have a shot with me is insane. I'm nobody. Literally nobody. If you're asking me if I want to be with you, of course I do. Always and only you. But the way you talk to me, like I'm something you're hoping for, it's very confusing. I feel like it's a joke that's going to come crashing down on my head the second I believe in it."

It was all the confirmation Henry needed. He scooped her up from her seat and wrapped his arms around her, swaying her in his embrace with an expression of gratitude over having her so near. "All I heard was 'blah, blah, blah. Henry, be mine.'"

"Well, that's exactly what I said. Stellar job listening," she teased him, relieved at his elation. A portion of her insecurity poked out. "You want to be with me?"

Henry's eyes lifted to the ceiling, as if in silent prayer for patience. "Only every day since I met you. Always and only you. We can be as public or private as you want about it all, but I haven't been able to stomach the thought of being with another woman since we met." His thumb traced up and down her spine with a slowness that communicated how long he'd wanted to hold her exactly like that. They didn't need to rush. Ella felt in his touch that Henry was certain about her, no matter what surprises came their way.

So she let him take his time as his thumb acquainted itself with the curvy slope of her hip. She savored the moment as he brushed his nose across hers, relishing the quickening of his breath. He didn't rush a moment of the kiss she'd been anticipating for far too long. With much trepidation, she savored the light caress of her lips against his.

16

READING BETWEEN REMUS' PAGES

Ella's lashes fluttered against Henry's cheek as the kiss took on a life of its own, growing in pace and passion once they got through the initial sating. There were too many weeks of subtle build-up to keep their attraction tame. It didn't take long before his tongue found its way past her lips, dancing with hers while they gripped each other with an edge of desperation to be closer—forever closer.

Ella's mind flashed as her Sight went out without her consent, alighting on the people in the house without preamble. She saw the chef, who had a curly mustache and a pot belly, but a relaxed expression as he did the dishes. She saw Remus jotting something down in a leather-bound notebook, using a fine-tipped fancy pen that made him look like a scribe. He leaned back in his chair and ran his hand over his shirt, brushing a stroke of pink across the breast, and then green, and then blue, all while deep in thought. He made a few more notations, but then looked up at the ceiling with sudden worry.

It wasn't until then that Ella realized the ground was vibrating beneath her feet. Her lips regretted the moment she shot back from Henry, missing the taste of him she had to forfeit for the greater good. Henry's eyes were still lidded, his hand moving over his heart as Remus tore into the dining room, eyes wild. "What was that?"

Ella backed into the corner, covering her face with her hands to hide her sins. "I didn't mean to!"

Henry fought his way through the haze of lust to take a stab at being helpful. "When we almost kissed before, the same thing happened. Walls shaking, and her Pulse went mad. Are you alright, Ella?"

"How can you ask me that? I almost just murdered you with my kiss!"

Henry tilted his head to the side, overcome with compassion as he closed the gap between them. Despite her misgivings, he held her in his arms, resting his chin atop her head. She wanted to run far away, so she wouldn't have to bring so much drama and danger into his life, but when she told her feet to move toward the exit, they planted themselves firmly in front of Henry's. Her body knew where it belonged. Her heart knew, as well.

Running his fingers over her back as if to soothe her angst, Henry kept his voice calm. "We did better that time. I finally got to kiss you, and your Pulse didn't do anything we couldn't back out of. We can do this, Ella. We can make this work."

"My Sight went out while we were kissing! I saw the chef washing dishes, and Remus writing in his journal. I can't control it when we're..." She couldn't bring herself to say the word "kissing" in front of Remus, who was still trying to rein in his shock.

"Yet," Henry reminded her. "You can't control it yet. Remus can help us. Please, Ella. Don't run away from me. If this is what we both want, then it's worth fighting for."

Ella's desire to bolt flitted away at his sincere plea. "You're not afraid of me?"

Henry shook his head and tucked his finger under her chin, lifting so he could get a full shot of her stunning features. "Not afraid. Crazy. I'm crazy about you, blue eyes." Then to prove his point, he carefully delivered a closed-mouth kiss to her full lips, as if needing to connect with her when she was so very shaken.

This time, the walls didn't tremble, nor did her Pulse go off on its own tangent. The kiss was just simple enough to give her a hit of something incredible without sweeping her away into the land of steep consequence. "Henry," she whispered his name like a prayer for clemency, begging him to be patient with all of the things she wanted to be, but wasn't there quite yet. She wanted to be a woman who could make-out for hours with the man she desired, but she had to be measured and careful.

She buried her face in his chest, memorizing the smell

of him. His deodorant was the right amount of fragrant, giving her a hit of masculine sweetness mixed with cloves that made her swoon. The planes of his chest were firm and broad enough to make herself a pillow out of his hugs. His body welcomed her to rest, always to rest. She hadn't been comforted like that in so very long. She winced, so unaccustomed to the support that at first it registered to her sensibilities as pain. It took a few breaths, but finally she relaxed in his arms, taking what she needed without certainty of being slapped.

Remus backed out of the room to grant them their privacy, and Henry used their alone time to hold Ella's arm out to the side so he could turn her in a slow waltz. It was partially to romance her, but in the back of his mind, he wanted to equip her for the many social engagements where she would need to know such things. He could picture her in a sweeping gown, her hair done up. There would be a confident smile on her pink lips, replacing the cagey glances to which she often defaulted. He could see the life of status laid out for the woman who was used to the shadows, and resolved himself to ready her for his world.

"You're keeping up quite well," he commented as he started to turn them, picking up the three-count rhythm as he might with someone who was more adept at dancing. He'd endured many lessons to make sure he didn't embarrass his mother on the dance floor, and was surprised Ella didn't seem to need much coaching.

"My father taught me. I can't believe my feet still remember how."

Henry tightened his hold on her, pressing his pelvis to hers as they let the worries of their situation slowly fade away, melting into the background as the desire to be simply teenagers on a date took center stage in their hearts. "I love it when you smile at me. Every time, it feels like I've won some sort of lottery."

"What about when I smile like this?" She crossed her eyes as they waltzed, finally letting her silly side shine through. She usually only let herself be goofy in front of her animals, who didn't much value proper behavior anyway.

"Simply ravishing." He kept the dance going as he leaned in to whisper, "I think it's been too long since you've been ravished."

Ella's feet stumbled as her attraction peaked. The dance slowed to a stop, and she cast a scolding up at his boyish grin. "Well, we can't do anything like that. I nearly broke Remus' house just a few minutes ago, if you recall."

"Worth it." Henry proffered his elbow to her, and Ella judged that he was beaming with a smug pride at being the one who made her lose control like that. He escorted her through the burgundy-painted halls with his chin high, ready to show her off to the world.

Remus stilled his pacing back and forth in his leather and dark wood bedecked study when the two entered. He cast up a teasing smirk and feigned an ease that didn't touch his eyes. "I trust no children will be conceived under my roof? If there are, there may not be a roof left to speak of."

Ella burrowed her face in Henry's shoulder while the prince sniggered and kissed the top of her head. "None yet. I'm delivering your prized pupil, ready to learn. I'll leave you to it." He made to drop her arm, but she clung tighter to him, betraying her pride as her nerves began to bleed through. A wave of tenderness seemed to sweep through his body at her silent plea for him not to leave her in uncertain situations where she was still finding her footing. "Would you like me to stay?"

Ella kept her arm looped through his, but tried to shrug her anxiety off so she wasn't a bother to him. "If you like."

Henry shook his head, chiding her for playing it cool when they were both so thoroughly smitten. "I think you'll have to ask me."

Ella's lips tightened as she shot him a warning look that this was well beyond the confines of her comfort zone. She ignored Remus' probing stare, and dropped her voice to a whisper. "Oh, fine. Henry, would you mind sticking around for a little bit?"

"Forever," he promised. "I wouldn't mind sticking around forever. All you had to do was ask."

Remus tsked the two at their obvious cuteness, motioning to the two chairs on the other side of his desk. "It's surreal to see you so captivated, Henry. I always knew you had it in you, but you never found the right girl."

Henry beamed at his mentor. "Are you going to weep now? Sing me a song about how grown I am?"

"Oh, Henry. It's my sincerest hope that you never grow up." Remus rubbed his palms together and set about his evaluation of Ella's grasp on magic. There were the rudimentary things—recitation of credos and the history of their magic, which she knew as well as any graduate should. Then there was the practical display of levitating books, but Ella went beyond the basics, and opened them to specific pages without touching—a feat usually only professors could perform. Remus skipped on to the advanced things—stacking objects midair, and making them rotate at differing speeds and directions, which she did with only a few hiccups.

"I'm sorry. I'm not allowed to use magic in front of Lady Tremaine or her daughters, so I'm a little out of practice. It agitates her, because it reminds her that I can do other things I'm not supposed to." She tried to sound matter-of-fact, but the culpable look on her face betrayed the guilt she nurtured over being so very different.

Remus kept his expression kind and unruffled, making notes in his leather book every so often. "You're not taking exams, Miss Ella. This isn't a pass or fail situation." He snapped his notebook shut and set it on the wide desk that looked organized and regal with its polished wood. Everything Remus Johnstone did had a hint of sophistication and surety to it. He pressed his finger atop the notebook as he spoke. "I want you to read what's in here."

Her eyebrows shot up. "Yes, sir." She'd been curious about his annotations, so she extended her hand to him.

"Without opening the book. You can send your Sight out, but let's see if you can focus it."

Ella stayed very still. "Why?"

"Because you need to trust yourself. There's nothing inherently wrong with someone having a mutation to their magic. Incidentally, it says in your school's records that your Pulse is Kindness. Would you like to fine-tune that, as well, during our time together?"

Ella shifted uncomfortably in her seat. "They told me it was Kindness, but I don't have a regular Pulse. Mine sends itself out from me. Nothing happens when I touch a person."

Remus extended his arm palm-up for her to touch. "Try it on me."

Ella fidgeted, embarrassed that Henry was hearing her shortcomings. "If my Pulse really was Kindness, it would've worked on Lady Tremaine and her daughters a long time ago. My professors just labeled me with that Pulse because that's what they felt around me. Pulses like that are easy to fake." She hung her head, feeling like a fraud. "I'm a terrible person."

Henry draped his arm around the back of her chair, sensing her need not to be abandoned. "You naturally bring out kindness in people without the use of magic? I think that's pretty great."

Remus leaned back and sat on his desk. "People put too much emphasis on Pulses. Rory couldn't perform any magic most of her life, but she's still capable and contributed much to the council. You have new magic that you've been taught is dangerous, yet you're ashamed you don't have a Pulse. Who cares about Pulsing, when you can hear through whole buildings?"

Ella raised her chin to look at him. "You're not worried something's wrong with me?"

"I know exactly what's wrong with you. You've got it bad for Henry, here. That's the only thing that should concern you. He's quite high-maintenance."

Henry guffawed. "You're the one who gets regular manicures!"

Remus shoved his hands in his pockets, rolling his eyes bashfully. "Can you read one of the pages in this book, Miss Ella?"

Ella shrugged with uncertainty, but decided to give it a try. She leaned forward in her seat, resting her elbows on her thighs as she stared at the book, sending her Sight out a few feet from her body. It wasn't easy to control the tether, and she accidentally saw through three walls to the empty foyer before she was able to reel it back to the desk.

She closed her eyes, shutting out the distractions so she could focus on the notebook. A few times, she over-shot it and saw too deep, viewing the contents of his desk.

"You're low on paperclips," she observed, and then recalibrated her Sight.

Finesse like this took more concentration than she was used to, though she'd been practicing her Sight every day since she'd discovered the new leg of her ability.

"That's enough. She's sweating, Remus."

Remus was firm. "She can stop whenever she likes, but fine-tuning her magic will only help her get it under control. If you want to kiss her without the walls shaking, she needs to explore her magic in a controlled, safe environment like this."

Henry reached over and placed his hand atop hers, silently warning her that she didn't have to do this if it was too hard. When her eyelids squinched like she was in pain, Henry brought her head to rest on his chest, holding her tight, as if she was breakable.

Oh, how Ella wished she was allowed to be breakable.

Ella gripped Henry's forearm to steady herself when her world began to tilt. She felt pressure in her brain as she whittled the layers away, gasping when she burrowed through the cover and bored through to the back. She bit down on her lower lip and dialed upward by the tiniest of degrees. "The back pages are empty," she reported with a note of wonder that she was actually doing it. The beige pages were faintly lined, and as her Sight danced delicately upwards, she alighted on his neat calligraphy. The letters were tight and written with purpose, drawing her mind's eye with a fascination she couldn't turn away from.

"'Work on controlling his Push once he goes off the second dose of the pill. He should be able to electrocute with precision, not at random.'"

Henry's grip on her head tightened, and she heard him shouting at Remus, but couldn't focus on his words. She was tuned-in to her Sight, and wanted to read more. Suddenly, it felt like she was in kindergarten again, triumphing over reading through her first sentence. Elation filled her, and pride over being able to do something she never thought possible made her desperate to read more. It could've been a dictionary of bird parasites, and she would've been fascinated to drink in every word.

"'Also needs to work on controlling the voltage. See if he can toast bread, instead of burning it with electricity.'"

There was more shouting, but it only sped up her urgency, unsure when the hullabaloo would interfere with her quest to read every word.

"'His fingertips are heating up when he practices for prolonged periods. He needs to breathe through the Push at a steadier rhythm. He holds his breath now, and it exacerbates his metabolic system.'"

It wasn't until Henry released her head and pulled her to stand that Ella's Sight snapped back, bringing her with a dizzying spin to the fight at-hand. She didn't have the wherewithal to support herself as the room tilted beneath her. Henry broke his argument with Remus short so he could scramble to catch Ella when her knees buckled.

Remus hurried to Ella's other side, and the two

lowered her back to the chair with great care. "Henry, run and get her some water."

"You did this to her! Don't think I don't know when you're taking things too far. How long has Cordray been off the pill? Was that your idea as part of your insane experiments?"

Remus' jaw was tight. "You don't understand the situation." The space between his eyebrows puckered with consternation. "Cordray is outgrowing the pill, Henry."

Ella's breathe came out in heavy pants, but even she tuned in to the anomaly.

Henry was beside himself. "What are you talking about?"

"Cordray has to take two pills to mute his magic, but now even that's not working as well anymore. His body's adapting, so I took him off the additional dose. He still takes a single pill every month. We work on the root of the problem, controlling his electricity so he can dial it back. We're hoping he gets it under his control so much that he doesn't need to take the pill at all."

Henry's tone was shrill. "Do you hear yourself? Cordray is a Lethal! Are you honestly telling me that you've been advising him to dial back on medication that helps him not accidentally murder the future Chancellor of Avondale?"

Remus held up his hands. "I'm trying to help him when medication can't."

"This is wrong, Remus. This is wrong, and you know it.

How could you and Rory keep something like this from me?"

"Because we knew you'd react exactly like this!" Remus didn't indulge in any further arguing, but instead focused solely on Ella, kneeling before her and shining the flashlight feature on his cell phone in her eyes to test if they dilated correctly.

When Henry took in her sickly pallor, he came back to himself and ran out to fetch her some water.

Remus instructed her to focus on his finger as he moved it from left to right to make sure she could track it. "Tell me your symptoms, Miss Ella. Don't leave anything out."

Ella tried to wipe the sweat from her brow, but only managed to smack herself in the face. She closed her eyes at the sweetness when Remus pulled a handkerchief from his pocket and dabbed at her forehead. "Just dizzy. Sweaty. Weird headache."

"Weird, how?"

She tried to put words to it as she came down from the intensity. "I can't explain. Just weird."

His voice lowered. "Is there a pressure behind your temples? Does it feel like your brain is too big for your skull?"

Ella's mouth popped open. "How did you know that?"

Remus brought Henry's abandoned chair to sit across from her, their knees knocking as he leaned forward. He brought her head to rest on his shoulder, as if they knew each other well enough for such intimate consoling. "Because I've seen others do variations of what you can do—stepping outside the normal confines of a Pulse. When Henry told me about your abilities, I knew I needed to meet you. You're not alone, Miss Ella."

His last sentence rang in her ears, striking a chord of acute yearning she'd long given up on satiating. She'd desperately wanted to find someone else like her, but had shouldered the burden of abnormalcy by herself. She steeled herself against breaking down in tears all over Remus' shirt, and settled on clutching him as tight as she could around the ribs. Remus was solid and steady, and as her worldview rocked, she clung to her new tutor, hoping that when the waves settled, he could explain all the things that haunted her.

17

HENRY'S BEDROOM

Henry was fuming as he showed Ella to the guest bedroom. The dozens and dozens of flowers he'd bought had been arranged in various vases and placed about her room, but neither of them could enjoy the sights or smells, because Henry was so worked up. "I can't believe he'd let Cordray go off the pill just to test his abilities."

Ella didn't contradict him, but she didn't agree, either. She kept her mouth shut, knowing when someone was in a tirade, it was best to let the fit run its course. She stayed in the doorway, her hands folded in front of her while she waited for him to wind down. After he'd blown up at a shockingly calm Remus yet again, he'd ranted for a good five minutes, and all the way up to the second floor.

"I mean, there's being scientific, which I understand, and there's being purely and simply homicidal! What I don't understand is that it's Remus doing this! Remus! He sacrificed five years off the back end of his lifespan to give Rory a fighting chance at surviving Malaura's curse. Then he goes and lowers her husband's medicine—for what? Pure curiosity? It's insane!" Henry gestured wildly with his hands as he paced the plush beige carpet, his white dress shirt standing out against the lavender walls that had gray trim along the baseboards. The comforter was the same shade of gray, making the bed look like it was from a designer's collection. There was a dresser and a nightstand, but that was all that took up space as Henry stalked back and forth. "Why aren't you more upset about this?"

Ella kept her lips tight together and shrugged, hoping he wouldn't require more from her on the subject.

When Henry sensed she was keeping herself from him, he stopped walking and stared at her. "You don't have to be silent."

"You're angry," she observed carefully, her hands still folded in front of her. "If I talk, it might upset you more."

Henry made to say something, but deflated at her decorum that had a note of anxiety to it. "I won't be mad at you. I'm angry at Remus. Ella, you don't have to be afraid of me."

Ella's cagey glances told him that she needed time to be the determiner for that promise, not merely his word. "I was thinking of turning in. Can you show me where I'm supposed to be sleeping?"

Henry motioned around the room. "Your new home away from home."

Ella frowned. "No, not where you sleep. Where I'll be sleeping. My head still kinda hurts."

Henry softened and moved over to her, holding his hands out to invite her to hold onto him. He relaxed when she moved into his body space, squeezing his hands and trusting him enough to let him lead her forward into the room. "This is where you'll be sleeping. Is that alright?"

Ella gaped at the room that was far too large for her. "But it's only just me in here. I don't need all this space. Where do the servants sleep?"

Henry's eyes softened around the edges, donning the patience he was learning to produce as needed. "Remus doesn't have servants. He has employees who go home after they finish working. This is Rory's room when she stays here, and you can use it now."

She shot him a baleful look. "I really don't think the Chancellor's daughter would like me sleeping in her bed."

Henry pulled out his phone and called his best friend. "Rory, quick question. My girlfriend is staying at Remus' place for a few days." He didn't get through his actual reason for calling for a solid minute, holding the phone away from his ear while Rory squealed and shot a string of rapid-fire questions at him.

Ella covered her mouth, unsure if she should be horrified that Henry was asking such a bold request of the elite woman, or if she should let herself be entertained by the steady stream of queries.

"I can call you that, right?" Henry whispered to Ella while Rory babbled on the other end.

Ella couldn't believe the life she was now living, where the Prince of Avondale wanted to ask her such things. "Of course."

Henry let out a gust of victory, and then reached out to hold her hand. Putting the phone back to his ear, he tried to rein Rory in. "Alright, alright. It's not that shocking. I was just wondering if she could sleep in your bed tonight."

"Yes!" Then, upon further thought, Rory shouted, "No! She can't sleep in my bed. She has to sleep in your bed with you."

Henry chuckled at his friend's attempt at meddling. "Thanks, Rory. Tell Cord... I dunno, something nice." He hung up the phone and used his grip on Ella to twirl her in, making her look and feel like an elegant dancer who was meant for such things. In that moment, they forgot their limitations and frustrations. They forgot about her black eye, and its many implications. They put aside the evolution of magic that was uncharted, and the dangers of magic unchecked, and simply were.

Henry nipped at her lips, but Ella wasn't in the mood to be teased. She reached up and slid her fingers along the nape of his neck, deepening the kiss and parting his lips with her tongue. She was high on the thrill of exploring her magic and being so far from her responsibilities. She had been old for so very long, but on this night, she wanted to be a teenager. She relished Henry's soft noises of passion that sounded equally hungry and fearful of how easy it was to fall.

When Ella's Listening went out, her knees buckled, and she slumped in his arms, panting as he broke the kiss to press his cheek to hers. Without having to be told, Henry spoke her quandary aloud. "Breathe through it, blue eyes. Take a minute. We've got nothing but time to work through this." He made a show of breathing deeply, stroking her hip until she could stand on her own again.

Ella burrowed her face between his pecs, which was rapidly becoming her favorite spot on his body. It was always warm, no matter how cold the world felt. She could feel his heartbeat, and that steady rhythm was a soothing balm that spackled over the gaps in her psyche. "Home," she murmured as contentment washed over her, rinsing her anxieties away for the moment.

Though the longing in Henry's eyes made it clear he wanted nothing more than to ravish her, his arms coiled around her curvy frame, gathering her to him as if they both needed to never let go. "Tell me I'm your home again. I think I need to hear it."

She pulled her face back a few inches so she could rub her favorite spot on his body, making slow circles with her palm as if it truly was the one space in the world where she belonged. "You're my home, Henry. This spot right here. You can have the rest of you. I just want this part."

"You can have all of me," he pledged, placing his hand over hers and holding it to his heart. Then he leaned in and pressed his cheek to hers, as if the secret admission was something that needed cover of darkness and whispers. "I want to stay with you tonight."

Ella's mouth drew to the side, clearly torn. "You might be disappointed when all we do is sleep."

"Of course." Henry's face lit up, and he pulled back to press a kiss to her lips. "Anything more might bring the house down. We can't have that."

Henry took her hand, gave Ella her bundle of clothes, grabbed up the nearest vase of flowers, and moved backwards out of the room and down the hallways, a look of pure rapture on his face as he led her to his bedroom. "Welcome to my room."

She couldn't take her eyes off him, standing in the space and looking like the one thing that had been missing from all the rooms in her life. "That's nice Remus has a room just for you here."

He dropped her hand and went to the dresser to pull out pajamas, setting the blue carnations on the surface to add something to the room that enchanted her. "Yes, well, it used to be for Adam and me to share. There's a trundle underneath. But Adam doesn't leave his castle much anymore." Before she could protest, he held up his hand. "And no, Adam won't mind you sleeping in here. Adam doesn't care about much of anything these days. Remus doesn't mind, either, so long as we don't break his house."

Ella took her bundle and unwrapped it, fishing out a tank top and shorts to sleep in. She leaned up and pecked his lips before disappearing into the en suite bathroom to change for the night.

After she brushed her teeth and prepared for bed, she came out to find Henry in green flannel pajama pants and a white undershirt that looked somehow formal and expensive, even though it was a normal t-shirt. Everything he did and every item he wore looked tailored and upscale, making each movement a sight to study.

Henry looked down and frowned. "What? Did I put my shirt on backwards or something?"

Ella swallowed hard and tried to remind herself that making out was harder to slow down when a couple was already in their pajamas with a freshly made bed right beside them. "You're handsome like this."

Henry's smile pulled to the side as he watched her fidget. Her white cotton tank top was faded and had a few stains on it, but made it delightfully obvious that she was a woman who was clearly in shape. When paired with her lavender cotton shorts, Ella noticed the deliberate steady breathing that was Henry reminding himself to be a gentleman.

He pulled back the covers and motioned for her to take the spot furthest from the door. "Under the covers with you. I don't want anyone else seeing you so scantily clad and delicious looking." He grabbed a book and climbed in on the other side, leaning against the headboard as he flipped open to the marked page and flicked on the antique lamp atop his nightstand, trying to slip into his normal routine with Ella by his side.

"It's weird how natural this feels," Ella commented as she shifted her pillow into place, supine next to his seated form. Her eyes drifted to the four dozen blue carnations, cherishing the look of something so beautiful existing just to make her smile. "You're sure you don't mind me in your space?"

"Are you kidding? I'm contemplating moving in, just so we can be exactly like this every night. Does it bother you if I read for a little bit?"

"Only if you don't read aloud. I'd love to hear whatever it is you're into."

Henry snorted as he showed her the cover. "My dad insists I reread this one every year."

"*War Strategies and Artistic Battles*? Not into light reading, eh?"

"I don't mind it. It's a little dense to plow through, though. Thin book, but it takes me forever to finish." He flipped back to the beginning and started from the top for her benefit. He'd had to read aloud many times, and in far more formal settings. He'd read public statements and country addresses, but tucked away in bed with Ella, he looked truly vulnerable. He cleared his throat too many times, as if worried he might trip over the words.

Ella saw his quandary and tugged him down to lay next to her, bending his arm out across her pillow so she could rest her head on his bicep. She turned on her right side, her body tangling through his when he kissed her, biting lightly on her lower lip just because he could. They kept the pacing slow, and Ella only ended the kiss when she deemed Henry calm enough to read to her.

His voice was velvety and soothing as she leaned her cheek to his chest, treasuring every moment they were together. He read in various accents just to entertain her, switching nationalities between stanzas to make her giggle. If she ate up every word he read, he devoured every smile that graced her lips. Her black eye was starting to fade, and they both wished for the day when he could hold her exactly like this without the reminder of the people who were so very cruel to her.

18

THE CENTER OF TOO MUCH ATTENTION

The next morning, Ella woke with sunshine harbored in her heart that she'd been able to sleep next to the man she adored. That simple shift unleashed so many things inside of her that had been waiting for something incredible to come along. She watched him sleep with rapt fascination, studying his pouting lips.

He stretched like a cat, not missing a beat before his arms wrapped around her, drawing her nearer, even though he was barely awake. "Good morning, Henry."

"Good morning, blue eyes." He kissed her the moment she finished yawning, and the two spent ten entire minutes rolling around and making a perfect mess of the sheets. Even when Ella's Listening went out, ending their morning make-out, they both noted how much better she was becoming at controlling her errant magic. "That was longer this time," he commented from his position atop her, his arms caging her in so he could occasionally lean down and suck on her lower lip. "How's your head?"

"A little tender, but worth it for an alarm clock like that. So weird. I never sleep in this late. I'm always up before the sun."

"I must be good for you." He kissed her nose, smiling when it scrunched as she wiped off the slightly wet remnants.

When he finally parted from her body to take a shower, it was with the express instructions that she remain in bed, lounging around. He showered as quickly as he could, and then ran a bath for her.

Ella's hand flew over her heart, her eyes lighting at the romance when she saw the extravagance of the bubbles. Orange and jasmine called out to her, flooding her senses with pure happiness. "What did you do?"

"For you, while I make some phone calls. Believe it or not, I have a little work to do that doesn't involve seducing you. Stupid government job." He kissed her cheek, wrapping his arms around her from behind. "Then we'll have breakfast, and we can start our day."

"I'm still reeling that my day will start at like, nine in the morning. I'm usually up and working for three hours by now. You're turning me soft, Henry. Pretty soon, I'll be sleeping till ten and reading books all day long."

"You can have all of that," he promised, and then lowered his mouth to her ear. "Let me protect you. Let's go public. Lady Tremaine can blabber your secrets. No one will care, and those who do won't be a bother to you."

While Ella wanted nothing more than to believe in the dreams he tried to sell her, she knew it wouldn't be that simple. "Your father might think he has cause to lock me up. If I wanted to, I could hear straight into his palace, Henry. I could be a threat to national security."

"But you're not. You wouldn't have to hear through buildings to get to the royal chambers." He trilled his fingers across her abdomen. "You could live there with me."

Ella gasped, her heart swelling to near bursting at his grand words. She closed her eyes, envisioning a life so beautiful that she could be permitted to maintain a permanent place in his world, and in his home. "It's a lovely dream." She slid her palm over the back of his hand and let him hold her while the dreams hit a crescendo, and then deserted her. "I've got to warn you; I haven't had a bath in years. Usually I just jump in the shower real quick. I might be a while in here."

Henry took a chance and skimmed the strap of her tank top over her shoulder, just so he could kiss the creamy skin that had teased him all night long. "Take your time. I'll be here when you're ready." His words held many meanings, and Ella appreciated all the nuances to his pledge.

He left her with the frothy, scented bubbles, granting her a morning where she could truly relax. She didn't emerge for half an hour, unable to recall the last time she'd felt so refreshed.

When she came out, Henry looked at her old jeans and red and blue flannel shirt as if she was the most beautiful woman he'd ever seen. "I'm torn. I want to blow the day in bed with you, but Remus needs us downstairs for breakfast soon, so you can start your lessons."

Ella's eyes widened as she slid on her socks. "Did he sound angry? I took too long in the tub, I know it."

Henry sniggered at her fretting. "Remus doesn't get mad at anyone, unless they're trying to like, murder someone he loves. Then he can get a bit snippy."

When Ella noticed a shadow of something more serious flicker across his face, she tilted her head to the side. "You alright, chief?"

He pursed his lips, as if debating between telling her the G-rated version of his mind, or going in for the truth. "I'm all over the place today. One of the calls I made while you were in there was to Adam."

"Adam Fontaine?"

Henry nodded. "I thought the closer he got to his transition, the meaner he'd get, but he was actually civil on the phone, if not on the edge of cordial. I haven't seen that shade on him in years."

Ella waited a few beats before she spoke quietly. "How much time does he have left?"

Henry drew in a long breath, as if he needed to be

steadied before smacking himself in the face with the truth. "Less than a month. Far less."

Ella moved over to Henry and held his hand. "Do you want to go spend some time with him? I'll be fine here without you."

"But *I* won't be fine without *you*." The shadows were quickly replaced by a grin of forced bravery. "He doesn't want me around, and I've accepted it." Then he stood straighter, staring at their joined fingers as if the sight was something at which to marvel. "I don't want to be sad. I want a good day with you, so that's what this is going to be."

"Well, it sounds like it's all decided, then." She leaned up on her toes and pecked his lips, letting him know she would drop the subject, if that's what he needed.

He held her hand as they moved through the hallways and skipped down the stairs. They bumped each other with their hips and laughed like children on a mission of mischief.

Ella's blonde curls were in a messy bun atop her head, but the moment her eyes fell on Remus' guest at the dining room table, she wished she'd opted for something nicer. Her grin melted to a more composed expression, and her hand fell from Henry's to clasp in front of her as she assumed a subservient posture.

"Good morning," the woman greeted them as she stood. "You must be Ella. I'm Rory."

Aurora Johnstone was slender like a ballerina, with a

gentle smile that looked as if she was well-practiced at dazzling the cameras at a moment's notice. Even at an affair as simple as breakfast, Rory wore black dress slacks and a delicate pink blouse with a silver brooch that was littered with diamonds surrounding a large ruby in the center. Her nails were perfectly manicured, and her black hair was swept back with two ruby-encrusted barrettes that didn't dare fall out of perfectly level alignment.

Ella expected to exchange a quick greeting, and then be dismissed to the kitchen to eat her breakfast. Instead, Rory threw her dainty arms around Ella, squeezing her with all her tiny might. They were similar in height, but Ella was slightly curvier. She shot Henry a look of silent alarm at the jubilant embrace, but said nothing other than, "Very nice to meet you, Your Grace."

Rory released her only a few seconds before she scooped Ella's hand up and led her to the seat next to hers at the large table. "You're to call me Rory, and I'm to call you my new best friend. Tell me everything about your-self. I can't tell you how long I've waited to meet you. Henry's been keeping you secret for far too long. I knew something was different, though. I knew he was smitten. Now that I can see you in person? I can tell why he's so taken with you. You're absolutely lovely."

Remus covered his mouth when a chuckle slipped out. "I don't think I've heard you speak that much in a row ever in my life. Did you even pause for a breath?"

"Who has time for boring things like breathing?

Henry's got a girlfriend!" She clasped her hands together under her chin. "Oh, Henry. I never thought this day would come."

Henry grumbled good naturedly as he sat on Ella's other side. "You act like I have no social skills. Like it would be a miracle for any woman to fancy me. I'm not a mutant, you know." Then he raised one shoulder higher than the other, lifted his hands to look like claws, bugged one eye and twisted his mouth into a roar. "Oh, no! You've discovered my secret! I really have been a mutant all these years." He growled, and then swooped in to mime taking a bite out of Ella's neck.

Ella let a giggle escape, but then swatted at his antics, pursing her lips to scold him. "Would you shush? I'm trying to make a good impression, here."

Rory's hand flew over her heart, worry widening her brown eyes. "Oh, no! You shouldn't think I'm anyone to impress. We're going to be the very best of friends; I'm certain of it. Henry tells me you'll be staying here, which means we'll have nothing but time to get to know one another."

Ella shifted uncertainly, but couldn't see any hint of falsity in the woman who positively beamed at her. She wasn't used to unfettered approval, and wanted to mistrust it on instinct, but there was something about Rory's wide, accepting eyes and joyful bob on her toes as her legs danced under the table that made Ella wonder if there really might be good people in the government after all. "That sounds nice."

"This evening," Remus interjected. "Rory, you have your lessons this morning. I was thinking Ella might want to sit in on them."

Rory's face fell as she turned to her uncle. "Are you sure? I thought you said we were going to keep those lessons private."

Ella shirked back, worried that her presence was going to upset the girl who seemed perfectly delightful. "I don't see why I should intrude, Mr. Johnstone."

Remus was dressed for a day at the office. He presented himself as the professional the rest of the world knew him to be—wearing gray pants, a light pink pressed dress shirt, and a blue tie that he kept brushing other colors across in ribbons while he sized up the three. "It's unfair that Ella's been expected to divulge all of her secrets, while we have our own that might help her understand hers. She's gifted, Rory. Much like Cordray is. I think watching your lessons will help her tremendously. I trust you can be discreet, Ella?" His eyes focused in on her, uncrinkled around the edges, as if unperturbed by her response, because he already knew what sort of character she possessed.

"Of course, Mr. Johnstone."

At this, he tilted his head at her and squinted one eye. "I believe I asked you to call me 'Remus.'"

Ella flushed, her fingers tightening as they remained

clasped in front of her, but she didn't waver. "I'm working my way up to that, sir."

Remus broke his formal demeanor and covered his face, letting out a handful of soundless laughs of frustration into his palms. "Very well. Get some breakfast, and I'll see you ladies in the study when you're finished."

Ella's posture remained stiff in her chair, but she tried to sound calm as she answered all of the questions Rory fired at her in rapid succession. It was a struggle to maintain a breezy demeanor when her stomach was in knots. Under the table, her ankle was coiled tightly around Henry's to calm her nerves at being the center of too much attention.

19

PEACE FROM RORY

"Again, Rory. You're afraid you'll make Henry pass out, but I assure you, he doesn't mind."

Rory balked at her uncle, arms akimbo. "You should assure me that I won't Pulse him so hard that he passes out, not that he won't mind if I accidentally render him unconscious."

Remus shrugged and pointed at Henry, who was laying on the leather couch that was pressed against the wall across from Remus' desk. "Henry and I only care if you quit, not if you make a mistake."

Henry rested the back of his hand against his forehead like a damsel in distress. "Oh, Rory! You're the evilest villain I know! What shall I do to counteract a Pulse of Peace? I'm powerless!"

Ella sniggered at his theatrics, but made sure to keep

her presence as silent as possible. It was clear Henry enjoyed putting on a show for her, casting her furtive glances every time he made a joke to ensure she shared in his humor. It seemed Henry was intent on collecting as many giggles and grins from Ella as he could draw out of her. Finally his charm had purpose, and he seemed determined to put it to good use.

Rory touched Henry's forearm with the delicate grace of a butterfly alighting on a flower. Everything she did seemed like a dance to Ella as she watched the lesson unfold. Within a few seconds, Henry's smile grew lax, and his arm slumped across his forehead.

Rory jumped back, her eyebrows furrowed. "See? I told you I'm no good at this! All these years I was desperate for a Pulse, but now that I finally have one, it's so troublesome to use correctly. I'm doing something wrong, Uncle Remus."

Remus moved around his desk and leaned his backside on the surface. "You're doing nothing wrong. You're simply more powerful than most, which is something I never doubted for a moment. It's difficult to wield, so be patient."

Rory's lips tightened. "If I had a gold coin for every time you told me to 'be patient,' I'd have about ten million useless piles of gold."

"Perhaps I'll try saying it again just once more. Do you think that might help?"

Ella concealed her smirk when Rory grumbled at her

uncle and turned back to Henry, who was gazing content-edly up at the ceiling. His eyes bore the same look Ella's stepsisters had worn when they'd emerged from a massage. "I think we don't play outdoors enough," he commented dreamily. "I mean, when was the last time I trounced you at... What's it called again?"

"What?"

Henry mimed shooting a ball into the air with both hands. "The thing with the hoops and the baskets."

Remus laughed through his nose at Henry's loopy cadence. "Basketball?"

Henry frowned as he considered the answer. "No. That's not it. It's got boops and haskets."

Ella stood when the door opened, and pressed her back to the wall with her head down and her hands clasped in front of her, hoping it wouldn't look like she assumed she belonged with the elite. She recognized Cordray Phillips from the papers. There wasn't a citizen in Avondale who didn't know about the man who'd won the heart of Aurora Johnstone. It was his kiss that had awoken her from the counter-curse, and his ring that had taken up a permanent space on her finger six months after. The fact that he had Lethal abilities was just icing on the gossip-laden wedding cake. The 'Sleeping Beauty,' as the tabloids called her, had been brought back to consciousness after her months-long coma, only to attach herself to someone who could kill her with an errant touch.

Cordray Phillips crossed the room and greeted his wife with a light kiss. "I see you decided to start without me."

Rory harrumphed up at him. "You didn't miss a thing, other than yet again, me not being able to control my Pulse." She motioned to Henry, who was still staring up at the ceiling with a contented wonder, as if finding shapes in the constellations of a starlit sky. Rory perked up when she recalled the newcomer. "Oh, but you get to meet my newest best friend. This is Ella, Henry's girlfriend."

Cordray's eyebrows rose as he spun to take in the woman who was very much trying to fade into the background. He was taller than Remus, dark-skinned and wore black driving gloves, which stood out against his jeans and maroon plaid button-down. Cordray lit up at the sight of Ella and cleared the space between them in three long strides.

Ella squeaked as Cordray wrapped his arms around her, squeezing her as if they'd been old friends separated by an ocean, and freshly reunited. "Ella! I love you already. Thank God for you. You're the key. You're the ticket to me not wringing Henry's neck. You've saved the royal bloodline, I hope you know."

Ella's eyes bugged, glancing at Rory in confusion.

Rory sniggered, shaking her head at her husband's relief. "Henry's not that bad."

"Not that bad? The git proposes to you every chance he gets just to make my blood boil."

Ella shirked out of his grip, her shock falling to discomfort and worry. She shoved her hands in her pockets and cast Rory a wounded look that begged for some sort of explanation.

Rory shook her head repeatedly as she moved over to Ella, looping her arm through hers to make sure the new girl didn't vanish. "No, no. Cord's saying it wrong. Henry knows how easily I get embarrassed, so he does everything he can to act up when we're in public. It's a joke on the press, who cover our lives so intrusively. You know about our betrothal?"

Ella swallowed hard and bobbed her head.

"Henry and I were promised to each other when we were born. Then when Malaura cursed me as a baby, my parents let Henry's parents out of the agreement. We stayed very close and grew up like siblings with Adam Fontaine. Never more to it than that."

The way her tone soured on Adam's name made Ella want to ask questions, but she balled her toes inside of her shoes and kept quiet.

"Henry proposes as a joke, and the press eats it up— the two promised to each other, finally finding their way back after all these years. It's ridiculous. I'm very much married to Cord, and Henry's woefully taken with you." She squared her shoulders to Ella and cupped her arms. "Please don't be cross with him, or me. I want nothing more than for Henry to find exactly you. And Henry has never, ever wanted to be with me. Cordray shouldn't have said anything." She shot her husband a glare that lasted two whole seconds, but then softened when her eyes fixed on Ella's uncertainty.

"Okay," she murmured, unsure what one was supposed to say in this situation. "Thanks for clearing that up. Have you and Henry ever kissed?"

Rory's expression faltered. "No more than he's kissed Adam, I'm sure. He used to do that to embarrass him, as well." She lowered her chin in shame. "When I was in my coma, I begged him and Adam to try and wake me with true love's kiss if Cord's wouldn't work for some reason. So yes, Henry kissed me, but it was an attempt to save his oldest friend's life, and only because I asked him to. Please don't hold that against him."

In that explanation, Ella saw clearly how deep their friendship went, and how loyal Henry could be. She took a chance and sank into Rory's open arms, hugging the woman for the sister she wished they'd always been. "How much easier my whole life would've been if you were my sister."

Rory gripped Ella hard, having needed the same female camaraderie through her lonely childhood. "Then I will be from now on, and life will be so much better for the both of us."

It didn't feel natural for Ella to rest her head on Rory's shoulder, but she found she couldn't resist the woman's transparency and utter acceptance of her. The hug didn't stop for nearly a minute, while both women silently unburdened a portion of their ostracism onto the other's shoulder, trusting that a sister could handle such things.

20

CORDRAY'S SECRET

Seven hours of lessons in Remus' study were interrupted only by meals and the occasional phone call that Remus or Rory couldn't ignore.

It had taken a few hours, but eventually Ella's secrets came out to the newcomers. Remus ran Cordray through his lessons before they moved on to Ella, which was what helped loosen her tongue. No matter what Ella had to deal with, it was nothing to the stigma that came from being a Lethal. Besides which, Remus had prodded Cordray to reveal his closely-guarded secret to lessen Ella's anxiety that she was the only strange one.

"You're so powerful that not even two pills were muting your Lethal abilities?" Ella gaped at him, having lost her timid demeanor a few hours back. Cordray was easy to get along with, and a little less intimidating to talk to than the royals she was constantly surrounded by in the study. "Isn't that a little dangerous?"

"I'm trying not to let myself be dangerous. That's why I'm here."

"Did Malaura know? Is that why she took you?

Cordray sat on the leather couch, shoving the blissfully peaceful Henry to the side. "No. Malaura knew she couldn't get her hands on Rory, since she was so closely guarded. So she stole me, knowing that Rory and I were in love, and if I was gone, Rory would be stuck in her sleep, and Malaura would win."

"I read about that. You uncovered a band of Lethals she was gathering."

Cordray bobbed his head, a haunted look crossing his features. "Months and months of torture. See, most Lethals don't actually kill much of the time. Sure, they can make you think you're drowning, slow your heart or whatever, and sometimes that kills you, but none of them are trained to make their Pulse last for more than a few seconds, so they don't often finish the kill. Still, their gift makes them capable of murder, so they're all lumped into one category. My Pulse is different."

Remus raised his finger in warning. "No, Cordray. *You're* different. With hardly any training, you were able to kill many of your captors, as well as Malaura herself. That's nothing to downplay."

Cordray shot Remus a withering look. "It's nothing to brag about."

Remus pressed his hands to his desk that he was leaning back on and hoisted himself up to sit on the polished wood. Though his body language was boyish, Remus still looked like the only adult in the room. He addressed Ella, who was trying to keep her opinions about it all to herself and just be a polite listener. "You see, Ella, people can learn skills under duress that they wouldn't be able to master with years of study. Cordray was able to kill his captors, but he also stumbled upon a unique ability no one knew was possible. Perhaps if he'd had me as a tutor growing up, I would have limited him by my knowledge, and he'd have never figured out that he can cast his Pulse."

Ella's eyes widened. "You can cast your Pulse, Cord?"

Cordray's brows furrowed that Remus had divulged his secret. "I thought we were keeping that quiet."

"We are. She's a mouse, Cordray. Plus, she's signed a confidentiality clause. Your secrets are safe with her. More than that, they're important to her." Remus turned to Ella, his expression that of a patient tutor. "One of Cordray's closely-guarded secrets is that he learned he can cast his Pulse. The king's known about Cordray for months now, almost a year. He's never been taken in for a formal testing. He's never been experimented on, or coaxed into using his unique gifts for the government. He works with me once a week. We're trying to get his magic under control so he doesn't need additional pills to ensure Rory's safety. We're also working towards him being able to control his casting, so he doesn't accidentally electrocute someone without meaning to. Casting one's Pulse is something no one thought to train anyone to do." His eyes narrowed in on her. "Do you know anyone else who can do something like that—push Pulse magic out from themselves without the use of touch?"

Ella froze, knowing that this was the moment Remus had been building up to. It was no coincidence that Cordray had been brought in to be tutored while she was staying at Remus' home. She didn't know what to say. So many people knew her secret now. To add two more to that list felt like a gross invasion. Still, she went out on a limb and decided to trust Remus, if for no other reason than that he fed her, and the reason for divulging her secrets seemed to be for camaraderie. "You brought Cordray here to show me that I'm not the only one."

Cord's head whipped toward Ella, his mouth falling open in shock. He stood, rubbing his gloves together and then crossing his arms over his chest, squaring his gait to hers. "You're a Lethal?"

Ella shook her head perhaps too rapidly, and then stopped, wondering if it was offensive to so adamantly make it clear that she wasn't like him. "I don't have a traditional Pulse," Ella admitted, feeling oddly lighter at releasing herself from the lie that her Pulse was Kindness.

Remus pressed his hands together under his chin. "That's true. What Ella has is a mutation. She can send out her abilities, just like you, Cord. But she can't use her Pulse by touching, like everyone else can."

Rory and Cordray both gaped at Ella, as if seeing a giraffe with three heads.

Henry giggled drunkenly from his place on the couch. "You should see your faces! Duh." He imitated their flabbergast, and then gave in to the laughter he'd gifted himself. Then he went back to studying the ceiling, which had kept him utterly fascinated for hours.

Remus smirked at Henry before coming back to the matter at-hand. "Ella, Cordray's gifts are far more controversial than yours. No one knows that he can send his Pulse out, except for the king and the people in this room. King Hubert's done absolutely nothing to harm or exploit Cordray, and no one on the council knows, except for Rory's father and mother, and myself, of course." He lowered his urgency to soothe her nerves, holding his hands out as if she were a wild animal in danger of spooking and running. "You're safe here."

Ella banded her arms around her stomach, worry scraping at her insides. Though she wanted to run from all of this and deny every shred of it, part of her understood that this was her one chance to learn with someone who was in a similar predicament as she, and she couldn't justify passing that up. Ella bobbed her head in a tight, jerky motion, but refused to speak. Not bolting for the exit was a grand feat, and she wasn't certain she was capable of much more.

Remus Johnstone was the greatest tutor in Avondale, and one of the reasons for the accolade was that he knew when to push his pupils, and when to back off. He didn't let up, though Ella's obvious fight or flight was peaking as she kept glancing at the exit. "Ella, you now know more about Cordray than most people in his life. Before Henry brought you to me, I thought Cord must be the only one of his kind – to be able to cast his Pulse as he did. How lonely and scary it is to have to keep such a large secret. I'd like to tutor the two of you together, with Rory and Henry learning alongside you both to see if casting one's Pulse can be taught." Remus straightened, though his tone was still low and nonthreatening. "But you have to be willing to open up about your gift. I'll not be brave for you. That's something you'll need to choose for yourself."

Ella was just frustrated enough to respond with a glare. He'd pushed her to this point, so to act as if any of it had been her choice to expose was laughable. Still, this final decision was for her to make, and she knew she was in too deep to back out now. She pinched her side, hugging herself as she lowered her chin to the ground, her voice coming out barely above a whisper. "If it's my Pulse that I'm casting, then my ability is Listening. And Seeing, I guess." When they only looked more confused, Ella shifted from side to side, wishing she didn't have to be brave. She wished she could run to her father and hide away from all the things that threatened her sanity. There so many things she wished for in that moment, but she sucked in her lower lip and pressed on, choosing courage over running into the shadows. "I can hear through walls. Sometimes through whole buildings and down streets. I can see through walls, too."

21

COMFORT AND CHAOS

ory and Cordray gasped, With Rory taking a telling step back.

When Ella saw Rory's hand fly over her mouth, she panicked. "But I don't mean to do it sometimes! When I get overwhelmed, it sort of just happens. I don't mean to eavesdrop most of the time." Guilt swept over her, and she hung her head. "But other times I do it on purpose."

Remus' shoulders rolled back, breathing easier now that the cards were all out on the table. "That's far better, isn't it? Now we all have a reason to keep our little group quiet. We can study with each other, and learn together as we figure out how this has happened twice, and what it means that magic is evolving right before us."

Rory was still processing while Cordray took a step forward, his expression earnest to both hear Ella's case, and for his own to be heard. "When did casting first happen for you? Mine was when Malaura was about to kill me. I didn't know what I was doing. It sort of just blasted out of me. Was it like that for you? How long have you had your abilities?"

Ella glanced toward Remus again, seeking out the silent push she knew he would give her with a simple nod. "My first time was when I was a little girl. My mother was sick." She choked on the word "mother," but forced herself to speak her piece. "They wouldn't tell me what was happening, but there were too many doctors, and she looked frail. My mother was never frail, but that day, she was." She paused, wishing she didn't have to tell anyone. "I don't like this story. Can we be done with this?"

Henry was fighting to focus, his voice vacillating between dreamy and compassionate. "Oh, blue eyes. Come here." He patted the spot beside him on the couch, a pleasant adoration on his face when he took in her squirming. He sighed as if she'd been the rib missing from his side when she slid in next to him, tucking under his arm and returning to where she belonged.

Ella didn't care if they saw her snuggling into the comfort Henry offered; she only cared that he was there, and that she didn't have to get through this terrible story alone.

Henry played with a few curls that had come loose at the base of her neck, relaxing her in an attempt to seal themselves off from the others, so it was only her and only him invited to her childhood traumas. "Tell me, Ella. There's not a thing about you I don't want to know."

She rested her head on his shoulder, her hand finding its way over his heart, so she could rub her favorite spot on his body. "She used to make singing pies. Pies so good, they made my dad sing."

Henry gave an airy, one-noted laugh through his nose. "That's cute. Which kind was your favorite?"

"All of them. Well, peach crumble," she admitted. "But I told her I was still searching for my favorite kind, so every Sunday, she would make another pie in a different flavor, and my dad would sing through the house while it baked." She pictured her father, younger and far more carefree. He'd had brown hair with no gray when she'd been little. "I got my blonde curls from my mother. She always wore her hair pinned with a pearl clip. So fancy. No matter what she was doing—scrubbing the floors or going out to a show with dad—she was always the most spectacular woman in the room." Ella's voice drifted as she unlocked the memory box she tried not to open in mixed company.

Henry smiled and eased into the cuddle, as if there was nothing harrowing at all in their lives, and they were sitting alone, trading stories to pass the time. "What was her name?"

"Cindy. They said she'd be okay, but I knew they were lying. Or maybe not lying, but telling me things I wanted to hear. I was kept out in the hallway while they worked on her, and that's when I sent out my Listening for the first time." She squirmed, still hoping for acceptance. "I didn't mean to. I was just trying to hear what they were saying about her condition. Then, when my father took me down the hall to the vending machines, I could still hear the doctors as if they were right next to me. It was a long time before I told my dad, but when I did, everything changed." She rubbed Henry's sternum. "He started to go gray after that. He stopped singing, too. Though, that was because there was no one to bake pies anymore. Neither of us had the stomach for them after mom died."

Henry's fingers stroked slowly up and down her arm as he gathered her closer. He was warm when the world felt impossibly cold. The others remained silent, respecting the somber story, and the woman who'd lived through it and tumbled out the other end changed.

Henry's voice was low and soothing. "Cordray's dealing with his ability to cast his magic, but it's hard for him. It's uncharted territory. To go through that when you were just a girl, while losing your mother on top of it? We have Remus to help us figure things out. You didn't have anyone." He turned his chin and kissed her forehead, letting his lips linger.

"I had my father, who helped me control my... whatever it is. My Pulse, I guess. But we were afraid. That was back when Malaura was gathering her collection of Lethals from the shadows. We only had each other, so we kept everything just between us." Her nose wrinkled as a foul memory came over her, shredding her heart with the bleakness of her life. "Then my father was coerced into marriage with a horrible woman who used her Pulse of Submission on him, and he told her my secrets. She's kept me hostage with the threat of letting it all out for two years now. Two years of being her servant and letting her get away with whatever she wants. All while I stand there and shine the floors my mother danced on so that she can entertain the Baron, who sat in my father's chair at dinner."

Henry examined his fingers curiously. "Rory, your Pulse is starting to wear off. I'm getting shooting pangs of rage. It's stripping away your Peace."

Remus held up his hand to stop Rory from giving him another dose. "That's a healthy anger, son. The Baron made a pass at Ella, and Lady Tremaine gave her a black eye for drawing his attention."

Rory blanched and covered her mouth. "The woman who came to the Dinner of the Elite with the Baron? Is that her? *That's* your stepmother?" She cast aside her decorum and gagged. "Ack! She's horrible! Going on and on about locking up Lethals while Cord is at the table, minding his own business and just trying to get through a meal!"

Remus slid off his desk and slowly moved toward Ella, squatting down before her with an earnest understanding in his gray eyes. "My Pulse is Comfort. May I..." He offered up a hand, but didn't touch hers until she consented with a tentative nod. He wound his fingers through hers, and after a few beats, Ella's shoulders began to relax.

"Wow, that's..." Ella's head tilted to the side as her face pulled with an expression that could've been misconstrued as pain. "I could see getting addicted to that."

Remus gave her half a smile. "I try not to use it all that often."

Ella could feel the Pulse fading in potency, but his fingers remained twined through hers. With Henry allowing her to mold her body into his side as much as she wished, and Remus holding her hand, she wondered how anyone could be unhappy when surrounded by such warmth. "Thank you." She glanced around at the others, who seemed united in their sadness. "I think I like it here."

"I'm glad to hear it." Remus remained kneeling before her as he pressed on. "We're fairly certain the Baron knew about Cordray's kidnapping before it happened, but we haven't been able to prove it. I believe it's only a matter of time before you'll be at risk, as well. It's the not the king we need to keep our secrets from, but other, less reputable government officials."

Ella nodded slowly, letting his words sink in.

"Malaura's dead, but people are still afraid. They don't trust new magic, because uncovering and exploiting it was her obsession." Remus sandwiched both of her hands between his. "I don't know how to get you away from Lady Tremaine without her potentially blabbering to the world all about your abilities. Your father was right; you'll be at risk by those who fear such things."

Henry kissed her temple and kept his lips there while he spoke, inhaling the fragrance of her skin. "Then she'll move in here, or into the palace. Father won't hang her out to dry." He glanced at Cordray. "He didn't give Cord any trouble."

Ella stiffened against Henry, but the others continued on figuring out their next move. She leaned up and whispered, "Can I talk to you in private?"

Henry quirked his eyebrow at her, but obliged, standing with a lax deportment as they excused themselves from the study.

The moment the door shut them in the hallway, Ella's tongue loosened. "Did you seriously just ask me to move in with you?"

Henry mulled over his last few exchanges, and then shrank. "I guess I sort of did. Probably should've asked you with flowers or something romantic."

Touching her forehead, Ella began pacing back and forth. "We only just kissed for the first time yesterday. That's insane!"

Henry held up his hands. "Look, Rory's Pulse was messing with me. Of course it's too soon to move in together. But honestly? I can't imagine I'll feel any different in another half a year. I love being near you, and if you move in, then we'll be together all the time. I'm not seeing a downside."

Ella shook her head, trying to think rationally. "We haven't even been on a real date, Henry. We have no idea how we can be together without Lady Tremaine blowing it all up. Do you think Cordray enjoys being ostracized? Abducted? That's what we're talking about if my gifts go public—which is what will happen if people know we're together. I'll be under a microscope."

Henry leaned against the wall, shoving his hands in his pockets. "Look, you can keep your secret as long as you want. I'm not denying that there are sizeable downsides here. But I don't like the idea that the woman I'm crazy about can't see being with me as a pro that outweighs all the other cons."

Ella stopped in her tracks, horrified that this was the conclusion he'd drawn. "Henry, I'm risking my freedom to be here with you. If Lady Tremaine found out that I wasn't shining Remus' silverware right now..."

"You call this free? You're not free, Ella. You're trapped in that house with the sword always over your head. So your secret gets out. What's the worst that could happen?"

She got so worked up that she began talking with her hands. "Um, why don't you go ask Cord? Abduction? Torture? Near-death escape?"

"Malaura's dead! What else you got?"

"Her followers aren't!"

"They were targeting Lethals, which you are not."

Ella folded her arms over her chest and shook her head, her eyes fixed on his shoes. "You have no idea the damage I could do if pushed. The wrong people will do all they can to exploit me."

"That's always going to be true. Wouldn't you rather I'm there by your side to help you when you do get pushed? Not if, but when, Ella. Make no mistake, your secret will come out someday. The question is, do you want me with you when it does?"

She took in the tightness of his eyes, his stern jaw, and the guarded body language that made her wonder how she'd missed that he was worried about losing her. Wanting to be closer was the cause of his obstinance, and she knew she couldn't fault him for that.

Her shoulders dropped, and the fight went out of her. "Of course I do. I just... I don't know how this works." She stepped back to lean against the opposite wall, rubbing her temples. "We haven't even been on a proper date yet, and things are already so chaotic and serious. I like being serious with you. It's the chaos part I'm having trouble with."

Henry began to breathe more evenly, and his voice lightened. "Well, I might not be able to give you all the answers tonight, but that one can be solved."

"We can't be seen in public," she reminded him.

"Not to worry. I know somewhere very out of the way that would be perfect. I'll set it all up for next week." He moved over to her without his former frustration, reaching out to hold her hands so their wrists could sway gently between their bodies. "You're right. There are too many complications. And I did all of it in the wrong order. I shouldn't have asked you to move in with me before I've taken you out." He leaned in to kiss her, sighing contentedly at the contact. "I don't do things halfway, Ella. You should know that about me."

Her chin tilted to the side. "You don't say."

"I can move slower, but I'll be shooting down any suggestions that land you in a separate bed than mine. Best night's sleep of my life, last night. When you're here, will you stay in my bed?"

Heat colored Ella's cheeks at his request. She was grateful he'd insisted on that one stipulation. Now that she'd slept in his arms, she wasn't sure how she would ever rest anywhere else.

22

RED AND RAFE

By the end of her four days at Remus' home, Ella had truly found her stride among the closely-knit group. Cordray had taken an easy liking to her, claiming her as his twin sister, since they were the only two of their kind. Being able to cast magic had bound them more quickly than any other commonality. Rory and Cordray stayed a few nights at Remus' just so the five could study together by day and hang out as friends in the evening. Each time Cordray went out, he always made sure to come back with a small trinket for his wife, and a second small something for Ella.

"Cord, I can't take that home. But it can stay in Henry's bedroom here, so I can enjoy it when I come back next week."

Cordray's face fell as reality began to dawn on him. He removed the card game from the town car with a frown that stood out against the snow. "I don't like this. This is really the plan, Remus? Her black eye only just faded yesterday. What if that woman returns Ella with a broken leg?" Cord had taken to calling Lady Tremaine "that woman," which made Ella smirk every time.

Remus paused in the moonlight outside the driver's side of the town car, having waited until the last moment to return Ella, as promised. "I don't like it any more than you do. But until we find a way to make sure Lady Tremaine stays quiet about Ella, this is the boat we're in."

"How about reporting her for knocking around her stepdaughter? That should take her down a few pegs," Rory suggested, wrapping her arms around Ella as the brisk night air kissed their faces.

Ella didn't mind the cold so much anymore, now that she had a proper winter jacket. She would have to leave Henry's coat in the back of the town car, but the oversized shield from the fast-falling snow felt snug as winter warned them it was finally here.

"You can't embarrass a woman with no shame," Remus replied sagely. "She paraded Ella in front of us and admitted to using force to keep her servant in line." He leaned his forearms on the roof of the car. "Unless Ella's willing to go public with her abilities, I have to return her." He met Ella's eyes across the top of the car and turned his palms up to give her one last chance to change her mind.

Ella swallowed hard, wishing for an option with no damning ramifications. Her father's wisdom had always been "Have the courage to be kind," but Ella couldn't find courage anywhere in her choice, nor was she going back out of kindness. She was returning out of fear, which she knew wasn't a good reason to do anything.

She leaned into Rory, suddenly feeling the weight of how terrible it would be to leave her side. She had been Ella's cheerleader through the steep learning curve that was fine-tuning her Pulse. When it was Rory's turn to flail and falter, Ella had cheered her on all the more, teaching her meditation techniques that actually did help Rory control her Pulse of Peace far better than she'd been able to four days ago. The girls worked in tandem, braiding each other's hair to match, playing cards with the guys, and staying up far too late sharing secrets and childhood stories. Ella's father had kept her away from children for the most part, and Lady Tremaine didn't allot much time for Ella to have a social life, so she cherished every sisterly moment and exuberant hug.

Finally, Ella squeezed Rory before releasing her, and slid into the backseat of the car. "Tell Henry I..." There were so many things she wanted to say, but she knew none of them would be enough.

Rory's lips pulled to the side. "He knows. He'll wake back up in a few hours, and Remus can deal with him then." Then Rory shut the door, and pressed her palm to the window.

Ella mirrored the action, wishing her life could be so very different. She was still wearing her old jeans and flannel button-down, looking vastly different than Rory's manicured and couture look, but the two understood each other, which was a rare treat for them both.

Remus started up the car and left Rory and Cordray standing in the driveway as he pulled down the lengthy, topiary-lined blacktop, and out onto the street. "I've never seen Henry so worked up. I can't remember the last time I heard him shout like that."

Ella watched the world blur by through the tinted windows, pursing her lips through the memory of the vein in Henry's neck pulsating so angrily. "I knew he wouldn't be able to accept it when I had to go home. We both wish the world could be different, but it's not." She shrugged, as if the whole thing didn't devastate her. "I'm sure Rory didn't mean to make him pass out."

Remus paused, and then glanced at her in the rearview mirror, his eyebrow raised. "I'll let you believe that, if you need to. She knew there was no way he'd be able to handle watching you leave. He's utterly smitten. It's a strange shade on him. Though, when Henry has his mind set on something, his fire burns too hot for most to handle. I guess I shouldn't be surprised that when he finally gave away his heart, there would be no holding him back. That's what you're doing, you know. You're asking him to hold back."

Ella hung her head, leaning forward to rest her elbows on her knees so she could cover her face. "I know. But the alternative isn't much better."

"I want a good life for Henry, for him to find all the things that make him come alive. I see it when you're near him."

Ella turned over his words, but decided to voice the thing that had been tugging at the back of her brain since one of their tutoring sessions. "Is this your good life? Does passing down your wisdom make you come alive?"

Remus blinked at her in the rearview mirror. "I suppose so. I do enjoy studying, so being around others who have the same passion feels natural."

Ella didn't know how to voice her concern with tact. Her fingers twisted in her lap as she worked out her worry. "Was Malaura a good teacher?"

Remus tightened his grip on the steering wheel. "Why would you ask me that?"

"When you were talking about Cordray learning to cast his Pulse because Malaura pushed him past his breaking point, it made me think she'd probably done the same to you when you were young."

Remus' voice was a taut whisper when he finally responded. "Yes, well. That was years ago. I was twelve years old when she was cast out. I've had plenty of time to heal from those wounds."

Ella kept her voice quiet and respectful, sensing this was pain that didn't often see the light of day. "What kinds of wounds?"

The answering silence stretched on for so long that Ella assumed she'd stepped too far into his business.

When he finally spoke, she had to lean in to hear the horrors. "Malaura was a believer that the darkness purged our powers to the surface. It's no surprise to me that Cordray was kept mostly in pure black for much of his incarceration. I endured the same trials. Weeks of being alone in the dark with Malaura's voice reading ancient spells in English, then in Latin, and then Greek. Over and over, that's all I had. I was let out when I could recite them in all three languages. Then I was put back in for more of the same."

Ella closed her eyes, her hand over her mouth. "That's terrible. How old were you?"

"I don't remember much of my eighth year, aside from her voice. She was so pleased when I got the incantations right. I was her favorite." When Ella didn't respond, Remus continued, digging into the sore he never allowed the air to touch. Now that it was out in the open, the sting of the cut sizzled and begged to be explored further. "She didn't like it when the other children came near me, so I was kept away from them for the most part, studying instead of playing. When I returned from boarding school, my brother tried to hug me, but I pushed him away. That's when my parents decided I shouldn't go back to study under Malaura anymore. It took me a long time to understand how to be normal after that, but I think I manage well enough now. When Rory was born, something in me clicked—came back to life perhaps. I was only twelve, but I felt responsible for her. When she woke up crying in the night, I went to her with her mother, Leah." He cleared his throat. "I'm sure you didn't want to know all of that. Apologies, Miss Ella."

Ella's words were filled with sorrow. "You were a little boy. A little boy who didn't know how to hug. That's tragic."

He ran his tongue over his teeth before speaking. "I am not so little anymore. I've long since recovered from my time under her care. That she's dead now? The world is better off. Still, there's this sadness that sometimes finds me, and I can't reason with it. I don't want her to be alive, of course. I mean, I had a hand in her death. I was there, fighting alongside Cordray to help deal the final blow. Still..." He shook his head. "Ignore me."

"Never." Ella reached forward and cupped his shoulder. "I understand. It is sad. It's sad when anyone dies having never learned to love or be good to those around them. When Lady Tremaine passes someday, I'm sure I'll have that same pit in my stomach. We all want our kindness to be big enough to bring life to the people around us. When evil is bigger than love, and that's how it ends? You're right; it is sad."

Remus' shoulders moved slowly up and down with his weighted breathing, as if he was trying to exhale the demons that were supposed to be long dead. He reached across his chest and placed his hand atop hers that still rested on his shoulder. "I never expect anyone will understand, so I've kept much of myself private. That you see me clearly? It's a gift I don't take lightly. Thank you, my dear. Now that I met you, perhaps I won't be quite so sad any longer."

"Well, I'm here—for the giddy moments and the grim ones."

"Thank you," he said in a choked whisper. Remus allowed a soothing silence to settle over them for several minutes after Ella pulled her hand away so she could sit properly in the back. When he pulled onto the freeway, Ella realized the teacher inside of him could only be quiet for so long. "Would you mind a detour?"

"Sure. So long as I'm back sometime tonight, that should be fine."

The turn he took led down a road Ella hadn't ever had cause to travel. It was overgrown in parts, and as the minutes turned into almost an hour of travel, Ella finally spoke up. "Where are we going?"

"We might not even get out of the car. What do you know about the Lupine?"

Ella sat back and rested her head on the window. "Only what everyone knows. A bunch of people were cursed by Malaura to live out their days as huge wolves. They've got the minds of humans, but are trapped as wolves." Ella didn't bring up the fact that they were largely feared, as that seemed unkind to mention.

"That's accurate. Quite the surly bunch. The two communities don't really understand each other. Humans assume the wolves are prowlers, so they do their best to keep them out, and the wolves don't seem to like being around humans. I think it makes them sad to see bipedals, and remember the lives they'd once lived that are now gone forever."

"That makes me sad for them. We don't see them much in our village, but perhaps that's because we're a more populated city."

"People assume a lot about me, most of which is wrong. But one thing I'll concede to is that I love to study. Not just books, and not just people. I daresay I knew Henry was in love before he did, because I watch the people around me."

Ella squirmed in her seat, a bashful smile playing on her lips. "Henry isn't in love. It's far too soon for that."

Remus chuckled. "Enjoy the denial. Enjoy the small span of Henry holding himself back. When he finally does declare himself, expect there to be fireworks and a parade."

He turned down a side street that was even more overgrown, the trees brushing the car as if the vehicle wasn't welcome in these parts. The night seemed impossibly darker all of a sudden, and Ella realized the lack of streetlights, or any businesses or other cars nearby. "Where are we going?"

"The Lupine are easier to study than most people assume. No one wants to acknowledge their place in society, but we are not no one. We're going to visit one of the packs as part of your training."

Ella balled her toes inside her shoes and rubbed the skin on her knuckles. "Um, isn't that kind of dangerous?"

"Normally I'd say maybe. But I know this wolf and his keeper. I know their pack. Rafe is a very old wolf who doesn't hold the same stigma about humans as the other Lupine. I think it's because his keeper softens him. They live together out in the woods."

"These woods?" Ella glanced out at the snow-covered ground. "It's snowing out."

"One of the many quirks that will paint a more detailed picture of the two. I want you to meet them for many reasons, but the main one is because I want to test your Listening. The pack has its own language, which the wolf we're about to see can speak. But this particular one has been able to maintain a human connection with his keeper, whom he came across after his transition. Rafe is the only one who can be heard by both the Lupine and a human. I want to know if you can hear him, as well."

Ella's eyes darted around, and she chewed on her bottom lip. "This seems like something we should've had a longer conversation about."

"I've found that no one's ever ready to jump into the ring with a member of the Lupine. Besides, Henry would never let me hear the end of it if he'd known."

Her brows pushed together to display her unhappiness. "How did you know I could communicate with animals? I was so careful here."

Remus locked eyes with her. "Pardon? You can talk to animals?"

Ella shrank. "I figured that's why you brought me to meet the Lupine. I don't hear animals say words. I don't hear voices," she explained, as if she was a guilty child trying to hide her chocolate-stained fingers behind her apron. Then her voice lowered to just barely above a whisper. "It's more that I can understand what they're thinking, and they understand me. You really didn't know?"

"I didn't. But I'm glad to hear my assumptions weren't entirely faulty. I guessed that if you could send out your Listening, you might be able to twist it to Hear things normal people can't. That you've been able to achieve this without any formal training?" He shook his head, perplexed.

"Talking to precious birds and squirrels isn't the same as reasoning with the Lupine." She tried not to let her voice sound accusatory, but kept her tone conversational. "I've seen articles that have photos of the Lupine tearing people out of their homes and dismembering them in the streets."

"I've seen those pictures, as well. And I've seen humans do far worse, and yet we can still look each other in the eye. Imagine the rage the Lupine must feel. One day they're walking to the grocer's, then Malaura curses them, and they lose their families, friends, homes, and the language they've always been able to speak. Imagine seeing your wife marrying your best friend after she grieves on his shoulder over your loss. Only you're not lost. You're still there, fully aware of what's going on. You can see it all, but suddenly, you're not counted as a person."

Ella considered his words, letting them fill her with compassion, which she always tried to keep on tap. "That's... I never considered that perspective before. I wish things like that were printed in the paper."

"You and me both. They're a lonely bunch. And I happen to know what dismemberment story you're talking about. I know the wolf, actually. Even though his wife wouldn't let him in the house anymore after his curse set in, he still watched the property for her. One night, he caught a prowler, which is the man he dragged out into the street and dismembered with the rest of the Lupine. The papers didn't cover that aspect."

Ella covered her mouth and closed her eyes as Remus pulled the car to a stop at the end of the road. "That's terrible! Wait, I thought you couldn't hear them. Only that woman could."

"That's true. She goes by the name Red. Rafe is her wolf, so he's attuned to the pack, and tells his stories to Red. On fortunate occasion, Red confides in me."

"Why you?"

Remus turned in his seat and cast her a small smile. "Because I asked, and then I listened. Same as I did with you. For all my studying, I've learned there's not many remedies more magical than that."

23

GUADALUPE, CONNOR AND ERROL

Remus got out of the car and opened the trunk, pulling out a duffel and opening Ella's door. "Rory's snow boots. It gets quite deep the further in we go. Can you carry this?" He held out a second duffel from the trunk.

"In a second, yes." Without preamble, Ella threw her arms around Remus' neck, holding him close through his surprise.

"Oof!" Remus dropped his duffels and awkwardly patted her back. "Are you alright? What's this for?"

"This," Ella said as she rose up on her tiptoes to press her cheek to his, "is a hug. After my father passed, and before I met Henry, no one hugged me, either. I made you talk about that whole awful Malaura story without being able to hug you through it. If you're going to teach me how to understand my Pulse, then together we're going to learn how to be better at hugging. Any time you feel lost, I'll have one ready for you."

Remus melted at her sweetness, his arms curving around her as his lashes fluttered shut. Their hearts beat in a perfect rhythm, as two people who spent much of their days shrouded in secrets finally unburdened themselves of the weight of such loneliness. "Never stop being exactly like this," Remus whispered in her ear. "Kindness like this can move even the most stalwart mountain."

Ella tried not to worry about going into the dark woods in the night, and clung to her belief that Remus wouldn't lead her into danger. He'd been the one to devise a plan to get her out of Lady Tremaine's grip for a few days. Ella decided to suck down her fears, sling the duffel over her shoulder, and shove her hands deep into the pockets of Henry's thick winter coat to keep her fingers from fidgeting.

The snow was deep enough to come up to her shins the further in they went, led by a high-voltage outdoor lamp Remus had stowed in his trunk. He offered his elbow to her, linking them together as they trudged through the thick packing snow. After their hug, Remus' body seemed more attuned to hers, bending as she bent, and stiffening when she needed extra strength to lean on. "Thank you for trusting me. The work I do requires a fair amount of off-the-beaten path ventures. Not many are willing to give those a try."

"I keep thinking of what you said about the Lupine. I

guess I never thought of them as ostracized, and wishing they could get back into society. It's so sad."

"The world moves on without you, as if you'd died."

Ella jerked her chin to stare at his barely visible features. "Are you a veterinarian on the side?"

"That would make things so much easier, but no. King Hubert has a veterinarian degree, so I borrowed a few of his schoolbooks as I saw fit. The Lupine don't need me, though. They allow me to learn from them, which is what we'll be doing tonight." He stopped their progression and opened his duffel, pulling out a short bow and arrow that had jingling bells on the feathered end of the arrow. He ignored Ella's confusion and shot out it through the woods, releasing the light tinkling sound into the forest before it sank it into a tree several yards away. "They'll be here soon."

"That's how you call them?"

Remus nodded. "It's how I request an audience. Remember that they're people. I don't click my fingers at them, or anything that might seem like a slight. Open up your bag and set it on the ground in front of you."

Ella complied, grimacing when she realized she'd been carrying around a plastic bag filled with raw chickens, freshly skinned. "Peace offering?"

"I never show up to a party empty-handed. That just seems rude." He looped her hand back around the crook of his elbow as they waited in the woods.

It was the small things Remus did that made her trust

him. The fact that he didn't hesitate to keep her close, and the protective tilt of his shoulders made her feel like she belonged in his universe, all evidence to the contrary. She'd been deprived of the good kind of touch for too long, and naturally gravitated toward Rory, Cordray, Henry and Remus, who doled out the kindness without hesitation. When Henry was not there to take her hand, Remus offered his for her to hold onto, as if he knew that's what she needed, but could never ask for aloud.

Though the snow couldn't fall on them directly through the canopy of the trees, the wind still found a way to whistle between branches, sending a chill through them both.

Ella was too nervous to indulge Remus in the few attempts he made at small talk. When the bramble crackled a stone's throw from where they stood, Ella's nerves hit a high note, and she squeezed his arm as if it was the only thing holding her to the planet. "It's them!"

Remus chuckled at her trepidation. "Yes, Ella. Try to stay calm." He patted her arm with his gloved hand. "See if you can send out your Listening. Nothing that would make your head hurt. And there's no need to send out your Sight. Just your Listening is enough."

"Remus, this is..."

They'd been working for the past three days on separating her Sight from her Listening, so she could more easily access one without overwhelming herself by pressing both internal buttons. "If you've graduated from calling me "sir" to finally referring to me by my first name, then it's a safe bet that you're finally confident enough to handle using your gifts out in the open without fear of being found out." Still, he steadied her, making sure she didn't sway on the spot.

Ella took a steadying breath and sent out her Listening in the direction of the shifting bramble. She rolled her shoulders back, assuming a position of ease, which Remus had trained her to do. A long drag in through her nose, followed by a cleansing breath out through her mouth pushed her Listening farther, spreading it from her like slow-creeping vines along the snow. She did her visualization exercises, imagining herself to be a ballerina, lengthening her posture and reach with grace, rather than tumbling through hard surfaces, as she was used to doing. Remus' way was slower, but far less taxing on her body and mind. It was easier to control, doing things his way, and she was starting to get more accurate results the more she practiced.

Remus had sent Cordray, Henry and Rory to separate rooms right next to each other, and instructed them read a string of nonsense. Ella's task had been to hear only one of them, and then broaden her Listening, so she could take it all in. Then back to narrowing her focus, and then widening again. It had been mentally exhausting, but now that she was in the woods, searching for voices she wasn't sure she could hear, she understood why he'd gone to such lengths to make her a pristine Listener.

As the wind whistled through the trees, she tuned out nature's dull shriek, and instead heard only the soft crush of paws on snow. More than that, she tuned in to a frequency that had a radio static quality to it. The sound crackled behind gravelly voices, which suddenly became clearer.

"Remus is back," one of them mumbled. *"It's a good thing he is. I'm starving."*

"Who's the girl he's got with him? Doesn't he know better than to bring outsiders to us?"

Ella stiffened, but didn't retreat as their bodies finally emerged from the thick of the woods. It was too late now; if she ran, they would surely catch her. They were huge— easily the size of mid-grown bears. Their fur was thick, and their eyes glowed through the night with an eerie quality that made Ella wonder if they could see straight through to her very soul.

A brown-spotted wolf said, *"Maybe he's taken a wife finally."*

"Woman, you know Remus is gay. And that girl is about fifteen years too young for him." He looked Ella up and down. *"Nice legs, though."*

"Shut up, Errol. I don't need to hear every lustful thought that pops into your head."

Ella swallowed hard, realizing why it was that the great Remus Johnstone had never settled down with a woman, even though he was a highly sought-after bachelor. She

vowed to keep the secret he hadn't meant to reveal to her, and still didn't realize she knew.

"Can you hear them?" Remus whispered.

Ella gave him a tight nod, clinging to his arm. "They're not thrilled you brought me. They seem to like their privacy, and distrust outsiders." She kept her eyes on the wolves, counting three of them. One of them was limping, and all were littered with deep abrasions marring their thick fur.

Remus' arm flexed with excitement, and he all but bopped from side to side with glee that he'd shifted the puzzle piece into the correct spot. "I knew it was possible! Ella, do you realize what this means? You can be a witness for them! You can be their voice in court!"

Ella's chin jerked to him in surprise. "What are you talking about?"

"So many crimes have been committed against them. I mean, their property was seized, for one, because they were deemed unfit to speak for themselves. Ella, you could grant them so much by just giving them back their voices!"

"I... But that would mean going public, which I've told you isn't a wise thing to do!"

Remus' eyes tightened, and his chin jerked up and down once. "Of course. I'm getting ahead of myself. For now, let's just celebrate that we're learning what nature intended for your gift."

Ella's mouth went dry as Remus broke from her to greet his old friends. Though he couldn't hear them, Ella observed that they'd worked out a basic one paw stamp for "yes", and two paw stamps for "no". He breezed through explaining Ella's abilities in such a rush, the wolves barely understood him, and conferred their confusion to each other with quizzical head-tilts.

"Do you think it's possible more people can hear us?"

"No. Remus is just trying to be helpful, grasping at straws. She's pretty, though. Think she'll let me nuzzle her tits? It's been a long time since I've felt a hearty pair like those."

The wolf with brown spots scoffed. *"And you never will again, Errol. You're disgusting. Connor, knock some sense into him. If I do it now, I'll draw more blood than he's got to give."*

Connor, the wolf with pure slate fur, sighed. *"Errol, honestly. Even if you were human, you wouldn't have a chance with a woman that beautiful."*

Errol blew off their chastisement with a hearty snuff. *"She can't hear us. Only Red can, and she's angry with us."*

"Why is Red mad at you?" Ella asked. Then she crossed her arms over her chest. "And don't talk about my body. It's rude. I'm surprised you can see my shape through this bulky coat."

There was total silence, and then the radio static was back as they all clambered to be heard. They'd gone from woodland menaces in one breath, to excitable puppies in the next. They raced to Ella, startling Remus, so they could lick her face and jump on their hind legs to get her attention. If someone was listening, it seemed they were ready and desperate to be heard.

24

PART OF THE PACK

Ella hadn't been expecting such a greeting, and was just grateful she hadn't lost a hand in the exchange. The more they licked her face, the more she let her guard down, giggling as they tickled her cold skin. They jumped over her body when she fell backward in the snow, laughing at how quickly they'd gone from feared nomads to loveable pets.

Remus shooed them off of her, his expression vacillating from horrified to amused. He hoisted her back to her feet, shaking his head at them while she dusted the snow off her jeans. "It's working? You can hear each of them?" At Ella's excited nod, he ran his hands through his hair, messing it as his mind raced. "There's so much I want to know!" He pulled a binder out of his satchel and clicked his pen, scribbling as fast as he could every time he called out a question that Ella answered for the pups.

"Why didn't this Red person translate these things for you?"

Remus kept his wide eyes on his notebook, flipping the page to get to the next slew of questions. "She interprets what she likes. Many of my questions go unanswered because she doesn't like humans knowing too much about the Lupine. Doesn't trust us. Plus, she's not always around. Her and Rafe like to travel without the packs, moving in and out of each group as they please." He glanced to the wolves, who were devouring the carcasses at their feet. "I could tell for a while now that they want to answer me, but Red wouldn't give them that freedom. They know I'm not some follower of Malaura's. I'm a student who only wishes to learn about them so I can help."

"Maybe we don't need Red anymore, if we have Ella. She can help us find shelter."

Ella frowned. "Okay, what's the deal with Red? Did you guys have a fight or something?"

They went back to eating, bending their necks down to avoid eye contact. Finally, it was the brown-spotted wolf who spoke up. *"One of the other packs attacked someone, based on information we reported. Red doesn't like when any of us maim humans, so when one pack does, she punishes all of us by pulling back from everyone until we get the hint."*

"The pack who fought the human, were they in danger?"

"No, she would've understood that. It's Adam. Adam Fontaine. Do you know him?"

Ella shook her head. "I know *of* Adam Fontaine, but everyone does. His story's not exactly a secret. Why was it necessary to attack him?"

Remus went very still, tuning in to every word. Ella recalled Henry mentioning that Adam had stayed at Remus' home many times, and was tutored by him as a boy, before his run-in with Malaura that cursed him into a slowly-transforming beast. He was doomed to join the Lupine on his thirtieth birthday, which everyone knew was coming up this year.

"*Adam doesn't belong in your world, and he'll never belong with us. Our pack is the only one that's tried to welcome him to ease his transition, but the others want him ostracized.*"

"Why's that?"

"*A while ago, Adam set traps for us when one of the packs grew overzealous and trespassed on his property. Killed one of us.*" The brown-spotted wolf lowered her head. "*Plus, he's got the kind of money that could really help us gain more favor with the people so we're not cast out, but he doesn't. Even though he's going to become one of us, he won't fight for change. Us three will still take him in when he transitions, but the other packs won't.*"

Ella chewed on her many responses, but tucked them away until she gathered more information.

Connor slowed his feasting and brought a chicken's head to lay at Ella's feet. It was an odd peace offering, but Ella respected the gesture all the same. "Thank you."

"You are the loveliest sight this forest has seen in far too long. Had I a hat, I would've laid that at your feet, instead."

The corners of Ella's mouth pulled upward as she indulged him in a curtsey, to which he bowed, as if they were two members of proper society making pleasantries. "Thank you, kind sir," she teased.

"You're a wolf, Connor," the brown-spotted wolf next to him said glibly.

"And what's your name?"

"Guadalupe," she replied. The nuances of her long maw made her look perpetually serious. She was stuck with a romantic, and a perv, so Ella couldn't fault her for being the one to force logic into the mix. *"Once we found that Adam took a wife, the more aggressive pack began making plans to take her out, just to make his human life more miserable. They found her driving and attacked, but Adam showed up, and things got complicated."*

Errol huffed at Guadalupe. *"Shut up, Lupe. We finally have someone who can speak with us. Don't go scaring her away with things she won't understand."*

Connor bumped him out of the way. He had pure gray fur and was the largest of the three. *"Enough, Errol. It's clear she can hear us. Remember what little manners you had in your human life."*

Ella knelt down in the snow, not caring that her jeans were thin and soaking through. She extended her hand and ran her fingers through Lupe's fur, and then Connor's. "Explain why attacking Adam's wife helps their situation."

Connor leaned into the touch, practically purring with affection. *"It doesn't, but some of the Lupine feel that it's all the justice we have. We can't exactly press charges in a courtroom setting. We don't have rights, and people are allowed to hunt us without cause. We didn't join the pack that attacked Adam, but we understand it well enough. We wish Adam would fight for us, too."*

Ella nodded, her face solemn. "I see."

Guadalupe rested her maw on Ella's shoulder in total submission. *"Red didn't like that they attacked Adam and his wife. Said that doing it made us exactly the monsters the world has written us all off to be. She and Rafe left us, and they haven't been back since. They do that when she's angry, but they come back eventually."*

"What can you tell me about Rafe?"

Connor shook his head at Remus, and nuzzled closer to Ella as if to protect her from the world. *"Your teacher should've educated you on this. He really brought you to us without telling you our names?"*

Ella shifted uncomfortably, and then stood, brushing off her jeans. "I'm a servant. People—including Remus—don't tell me things unless I need to know." She kept her scolding confined to that, taking Remus' apologetic bow with a polite nod.

Connor shook his head. *"What a backwards world, that they'd take someone like you, who clearly has more magic in her little finger than most, and confine you to housework."*

Ella could hear the disgust in his voice at the state of

the world that had cast him out, as well. "Tell me about Red's wolf."

"Rafe is the alpha. The oldest of the Lupine. Pure white coat. Bigger than the rest of us. He's Red's favorite, though they bicker like children all the time."

Ella touched her forehead, unsure of all the details. "I've never met Adam, so I can't speak to what kind of person he is. But I'm guessing they'd never met his wife before they attacked her, so they don't know what kind of redemption she's bringing into his world." When the wolves didn't speak, she pressed forward to make sure the disgruntled demeanor that dictated the actions of the more violent pack didn't bleed into this one, as well. "Wouldn't you want that for your enemy? For him to find something as transformative as love?" Her eyebrows bunched as she turned to Remus. "Did I miss some big news announcement? I would've thought Adam Fontaine getting married would be a huge deal. Does Henry know?"

Remus shook his head. "No. Adam's not married. Henry hired a woman who's a housekeeper and a nurse to look after him. Adam's... He's not well."

The wolves exchanged culpable looks of horror. *"No. No, no."*

"We saw them walking and talking together in his home through the windows."

"We saw the way they were looking at each other. Of course they're married."

"She lives there! She has to be his wife!" The more they

argued, the more they realized how very wrong they'd been when they'd reported the new staff member to the Lupine community.

"They attacked a housekeeper? You realize that's what I do, right? And did *she* set those traps for you guys?"

They each laid on the ground at her feet and buried their noses in the snow, keeping their eyes scrunched shut. Errol whined for forgiveness at not trying harder to stop the renegade pack, but Guadalupe seemed to understand that mercy was a thing they didn't deserve. *"Please don't leave us,"* she begged quietly, her nose inching through the snow to touch Ella's boot.

Ella shoved her fists in Henry's pockets, wishing he was with her. Even through the chill of the outdoors, she could smell his soft cologne on the collar of the jacket. She took a long, deliberate breath, locking his scent in her lungs before she exhaled her verdict. "I think the best way to get people to stop hunting you and give your voices serious consideration is to make sure you're not the monsters they assume you are. You're in a tough spot, and I get it, but if you don't have any clue who you are or how to be kind, then what good is your voice? You may not have attacked Adam's housekeeper, but you set it all in motion, giving that info to a pack you knew wouldn't be able to see things calmly." She shook her head at them. "You didn't have the courage to be kind."

Guadalupe whined in distress, resting her throat atop Ella's boot. It was an act of total trust that stilled any further lecturing. When Connor mirrored her actions on Ella's other boot, she exhaled, unsure what the right move might be. She leaned down and ran her fingers through Guadalupe's brown spots and Connor's gray fur, softening when she saw how starved for touch they were. She reached over and scratched behind Errol's ears as well.

Remus pulled out his phone, but frowned when he realized they were too deep in the woods to get a proper signal. "You're saying Adam is hurt, as well as Belle? Did they make it back to his castle?"

"They made it back," Errol replied with a nod, leaning into her touch. *"They weren't mortally wounded. If she's a nurse, she would've been able to stitch them both up just fine."*

Ella's mouth drew to the side. "Maybe we should go check on them."

Connor inched closer, leaning his ear against Ella's shin as he nuzzled the outside of her calf. *"You can't go there. I don't want you near him. He's not a good man."*

Ella's heart tugged in her chest that so tight a bond had been formed already. She wanted to scoop him up in her arms, but Connor was the size of a muscular, oversized Saint Bernard, and she wasn't sure if he would fit in her arms. Instead, she lowered herself to her knees again and wrapped her arms around his neck, kissing his fur. "I'll be alright."

Connor took a chance and licked her earlobe, and then her cheek. *"We've needed someone to hear us for so long.*

I won't let you go to Adam's castle. He's unbalanced. People who set traps for the Lupine aren't the sort I want you near."

Ella held tight to Connor, resting her temple to his. She relished the warmth of his fur, and the way it tickled her nose. "If only you understood how much of a nobody I am."

"You're not nobody. After tonight? After tonight, you're our somebody. You're our only somebody. Finally, we have someone to listen to us."

"Where are you staying? How can I help?" The snow was falling too fast. Ella wondered in the back of her mind how they would get the town car out of the snow if they didn't leave soon.

Connor licked her jaw. *"We have thick coats, but food is hard to come by in the winter. Tell me where your home is. Let me watch the grounds for you."*

Ella's lashes swept shut. "I don't make the rules for my home. But if I did, of course I would take you all in. Of course I would give you a place to rest." She glanced up at Remus, who was too shocked to speak. "Remus, how can we help them? Rafe and Red left them, and food is getting scarce. They're scared."

Remus put his notebook away with a wary expression. "Ella, I can't take them in. If people knew I was harboring the Lupine? They wouldn't be safe on my property. People would hunt them, and they'd be easy targets if they were confined to my grounds."

"We can't just leave them here! They'll starve. I can't

sleep with that on my conscience." Light danced in her eyes. "The barn. Lady Tremaine and her daughters never set foot inside it. It's far too dirty for them."

Errol snarled at the attention Connor was getting. *"I thought you said you didn't make the rules for your home."*

Ella lowered her chin. "I don't. It's the best I can do."

Remus shook his head, buttoning his satchel. "Ella, your stepmother would have them killed the moment she finds out about them. Sometimes they howl in their sleep. They would be found out the first night."

Ella clung to Connor's neck. "That can't be it. There's got to be a way for me to help you."

Connor's voice was low and smooth, offering comfort, though he was the one in the rough spot. *"We'll be alright, amorelux. We've survived worse winters."*

"Worse than this?"

Guadalupe hissed. *"Don't call her that. She's not likely to take a mate from the Lupine. Look at her. She's gorgeous. She probably already has someone warming her bed. You're barking up the wrong tree, Connor. Always romantic but never practical."*

Ella's eyebrows rose, and her cheeks pinked. "Oh! I... Um..."

Connor chuckled, as if nothing could ever ruffle his feathers. He licked her cheek before pulling away to stand with his pack. *"When will I see you again?"*

Ella glanced at Remus. "They want to know when we can bring them more food."

Connor tsked her with a slight tease, circling her and dragging his tail around her legs. *"You know very well that's not what I asked. It's been a long time since anyone's been as compassionate to us as you. Tell me I'll see you again soon. Sometimes we have Remus, but feeling your arms around me? Tell me you'll come back to us."*

Ella's cheeks reddened, and she looked away with a bashful smile that Connor chuckled at. "That's up to Remus."

Remus extended his elbow to her. "Depending on the weather, we can make another trek out here in three days' time. That's when I pick Ella up for her tutoring. I can bring more food then."

Connor's tone turned sharp. *"You're shivering. Tell Remus he shouldn't bring you out here unless you're dressed for the weather."*

"I'm not that cold," she insisted, but didn't pull away when he moved forward to shield her legs from the chill, and instructed Guadalupe to hem her in on the other side. Errol moved around to her back, and the three formed a tight circle around her to keep her lower half from freezing. "You guys are wonderful. I don't..." Ella gulped back her emotions, but decided she wouldn't chicken out on making her gratitude known. "I've been cold for a long time, but not many stop to show me any warmth. Thank you."

"You belong to our pack now," Connor explained. *"I'll be counting the days until your return."*

Before she left on Remus' arm, Ella indulged the three in embraces, tummy rubs and cheek kisses. She wanted to stay with them, but knew she'd indulged in enough affection. She'd long understood that her life wasn't meant to be filled with snuggles and companionship, so the breaking of her heart wasn't anything she hadn't soldiered through before.

Still, as she trudged through the snow on Remus' arm, the howls of Connor, Errol and Guadalupe stayed with her, bringing emotion up to tighten her throat.

25

BECAUSE YOU'RE MY SISTER

Ella had known life back at her house wouldn't be filled with the same joy she'd been lavished with while staying with her new friends at Remus' home, but the steep divide was harder for her to swallow, now that she knew there was a possibility of freedom. It dangled like a shiny bauble just to tease her. She knew the freedom was tainted. If she went off with Henry and let Lady Tremaine spread what rumors she wanted, there wouldn't be more than a few days of liberty to revel in. Still, Ella considered the offer more heavily when, every twenty minutes, she was bombarded with yet more inquiries of how she'd spent her time at Remus Johnstone's home.

She recited the lie that dug at her soul when she did anything terribly duplicitous. "Every morning I started cleaning all the bedrooms. Then I helped the chef in the kitchen. Then I cleaned the kitchen until every surface sparkled. Then I started fixing Mr. Johnstone's lunch."

"What does he eat?" Anastasia asked, leaning forward on her pudgy elbows. She remained seated at the table while Ella scrubbed out the congealed mass that had crusted on the bottom of the oven. Ella couldn't even tell what it was, it was so bubbled and blackened. She'd chiseled at it for twenty minutes, her head swimming from the harsh oven chemicals.

"Nothing too wild. He eats pretty healthy. Oatmeal, vegetables, fruits, baked chicken. Things of that sort." Ella tried to stick to the scripts she'd worked out with Remus. She'd known she would be grilled for information, so he gave her tidbits she could divulge.

Lady Tremaine sipped her morning coffee while she watched Ella. Her tight smile was always most smug when Ella was on her hands and knees. "How does he take his coffee?"

"Black." Ella was resolved not to be obstinate, but loathed every bit of information she shared. Remus had been wonderful to her, and she felt like a traitor for revealing even the smallest of details about him.

"Does he have our slow drip model, or has he upgraded to the new ultra-slow?" She glanced with a prideful sneer at her coffee contraption that Ella loathed.

Ella kept her face hidden in the oven, and her tone light. "Actually, he has a regular coffeemaker with an espresso feature on the side. Swears by it." She left the bait at that, hoping it would sway Lady Tremaine to turn in the slow drip mechanism for an easier to use machine.

"Oh? What brand?"

Ella responded with no hint of persuasion, and continued scrubbing.

"What of his sheets? What's the thread count?"

Ella hadn't changed Remus' sheets, so she picked the thread count closest to what Lady Tremaine preferred. She grimaced in the privacy of the oven, feeling dirty discussing the man's bedding.

"Did he have any women over while you were there?"

"His niece visited for dinner once, but she didn't stay long. I stayed out of sight, so I didn't have much interaction with Lady Aurora Johnstone."

Ella's response seemed to cause Lady Tremaine pain. "What is the point of having you there if you're not going to bring us back any useful information? Is Remus Johnstone single?"

Ella cast around for the correct response. "He doesn't talk to the help about his private life. You taught me to stay out of the way when important people are in the room. Do you want me to be more visible next time, so I can try to find out more?"

Lady Tremaine let out a labored sigh. "Honestly, it's like you have no interest in getting ahead in life. Of course I want you to be useful to us while you're there. If he's seeing someone, we can bend her ear about the vote on

Lethals. Then perhaps she can sway him. Think it through, you idiot."

Ella bit her tongue to keep from spouting back that it was entirely condescending to both genders to assume that one could sway another's political views with mere flirtations. "I can keep an ear out, sure."

Drizella ran into the room, her phone on display as if it had news that was sure to blow the world away. Her hair was still partially in sponge curlers, and she was wearing only her slip as she bounced up and down on the balls of her feet. "Did you see the news on Royal Watch? The event after the yearly votes are cast isn't going to be just a Dinner for the Elite, but a grand ball open to everyone! There's even a note at the bottom that all eligible women should be ready to introduce themselves to the king for consideration for marriage to his son, Prince Henry!"

Anastasia leaped up from her seat and seized Drizella's phone, which led to a chase around the kitchen and into the living room. Drizella pulled Anastasia's hair, and Ana slapped Drizella across the face.

"Ladies, ladies," Lady Tremaine tsked them, plucking the phone from Anastasia's grip seconds before her daughter tumbled over the arm of the couch and slumped onto the floor. Her eyes skimmed the webpage with satisfaction. "Why, yes. The Baron mentioned this was in the works. Though, I did think you'd be presenting yourselves to Prince Henry himself."

Ella kept her head in the oven, her chest tightening at

the news that was certainly new to her. Had Henry known about this? She listened to one of her birds cheeping on the sill quietly, singing her a song to soothe her palpable ache. Last night when she'd checked her secret phone, she'd found fourteen missed calls from him, and several panicked texts. She'd sacrificed one of her five allotted hours of rest, texting back and forth with him, but he hadn't mentioned anything about the ball—only that he wanted to bring her to the palace to meet his father.

Ella had declined the invitation, warning him that it was too risky and far too soon. But now, as she was covered in oven grime, woozy from the chemical stench with her fingers aching, she wished she could tell him anything that would get her out of this mess. The thought of her stepsisters posturing and posing for him made her stomach turn. When Ella factored in every eligible woman in Avondale prancing about for their chance to have a place next to Prince Henry, she felt bile churn in her gut. She wanted to be selfish and ask Henry right then to forgive her for putting him on hold, but part of her knew that his life would be far more complicated with her in it. Perhaps he deserved better than what he wanted. Perhaps his father already knew about them, and this was his attempt to force Henry to widen his prospects to someone more suitable.

A solitary line of sweat dripped down Ella's face, and when she swiped it away, she accidentally brushed soot across her cheek.

She didn't have time to rectify the mess, squeaking in frustration when one of her stepsisters yanked her out of the oven by her ponytail. "Come on, dummy! Why are you wasting time doing that? No one cares about the oven right now."

Lady Tremaine's upper lip curled in disgust at Ella's appearance. "Do whatever my girls require so they're ready to meet the prince at the ball. I don't think I need to explain to your tiny brain how important it is that they look their best for the occasion. It's in three weeks, so there's no time to waste, especially if you're to earn your keep four days a week at Remus Johnstone's house."

"Yes, ma'am," Ella responded with her chin lowered. She removed her gloves and plopped them in the sink, leaning in to splash water on her face, but she was cut short.

"Come on! Take this seriously, Ella. Nothing we have in our closets will do for a royal ball." Drizella rose up on her toes again, clapping like a little girl being promised a toy. "A royal ball! I can't believe it!"

Anastasia danced around with an imaginary date, raising her chin and composing her face to look like a proper lady. "When Prince Henry chooses me, I'll let you stay in the palace, Drizella."

Drizella reared back, a haughty head-swivel controlling her tone. "Oh no, you don't. *I'm* marrying Prince Henry. I'm the only one who cares enough to know his favorite color, what he drinks at clubs, and that his childhood goldfish was named William Sharkskin. I'm clearly a perfect fit for him."

Ella bit down on her bottom lip as it dawned on her that she knew none of those things. She knew what his tongue tasted like, but not even something as basic as his favorite color.

Drizella and Anastasia went into heavy planning mode, shoving a pen and paper at Ella so she could make sketches of the dresses she was to design for them.

"I want something sleek and form-fitting," Anastasia rattled off. "With gold trim around the cleavage." She motioned to a spot just above her belly button. "Cut the neckline down to here. Give him something fun to chase." She gave a little shimmy, causing not just her breasts to jiggle, but her tummy, thighs, chins and backside as well.

Ella's mouth drew to the side. "I'm not sure I can make that work. What sort of bra will you be wearing?"

"The best kind." She waggled her eyebrows and giggled. "None at all." She grabbed her breasts in her fists and pushed them up. She frowned as she glanced down to see the shape of her round body. "You'll figure something out."

When Anastasia grabbed a carton of ice cream from the fridge, Drizella knocked it out of her hands, not caring that it splatted on the freshly-cleaned linoleum. Her finger leveled in Anastasia's face. "Don't you dare eat ice cream right after breakfast. You're going back on a diet first thing. It won't do to wow the king and get him to give me his blessing, only to take one look at you and renege on the whole thing." She whirled on Ella, her pointy features stern. "See to it she doesn't eat a thing until the ball. Not a single grape."

Ella's mouth popped open. "Lady Tremaine won't let you starve your sister."

Ella knew she'd grown too bold with her time spent able to speak her mind at Remus' home. Never would she have dared contradict Drizella openly before, and she quickly realized her mistake when Drizella smacked her across the face, and then repeated the action twice more for good measure. It wasn't until Ella remembered the way to end Drizella's assaults was to get down on all fours that her stepsister's temper passed.

"Would you look at what you did? My hand is filthy now! Wash it off, or I swear, Ella..." Drizella's fingers dug into Ella's ponytail, and she hefted her up just so she could slap her again.

Ella turned quickly to the kitchen faucet, cranking on the water and guiding Drizella's hand under it to wash off the soot from the oven. She flinched, but didn't make a noise when Drizella body-checked her into the sink, making Ella Heimlich herself so hard she almost vomited. "That's too cold!"

Ella didn't speak up for herself, but bit her tongue as she adjusted the water temperature and scrubbed soap into Drizella's palm.

When Drizella finally stomped away, Ella turned

around. Her attempts to recollect her bearings fell to disrepair when she caught sight of Anastasia sitting on the floor, scooping ice cream off the linoleum and shoving it in her mouth with gusto. "No, sweetheart! You don't want to do that. The doctor said it's not healthy for you to have this much sugar. Let me make you a fruit salad. That's every bit as sweet."

Anastasia glanced up with a sadness that looked like self-flagellation as she popped the spoon from her lips. "It's hopeless! I'll never lose enough weight to fit into a pretty dress."

Ella fell to her knees, ignoring the sting of her own cheek as she threw her arms around Anastasia. "We'll find you something lovely for the ball. You don't have to be rail thin to look nice. But you do have to stop eating ice cream in the morning, because the doctor said so. You're going to make yourself sick, eating like this." She gently pried the spoon from Anastasia's mouth, giving her a second squeeze. She couldn't understand why Lady Tremaine would allow sweets in the house, if Anastasia wasn't allowed to eat them. It was as if she wanted to taunt her daughter, constantly lording the precipice of failure over Anastasia's head.

Anastasia's tears fell hard and fast on Ella's shoulder. "It's no use! Prince Henry will never want me."

"Then you'll be no worse off than every other woman in the kingdom who also gets passed over for nebulous reasons. Who cares what Prince Henry thinks? Let's dress you up for you, not for him. You don't even know him!" She forced out a chuckle, trying to soothe Anastasia, who was now pliable in her arms.

Ella didn't pull away until Ana wiped her tears on her shoulder and blew her nose in Ella's shirt with a hearty honk. She kept her grimace internal, and moved to the ice cream to scoop it up and deposit the sloppy mess into the sink. "I'll make you something spectacular to wear for the ball, Anastasia. Your eyes are such a pretty shade of brown; maybe we should make a dress to match them."

She sniffled on the floor, legs spread, licking her fingers clean of the sticky ice cream. "That might be alright."

"And as far as the low-cut option you had in mind, you might want to consider making him wait to see the goods. If you put it all on display the first time you meet him, that might not give him something to wonder about."

Anastasia hefted herself to her feet. "Okay, yeah. Maybe something with just a peak at my boobs. Can we make a slit up the side? I like my calves."

"Of course, Anastasia. Whatever you like."

There was a pause, and Ella almost let out the breath of total devastation she felt whenever one of the Tremaines struck her. But she knew if one breath escaped, a tear might, and she couldn't have that. If one tear fell, they all would, so she sucked in her breath and spackled up the dam to keep her heartbreak tucked inside.

Anastasia's voice was small when she finally spoke. "Ella?"

"Yes, sweetheart?" Ella glanced over her shoulder to see Ana's mouth pulling to the side in thought.

"Why are you nice to me?"

It was a question Ella had asked herself many times, and had defended to Henry during their days together. "Because at the end of the day, I want to always be myself. In my heart, I like that I'm a nice person. I care about other people, whether or not they're capable of loving me. I don't have to answer for anyone's behavior, except for my own."

Ana harrumphed, her upper lip curling in distaste. "That's boring."

"Well, then how about because you're my sister?"

Ana was quiet for a few beats, but then scoffed off Ella's answer. "Whatever. When you finish cleaning up the kitchen, my bedroom needs straightening."

Ella turned back to the sink, rinsing her hands and trying to ignore the globby, green-tinged snot stain on her shoulder. "Yes, Anastasia."

26

SICK, SICK, SICK

Ella barely slept during her three days spent in her house. The women had left the place a wreck for her to clean, with no expectations that it would not be spotless before Remus Johnstone came to pick her up Friday night for her four days of service in his home.

She whipped around the house, employing the birds and squirrels who came out when the Tremaines weren't around. The animals put themselves to good use, helping Ella with the many chores. The squirrels dusted, the birds picked up errant misplaced items from around the house and put them away, and a skunk offered her services to help Ella wash the windows with her tail.

She tried to send out her Listening to them. She'd always been able to understand them, but without getting direct words. It was almost intuitive, while communicating with the Lupine had been more of a two-way conversation.

Ella reasoned that perhaps it was more direct with the Lupine because they had once been humans, so parts of their minds were still the same. Normal animals didn't have such advantages.

Ella was covered in dust from her inside chores. It was slightly better than her work yesterday, which had been mostly done outside, and had left her socks soaked through. She'd bought herself winter boots before, but they had been confiscated by Lady Tremaine, who claimed she dawdled during her outside chores if her feet were too comfortable.

Ella was nursing a bone-aching cold virus, but didn't dare ask for time to lie down. The Baron was to come over for dinner that night, and she knew that meant Lady Tremaine would tolerate nothing out of place. Despite her runny nose and foggy brain, Ella made individual soufflés for the meal, along with blanched vegetables with a lemon butter sauce drizzled over. The table was set to perfection, including Lady Tremaine's scrutiny of the silverware, which Ella had polished that morning.

"This one is spotty." Her tightly pulled bun permitted only the slightest hint of a frown. "Clean them all again."

"Yes, ma'am." Ella didn't mention that the spot Lady Tremaine was seeing was her own thumbprint. She did the chore again, and then hurried to arrange the flowers with the red roses facing Lady Tremaine's seat, since they pleased her most.

Ella moved to the bathroom on the main floor,

knowing she had very little time to clean it before the Baron arrived. She nearly dropped the bucket when she opened the door to find Drizella on her hands and knees, her fingers down her throat, forcing a stream of vomit into the toilet.

"Oh! No, Drizella! This isn't the way." Ella took a clean rag from the cupboard and ran it under cold water, pressing it to the nape of Drizella's neck. "Why are you doing this to yourself?"

"Because the ball is in less than three weeks' time, and I haven't lost a single pound! Less than three weeks!"

Ella flushed the toilet and dabbed the puke off Drizella's chin. "How much weight do you imagine you need to lose? You're rail thin as it is."

"I have to catch the eye of the prince! You wouldn't understand. You don't know what it takes to nab a royal. Mother understands. She landed the Baron. Don't you see that I have to do better?"

Ella didn't argue with Drizella, but fanned her sweaty face and leaned her back against the wall. "Sweetheart, you have to eat something. I made your favorite soufflé with plenty of porcini mushrooms."

"Don't you dare serve me that! Do you know how many calories are in a soufflé?" Her voice was sharp as a slap, and made Ella wince. "If you give me that, I'll beat you till I burn off the extra calories."

Ella bit down on her lower lip, knowing that whatever she suggested would only get her into trouble. "Yes, ma'am." She stood and exited the bathroom, sneezing twice in the hallway. She didn't see Lady Tremaine coming her way, which usually would've been her cue to make herself scarce.

"You stink like vomit," Lady Tremaine commented. "Go wash up. It won't do you any good to parade yourself around covered in dust like this. The Baron should be here in twenty minutes. Do not disappoint me."

"Yes, ma'am."

Then Ella watched in horror as Lady Tremaine opened the bathroom door, took in her daughter on the floor hovered over the toilet, and gave a tight nod. "Carry on, Drizella. You must fit into your gown."

Ella hadn't possessed the urge to speak up for herself in ages, but the words nearly bubbled out of her mouth to defend the stepsister who had always despised her. She wanted to shout at the injustice, but shoved her filthy fist into her mouth to stave off the chastisement that would surely produce nothing good. Ella turned on her heel, determined that she wouldn't greet Remus Johnstone with a black eye this time.

Ella was quick in the shower, knowing that two minutes in, one of the girls would flush the toilet to douse her in freezing water. How she needed the hot steam to fill her aching lungs. Her cold felt set deep in her bones, making her nearly weepy for her bed.

She dressed quickly in her white serving blouse and black slacks, wishing she could wear fifteen flannels and fourteen woolen scarves. Her socks had holes in them, and she tried not to shiver in the drafty attic as she bundled her meager possessions up to take with her when Remus arrived.

Her hair was still wet when the doorbell rang, and Drizella's nasally voice echoed through the house. "Ella! Get the door! Proper ladies don't answer their own door."

Ella shoved her thin, holey shoes on and stumbled down the steps, blowing her nose once more before shoving her tissue in her pocket. Her hair was fashioned up using two pencils, forming a messy, wet bun atop her head that slowly dribbled down her neck. She kept her chin down as she opened the door, her eyes falling on the pointy black leather shoes of the Baron and his guest. "Good evening, sirs. May I take your coats?"

The Baron tsked her, his garlicky breath brushing her skin with all the intentionality of a hand across her neck. "Now, now. Where's my smile? What a waste of a beautiful servant. Come, Ella. Let's see that smile. I didn't come all this way for the food."

Ella's eyes were puffy and rimmed with pink. Her nose was red around the edges, and her lips were dry from not sitting down to take a drink in the past twenty-four hours. Still, she obeyed, her skin crawling as she mustered up a wan smile for him, which was aimed at his shoes.

His long, bony fingers reached out and curled under her chin, lifting her face so he could study it, as if she was a show dog. "Didn't I tell you? Beautiful. There's nothing more luxuriant than having something spectacular under your feet."

Mr. Herchon had a round belly and a nose too wide for him not to make low snorting noises while performing the simple labor of breathing. "She makes my servant look like an old maid."

The Baron released Ella's face, turning her chin forcefully to the side. "Yes, well, your servant is an old maid. Go on inside." His voice carried to Lady Tremaine, who was standing a few feet behind Ella, her pleasant expression frozen in place to hold back her indignation over the Baron showing an interest in Ella yet again. The Baron gave Lady Tremaine a slight bow with a simpering smile. "Good evening, Lady Tremaine. Lovely as ever. Your little servant made us wait in the cold out here for an entire minute. I'd like a word with her to educate her on how your household should be run."

Ella turned and begged Lady Tremaine with her eyes not to allow her to be alone with the Baron, even on the front porch, but Lady Tremaine's flash of rage was glossed over with a breezy smile. "Of course, smookiepoo. Whatever you like." Then she shoved Ella out the front door to stand on the porch with the Baron, welcoming Mr. Herchon into the house and shutting the door behind him.

Ella took a step back until she was teetering on the edge of the icy stoop. She kept her chin down and crossed her arms over her chest while she shivered, the winter weather catching in her wet hair, and taking the freeze deep to her innards where she was sure it would never leave. Even without help from the weather, the Baron's gaze always left her feeling cold.

"Come here, Ella."

She was too scared to comply, frozen solid on the precipice of the stoop.

The Baron chuckled at her resistance, and reached out to cup her elbow. "What are the chances I could parade you around naked in front of Lady Tremaine, and she wouldn't say a word?"

Ella knew speaking in her own defense would only be seen as a challenge, so she remained silent. She was too tired and sick to put up much of a fight when he moved her to face him, and backed her up against the front door, shielding her body from view of the neighbors. Her limbs were stiff, and she felt herself float up out of her body, watching with horror as the Baron plucked open the top two buttons of her white serving shirt.

Her arms moved to shove him off, but his thick fur coat afforded his limbs movement she simply didn't have. Another button opened, and he eyed her no-frills beige bra with unconcealed lust, hissing through his thin lips at the sight of her breasts—buoyant and on display for him. He thumbed the peaks as she struggled against him, vomit rising in her throat. "Leave me alone!" she shouted, finally pushing him off the porch.

"I could have you arrested for that."

"I could have you arrested for this!" Ella spat back, angry and embarrassed as she buttoned up her shirt.

"The top three buttons will remain open throughout the entire meal," he ordered, running his hand down his long coat to appear like a dignified official giving a command. "If I don't get to see you as I wish, I'll pay Lady Tremaine for the rights to take you back to my home. Remus had his turn with you. Let's see how well you fare in my bed for four days."

Her eyes widened with terror, and her limbs ceased all movement. "Is that what you think happened?"

The Baron laughed. "That's right. I know all about Remus' offer for you. Smart man, taking you home so he can do with you as he wishes. He may be younger than me, but I can afford to buy you for far longer."

Ella whirled around to open the front door, but he swooshed his hand in the air to keep the door magically shut. "Leave me alone!"

"The top three buttons, Ella, and I'll be satisfied. Remus can have you for now, so long as I get a peek."

Ella's fingers were numb, not unlike the rest of her. She hated herself and the world as she popped open the top three buttons on her shirt.

The Baron pinched her when he moved past her to open the front door. He greeted Lady Tremaine with a kiss to her cheek and a smile that didn't bother hiding all he'd done when she glanced over his shoulder and saw Ella so disheveled.

Lady Tremaine's tone was tart as she shoved Ella backward when Ella tried to move into the house. "No. You've upset us enough. You can wait out here until we're ready for you to serve dinner."

With that, she locked Ella out of the house, leaving her to shiver on the front porch while the snow fell in thick sheets.

ELLA COLLAPSED IN THE LIVING ROOM ATOP THE RUG WHEN Anastasia was sent to let her inside. Ana glanced around to make sure no one could see from the dining room when she bent down and blew on Ella's fingers. "She shouldn't have left you out that long! And with wet hair?" Anastasia slapped Ella's cheeks to bring some life into them, finally rousing her and getting her on her icy feet. She gripped Ella's shoulders with a look of actual concern. "Just get through dinner service, and then you can warm up in your bedroom."

Ella couldn't feel her fingers or her toes, but managed an open-mouthed astonishment at Anastasia. She didn't speak her confusion at the offer of mercy, but worked out a nod.

Anastasia directed Ella to the kitchen and popped a spear of asparagus into Ella's mouth, glancing with paranoia over her shoulder, scared to get caught in the act of being mildly humane to her lowly stepsister. Then she pointed sternly in Ella's face, as if warning her not to mention the kindness before she moved back out to the dining room.

Ella was starving, but too tired to wish the food she'd made could be meant for her. Breakfast had been a strange affair that morning—not because Anastasia had left a handful of grapes on her usually cleaned plate, but because when she'd walked in and caught Ella eating the discarded food, she didn't tell on her to Lady Tremaine. Then at lunch, she'd met Ella's eyes and moved a few cubes of cheese to the side, leaving them there for her, as well.

Ella didn't understand the gesture as kindness—the thought was so foreign to her—but she ate with caution all the same the moment she was alone in the kitchen.

She lit the gas burner and warmed her fingers over the small flames, though she couldn't feel any difference. Thirty seconds of self-care was all she would allow herself before she set the tray with salads, trembling for too many reasons as she moved out into the dining room. She managed to keep her eyes down and avoid being brought into the conversation by the Baron as she served each course of the meal. A deep-set shiver wracked her bones and rattled the tray. She slipped upstairs only once to send a text to Remus and Henry, begging them to hurry.

How she'd missed the sound of Henry's laugh, and the way he banded his arms around her. There were too many things tugging at her insides, but in his embrace, the harrowing aspects of her daily life felt simpler and somehow manageable. She wanted a safe place to hide for just a little while. The bed she'd shared with him had been warm and inviting. What she wouldn't give to feel the glow of his warmth again to stave off the coldness of cruelty.

The moment dessert was served, Lady Tremaine followed Ella back to the kitchen, her grip too hard not to bruise as she grabbed Ella's arm and yanked her down the hall. "That's the last time you draw the Baron's eye. You'll stay in here until he's gone."

Ella didn't allow more than a bleat of agony when Lady Tremaine shoved her into the utility closet that was too narrow for her to sit down in, and locked her in the suffocating darkness.

THE DARKNESS OF REMUS
AND ELLA

Ella had much practice struggling to fall asleep while standing up against the door. The trick was to kneel against the bucket, so her shins carried the brunt of her weight. Ella soaked through four rags as she blew her nose and attempted to dry her frozen hair in the darkness. She tried not to let the black void of claustrophobia gnaw away at her insides, but her nerves felt scraped raw all the same. She knew from experience that hyperventilation wouldn't help anything, but the temptation to topple over the edge of sanity was always there, inviting her with its crooked finger to give in to the panic that would surely never leave her.

It was half an hour later that hope sailed in her heart. The doorbell rang, and though Lady Tremaine never preferred answering it herself, her burning anger toward Ella outshined her pride at projecting a lifestyle of wealth.

Remus' voice made her heart stutter in her chest, but no sooner had it soared did it go crashing into the depths of her stomach. Henry's voice carried with it a hopefulness that crushed her. Though she'd wanted nothing more than to see him again, this was not how she wanted to be seen. She shivered in the dark, clinging to her damp shirt that was now buttoned all the way to the collar. She wiped her sweaty face on the dirty rags and shoved them in the bucket. She straightened her shirt, as if that would undo all that was wrong. She tried to stand straight, but the dark was disorienting, so she placed her hands on the door to steady herself, knowing that at any moment, she would be free of her prison. The darkness made her dizzy, and her cold was taking a downward turn, making her weak and nauseous as she breathed in the stink of cleaning products.

The pleasantries took agonizing minutes, each of which made Ella want to scream out for help. She bit her tongue, closing her eyes, so the darkness felt like her choice, instead of a punishment that had been inflicted upon her. She nearly clawed at the door when she heard Lady Tremaine's long strides accompanied by Remus' light, conversational tone. "Yes, we were in the area a little earlier than I anticipated. Apparently, we missed all that traffic everyone's always complaining about. I hope I didn't interrupt your dinner."

"Oh, of course not. We were just finishing up. Would

you care for some dessert? I can have Ella whip up something sweet for you and Prince Henry."

"I wouldn't dream of putting you out. Where is Ella? I'd like to get back to the house soon. I was hoping she could get started scouring the bottom of my sailboat tonight."

"Sailboat? Surely it's too cold for sailing, Mr. Johnstone." Lady Tremaine let out a throaty chortle as she fished through her keys.

"Indeed. I have a buyer for it, though, who wants to take a look at it in the morning. I do hope you haven't worked Ella too hard. She'll need to be scraping fungus and barnacles off the bottom all night if it's to be ready by sunrise."

Ella nearly snorted at the ridiculous lie that made Remus seem like the grueling taskmaster Lady Tremaine would approve of.

"I'm sure she'll manage." The key shoved into the door, but she didn't turn the lock. "You know, there's been another bid for Ella's expertise. The Baron offered to pay more for her than you did last week."

Ella's breath quickened as panic welled in her chest. Remus' pause scared her, but she let out her breath when his words reassured her fears. "Lady Tremaine, I'd hate to think you were considering backing out of our deal. Surely you don't think the Baron wants Ella for her ability to shine shoes. Neither of us are that naïve. I put Ella to work for her intended purpose, and nothing more. Do you want to sell Ella to the Baron? Forgive me for speaking out of turn, but I thought I saw you on his arm at the last Dinner of the Elite. Selling her to the Baron seems quite the conflict of interest."

Lady Tremaine's voice was terse, though her words were well-chosen. "I don't wish to sell Ella to him, no. But if you could only match the Baron's price. He offered two hundred more than your fee."

Ella winched her eyes shut and silently begged Remus to free her, no matter the cost.

Remus chose a different argument, his tone growing indignant. "My dear lady, if you're in the business of selling your servants for sexual favors, then I can't be seen doing business with you. In fact, if you're insinuating what I think you are, then I'll have no choice but to report you to the king!"

Lady Tremaine faltered, her tone turning dulcet and syrupy. "No, no! Of course, I would never. And I'm sure the Baron wouldn't have wanted her for such things, anyway. How your imagination does run away with you, Mr. Johnstone." She let out an airy laugh that made Ella cringe, which incited a coughing fit that rattled her bones.

"What… Is someone in the closet?"

Lady Tremaine brushed off his inquiry. "Ella's yours for four days, and then you'll return her, as discussed."

"That's much better. Where is she?"

"Right here."

When the key turned in the lock, Ella was determined to keep herself upright. It was when the bucket her shins were propped up against toppled over that she fell forward with the mop, tumbling out with a shriek onto the floor at Remus' feet.

"What's all the commotion?" The Baron rounded the corner just in time to see Ella floundering on the floor, knocking herself in the back of the head with her broomstick. "Oh, Ella. Always so clumsy."

Remus shouted his shock, but stuffed his more coherent exclamations back down his throat as he knelt to untangle Ella from the mess of cleaning supplies. When Henry craned his head down the hallway, Remus used his body to partially shield Ella from view. His tone turned sharp to warn Henry to keep his mouth shut. "Henry, you don't deal with the servants. That's my job. Go out and entertain Lady Tremaine's daughters." When Henry took a step toward Remus instead of away, Remus didn't hold back the command in his voice. "Now!"

Henry's eyes glinted with anger, and then wilted to misery when he took in what he could make out of Ella's downcast state. For all the power his throne afforded him, he couldn't go against Ella's wishes. She'd been firm that he was to let things continue on in the cycle of abuse she was stuck in, for fear of tumbling out of the cycle and landing in something far worse. "Of course, Remus."

Once Henry was out of sight, Remus lowered his voice to a threatening whisper, his hand resting atop Ella's head. "What's the meaning of this, Lady Tremaine? You kept her locked in the dark?" His tone was pure horror, and Ella knew he was reliving his own time locked in the dark under Malaura's cruel tutelage. His fingers trembled with barely contained torment as they floated atop her tangled curls.

"She displeased me."

"She's shivering, and sick as a dog! I didn't pay you for a barely upright servant. Come, Ella. On your feet." His words were brusque, but his hands gentle as he pulled Ella up, taking in her pallor with a tightness to his eyes. "Go fetch your things. There's much work for you to do at my house. Quick, now. Prince Henry has many important errands to attend to this evening, and doesn't wish to linger."

Ella read between the lines, understanding that Henry's patience could only be expected to last so long in this place. "Yes, sir."

Remus touched his forehead at her formal address. "Actually, I wanted to see your bedroom, Ella, if it's alright with Lady Tremaine. My servants have too many trinkets in theirs, and I wondered if I was indulging them too much. May I escort her upstairs, Lady Tremaine?"

"Do what you like with her." Lady Tremaine waved her hand dismissively in Ella's direction. "When you leave, make sure you go out the back entrance, Ella. I don't want anyone to see you so filthy, and assume that's what I allow in my house."

Ella's cough was deep and rattled in her chest, but finally she eked out a croaky, "Yes, ma'am."

28

COMFORT TO END THE DARKNESS

*E*lla's legs were unsteady from not being able to bend for so long, but she made it up the steps by bracing herself on the railing, cursing her life that Remus had to walk behind her and watch her struggle.

The moment they reached the top of the steps and turned the corner, Remus swept her off her feet and kissed her cheek, his whisper frantic. "I'm so sorry, my darling. Say the word, and I'll do whatever you need."

Ella permitted one long breath in his arms, and then struggled to get down. "You can't hold me like that."

He didn't take offense, but set her feet down gently and stepped back. "Of course. Apologies. You only looked like your legs might be aching you. I didn't Pulse you with Comfort. I would never do that without permission."

Ella shook her head, emotion making its way to her throat. "No, it's not that. You can't be nice to me here! I'll start crying, and I can't break down like that right now. Please get me out before the Baron buys me from her!"

"Of course, Miss Ella. Which one is your bedroom?" He glanced around at the rooms on either side of the hallway.

Ella reached up and tugged on a cord that hung overhead. "Right here." She pulled, and a rectangle in the ceiling opened, revealing a staircase that fell from above.

Remus paled, looking as if he might be sick. "You sleep in the attic?"

"It's not so bad." Ella climbed up the steps that gave a slight bounce to them under her weight. She wasn't expecting Remus to follow her up, but moved to the side when he entered the tight space that had welcomed her when nowhere else had. "My things are right here." She picked up the bundle atop her quilt and rested it under her arm against her hip.

"You should change into something that's not damp. It's freezing out there."

Ella shook her head. "Lady Tremaine will be happier if I'm uncomfortable. Let's just go."

Remus ran his fingers through his black hair, looking younger and completely lost. To Ella, he usually appeared so very in control, but standing in her bedroom, she could see his struggle to find the right thing to say. "That horrible woman locked you in the dark."

Ella gave a curt nod.

"I want you to pack up all your things. Quick, now. Where are the rest of your clothes?"

Ella was cautious as she pointed, shivering toward the small chest in the corner. "That's everything I own. Most of my parents' stuff is locked in a storage unit that's under my name only."

Remus darted to the chest, swallowing hard at the meager possessions that amounted to a pile of worn clothes. "Is there anything here you have an attachment to?"

Ella hugged herself with her right arm, trying to rub feeling into her body. "No. Why?"

"Because you're not coming back here, so take whatever you like, but then we're leaving. We're not looking back until you go public. Then you can return here as the lady of your own house."

Ella tried to reply, but instead lost her words to a coughing fit. Remus shoved her tattered things into his messenger bag, and then met her in the center of the room to wrap her in his arms. "Not to worry, darling. I'll get you out of here. Soon this will all be a distant memory. Say a fond farewell to this space. The next time you step inside, this will be an attic, and no longer a bedroom."

Ella made to argue, but only ended up coughing.

Remus' pitch climbed with a tinge of desperation. "I couldn't save myself from the darkness, but I can save you! Do not fight me on this!" His eyes squinched shut as he squeezed her through her next bought of coughing. "You don't even have a bed! You sleep on a mattress on the floor!"

It wasn't until she saw the full breadth of his panic that she began to understand the mess for what it was. Far less than ideal, it wasn't sustainable. No matter the outcome, she knew she couldn't live like this any longer. Reality crashed over her with all the subtlety of a wrecking ball. "It's only a matter of time before the Baron convinces her to sell me to him."

Remus gagged, his face twisting with torment. She could tell he had whole epistles of arguments to persuade her to leave the life of misery, but in that moment, she didn't need a single push to finally take that first step in the right direction.

"Remus," she whispered, and finally let her head rest on his shoulder. So many things he'd done had confused her or given her pause, but his hug was filled with a desperation to make her life better. She decided to trust in the kindness, since that was the language with which she was most familiar.

Remus lowered his volume to match hers, but his words flowed out no less tensed. "Your parents wouldn't have wanted this life for you. Let's honor that, shall we? Let's honor your parents, who loved and protected their daughter as best they could."

She caught the sob in her throat before it birthed from her. She quickly shoved it back down and replaced it with a quiet plea. "I need you to do something for me. Please."

"Anything."

She pursed her lips, wrestling with her anxiety that came whenever she had to weigh the pros and cons of asking for help. "Pulse me, Remus," she begged with a quiver slicing her voice.

His breath of relief relaxed his shoulders as he fanned out his fingers across her back, thrumming a steady dose of Comfort into her spine. When Ella's syncopated panting calmed to light puffs of breath fanning across his neck as she lay her temple on his shoulder, Remus' frustration visibly melted. "There we go. Any time you need me, all you have to do is ask." He turned his chin and kissed her forehead. "See? You trusted me with that; you can trust me to help you leave this life."

Slowly, Ella nodded. "Okay. I trust you."

Another kiss pressed to her forehead, and he donned a pleasant expression he tried to force to appear sincere. "Come now, I can make you some chicken soup the moment we get home—your new home with me."

Her arms were weighted with weakness, but she managed to summon enough strength to hold onto him. "You'll let me stay with you until I get back on my feet and make a plan?"

"Silly girl. I'll let you stay with me forever. As long as you like."

His words were honey to her soul, and she savored the sweetness she so desperately needed. Though she wished for more eloquent musings, she choked out a raw, "Thank you."

"Of course, darling. There will be no more darkness for us." Remus Pulsed a few more beats of Comfort into her skin. "And do make sure to tell Henry exactly how sick you truly are. He won't hesitate to wait on you hand and foot. He's got a cold remedy he swears by that's absolutely dreadful. I can't wait to see your face when you choke it down."

Ella chuckled, but then coughed so hard, she nearly collapsed in his arms.

"Or perhaps we'll make a quick stop at Urgent Care first. Is that everything, then?"

Ella nodded, blinking back tears, lest they fall and break her perfect track record. For better or worse, her nightmare of living with the Tremaines was coming to an end.

"Can you make it down the steps and to the car? It's unlocked. Get in the backseat and wait for us there."

Ella was careful as she moved out of the attic down the steps, and then onto to the main floor. She carried her bundle, shivering as she tiptoed out the backdoor, leaving Remus to fetch Henry. She slipped into the back of the town car and let loose a tearless cry that was a catharsis of both joy and anxiety, knowing there was no turning back now.

29

SOMEONE TO LEAN ON

*H*enry's hands were careful with Ella as he guided her up the two steps in the garage that led to Remus' home. With an arm curved behind her and his other hand clutching hers, he moved as if escorting a delicate woman in her nineties.

Now that she had the freedom to breathe without threat of Lady Tremaine's vindictive nature, Ella was finally allowed to feel the aches and pains of the common cold, which had been made worse by going outside with wet hair. The sound of her rasping coughs scared her as they moved further into the house.

Remus pushed past them and darted up the stairs, while Henry lowered her to sit on a stool in the kitchen. He fished around in the fridge and pulled out a pot of freshly made chicken soup Chef Lionel had whipped up before going home for the evening. In front of the pot was a Get Well Soon note from him, at which Henry frowned. "Hey, now. Lionel has never given me a card when I've been sick. Back when I had my tonsils out, he force-fed me ice cream and kept asking me questions I couldn't answer, because I couldn't talk." He shook his head at Ella, who was slumped with her elbows atop the granite counter. "You've enchanted him, you minx."

Ella blew her nose. "What can I say? I've got it going on."

"Indeed." Henry heated up her soup, and then stood next to her stool so she could rest her head on his chest. He ran his fingers through her hair while she ate, not looking up when Remus trotted back down the stairs toward them, his sleeves rolled.

"The bath is ready for you when you're finished with your supper, Miss Ella." Remus always spoke to her with respect, as if he were the servant in his own home, content to wait on anyone who should need it.

Ella's nose was runny, her head ached, and she was too tired to examine anything, save for the gratitude that rose up in her ribs, which were sore from coughing. She moved from the comfort of Henry's chest only to stand and wrap her arms around Remus, finally accepting that he was who he claimed to be, and nothing more duplicitous. "Please," she asked, hoping for a dose of his Pulse to quell her anxiety.

"Of course." Remus didn't hesitate, engulfing her in

the hug she craved, while giving her a little something extra to take the edge off. "Good for you for asking."

"You're not trying to use my abilities for anything selfish," she whispered as she gripped him.

Remus melted around her. "Of course not, darling. The best teachers are perpetual students. I merely want to understand, and then to help."

"I see it now." She didn't stiffen when his hand cupped the back of her head to lean it on his shoulder. She felt protected with her head resting there, which wasn't a feeling she was altogether used to yet. Oh, how she'd needed a place to rest. "You're sure I can stay here until I figure out my next move?"

Both Henry and Remus didn't hesitate. "Of course." Remus gently swayed from side to side, rocking her as if she was his treasure. "Stay as long as you like. Make this your permanent address. As long as I'm in your life, there will be no more darkness. I'll keep you safe."

"Safe?" Ella echoed, turning the word over on her tongue to test how it tasted. There was too much beauty in that one word for her to feel like she belonged in the same room as it, but Remus held her to the spot, assuring her that she very much did.

Too many emotions swam to the surface, breaking through the dam she'd needed in place to keep her head above water, day in and day out. An avalanche of shame crashed around her when she broke down in his arms, sobbing into his clean dress shirt. Fearing that something so perfect might be snatched away, she gripped the pressed fabric, threatening with all of her resolve that this one good thing wouldn't be stolen from her fingers. Of all the things Lady Tremaine had taken from her, this one word, this concept too grand for comprehension, would remain forever hers.

Remus didn't shy away from her tears. The only thing he asked was for Henry to fetch a box of tissues, and to make her some tea. By the time her tears had quieted to mere hiccups of exhaustion, the tea was ready, and Remus lowered her back to her stool so she could drink it, his hand never leaving her back. That simple touch assured her that the stability she craved wouldn't be gone in the morning. She didn't resist it, but leaned into the touch, silently begging for the Comfort he had on tap.

Henry was careful with her as he led her up the stairs once she'd finished with her tea. He only whispered words of love and loyalty as he led her not to her bedroom, but to his. "Go on into your bath and relax. I'll make you a sandwich while you're in there."

Ella's heart seemed to be on perpetual swell and shatter mode, causing new tears to trickle down her cheeks. "You don't have to do that. You're both being too nice to me; it's all so confusing."

Henry tilted his head to the side, as if to ask her how she expected a boyfriend might behave under the circumstances. He didn't argue with her perplexed expression, nor did he sweep away her tears to pretend they didn't exist. Henry kissed her cheek, and then pulled her into his arms, letting her feel his solid body.

Ella permitted herself to rest against his chest, finally understanding that the beacon of safety she'd only just begun to trust wasn't going anywhere if she let herself lean on it.

30

FINDING HER ROLE

One might blame Ella's deep sleep on the nighttime cold medicine Remus gave her, but wiser minds would argue that she slept so soundly because of the arms that banded around her in the night. The gentle glow of the moon lulled them both to indulge in ten hours of unfettered rest. They woke only when the sun decided it had been ignored long enough.

Ella shot up in the bed, turned around after indulging in so much sleep. "Oh! It's almost eight o'clock!"

Henry shifted, his full lips pulling into a pout, now that his arms weren't wrapped around her. "Go back to sleep, hun."

She gasped, scandalized. "Are you serious? I haven't done a thing to help." She cast around for her bundle. "Where are my clothes?"

Henry mumbled something that sounded like "Inna fresser," which Ella translated to mean "In the dresser."

She darted to the drawers, pulling them open until she came to one that had been cleared just for her. Her panic at not being useful was put on hold when the significance of Henry putting her things in with his hit her with the obvious smack of permanence. Her shoulders lowered, and she pulled out one of his shirts, pressing the expensive fabric to her nose. The fragrance of Henry was wildly addictive. She wondered if her garments would begin to smell like his if she kept her things in the drawer long enough. Henry smelled of cinnamon-laced cologne that had faint notes of peach to it, but was still somehow masculine and alluring.

"Come back to bed. It's still early. I don't have anything until nine."

Ella turned her chin over her shoulder, soaking in the cuteness that was Henry before he awoke. No doubt Drizella would drool over pictures of him with no shirt on, tousled hair, and sprawled out on the rumpled sheets, full lips extra puffy from rest.

"Go back to sleep," she whispered, and Henry was just drowsy enough to comply without too much more of a fight.

She sniggered at his cuteness, and then changed into her jeans and flannel, blowing her nose and rubbing out an ache in her chest. If this was to be her new home, as

Remus suggested, she wouldn't make him regret his kindness.

She found her morning cold medicine, and prayed it would hold as she filled a bucket with cleaning solution and water. Her stomach was roaring, but she knew that at least a few chores should be done before anything else. Dusting, polishing the long oak table, and then thoroughly sweeping the dining room took only twenty minutes, but washing the floor took longer, drawing out her cough as the harsh chemicals coupled with the polishing done on her hands and knees. She felt far more tired than she usually did this early in the day.

"What are you doing?" came Remus' agitated voice from behind her.

Ella leaned back to sit on her heels, mopping the sweat from her brow. "I don't know what your regular routine for chores is, but I figured you can't go wrong starting in the dining room. That seems to get a fair amount of use."

Remus swore, and then bent to draw her up, a horrified grimace pulling at his usually composed features. He sat her down on a chair and pried the rag from her fingers. "I didn't bring you here to clean my house. You're my guest, not my housekeeper. I already have one of those, and I can't imagine she'd be willing to forfeit the job she's had for ten years."

Ella's lips pursed as she mulled over several responses, wishing she could just finish the job already. "I'm not lazy," she countered, her knees half a foot from his when he turned a chair so he could sit and face her stubborn expression.

"I'm not sure where you'd assume I might draw that conclusion. This has nothing to do with being lazy. It has to do with you punishing yourself for who knows what, or trying to earn a space here that's been freely given."

Ella studied him with caution. "I'm not sure what my role here is. I mean, if I don't work for you, then what are you getting out of the deal? How is that fair to you? I don't want to be a taker."

Remus took in her red nose and the pink around her eyelids, leaning his elbow on the table with a compassionate sigh. "Darling, in what world do you imagine yourself a taker? Sometimes it's my turn to accept help, while others it's my turn to give it. What do I get out of having you here? Friendship, for one. Also, there's the matter of my rabid fascination with the unknown. Our tutoring sessions are every bit the education for me as they are for you. I live for that. I would pay for that. The fact that you'll be here every day only expedites any progress we're trying to make."

Ella pulled a tissue from her pocket and blew her nose for the eleventh time that morning. Then she rubbed her temples to alleviate the tension that only seemed to build the longer she was awake. "All that sounds fine, but I'm not ungrateful. Please let me help out."

"'Help out' means picking up after yourself, not everyone in the house. Back to bed with you, darling. The doctor said you're a breath away from pneumonia, and housework won't help with that. Today is for rest. Tomorrow we can think about starting up our lessons again."

She couldn't stifle the lost look in her eyes. "What am I going to tell Lady Tremaine? This is going to go south real fast."

"You're not going to tell her anything when you're this ill. A stiff breeze could knock you over at this point, and that woman is a hurricane. You're not in any shape for the battle it's going to be when you openly defy her." At Ella's sharp intake of breath and the panic welling in her eyes, Remus held up his hands. "Which isn't something we're going to worry about today. For all she knows, you're merely staying here to clean my house for your usual four days. There's no need to add stress to our lives prematurely. Rest today, plan tomorrow."

Ella's one-track mind wasn't easily derailed, but after a few more back-and-forths, she consented to going back to bed if she could finish the floor. "It'll be uneven if I don't finish. Then it's like I didn't do anything helpful!"

Remus sighed, but handed over the rag with a resigned look that she was who she was, and it wouldn't be an easy road deprogramming her.

When Ella went back upstairs, she showered and then slipped back into her pajamas, feeling scandalous that her grand plan was to sleep the day away. She shivered in her clean flannel and shorts, but her limbs calmed when, in sleep, Henry reached for her, warming her body with his. She melted in his arms, allowing the guilt to slide out of her mind so she could rest contentedly with the man who seemed to crave her presence every bit as much as she desired his.

31

A WORD FROM THE KING

A bit of dozing was brought to a halt by Henry's phone ringing on his bedside. He groaned and rolled over, answering it without opening his eyes. "Hallo?" He tugged Ella to curl around his body, his arm under her head, and her hand atop his chest. "Yes, Dad. I've got it noted in my schedule. I'll be at Remus' for a few days, so I won't see you for a bit. I know, I know, you'll miss me terribly. I don't blame you; I'm quite adorable."

Ella loved the way his chest vibrated when he chuckled. She stroked the space over his heart, wondering if there was any better place in the world than this bed, in Henry's arms.

"Now, now. Don't say, 'That's fine, Son.' I want to hear your anguished cries at not being able to see my handsome mug for several days." He paused, and Ella giggled silently that King Hubert himself indulged his son in a few dramatic sobs, begging him to come home that instant. "That's much better. Next time, if you could work in the phrase, 'Henry, you're the light of my life,' that would also be acceptable."

When the king started going over details for the upcoming royal ball, Henry's smile faded as his eyes opened, his mind kicking into full gear. "I told you, I don't want the charade of a ball. The whole thing is barbaric and unnecessary."

King Hubert's voice left no room for arguing. "The kingdom has gone through too much, what with Malaura finally being killed, and now this whole Lethal vote coming up. The fact that she was queen before me makes everyone wary of anyone in power—no matter how tight of a job I'm doing. The people need something fun to distract them from the fact that no one can agree on anything. It seems the only thing the majority agrees on is the one thing I won't give them."

Henry groaned. "Don't tell me there are still people on the council who are insisting on installing the Lupine trackers. We voted that down last year."

"The Baron's trying to go over Stefan's head, insisting it shouldn't be a matter for the council to decide, since the Lupine aren't technically citizens."

"Whatever you need me for, count me in. Unless, of course, you want me to actually attend this ball where I'm to be auctioned off."

"It's hardly that dramatic. You'll merely select someone

to spend some time with. If it doesn't work out between you and your date, then we can revisit the idea of auctioning you off. Might be able to slash the budget considerably if we did that."

"Hysterical. I'm simply rolling on the floor over here. What if I told you I was seeing someone? It's serious, too."

Ella picked out the king's measured reply. "I was wondering when you would tell me."

"You knew?"

"Perhaps it's time you were introduced to women who aren't so..." She could tell he was censoring himself, fishing around for the right words but coming up empty.

Ella's stomach churned with sudden anxiety at the king's obvious disapproval.

Henry shifted, his brows pushing together. "Are you implying something, Dad? Do you know more about my love life than I do? Who do you imagine I'm spending my nights with? Remus is sexy, but he's hardly my type."

"Hilarious. It's not a secret if I'm seeing photos of you with that girl on Royal Watch. I do wish you'd confided in me first. That girl is... Well, she's not who I would've chosen for you. Though, kudos to you on picking her up from her house. I know what a serious gesture that is for you."

Henry sat up in the bed, taking the call away from Ella, who shrank under the covers. She'd been so content and peaceful mere minutes ago, but now she was awash in shame, wondering when it was that she'd allowed herself to entertain fantasies that anything could ever work out between her and Henry. The king hadn't even met her and he already knew what she understood to be glaringly obvious—that Prince Henry could do lightyears better than her. She knew it was childish, but she pulled the comforter over her head, hiding from the world so she could be alone to wallow in her rejection.

When Henry came back into the bedroom fresh from his phone call, a shower and getting dressed for the day, he sat on the edge of the bed, feeling around for her knee to give her a little squeeze. "Any chance you didn't hear a lick of that?"

Ella's voice was small under the covers. "Your father hates me. The King of Avondale knows I'm not good enough for his son. It's what I've been trying to tell you this whole time."

"He's never even met you. I don't know what his deal is. He's rarely so sharp with his opinions. Apparently there was some photo of us on Royal Watch, but our press agent had it taken down before I could see what got him all worked up. Who could've taken our picture?"

Ella bit down on her lip to keep her heartbreak tucked away. "Let's just hope not too many people saw you with me. It won't do well for your reputation."

Henry ripped the covers off her in a burst of temper, his brows squeezed together in consternation as he stared down at Ella, who squeaked at being suddenly revealed. "Do you think I care about any of that? I'd take a picture right now and post it myself, if you'd let me. I'm upset because my dad's acting out of character, and you made it clear you wanted things private, which now might not be the case. I'm trying to do everything I can not to spook you, so you don't disappear on me. It took me an entire week to get your first name out of you! Don't you know that I understand you? I see that this whole thing scares you. I just need to know how much."

Ella sat up against the headboard, holding her flannel tighter around her as she shivered. "I don't know," she admitted, feeling lost.

Henry took pity on her chill and covered her lap with the comforter. Then he went to his dresser and pulled out his gray sweatshirt, threading her arms through it and zipping her up. He sat down on the bed facing her and gathered up her hands in his, kissing her knuckles as if they were the soft, untarnished skin she wished she had. "Ella, my life is public. My first haircut was televised. The girl I first kissed was interviewed the next day by dozens of gossip sites, all of which concluded I was a terrible kisser."

Ella's face pulled into a look of horror. "Are you serious?"

Henry pressed her knuckles to his cheek to warm them. "You guard your privacy, and that's your right. However, if you're to date me publicly, nothing will be private again. I need to know that if I make a stand for us, you'll be by my side. I couldn't take it if I made an announcement that I'd finally, finally found someone incredible, too many cameras flashed, and you vanished on me."

"Why would they need to know about me?" Her wary expression gave away that she hadn't considered this all that thoroughly before. She'd seen it all through the lens of government officials trying to snatch at her and control her for her abilities—not gossip sites clambering to know if Henry was a good kisser.

"Because no one's ever captivated me the way you have. They'll be obsessed." He held her hands between them, looking down at her fingers with palpable sadness in his eyes. His voice was quiet with the urgency of a plea when he spoke again, his chin lowered. "I would give you everything you could possibly ask for. I would move whole kingdoms for you. Always and only you. But this one thing —privacy—I can't grant you. So I need to know now if that's a hard stop for you."

Ella's arms felt weak, and her whole body ached as she withdrew so she could cough into her sleeve. This wasn't the way she'd imagined she would fall in love, but there it was, her heart beating in his open hands. Soon all the world would see her exposed organ for the vulnerable mess it was. "I might say the wrong thing."

Henry's head shot up, swelling with elation that she hadn't immediately called the whole thing off. "Then you won't have done anything I haven't. And you don't have to say anything. You can 'no comment' everyone until you're blue in the face for the next sixty-five years."

Ella's intake of breath was followed by a stream of hacking into her sleeve. When her lungs finally settled, her eyes locked in on his, wide and filled with disbelief. "Sixty-five years?"

Henry shrank from her shock for only a second, and then leaned forward with a determined look. "Yes. And if that scares you, then I need to know how badly. I'm not in this for a casual date every now and then. I'm in it for the next sixty-five years."

Ella tugged a tissue from the box on the nightstand and blew her nose. "You can't say things like that to me when I'm sick and pathetic like this!"

Henry chuckled at her frustration and handed her another tissue. "I don't need an answer now, and I'm not officially asking until I've got a ring, a flock of doves, a string quartet and the whole nine yards. And clowns. Proposals are supposed to have clowns, right?"

"Naturally. I won't say yes without a slew of clowns."

"I figured."

Ella shook her head at him, a small smile playing on her lips. "Now I'm hurt. You only want me for the next sixty-five years? What happens after that? Planning on leaving me already?"

Though Henry was dressed for the day, he moved to sit next to her under the covers, tucking her slight body under his arm. "I figure you'll start to grow tired of my jokes by then."

"Never," Ella promised. In that simple exchange, Ella

knew that whatever frustrations and complications might come their way, at the end of the day, and at the end of sixty-five years, it would all be worth it if Henry was by her side. "Okay, then. Yes."

"Yes?" Henry shot off the bed as if it was suddenly laden with an electric current. His eyes were wide with disbelief, and he held up his hands as if to tell her she should be cautious when pulling his leg or tugging on his heartstrings. "Are you having a laugh? Is this real?"

Ella raised her finger to pause his quickly inflating glee. "Yes to going public, but give me like, a solid month to work up to it, okay? I can't go back to Lady Tremaine, so it's all about to hit the fan anyway. It's time. And the sixty-five years part? Let's give that a minute to digest."

"Finally! What tipped it?"

Ella held his gaze, muscling through to reveal a little of her raw underbelly to him. "When the Baron felt me up yesterday, Lady Tremaine looked the other way."

Henry stilled as the best news and the worst news warred for which would get top billing on his face. "The Baron touched you?"

"I shoved him away, but yeah. I can't go back there. Weighing a possible government-sanctioned lobotomy against the Baron's boney fingers on my body? I'll take my chances."

They were quiet for several seconds as the waves of elation and agony rippled through the room. Neither of them spoke until the tension settled enough for them to feel their connection more than the oceans of trouble that threatened to rock them both.

Henry ran his hands through his hair, his eyes darting from side to side as he processed that the person he'd been chasing after was finally slowing down enough for him to catch. Then he scrambled back to the bed, kneeling beside her and scooping her face in both his hands, so he could feel the dream and be sure she was real.

The kiss wasn't gentle, but neither of them needed it to be. Their lips crashed in a frenzy of elation as they finally were able to keep close what had always seemed so very far away.

THE BIGGER PICTURE

"Again. I'm not sure you're concentrating."

Ella bit her tongue to keep any sass locked inside. Her brain felt like it was seeing the world through a foggy mist, taking longer to process everything. "I'm sorry. It's the cold medicine. I'm not used to it."

Cordray turned a full circle in the swivel chair that he'd rolled to the side of the study to avoid Remus' agitation. Though Remus was never out-and-out harsh, he didn't hesitate to push when necessary. "Honestly, Remus. The poor girl's clearly sick. She's doing her best. Ella, the next time you sneeze, aim it in his direction so he catches your virus, and we can say condescending things to him while he muddles through."

Ella sniggered but that led to a coughing fit, during which she was pretty sure she actually did spread germs in his direction. "No, no. Remus is right. I'm not concentrating. We have to figure out what to say to Lady Tremaine tomorrow, and I'm in knots about it."

Remus leaned back on his desk, and then pressed his hands behind him to lift himself up to sit on the sleek top. His gray slacks and light green dress shirt were perfectly pressed, even though he'd worked nine hours that day at the Johnstone Foundation. He sighed and scrubbed his face with his hands. "Cord is right. I'm off-center. I was hoping to be further along than this, but it seems your cold is affecting your magic."

Ella shook her head. "It's not my cold. I could still hear through walls and whatnot when I was starting to get sick. It's the cold medicine."

"You're certain?"

Ella shrugged. "I haven't had any kind of medicine in years, so yeah. I can tell something's not firing correctly, and that's the unknown variable."

Remus stared up at the ceiling, as he often did when he was putting together equations and solving problems in his head. "Have you tried St. John's Wort before?"

Ella quirked her eyebrow. "That you think Lady Tremaine gives me access to any kind of vitamins or herbs makes me think I downplayed how miserable it was for me there. She barely gave me food." Ella sat back down in her chair across from the desk, her body groaning at being out of bed for this long. "Why do you ask?"

"Lethals have options. Cord doesn't have to wear his gloves, but he chooses to, because he's too powerful for the pill to mute all of his abilities. I don't want to mute your abilities, only make it so you can more easily control them. Take them down a notch so you can choose when you access them. Think of how nice it would be to kiss your boyfriend without fear of bringing down the house."

Ella thought over the last two hours of mental and magical exercises Remus had her do. Each one was designed around control. Levitate a chair, but only two inches, and then hold it there, never moving it up or down, for twenty minutes. See through the cover of a book, but find only a specific page while being timed to see how long it took, and then how long she could stay on that page before the vision fell away. "Do you really think it's as simple as an herb?"

Remus tipped his palms upward. "I think we can do a fair amount of practicing on you to see what we can get right. It's much more complicated troubleshooting with Cordray."

Cord flexed his gloved fingers with a look of a chagrin to him. "Sorry."

Ella's eyes fixed on Remus' feet that swayed lightly against the desk. "Henry doesn't understand why you aren't on as many pills as it takes to mute your powers, Cord. Isn't it safer if you are? Isn't that easier for you than going through all this testing?"

Cord stopped swiveling in his seat to stare at her. "Of

all people, I never would've pegged you as one to vote for the easy way out. I don't want to need a band-aid for the rest of my life. The pill isn't a solution, it's a temporary fix. Besides, my abilities seem to want to mutate past whatever dose I put in my body." He shook his head. "And it's not safer for me to be on the pill, even if it worked as it's supposed to. Rory has been abducted eight times in her life. Did you know that?"

Ella's eyebrows shot upward. "Oh, that's terrible!"

Cordray touched his chin, running his tongue over his teeth. "In those situations, I'm not going to just sit there and watch while they take my wife, kicking and screaming. I know what happens to the hostage." His dark eyes clouded over with a storminess that made Ella feel like his thoughts were too private for her to look at him directly. "It's not safer for anyone if I can't protect my wife. I'm very careful to always wear my gloves, so I'm not worried about accidentally electrocuting her, like I know Henry's afraid might happen."

Ella felt horrible for Cord's plight. She adored Rory, and couldn't stomach anyone hurting someone so wonderful.

When Ella coughed again, Remus said to Cordray, "Would you mind getting Ella some tea?"

"Sure thing. Hang in there, Sis." Cordray clapped Ella on the shoulder before leaving the study.

Ella took in Remus' serious expression, and the fact that he waited until Cordray was halfway down the hall before he spoke. "Have you read the fine print of Proposition 7?"

Ella turned her chin slowly from side to side, confused at the abrupt subject shift. "I just know the headlines. It's about privatizing the pill, leaving the original for the government to distribute. The plan is to release the formula to the highest bidder, so they can make mutations and try to work out the kinks." She frowned at him. "That would be good for Cordray, right?"

"On the surface, yes. But there's a little line in there that most people gloss over. 'If any harmful side effects occur, the manufacturer has the right to quarantine, treat, and study the subject for the duration of the effect.'"

Ella chewed on his words, but didn't see anything inherently evil about them. "Well, shouldn't they help if they do something that hurts Lethals? Doesn't that just give them license to clean up their messes?"

Remus remained seated atop his desk, but he leaned forward to meet her eyes in earnest. "'Harmful' is a broad judgment. Taking away Cordray's magic could be considered harmful, which would then give whoever's in charge the right to lock him away, test serums on him, and track his every movement for the rest of his life under the guise of medical research."

Ella's mouth fell open in horror. "Are you serious? Do you really think that could happen?"

Remus crossed his legs atop his desk, looking to Ella a little like a meditation guru in business casual. "If I was diabolical, my first move would be to lengthen the life of the pill, so instead of every month, it would last a year or more in a person's system. That way I could study them for much longer when they needed to be quarantined 'for their own good.'" His voice lowered. "If that bill is passed, the government would also have those rights."

Ella's head felt like it was swimming with too much information. "But King Hubert is a good man." She swallowed the shame at the king's scorn of her over the phone, and clung to his usually fair policies. "He wouldn't do that."

Remus met her eyes with a seriousness that revealed more sleepless nights than he would admit to aloud. "There have been two attempts on the king's life just this year. Henry can't leave the house without either myself or a guard. Once you two go public about your relationship, that will be your life, as well. The throne is in good hands now, but if certain councilmembers had their way, the king would be replaced. Imagine the damage that bill could do in the hands of the Baron. He owns a company that's chomping at the bit for this bill to pass. Would you want the Baron manufacturing your medication?"

Realization of the far bigger picture crashed over Ella like a ton of bricks, knocking her worldview. Reality began to chip away at the precious parts of her that needed to believe in happily ever afters. "Why are you telling me this?"

Remus straightened his tie. "Because Cordray won't

see reason. He wants this bill passed, which means that if it does, he'll be first in line to try a new pill that might let him hold onto his magic while keeping Rory safe. I don't want you to fall into the same trap. When your ability gets out, it might be suggested you go on the pill as well. That would be most detrimental."

Ella covered her mouth and sucked in too much air, which pushed her into a coughing fit. It wasn't until Remus hopped off his desk to rub soothing circles into her spine that she saw another layer clearly through all the politeness and politics. "You're not done studying me, and you're worried a new pill will pause our progress."

Remus shook his head. "That's like, fifth on the list of reasons why I don't want you to fall for this golden opportunity. Henry needs someone like you to watch out for him. What you did when you overheard the Baron plotting to take out members of the council? We were able to get ahead of that because of your gift. I sleep better at night knowing you can help the people we love."

Ella slumped against Remus' hip, letting him ease her assumptions that had been a bit too harsh. "I'm sorry. I'm just used to..."

"I'm not here to use you, Ella. No more than you're here to use me."

Ella's eyelids drifted shut as she rested her weary head against his side, marveling at how very comfortable she was with Remus now. She felt truly at home in his house, and knew that he was only expecting of her the standards he'd set for himself—to protect the people they both loved with the unique gifts nature had granted them. "If the bill passes, I won't take the new pill. Thank you, Remus."

Remus gusted out a sigh of relief. "Thank you for trusting me, Miss Ella."

33

REMUS' CONSPIRACY THEORIES

"Henry, I don't know about this." Ella shifted in her dress. She felt so formal; she wasn't sure if breathing was allowed in the corseted waist and long, flowing skirt. She studied herself in the bathroom mirror, seeing a stranger in the glass as Rory pinned the last curl up into the intricate knot.

Henry had insisted on an evening at the best restaurant in town, but Ella countered with a request for something private for their first time out together.

"Adam's no one to be afraid of," he said from the doorway, watching her nervous fidgeting with a careful eye.

"It's not that. Well, now it is, since you brought it up. It's just... Look at me." She motioned to the expensive dress with disbelief. "This isn't normal us. This is fancy us, which isn't real."

Rory remained quiet as she sprayed Ella's hair, and

started putting away all the accoutrements that were scattered atop the counter, allowing Henry to field Ella's concerns.

Henry shoved his hands in his pockets, looking like he was casually posing for a modeling spread that featured couture suits for men. "I hate to break it to you but every now and then my life requires a little fanciness. Now that it's going to be *our* life, this is something you need to try on for size."

Ella rubbed her arms in a hug, feeling strange that her shoulders were so exposed. "I guess it's good we're test driving this at your friend's house. I'm nervous I'll trip or something. Or that you're all thinking how ridiculous I look in a dress, but you're too polite to say anything to my face."

Henry's eyes combed her body, not bothering to hold back the lust that burned for her. "The only thing I don't like about you in that dress is that I can't peel it off you and throw you down on the bed right now. Like it or not, you look good in my world."

"It just takes some practice, is all," Rory assured her. "Would you prefer the flats instead of the heels?"

"That's an option? Yes!" Ella kicked off the heels, groaning at the unnatural feel of it all. She gripped the sink, her heart racing. "Remind me why we're doing this."

Henry studied her anxiety with a sadness that weighted his shoulders. "Because we're a team. Because we belong together everywhere—in this house, in the palace, in your house and on the moon." He was constantly afraid that one thing would prove to be too much for her, and she would run from him again. "Look, I'm sure about us. If you're not, now is the time to speak up."

Ella touched her stomach to calm the swarming butterflies. "I'm sure about us. Not so sure about the rest of the world."

"Then that'll have to be enough to see us through. Take a breath. Adam will behave."

Ella squeezed Rory's hand to steady herself as the trio made their way down to the kitchen, where Cordray and Remus were having tea at the counter. The men stood, and Remus inclined his head to Ella, taking in her nerves with a gentle smile. "You look lovely, darling."

"Like I was just scrubbing toilets last week?" She tried to pass it off as a joke, but Remus saw through her forced grin.

"Why don't you all get in the car? Benjamin's waiting for you. I'd like a word with Ella."

"Who's Benjamin?"

Rory shrugged into the coat Cordray held out for her, smirking as he planted a kiss to her neck from behind. "My guard. He's wonderful. Been by my side since I was a baby."

Henry cast Remus a furtive glance, as if begging him to talk Ella out of running away, if that was in her plans for the evening. Then he followed Rory and Cordray out into the garage, leaving the tutor with his pupil.

Remus waited until the others exited before he took Ella's hands, pointing her knuckles skyward. "I feel as if your father would've had many things to say to you about a night like this. It's a good thing you're doing, giving Henry a chance to show you his world." He kissed the back of her hand, instilling the idea that she was a proper woman who deserved such niceties.

"What if I don't belong there?"

"Do you belong with Henry?"

Ella's voice quieted to a whisper. "I want to."

"Then if you belong with him, he'll make sure that's true, no matter the setting."

"Tell me I look normal in this dress. Tell me meeting Adam will go great."

Remus chuckled. "I bought you this dress because it's anything but normal. And no one who meets Adam thinks it went great. He's impossible to please, so best just be yourself and enjoy the food, if he remembers to buy any." When Remus saw the last of her hope fall, he tucked his finger under her chin. "Darling, you belong here with me, no matter how tonight goes."

In the next breath, Ella's arms flung around Remus' neck, squeezing him to stave off the angst that welled up in her. "Thank you."

Remus held her as long as she needed, giving her the assurance that life would still find a way to turn, even if everything around them crashed. "Did you take your evening herbs yet?" He kissed her cheek, unable to hold back his fondness for her. It was a heady thing—the bond between rescuer and the rescued.

"No. I was just about to. I took two tablets of St. John's Wort this morning, but I haven't had my evening dose yet."

"Hold off on taking them for now. I don't want your magic dulled tonight. Adam is... He's not well. But you know me and my conspiracy theories. It's what led me to you."

"You've got a conspiracy theory cooking about Adam?"

Remus shrugged, as if unwilling to put a voice to something he was only mostly certain of. He checked over his shoulder to ensure the door to the garage was shut. "Everyone assumes Adam is schizophrenic, what with him seeing and hearing people who aren't there. But I've known Adam since he was a boy. I think we're missing something. Perhaps some bit of magic our minds are too small to quantify. I always assume my imagination is too small, which is how it's grown so large over the years." He released her and leaned against the counter with a sigh, folding his arms over his chest. "Malaura always said that our minds were too limited to understand all we were capable of. It's her that addled Adam's brains, and her curse that will turn him into a Lupine not too long from now."

"Sounds like a straightforward curse to me."

Remus shook his head. "There's more to Malaura

than strict hatred. People want to simplify her because it makes them feel safer. They don't know about the letters."

"What letters?" Ella felt like the more she asked, the less she understood.

Remus again glanced at the door, and lowered his voice. "Years ago before Adam's curse, he was voted Avondale's sexiest bachelor. He was quite handsome, and Malaura took notice. She was always a prize collector, and she wanted Adam. Wrote him letters from the shadows that he turned over to me when they grew too... intimate. When he spurned her in person that last time, she cursed him with the Lupine ticking clock."

Ella shrugged. "Well, sure. If she couldn't have him, she would make it so no one wanted him. Makes sense."

"Indeed. But hearing and seeing people who aren't there?" Remus' eyes burned into hers, communicating a puzzle his brain hadn't entirely worked out. "What if they *are* there?"

Ella's sharp inhale set her mind spinning. "What do you want me to do? How can I help?"

Remus softened, his shoulders lowering as he took in her selflessness. "I didn't know where Henry was taking you tonight, otherwise I wouldn't have started you on the St. John's Wort regimen. I wasn't expecting it to work so well this quickly. You can still access your Hearing and your Sight?"

Ella rubbed her forehead. "Sort of, but it's foggy, which

is actually much better for my dating life, since I date now," she declared with a puff of pride.

Remus smirked at her and motioned to her dress. "Do you like the color?"

"I like anything you buy me."

He narrowed his eyes, spotting the lie. He got down on his knees before her and pressed his palms to the skirt, dying it the lightest shade of pink. "Better?"

"I didn't want to insult you, but yes! Henry keeps making marriage comments, and I worried wearing a white gown might rush things too much. Plus, I don't want to have a clumsy moment and spill something, which I know will happen if I wear white." She held still while Remus stroked the expensive material, leaving the corseted bodice white, but transforming the skirt to a baby pink that matched the blush in her cheeks whenever Henry complimented her. "Oh, Remus, it's gorgeous!"

Remus stood, chuckling at her genuine grin. "There. That's much better. Any dress that makes you so nervous you look as though you may vomit, might not be the one for you. The right dress should make a woman glow, which now, you are." He stood and kissed her forehead, grasping her hands when he pulled back to look at her. "Tonight, I want you to have fun. But while you're there, do me a favor and send your Hearing and your Sight out to the candelabra."

"The candelabra? You want me to check if the candelabra... What? If it makes a noise when it's lit?"

"Not a noise, darling." He swung their arms lightly between them. "Now, I don't want you to involve Henry with this. This is to be our little secret. I'm working out several theories that need to stay private. I want you to tell me if you can Hear the candelabra speak."

34

HOWLING IN THE NIGHT

"It's nearing one in the morning. I was wondering if I would have to come in and get you myself," the mid-forties guard said as he opened the car door for them.

Henry cast the suited man a tired smile. "Oh, Benjamin, you old tease. Don't you know I'm a taken man?"

Rory's guard had a paperback Western tucked under his arm and the look of practiced patience on his lightly lined face, well accustomed to Henry's humor. He lightly shoved the prince into the backseat of the town car. Then he nodded to Cordray and offered his hand politely to Ella and Rory before sliding into the driver's seat. "I'll just be crying with all the other eligible maidens in the kingdom when they find out the tragic news that Prince Henry's off the market." His brows furrowed as he started up the car.

"Why is your father throwing you a royal ball? You're supposed to choose a companion from the single women. People are going crazy, trying to find dresses to impress you. I actually heard one woman ask the tailor to cut a slit in the back of her dress that went down to her..." He glanced at Ella and cleared his throat. "They're getting a bit overexcited."

A cloud settled over Henry's features. "Yes, well, Dad hasn't met Ella, so he can't be as disapproving as he claims."

Rory's wistful expression melted away. "I can't believe Papa Hubert would jump to conclusions that Ella isn't the one for you over something he saw in a picture. Did you see the photo before it was taken down? I mean, were the two of you skinny dipping or something?"

Henry rolled his eyes. "We can barely kiss without bringing down the roof, but sure, skinny dipping. You two were the ones making babies in Adam's castle, not us. I didn't see the photo, but it couldn't have been anything scandalous."

Ella's chin fell, and the levity of the beautiful evening crested at mention of the real world they'd escaped for a few hours. She swallowed hard and resolved herself not to recoil from the pain but to reach out instead. She laced her fingers through Henry's, anchoring herself to him and silently promising them both that she wouldn't leave. "Whatever happens, we're still us, right?"

"Always us," Henry assured her, squeezing her fingers.

"I'm not worried. If we made it through a dinner with Adam and you didn't bolt, then everyone else is downhill. Though, he was on his best game tonight. I've never seen Adam so calm and talkative. He winked at Belle, like he was his old, playful self again." Henry ran his thumb over Ella's knuckles. "Did his Lupine features freak you out? If they did, you did a brilliant job of hiding it."

"You prepped me well enough. He was lovely, and Belle was wonderful. I think it's sweet how you, Adam and Rory have clung to each other over the years, with Remus guiding the way."

Benjamin spoke up from the front seat. "I chatted with the police when they showed up, trying to bring Adam in on those false charges. I gave them my statement that Adam never left the castle while I watched the grounds. I trust everything is settled?"

Henry's expression darkened. "It was. I handled it enough to clear Adam's name. Why people can't leave him alone in his last days being human is beyond me." He ran his thumb over Ella's knuckles, swallowing hard. The interior of the car fell silent for a few moments while everyone processed the change that would surely come soon. "Thanks for letting me handle it, and I'm sorry our date ended with the cops showing up."

Ella shrugged. "No one can ever accuse you of being a boring date, that's for sure." She glanced out the tinted windows, pondering her brief time away from the group while the police were questioning Adam. She'd waited in the dining room, hoping that her first date with Henry could remain out of the public eye.

It was the candelabra that distracted her from the hullaballoo in the foyer. She wasn't sure what Remus was expecting her to discover, but she reasoned then to be her best window.

She'd sat at the table, her elbows resting on the surface with her fingers twined to cradle her chin as she stared at the brass two-foot tall three-tiered brass candelabra. Remus had started every session with deep breathing exercises, taking her and Cordray to an almost meditative state to open their minds before filling them with lessons.

The St. John's Wort she'd taken in the morning wasn't strong enough to make sending out her Hearing and Sight impossible, but the view was foggier, and the sounds weren't as easy to piece together into conversation. However, the tradeoff was that she'd been able to let Henry pin her against the wall in the ballroom when the others were off doing their own things.

Ella shivered at the memory of such unencumbered ravishing. Her lips still felt swollen from his hungry kisses that never seemed to find satiation. It hadn't been until Henry's hand had gripped her thigh beneath the fabric of her hiked-up dress that her Hearing accidentally shot forth, cluing her in to Adam's dilemma with the police.

In the privacy of Adam's dining room, Ella had gathered her Hearing up and pushed it out from her body with purpose in the direction of the polished candelabra. Remus had taught her to control the abstract as if she were conducting clouds to hover over a certain spot. She imagined the clouds gathering like cotton candy around the candelabra that kept catching Adam's eye during dinner. She wasn't certain what she was supposed to be searching for, but she gently peeled back the layers of logic that would advise her she was wasting her time.

"Mm-b-hmph. The Master should ust ask Belle to marry him uh-etty."

Ella's head jerked around, finding no one else in the room. "Hello?"

When no one answered, she wet her lips and went in for another attempt, this time adding Sight to the mix. Remus was adamant that she catalog every detail, no matter how small, but as much as she tried to focus, the edges of everything remained blurry. The St. John's Wort, though it was weak in her system, made it feel like she was hearing underwater.

"Mm-fl-sip-zoo should be more romantic. Make hi-lifsping."

Ella had cried out when she'd caught slight movement, as if the candelabra's top half had opened up and formed a mouth with which it spoke when it assumed no one could hear him. She wanted to hear him speak for hours just so she could observe the oddity, but the pressure in her temples began pounding with uncomfortable pressure.

"You look like your mind is somewhere far away," Henry commented, bringing her back to the town car that drove along the snowy backroads towards the freeway.

Ella was about to reply, but she realized belatedly that thinking about sending out her Hearing had done exactly that in real time. Panting sounds of *"It could be Remus! Don't lose the car!"* reached her ears, with that same growl behind it she'd heard when she'd conversed with the wolves last week.

"Stop the car!" she cried out, surprised when Benjamin obeyed.

"Is everything alright, Miss?"

Ella unbuckled herself and fisted the handle. "Everyone stay inside, understood?"

Henry held tighter to her hand to keep her in place. "Not a chance. The snow is at least a foot deep off the road. What's wrong?"

"It's the Lupine. I can Hear them speaking. They're trying to flag down Remus." She shook her head when the others gasped. She'd kept her field trip into the woods with Remus private.

This revelation seemed to push Henry over the edge. "You can talk to the Lupine?"

Ella slipped her hand from his. "I didn't think it was relevant to mention. I'm still learning all that I can do." When this didn't pacify him, Ella exhaled. "I'm sorry, Henry. I should've told you. But I really need to talk with them right now. It seems urgent."

Cordray pressed his hand to Henry's chest when the prince tried to exit the vehicle. "You stay in here. I'll go out with her."

It was a clear shot to Henry's masculinity, though Ella knew Cord hadn't meant any offense by it. He touched the edge of his gloves, but kept them in place for the time being. He tossed his wife a gentle smile when she warned him to be careful. "Of course, Story. I'm the most careful Lethal you know."

Benjamin didn't heed Ella's warning to stay inside but came out with the two, hemming her in with Cordray. "You can talk to the Lupine? That's really something, kid."

Ella muscled through the cringe that yet another person knew her secrets, but she understood this was a drop in the bucket. Soon enough, all of Avondale would be told by Lady Tremaine that Ella could Hear things she shouldn't.

She flagged down the wolves, who ran even faster when they saw it was her, and not Remus. They jumped like puppies when they neared, yipping and rolling in the snow with excitement. "Hi, guys! Is everything alright?" She fastened the top button of the gray wool coat Rory had bought her, but the wind was unmerciful as it whipped at her cheeks, beating color into the flesh that made them feel raw.

Connor noticed her shiver and moved cautiously toward her. *"Tell your friends I'm just going to warm you up. I don't want any trouble."*

"At ease, soldiers." She bent down, leaning forward so she could wrap her arms around Connor's neck, kissing the gray fur as she scratched behind his ears. "I missed you."

"*Oh, my queen. You have no idea.*" Connor shuddered at her touch, leaning into it like a starving man offered his last meal. "*I don't want you out in the snow like this, so I won't keep you as long as I'd like.*" He licked her cheek. "*How I should like to keep you forever.*"

Ella dimpled. "Oh, you charmer."

Guadalupe smooshed her body against Ella's other side, shielding her from the wind as best she could. "They put trackers in us!" she moaned, letting out a chilling howl into the night. The trees were the only other witnesses to her pain this far out, but nature seemed to absorb her sadness, hushing as the snow fell to respect her agony.

Benjamin and Cordray observed the exchange with mixed looks of curiosity and fear as they assessed how much of a threat the Lupine were to Ella, affectionate as they were to her.

"What? Who did?" She reached out and scratched under Errol's chin, taking in his whine with compassion.

"*We didn't get their names. They put trackers in us, and injected us with some serum. We're not safe anywhere now!*"

"Are they hunting you?"

"*Not yet.*" Guadalupe covered the nape of Ella's neck when she shivered. "*But it's coming.*"

"What did the serum do? Are you okay?"

"It muted our Pulses for a while, but they're starting to come back, thank goodness." Guadalupe's tone turned biting. *"They treated us like animals, forcing us into cages and injecting us with stuff we never consented to. Now we can never escape, because they'll always be able to find us!"*

Ella gripped Connor and then brushed her fingers over Guadalupe's brown-spotted fur as her mind rushed to put the pieces in the most logical order. "If they'll do that to you…" Her eyes climbed up to Cordray, whose fists were bunched as he tried to determine whether or not he should remove his gloves and clean house. Her heart clenched, and then began to beat rapidly as fear dawned on her afresh, connecting two scandals in her mind. "If that serum muted your Pulses, it's because you're the test subjects. They're gearing up to move forward with developing the pill before Proposition 7 even passes."

Errol howled into the night, and despite his stalwart body language, Benjamin let out a bleat of distress. *"They wore blue lab coats and took us into a huge warehouse. That's where they experimented on us. Find them, Ella! Don't let them do this to anyone else!"*

Ella shuddered from the cold. "Will you come to Remus' home with me? He might have a few theories. He's better connected than I am."

Connor's maw brushed her cheek before he licked her earlobe. *"I would go with you wherever you led, but we have to alert the other packs. We're telling you because Remus needs to know. He needs to understand that they're moving forward without government consent, which means they either know they've got the vote secured, or they don't care if the government sanctions this or not. I'm not sure which is worse."*

"You can't expect me to leave you out here!" Ella flung her arms around his neck, casting up a look of gratitude when Guadalupe and Errol moved in closer to shield her from the angry gust of wind that kicked up around them. Ella shivered against Connor, sneezing a few times until her eyes watered.

Connor hooked his maw over her shoulder. *"That's exactly what you have to do. I don't want to lead those men straight to Remus, or to you. I want them far, far away from you. Tell Remus the men were wearing blue uniforms with a white stripe across the breast. I bit into one of their legs, and Errol tore up one of their hands pretty badly. So check the hospitals for someone who was treated for those kinds of injuries two nights ago."*

"Two nights? You've been dealing with this by yourselves for two nights? How can I help?"

"Getting the information to Remus is all the help we need." Connor laved at the hollow of her throat, forcing a coo from her lips.

That was when Henry decided he was done waiting it out in the car. He stepped into the snow, his chest barreled. "Are you kidding me with this? I'm not about to sit back and watch while some guy licks my girlfriend's neck."

Ella craned her head up at him. "Huh? He's a wolf,

Henry. It's hardly the same thing."

"He's a man, Ella. It's exactly the same thing. Let's get home. You're not completely over your cold yet. I'll not see you back at Urgent Care again so soon." He sneered at Connor, who snarled in return.

"Enough," Ella chided them both. "We can go, Henry. Was that everything, guys?"

Guadalupe shot Ella a look of warning. *I'd listen to Henry on this one.* She barred her fangs at Connor when he growled at her. *Leave her be.*

Connor wrapped his tail around Ella's calf when she stood. *Until we meet again, my queen.* Then he farted in Henry's direction before he walked off with the pack into the woods.

When they all piled back into the car, the first thing to break the tension was Henry's incredulous, "Where was your Lethal status just then, Cord? Next time some guy cozies up to my girlfriend, the gloves come off."

Cordray merely chuckled as he shivered next to Rory, who cuddled into his side. "There's a reason nature didn't give you anything more than charm. You couldn't handle a day in my shoes."

Henry grumbled at Cordray and gathered up Ella's hands, blowing hot air onto her fingers. "Tell me you'll never do something so reckless again. Having a chat with the Lupine shouldn't be done unarmed. They're dangerous, Ella."

"Oh, honey. They're not the ones we should be afraid

of." She leaned into his shoulder, wondering just who was behind the attack on the Lupine, and what could be done about it all now.

35

EAVESDROPPING

"She's being dramatic. You wouldn't believe the wild stories she can concoct."

Remus ran his hand across the surface of his desk, keeping his face composed, lest he shout at the woman on the other end of the call. "I'm not speaking of Ella, I'm merely relaying the doctor's notice I was given when I took her to Urgent Care. Ella's got a severe case of pneumonia, I can only assume from being locked out of the house with wet hair in the dead of winter. She's to be confined to bedrest for two weeks. She hasn't been able to perform her housekeeping tasks that I paid for, so I'll put her up here at no cost to you until she's well enough to fulfill her duties. Does that sound reasonable?"

Lady Tremaine made a verbal show of huffing and puffing out her indignation, but eventually consented when Remus threatened to have Ella hospitalized for the duration of her illness, and the bill be sent to Lady Tremaine. "Fine. You can keep her until she can do her job. This is ludicrous. She's faking it."

"Faking pneumonia? My, she's utterly wasted as a housekeeper. I should book her for acting gigs first thing. Good day, Lady Tremaine."

Ella didn't speak until Remus ended the call. "I don't have pneumonia, you know. I'm perfectly healthy."

He quirked his eyebrow at her. "You wanted more time to be with Henry before going public. I just bought you a little privacy until the ball. You don't need the stress of dealing with the fallout of leaving her on top of it all. And frankly, Henry can't handle one more thing right now. After seeing Belle defeat Adam's curse two nights ago, I think he's had all the cameras in his face that he can handle. He could use some downtime with you every bit as much as you could use the time with him."

"I still can't believe that when we left, he was part Lupine, and then the next day he's full-on human again. Good call on him not being mentally ill, by the way. I thought I was going crazy when I heard the candelabra speak."

"I'm just grateful everyone's alright."

Ella's mouth drew to the side. "How about you? Are you alright? I know you left with Henry when he dropped us off here to go back to help Adam."

Remus tilted his head to the side, looking at her as if she was the first breath of fresh air he'd had in days. "It's exhilarating to be witness to a curse breaking. But yes, I'm glad the cameras seem to be aiming at Adam now, instead of at me."

Ella rubbed her throbbing temples. She'd been doing the mental exercises at length while Remus had been helping Adam field the voracious journalists with Henry. Something about stretching her abilities all day sent her to bed with a headache every night. However, it was starting to pay off. She'd been able to read a receipt Remus had hidden in his drawer upstairs from the study on the floor below. He'd paid entirely too much for her gown, so she took breaks throughout her studies to make it up to him by cleaning on the housekeeper's day off.

Remus set his planner down to take in her furrowed brow. "You look troubled. Anything I can help with?"

"I don't like that I know all this terrible stuff that's happening to the wolves, but there's nothing I can do about it. Like, literally nothing. I mean, is there a plan to storm the warehouse of Davin Industrial or something? Because I wouldn't mind being part of that."

Remus sat back in his leather chair and turned his focus to the ceiling. "Unfortunately, this isn't something the law can handle, or that the law would forgive if we handled. The Lupine aren't people, so they aren't afforded the same rights as we are. The Baron's company put trackers into wolves, which isn't humane, for certain, but it's not illegal."

"You can't honestly tell me you're okay with that policy.

It's an outdated, shortsighted law that needs to be changed."

"Ah, but as much as I'd love to accuse the king of being outdated and shortsighted, I'm thinking that's not the way to affect change."

"You're the Chancellor's brother. You're telling me we've got nothing? There's no way to help the Lupine?"

"I didn't say all that. I just said the law can't help us, and we can't act outside of its boundaries."

Ella stared at him dubiously. "I feel like you're enjoying your riddles, old man."

Remus smirked at her sass that usually only came about when her headaches were growing vexing. They'd tweaked the dosage of the St. John's Wort to perfection. It was doing wonders to control errant magic casting out from her, while still allowing her to use her abilities. The fogginess was starting to fine-tune itself as she dialed back the dose of her herbal regimen, but it was still a concerted effort to get her Pulse to perform properly.

Remus strummed his fingers atop his desk, his eyebrows dancing playfully. "I admit, I rather like leading you around the obstacles so that you can come to the most beneficial conclusion."

Ella's nose scrunched. "That's my point. I'm not seeing a conclusion. Are you?"

"Not yet. But if we narrow down what we can't do, then it makes a clearer path toward what we can."

Henry entered the study, pausing to greet Ella with a

light kiss. "Is Remus doing that annoying 'the answer is within you' thing again?" He shook his head, tsking his mentor. "Always trying to make us smarter."

Remus stood to hug Henry. "My eternal crime. Good to see you, Henry. How's your father?"

A cloud shadowed the prince's usually breezy smile. "Stubborn. Still intending to go through with the ball, even though I told him I'm already in a relationship. Ella, can I talk to Remus for a minute?"

Ella tried not to let the king's stalwart rejection strike her chest, but the arrow sunk in its usual spot all the same. "Sure. I'll be in the living room when you're finished."

Before she exited, Henry gripped her hand once more, meeting her eyes with a firm, "Always and only you."

She softened at the reassuring reminder that no matter what, they were in this together. "Always and only you."

Ella closed the door to the study behind her, knowing she shouldn't eavesdrop. She'd had many lessons with Remus about ethics, and the responsibility that came with unnaturally strong gifts like hers.

She moved up the stairs to the living room and sat on the caramel-colored leather couch. She didn't relax into the cushions but sat perfectly erect, her hands atop her knees. She closed her eyes, honing her Hearing to push through the floor and walls so she could listen to things that weren't meant for her.

"I don't understand how Dad can be like this about her. He's never even met Ella!"

"I admit, King Hubert isn't usually so snappish in his judgment. You can't get your hands on that photo?"

Ella pushed out her Sight, so she could see how worked up Henry was. She bit her lip when she saw him pacing and talking with his hands, his shoulders tight with agitation.

"No! My own press secretary won't give the incriminating picture to me. Said they destroyed all traces of it. Remind me again why I can't just drive her to the palace tonight and introduce him to Ella. He'll have to see that she's not whatever wretched monster he's concocted in his head."

"Is that how you imagine Ella would like to meet her future father-in-law? Don't you think she's had enough heartbreak?"

Ella's palms grew sweaty at using her Pulse in such a focused way. Her heart hammered in her chest when Remus slid King Hubert into the role of her future father-in-law. There were so many things she'd never allowed herself to want, but now that they were being dangled in front of her, part of her *needed* them.

Henry scowled, shoving his hands in his pockets. "I hate it when you're right. The throne makes things so much more complicated. If I was anyone else, I'd marry her tomorrow and everyone would just have to deal with it. But there can't be contention when there's a crown involved. I have to do this delicately, and you know how I hate that. Being in love shouldn't be so weighted with politics."

"Ah, but 'shouldn't' and 'are' might be two sides of the same coin."

Henry paused his pacing to glare at Remus. "You know I despise it every time you riddle me when I need actual guidance."

Ella's Sight was too foggy around the edges to clearly see the details of Remus' hands on his stomach, but she imagined him twining his fingers together, as she noticed he often did when he was holding himself back.

"You want advice?" Remus asked, his expression neutral.

Henry threw his arms in the air, exasperation flying out in his words. "I didn't come down to your study just to hear myself whine. Please, Remus. Any solution at all."

"Do nothing."

Henry blinked at Remus, and Ella could see his anger boiling. "You are being impossible on purpose!"

Remus stood, letting Henry know he wasn't the only man in the room, and that the prince needed to calm himself down. "Do nothing. Let your father think as he does for now. Ella will go to the ball and present herself as one of the many women hoping to win your affections. That girl won me over in the first minute I met her. Give her fifteen seconds with the king, and he'll see what's obvious to anyone who's not trying to use her. Trust your father to see the truth, and trust Ella to stand for herself."

Henry collapsed into the chair Ella usually took across from Remus' desk. He leaned forward, his elbows on his thighs. "And if it all falls apart? If he meets her, hates her still and breaks her heart? Then what?"

"Then you're in the same place you are now, and we'll deal with it then."

Henry shook his head, and Ella began to lose the details of his face. "I just don't understand. He was so adamant about it today. Wouldn't even have a conversation about it. Said point blank that he forbids me to marry her. Said that her politics were bigoted, and he couldn't believe I was drawn to someone who would only bring shame to the crown."

The harsh words cut Ella, making her feel as if the wind was knocked out of her.

Remus leaned against his desk, his arms folded over his chest in confusion. "I wouldn't tell Ella those things. She doesn't need the stress right now. I bought her another two weeks here before she has to stand up to Lady Tremaine, but it's coming." Remus rubbed his forehead, his shoulders tight with consternation. "What are you going to do if your father threatens to take away the crown if you marry her? Will you go through with it?"

Henry hung his head. "I love my father. I can't believe he would come down so harsh the one time I finally want someone in my life, which he's always encouraged." He paused, the shadows flickering as he considered the gavel that would inevitably fall. "My duty is to the people."

Ella lowered her chin, biting her lip to keep it from trembling. Her hands gripped her thighs as her heart hammered in her chest. She felt cold on the inside, and knew the chill wasn't something that would fade if things remained as they were.

Henry shook his head. "But a crown without her is a consolation prize. If I can't marry Ella, I'll fulfill my duty to the people, but I'll never take a wife. The lineage will end with me." He buried his face in his hands. "Either way, I destroy the crown."

Ella slumped against the couch, pulling her magic back into her body. Everything felt surreal, as if she was floating above her life so she could see the problems for what they were.

She didn't have to tell her body to stand—her feet were already on their way up the stairs. She packed up the meager possessions she'd come there with, leaving behind the beautiful clothes Rory had bought her. She ran her hand over the bed Henry had invited her into, lifting his pillow to inhale the smell of him one last time.

She turned corners and moved down stairs without calculating them, feeling as if the world was a thing she merely passed through, instead of enjoyed and explored. She opened the door to the study and didn't apologize for interrupting.

"I'm breaking it off," she declared abruptly, detached from her passion, which felt crushed inside her chest. "I won't be the reason you don't get the crown, and I won't be the reason you can't pass it on to your children. I'm out."

Remus hung his head, but Henry was on his feet, anger burning in his damp eyes. "This is how you stand by me? Listen in on my private conversations, and then go over my head to make decisions about me on your own?"

Ella blinked at the bite in his words but maintained her level chin and quiet demeanor. "This is exactly how I stand by you. Taking the crown is what's best for you, and what's best for the country. You and I both know that. If you don't rule after your father, then it's open to the Chancellor, the Baron, and whoever else wants to try their hand at making choices for Avondale." Anxiety over leaving him shredded her heart over and over, rending her insides to pieces. Still, she put Henry's welfare ahead of her own. "If you left the throne to marry me, our children might live under the Baron's rule. You'll resent me and curse yourself, wishing you could've done something." She shook her head. "I won't be the curse that holds you back."

Henry's anger melted into panic. "You don't hold me back! This is some crazy misunderstanding! Don't you see? If my father could only sit down with you, he would see what I do—that we're perfect for each other, and there's no one who would fit better beside me on the throne." He gestured wildly toward her. "See? You're already thinking of Avondale ahead of your own needs."

Ella glided over to him and lifted herself up on her toes to press a kiss to his lips. His eyes moistened, and a tear fell onto the curve of her upper lip. "Always and only you."

"Always and only you." Henry let out a sob as he pressed his forehead to hers. His eyes were winched shut, as if the thought of separation from her caused him physical pain. "Don't take away my always and only."

Her words felt like a slice across her chest, but they tumbled out of her all the same. "There's no other choice."

Remus moved to the door and shut it, pressing his hand to the center to keep her inside. "The ball. Promise him you'll come to the ball and present yourself. If you love Henry as you say you do, then you'll have an open and honest face-to-face with the king. If Hubert remains stalwart in his opinion, then we can examine that fallout. But if he'll give his blessing..."

Ella folded herself into Henry's arms that held her a little too tight, but still never tight enough. "If the king approves of us, then I'll let you pick out my wedding dress, Remus."

Henry kissed Ella through his anguish, his tears mixing in with hers before he pulled back in frustration. "Don't do this. There must be another way!"

"If I really love you, then this is the *only* way. You won't be able to live with yourself if you go against your father. You love him."

"I love you!"

"And I'll always have that. In my heart, I'll have always and only you." She let out a bleat of agony, fearing part of her would remain perpetually broken if separated from him. Her forehead rested against his as the world shifted around them. "Tell me a story, Henry. One that has nothing to do with this one."

A tear slid down Henry's cheek and touched onto her thumb as she held his face. His voice trembled with heartbreak and uncertainty. "Once upon a time, there was a prince who wanted…" His nose was red as a sob escaped him. "Ella, this is madness! I can't let us be over when we're clearly not!"

Ella held tight to him, her whisper shaking her insides as her eyes shut tight. "Once upon a time, there was a prince who wanted good things for his kingdom. He was noble, selfless and wise. The kingdom was so lucky that one day, the prince gave up his one true love so that he could rule his kingdom without division. And the kingdom lived happily ever after."

Henry gripped her hard. "That's a terrible story!"

"But that's how our story has to go."

With one last kiss, Ella tore herself away from Henry, holding her chin up as she walked out of the house to the bus station, taking herself out of the equation, and back to her town.

36

STANDING ON HER OWN

The crash of leaving Henry didn't hit Ella as she got off the bus at the police station. She kept the dam in place in her mind, hoping she could get through all the changes that needed to be made before she was crushed by the weight of it all. If she was truly going to stand on her own, she knew she couldn't go back to the life she'd once accepted as her only option.

She filed a police report for the black eye, showing them the photo Henry had taken of her on her phone as proof. She explained the whole story, proving that the house she'd let get taken over by the Tremaine women was, in fact, hers. "I need them out, but they won't go without a fight. I'd rather not get hit again, if I can help it."

"Eviction isn't all that simple. If they've been paying you rent, they have thirty days to leave."

"They've never paid a thing. Lady Tremaine's been

living there because she doesn't like my Pulse, and thinks I'm dangerous." Ella had kept the winter gloves Rory had bought her, and took a page from Cordray's book, flexing her gloved fingers to incite fear.

The police officer's eyes widened. "Are you a Lethal?"

"I'm a tax-paying citizen who's never harmed anyone. I'm asking for a police escort to get rid of abusive squatters who have no legal right to be in my home. I don't use my Pulse to solve my problems, which is why I'm here, abiding by the law." Ella met his eyes with a firm but kind smile. "I trust you can respect that."

The officer was sweating, but stammered through his response. "Of course. Lethals are protected under the same laws as everyone else. Let me look into the name on the deed of your home, and I'll see what I can do."

Ella didn't get up, but waited patiently for the help she requested while she called a locksmith, asking him to meet her at her address in an hour. Leaving Henry had been the hardest line to cross, which made everything else that had seemed so impossible mere hours ago look laughably simple.

Everything was expedited when a Lethal was involved. The officer she'd petitioned handed off the job to two cops who looked like they wrestled trolls for a living. Both of them were easily several inches over six feet tall, and kept their hands on their belts, as if readying to defend themselves against the meek woman.

Ella smiled up at them, brushing a few stray blonde

curls from her face. "I'm sorry I'm making you guys uncomfortable. If only I'd been born with a Pulse to make people laugh at my jokes, right?"

The corner of the mouth of the officer standing nearest to her twitched, giving in to the gentleness she couldn't help but radiate. She did her best to put the men at ease, wondering how Cordray did it so effortlessly.

In the back of the squad car, Ella's phone buzzed with a call from Henry. The moment she heard his voice, she felt a pressure behind her eyes. "Hello?"

"Tell me that didn't just happen. Tell me I hallucinated the worst thing in my life. Tell me you didn't leave me."

Ella cradled the phone as if it was his hand on her face. "I love you. The people we love never truly leave us. Don't you feel me in your heart?"

"I do, but I want to feel you in my arms. Come home. This is madness."

"Actually, I'm on my way home right now. Not to Remus' place, but mine. After tonight, it's going to be all mine. I'm kicking out Lady Tremaine and her daughters. I don't care what happens to me anymore."

Henry gasped. His next words came out in a rush. "I'm so proud of you. I'm on my way."

"No. This is something I have to do on my own."

"That woman is a monster! There's no way I'm letting you have a confrontation with her without me there in case things go south. Am I not allowed to love you now?"

Ella couldn't help the smile that played on her lips. "You really do love me."

Henry let out a sigh of exasperation. "It's like you're trying to vex me on purpose. Of course I love you. Always and only you."

"Stay where you are. Coming here would only complicate things with your father. I'm not going alone. I've got the cops with me."

"With you now? Hand them the phone. I want to speak with them."

"Now's not the time to go public."

"I only want to have a little chat with the boys in blue about my dear friend Ella. What's the harm in that?"

"Behave," she scolded him before handing up the phone to the officer in the passenger's seat. She sent out her Listening, feeling nervous using her abilities inside a police car, but it was worth it to hear Henry's voice just a little while longer.

"Officer, this is Prince Henry of Avondale. What's your name?"

"This is Officer Klein. Is this truly Prince Henry?"

"It is. I want you to make sure Lady Tremaine doesn't lay a hand on Ella. It would be considered a personal favor to me if you could keep an eye on the house until the Tremaines have collected their things and are off the property. In fact, I'd like you to stay until I can get a locksmith there."

"I already called the locksmith, Prince Henry," Ella

chimed in from the back, using his formal title so as not to appear overly flirtatious.

"Very well, then please stay with her until I can get a security system installed tonight." Then he raised his voice to be heard through the car. "Bet you didn't think of that!"

Ella smirked at his protective nature, grateful that, even though she couldn't be with him, they could hold their connection in their hearts, untarnished from the world that threatened to pull them apart.

37

ELLA'S SCANDAL

There were no expectations that Lady Tremaine would go quietly, but Ella had hoped for the sake of not looking like a family on a trashy talk show that her stepmother wouldn't take a swing at her.

The police cuffed Ella's stepmother, taking her to wait out her temper in the backseat of the squad car while the neighbors gathered around to gawk at the scene. Ella was certain they'd known about the abuse—known, and did nothing. Anastasia stood in the center of the living room, shouting obscenities at Ella, weeping openly that her own sister was kicking her out to a life on the streets.

Ella didn't respond, but stayed near the police officer as she gathered up her stepfamily's belongings and began shoving them into laundry baskets and trash bags. When Anastasia proved incapable of picking up the bags, Ella then took the loads to Lady Tremaine's SUV.

Drizella came home to the chaos, fresh from her date with Gary Herchon, who couldn't have squealed away quick enough after dropping her off at the curb. Drizella ran into the house, raising her hand to Ella, but then caught herself when it dawned on her that there were witnesses. "Where's Mom?"

"Your mother's in the back of the squad car out front." The officer explained the situation to Drizella and then told her to start packing. Drizella, of course, had no experience with actual work, so she stood in the middle of the living room with Anastasia, yelling at her sister to stop crying.

When Rory and Cordray walked in the front door, Ella dropped the laundry basket of Ana's shoes in the hallway and ran to them, throwing her arms around them both. "Thank you! Oh, I'm so glad you're here. Did Henry send you?"

Rory's eyes were wide at the sight of Ella's stepsisters throwing tantrums in the living room. "He did." She squeezed Ella and whispered, "He's in his car at the end of the street, waiting for you to say the word so he can come lend a hand."

Ella's heart flooded with warmth and confidence. Though she wanted nothing more than for Henry to be with her for the rest of her life, she knew him making an appearance would push their connection to the forefront of all the tabloids, which wouldn't help smooth things over with his father. "Now that you're here? I think we've got it."

"We brought boxes." Cordray pointed to the stack of brown flattened packing materials he'd rested next to the front door. "Let's get them out of here for good. What can I start packing?"

Ella hugged Cordray tight around the neck, feeling a kinship with the man who'd shared many a study session with her. "Thank you for being you. You're the best twin brother I've ever had. Any of the bedrooms upstairs. Let's pack everything up and get it in the SUV."

"Furniture?"

"Lady Tremaine bought most of the furniture. Everything that's upstairs came from her part of my father's life insurance. It all goes."

Remus strolled in through the front door as if he'd been invited over for tea, and wasn't put off in the least that there was a cop car out front. "I believe you've done enough to clean up after these people. I'll call a moving service to handle the rest. Do we have a forwarding address yet?"

Ella had been holding herself together just fine before she heard Remus' voice. There was something about his calm demeanor that felt reassuring, even though there was danger all around. He was Superman, and it wasn't until she saw his face that she realized how very much she'd wished for him to show up for her—his mere presence saving the day.

She'd promised herself that she would never cry in front of her stepfamily. When moisture started pricking her eyes, she ran in the other direction, tripping over the heap of shoes and crashing into the backdoor.

Remus was by her side in the next breath, his hand on the door to keep her from running. He didn't say a word, but extended his arm to her, wrapping her tight in his embrace when she finally let too many tears fall onto his shoulder.

Remus combed his fingers through her curls. "Now, now. Did you really think I'd let my prized pupil face her greatest obstacle without me there to help? I adore you, my darling."

Ella couldn't find words, but the sorrow didn't need them to articulate her brokenness that finally had a chance at healing. She gripped his dress shirt, knowing that Remus would allow her to call the shots. From now on, her life would be her own.

"I'm sure Rory and Cordray told you that Henry is at the end of your street, but I'll tell you again. He should be here for this."

Ella shook her head. "It's already a big ordeal, me kicking out my stepfamily. The neighbors are out on the front lawn, even though it's almost nighttime. It wouldn't go over well if Henry was mixed up in my family drama. It would only make King Hubert hate me more."

Remus closed his eyes and kissed her forehead. "I

thought you might say that. It's a noble thing you're doing, but I hate it all the same."

"Me too."

"Henry's here for you, as much as you'll let him. I hope you know how very loved you are."

She leaned up and kissed Remus' cheek, shrinking when she heard Drizella's gasp.

"That's the money shot!" Drizella clicked a few more buttons, and just like that, Ella became the overnight scandal—a young vixen seducing the eternally elusive bachelor who was more than a decade her senior.

38

REMUS' SECRET LOVER

*E*lla felt sick to her stomach the next day when she awoke. Remus had assured her that the quickly-spreading rumors didn't bother him in the least, but she had seen the worry in Rory's eyes that mirrored her own. "It'll blow over," she assured Ella. "Believe me, we've all had worse."

Though Ella had full reign of the house now, she was too overcome with anxiety to sleep anywhere but atop her mattress in the attic. When she finally stumbled down the steps at eight o'clock in the morning, she stopped short when she saw Remus sitting at her kitchen table with none other than Henry.

"What are you doing here?" she shrieked, and then bolted to the windows, confirming the blinds were shut. She yanked the curtains closed for a double layer of secrecy.

Remus motioned to the coffee drip contraption. "I can't figure out your coffee maker. Why can't people just leave well enough alone?"

"Oh, that was supposed to go with Lady Tremaine."

Remus' smile was devious. "I can drop it off. She's staying with the Baron. Imagine his face when he sees me—the man who was caught in the act of seducing the delicate flower he tried to steal and crush. Oh, I'm going to enjoy this."

Ella blanched. "But it's not true! Henry, I wasn't doing anything like that. You have to believe me. Remus is my friend, and nothing more. I'm just sick about the whole thing!"

Of all things, Henry chuckled. "I know, honey. I'm not worried about that. Remus is gay."

Ella gasped. "You knew?"

Remus' head snapped in her direction. "*You* knew?"

Ella shrank apologetically. "The wolves may have mentioned something about it. It's your business, and I didn't tell anyone."

"Clearly. Henry's known for years, and you didn't even talk to him about your suspicions. You're right that it is my business, and I thank you for your discretion. You're a good friend and a spectacular secret lover, if I do say so myself."

Ella blanched. "Stop it. I'm so embarrassed. I didn't know Drizella was going to..."

Remus held up his hand. "Ella, it's all fine, and just a

taste of what you'll get if things work out at the ball, and you two end up together."

Ella narrowed her eyes at Henry. "By the way, we're broken up. How'd you even get in here? I just had new locks put in last night."

Henry shrugged. "I have my ways. And we're not broken up. We're on hold."

"I fail to see the difference, or how either of those labels lands you in my house." She caught herself in her wording and glanced around the empty kitchen. She reached out and stroked the wall with wonder, feeling affection swell and a veil of peace descend upon her heart. "*My* house. It's finally mine."

Henry sighed as he studied her from head to toe. "It's lovely. You look good. Like yourself. You never looked like yourself in this place, but now you do. I like it."

Remus took a catalog from the messenger bag at his feet, and opened it on the table. "You'll need plates, cups, a bedframe, a real mattress—no secret lover of mine is going to lie on a thin mattress on the floor. I simply won't have it."

Ella buried her face in her hands. "Please stop saying 'secret lover.' I'm barely holding it together, here. Have I said I was sorry?"

"Only a hundred times in the past minute. Let's start with the kitchen. You need plates, cups and silverware. What else? She seems to have left you the pots and pans."

Ella snorted. "She's never used them before, so that's

not a huge surprise. I have enough stuff. My parents' things are in my storage unit downtown. I couldn't stomach them eating off my mother's china, so I had it all stored away."

"A bedframe?"

"I can sleep on the floor until I get a job and save up for it."

Henry took in her defiant expression with a delicate gracefulness to his tone. "There's a bed for you at Remus'."

Ella kept several feet of distance between them, knowing if she got too close, she would fall into the abyss of his blue eyes. "Hopefully some handsome prince will keep it warm for me."

Henry looked as if he hadn't slept all night, his eyes puffy and his hair mussed. Still, he was the picture of perfection, his charming features making every facial twitch a treat for her to watch. "I'm having lunch with my father today. If all goes well, you'll be back in my arms tonight."

Ella wasn't as hopeful, but she didn't dare crush his dreams. She figured it was good that at least one of them had remained an optimist.

"You need security, and more than the system Adam's company partially installed, and will finish putting up later today. Other than the fact that everyone will want to interview my secret lover," Remus paused for Ella's groan, "Lady Tremaine already told the Baron about what you can do. Though, she only knows about your Listening, which is truly the lesser culprits for potential security breaches. The Baron's called an emergency council meeting tonight."

"Already?" Ella touched her forehead, then her chest, then her forehead again. "I haven't even... I've had one night of freedom!"

Remus tilted his head to the side, reaching out to hold her hand. The moment her palm slid into his, he placed a kiss to the back of her hand. "And you'll have many more, but things are going to be rocky for a while, as you knew they would be. While we're waiting to see how it all settles, let's take preemptive measures by increasing your security."

Ella's stomach responded by rumbling for breakfast.

As if on cue, Henry stood and moved to the fridge, taking out a carton of strawberries. He smiled at the fruit. "The first time I met you, there were strawberries. Your first morning of freedom, here they are again. I think strawberries are a good omen, blue eyes." He washed them off and handed her the carton, resisting the urge to feed her just to watch her lips close around the fruit.

"Thank you. You don't have to wait on me."

His eyes met hers with the note of a promise. "You don't have to go hungry anymore."

Ella wanted to lean into Henry's shoulder, but knew she couldn't touch him or she'd never be able to let go. She took the berries and ate without pause. "I can't afford private security, and I don't want you paying for it. I need to get a job. That's the first thing on the list."

Henry opened his mouth to argue, but Remus held up his hand. "I did the same for Cordray when he first got back from his abduction. Whenever there's someone in my circle who's about to be thrown to the wolves, I'm afraid I can't help myself. Besides, you're my secret lover. What sort of gentleman would I be if I didn't look out for you?"

Ella exhaled through her nose, wondering how to get around Remus' logic. "I really wish you'd stop calling me that."

"Very well. Then should I call you my student?" He shivered. "Oh, that's even more tawdry. The teacher who seduced the young, impressionable student. I feel like I should call the papers and start suggesting headlines for them."

"You're ridiculous."

Remus' voice took on a more serious edge. "You'll still come around for tutoring, won't you?"

Ella shifted as she ate, and then something pinged in the back of her mind. "After the commotion dies down about us, sure. I like our lessons."

"Good. I look forward to them as well."

Ella put down the berries and moved to the front closet, laughing with delight when she found Anastasia's old pair of snow boots on the top shelf. "Perfect! She always hated these things."

"Where are you going?" Henry asked, following her into the foyer.

Ella beamed at him, latching onto the idea that was only half-formed in her mind. "To find myself some security."

39

ELLA'S NEW JOB

Working at the grocery store in town was a breath of fresh air for Ella. It had taken her exactly two days to find a job. When word spread that she was Remus Johnstone's secret lover, everyone wanted to hire her, just for the simple fact that wherever she went, people clambered to talk to her. Her instant celebrity was a boon to any business.

Her best patient smile lasted through each eight-hour shift, though by the end, she was tired of answering the same questions.

"Are you really Ella?"

"Yes, ma'am. Did you want to get two of these? They're buy-one-get-one-free."

"So, what's he like? Remus Johnstone is so sexy!"

"He's my tutor. He's professional and private, so I don't

think he'd appreciate us talking about him like this. Your total is forty-two seventy-five."

"Is it true you can send out your Listening Pulse? Like, are you doing it right now?"

"How did you want to pay for your groceries today?"

Over and over the conversation went. Ella soon became the fastest cashier because she wanted to get each customer out of her lane as quick as she possibly could.

She couldn't believe anyone was talking about anything other than Adam Fontaine's curse being lifted. He'd escaped transitioning to a Lupine, yet people were still desperate to gawk at Ella and the new twist of magic she was responsible for introducing to the world.

Rory made sure to keep Ella in the loop via an animated phone call every night. Apparently, things were progressing quite quickly with Belle and Adam. Every magazine in her checkout lane featured a cover that was split into two halves of Adam's face: Adam's beast-like cursed countenance on the left, and the cured version of Avondale's second-most eligible bachelor on the right. Though Ella only had eyes for Henry, she had to admit that Adam losing his good looks must've been a hard pill to swallow. Most of the human race didn't have quite so far to fall.

Ella wanted so desperately to call Henry and see how he was dealing with it all. She wished to offer any help she could, but she remained firm in her stance that Henry should put the kingdom first. Only if King Hubert gave his blessing would they have a chance at being together again. So much was riding on the ball. She knew Henry would be waiting for her to show up so he could properly introduce her to his father. She had to make a good impression. She had to convince the king that she could be good for his son.

For all the victories she'd found in her new freedom, the utter loneliness felt like a loss.

Most businesses closed down the evening of the royal ball, and the grocer's was no exception. Ella's nerves were starting to peak but she kept her focus clear in her mind. No matter what, she would say her piece to the king. He didn't have to like her, but he did have to meet her, since she was an eligible woman in the kingdom. Most of the women would use their time to flirt or talk about their achievements. Ella had only one topic she was burning to discuss.

After her drive home, Ella was welcomed by the quiet, which meant her security detail was out. She rolled back her shoulders, smiling that she had found a way to keep herself safe without taking yet more help from Remus and Henry.

Ella thumbed through the clothes Remus had dropped off from Rory, each garment lovelier than the last. It was when her hands alighted on the gown bag that her heart threatened to explode out of her chest. Everyone would be on their way to the ball already, so Ella made quick work of showering, pinning up her hair as best she could, and slipping on the ice blue dress Remus had bought her. Her fingers trembled as they ghosted over the material. It was the lightest of blue in shadow, but in full light, the gown looked almost matrimonial. She debated turning it pink with a few brushes of her palms, but paused, giving herself an honest look in the mirror.

She clasped her hands in front of her, and then realized she didn't have to imagine a bouquet. She tugged a stem from the vase on the table. It was the one concession she couldn't turn away. Henry gave her all the space she demanded was necessary, except for the bouquet of flowers that were sent to her house every third day. With each bouquet there was a card that read, "Always and only," and it melted her every time.

Studying herself in the mirror, Ella realized how very much like a bride she looked in the dress. She pictured her father standing at her side, walking her down the aisle toward the man she was certain he would approve of. She had done her best to be courageous enough to be kind, as he'd instructed. She only wished her father could see her so self-possessed, finally standing with her head held high.

Ella donned her fitted wool coat and moved out into the chilly garage, the rickety clinking of the doublewide door sounding in the background as she slid in to start her old red sedan. The rusty thing gave a few honest coughs, but Ella's heart sank when it refused to turn over. She sighed and popped the hood, worrying that she might get the beautiful gown dirty – a thing she'd never had to concern herself with before.

She didn't hear the muffled footsteps that crept into the garage. She didn't see the crowbar that raised before it cracked down on her head, knocking her into the wall before she crumpled into a heap of limbs on the floor.

The sound of Lady Tremaine's cold hatred rang in her ears. "I hope you enjoyed your time as lady of the house. You've seduced Remus Johnstone long enough. You'll not audition to take your chance with the prince."

With that, consciousness slipped through Ella's fingers, leaving her at the mercy of her wicked stepmother.

40

LOCKED IN THE DARK

Ella came to in the dark, waking to the thrumming of a pounding in her cranium. She bit down on her lip as a bleat of agony shot through her shoulder. She shifted as she tried to orient herself in the black. The sting of bleach and floor polish nipped at her nose. Without needing her sight, Ella finally understood where she was.

Tears threatened to spill from her, but she held them back as she renewed her promise to herself that she would never let Lady Tremaine make her cry. The tiny space made her stomach roil, and she searched frantically in the dark for the bucket, in case the contents of her stomach revolted. The moment her fingers alighted on the plastic rim, she hefted it up and clutched it to her chest, letting the fumes from the floor cleaner blast her in the face. She searched her pocket for her cell phone, but knew with a sinking dread that it was gone. If Lady Tremaine had stolen it, Royal Watch would have its top story in no time at all. Remus Johnstone's secret lover, pledging herself to Prince Henry via too many damning texts.

Ella leaned her forehead against the closet door, hugging the bucket as she willed herself not to throw up. It took her a few moments to suck her terror back inside of herself and gather together enough scraps of hope to assemble her bearings.

A few steadying breaths was all it took for Ella to send out her Hearing, listening for any signs of the security she'd put so much faith in. She sent her Hearing out beyond her street, and stretched it further than she was sure she could control. Too many conversations swirled in her mind, too many horns blasting as everyone fought for purchase on the same road that led to the palace. Ella was frantic to get to Henry, to let him know that she wouldn't bail on him during his vulnerable moment where he was patiently waiting only for her.

It wasn't until she heard steady panting that she pressed her palms to the closet door and closed her eyes, making the darkness her choice, rather than something that was inflicted upon her. She knew sending out her Sight wouldn't do anything to get them back to her sooner, so she leaned into Remus' sense of exploration when it came to new twists of magic, and tried her hand at sending out her Voice, calling to them in a low command.

"Guadalupe," she whispered, focusing on the brown-spotted wolf in her mind. "Come home."

Ella couldn't tell if the wolf had heard her, but that didn't stop her from trying again and again. "Errol," she whispered. "Come home."

She dropped the bucket and palmed the door as she began to sweat. She trusted the deep breathing Remus had taught her. She trusted the magic she'd taken great care not to exploit, hoping that it would be there to call upon in her hour of need.

She could picture Henry sitting on his throne next to his father, his face rising and then falling when each new woman was brought in to meet him. With every time the door opened, she knew she was breaking his heart when it wasn't her come to stand by him when he needed her. If she couldn't manage to free herself from the closet, he would assume she'd turned him away, and that he should look elsewhere for someone with whom he could share his dreams. He would assume she didn't deem him worthy of risking it all.

But he was. Oh, how much she would throw away if it would lessen the distance between their two beating hearts.

Ella pushed against the door with all her might, crying out with fervency for anyone to help her. "Connor!" she called, desperate for her Voice to make it to their ears. She'd given them a place to stay to keep them from being hunted, and in exchange they'd offered to protect her from

Lady Tremaine, the Baron, and anyone else that might come to take her away when her abilities came to light. "Connor, help me!"

She knew it was futile, but she called out to Remus, hoping he could hear her from miles away. The dress he'd bought her was covered in something sticky, and the left cap sleeve was torn clean off. The full skirt had been lovely, but now she felt cramped in the narrow space with too much material crowding her legs. The black around her felt suffocating—a thing she knew Remus understood all too well, and would free her from if he knew. "Remus!" she screamed, sending out her Voice to the man who had taught her to trust in abilities she hadn't been able to control or quantify.

Ella dug grooves into the wooden door over and over again until her fingernails splintered, panic choking her around the throat.

Ten minutes later felt like an eternity, but that was all it took for the Lupine to burst in through the doggy door she'd had installed for them. "Help! Help! I'm in here!"

Guadalupe's voice came back perplexed. *"Ella? How did you lock yourself in the closet? Where's the key?"*

"Lady Tremaine attacked me and locked me in here. She's got the key, and I can't get out!"

"Stand back!" Several of them pummeled the door, but in the tight hallway space, there wasn't much room for them to get a decent running start. *"Is there another key?"*

"No, and I need to get out! This is my one chance to talk to the king, and I'm wasting it locked inside of here!"

The wolves were talking amongst themselves, then Ella heard one of them go back outside. *"We'll get you out, my queen,"* Connor assured her.

Ella was too worked up to calm herself. She clawed at the door until her fingertips bled, finally breaking down in hysterics as the tight walls that didn't even leave room for her to bend her knees finally gripped her psyche and shook her insides until she was trembling with panic. "Help! Help!" She thrashed in the tight space, knocking into everything and banging up her body. Too much anxiety broke something precious inside of her, and she sobbed through the pain that radiated through her entire being.

She felt Connor's paws on the other side of the door, mirroring where hers were. She could feel his words coming from just a few inches away from her own mouth. *"Listen to me, Ella. Close your eyes and send out your Sight. Can you see me?"*

Ella gulped, trying to maintain a steady grip on reality as she sent her Sight the few inches necessary to give her hope that she wasn't alone. "Connor, I don't like it in here!"

"I know, honey. I'll get you out. Say, 'I trust you, Connor.'"

Ella leaned her cheek to the door. "I trust you, Connor."

"Guadalupe went out with Errol to find Remus. They'll crash the royal ball if they have to. We'll get you out."

"No! If they're seen, people might attack them. Call them back!"

"It's done. We know the risks. We can be stealthy."

It was then she realized that the risks they were willing to take on for her weren't as great as the risks she was ready to take on for them. They'd had trackers inserted under their skin, but aside from telling Remus, she hadn't been able to truly help them or make their cause known. "I can do better," she pledged to Connor. "I can protect you better than this."

Connor shushed her self-flagellation. *"We can protect you better than this,"* he countered.

Ella's lower lip trembled as she placed her blooded fingers against the door to center herself when the world wouldn't stop spinning in all of its blackness. "Please don't leave me."

She heard Connor's voice soften with affection. *"Never. We did all the hunting we needed to do, so I'm here until you're free. I'll watch the house for you. There's nothing to worry about if I'm here. Sit on down and rest while you wait. You'll be freed in no time at all."*

"I can't sit! I can't move much. It's so narrow, I can't even turn sideways!" Ella's chest heaved, and she felt another wave of panic creep up her spine. The utility closet had always seemed like a coffin to her, and the darkness felt like she was being slowly buried alive.

"What kind of sick person would... Ella, find the back wall and lean your shoulders against it."

Ella complied, her breath coming in rapid gulps that made her lightheaded. "Lady Tremaine used to lock me in here for hours, but I always knew she'd release me eventually when she needed something done. But now? Now there's no one to let me out!" Ella let out a terrified bleat and started clawing at the door again.

Connor did his best to soothe her but it wasn't until Remus' voice broke through her fright more than an hour later that Ella finally was able to pull in full breaths. "Ella? Ella, where are you?"

"Remus?" She hated how hoarse and scared her voice sounded, but she pounded on the door with her bloody fist. "I'm in the closet!"

Remus swore as he bolted toward her. "Ella? No! How did... Don't you worry. I'll get you out."

"Lady Tremaine has the only key. You have to break the door down somehow!"

After several failed attempts at ramming the door with his shoulder, Remus ordered the wolves out of the house. Then he lowered his voice, pressing his cheek to the door. "I can get you out of there without a key. Promise you'll keep another of my many secrets."

"Yes! Anything, just please hurry!" She bit down on her lower lip before letting loose the root of her fear. "I'm trapped in the dark!"

"Step back!"

Ella complied, sending out her Sight so she could comfort herself with the image of Remus. She watched him glance down both hallways to confirm they were alone, and then he pressed his palm to the keyhole. She saw him take a deep breath in, and then let it slowly out. With a quick turn of the knob, the door popped open.

Ella lost her footing and tumbled out, smashing against the opposite hallway wall. Remus threw his arms around her, gasping when he saw her bloody fingers and the red-streaked claw marks she'd left on the inside of the closet door.

Remus brushed a few stray strands of hair from her tear-stained face so he could kiss her forehead. "Oh, darling. It's alright. Never again, okay? I should've seen to tearing this door off its hinges when you first moved in. It'll be gone tomorrow."

Ella heaved in his arms, barely upright as she tried to orient herself in the moonlight that shone through the window. She floundered around for a few seconds before clutching Remus' shoulders, her chest heaving against his. "Tell me I didn't miss the ball. Tell me Henry doesn't think I stood him up!"

Remus made a show of taking in a handful of deep breaths to remind Ella to steady herself. His thumb traced the well of her dimple, and then kissed it for good measure. "No, you didn't miss the ball yet. And yes, Henry's afraid of exactly that. I'll call him, but I doubt he has his phone on. Go upstairs and change. We'll be to the palace before you know it. There's still time. The king said he'll hold the invitational until midnight."

Ella glanced down at her gown and grimaced. "I'm sorry I ruined your dress!" There was motor oil splashed over her frock, and it was torn in several places.

Remus tsked her worry. "Don't think on it another second. Hop in the shower and get some of this grime off you. I'll have the car ready for you when you come down. Hurry, now."

Ella stumbled up the steps and flung herself into the shower to wash the car grease and dried blood off her. It was the fastest shower of her life.

She hurriedly dried herself on the way from the en suite bathroom into her father's old bedroom. She threw on her jeans and a flannel, knowing that she wouldn't impress anyone with her clothing. She decided she couldn't care about that. She looked like herself, and knew that would be enough for the man who truly loved her.

Ella ran back down the stairs, her damp curls flying out behind her. She paused only to greet the wolves who had been let back inside the house, leaning over to let them lick her face. "Thank you. Thank you for risking so much to get Remus for me."

She looked into their eyes and knew that no matter how heartfelt her plea to the king might be, nothing was better than firsthand accounts. Perhaps she couldn't solve all the Lupine's problems, but she could tap into her courage even more than she had. They deserved more from her—especially after risking being seen and hunted when they went out to find Remus.

She kissed them each on the maw and stood, beckoning them to follow her, even if it was scary, even if it was hard, even if it was dangerous. "Nothing will change until we make them see there's a problem."

Remus didn't question her more than a raised eyebrow when she slid into the front passenger's seat of the town car after letting the three wolves take up residence in his backseat. "I trust you have a plan?"

Ella shrugged, her eyes wide as the reality of what she was about to do slapped her across the face. "I have hope," she countered.

Remus nodded, reaching over to squeeze her hand after he pulled out and started down her street. "That's good enough for me."

REMUS' DATE TO THE BALL

$\mathcal{E}$lla had never been inside the palace, but she'd driven by it enough times to feel intimidated by its splendor. The tall parapets stretched too many stories for her to make sense of, and the light-colored stone exterior looked like a welcoming, yet impenetrable, fort.

Remus' face was relaxed but his tone was firm. "Stay with me, all of you. And if anyone wants to back out, this is your one shot. Once we get in there, you're in, which means you can't change your mind. I can protect you, but only if you stay by my side."

The wolves nodded, lowering their heads in obeisance.

Remus pulled into the circular drive Ella first met Henry in, and parked, handing his keys to the valet. He got out of the car and walked around, offering Ella his hand like a true gentleman. "Miss Ella," he greeted her, taking her shaking fingers in his steady grip.

Her blonde hair had dried in a waterfall of curls that she'd swept into a harried ponytail on the way there. When she heard a camera's click the moment she got out of his car, and then two more, her nerves began to rattle around in her chest. Her eyes widened as she looked down at her flannel and jeans, knowing she wasn't the belle of the ball by any means. "Why are they taking my picture?"

Remus tucked her under his arm to shelter her body, bringing her hand to wrap around his abdomen to keep them glued together. The partial embrace soothed them both as they began to breathe in harmony. "Haven't you heard the gossip? You're my young secret lover, and this is the first time we've been spotted together in weeks. Can you imagine the scandal?" He smirked at the camera, keeping her tight to his side as he opened the car's backdoor to address the Lupine. "Come on out, and remember, stay close to us."

The cameras multiplied, and were soon joined by shouts of terror as Errol, Guadalupe and Connor emerged from Remus' town car. Ella's hand dropped from Remus' stomach to rest atop Connor's head. Errol stayed tight to Remus' side, and Guadalupe took the lead, her head raised high as if to tell them all that she belonged at the ball every bit as much as the gawkers did.

The five moved forward as a unit, turning a deaf ear to the many who shouted at them to get the Lupine out, as well as asking Ella how Remus Johnstone fared in bed. The guards at the front moved to block the way, but

Remus waved them off with a flick of his wrist. "I'm hand-delivering an eligible maiden to Prince Henry. Do step aside."

"I'm afraid we can't allow that. Lupine are dangerous, Mr. Johnstone."

Remus' eyes narrowed but he held tight to Ella. He pulled out his phone and called his first speed dial. "Hello, Stefan. The guards won't let me inside without authorization. Can you come out and tell them that I and my guests are to be let inside the castle?"

Ella moved the wolves to stand between herself and the door, in case anyone in the gathering crowd behind them decided they were brave enough to attack her friends. Though they could handle themselves in a fight, Ella knew that even if they didn't instigate a brawl, they would be blamed for it nonetheless. The three oversized wolves sat like gargoyles, perfect and statuesque, until the front doors opened and the Chancellor himself strolled out. He smiled at his brother but then stopped short, recoiling when his eyes fell on the wolves. His fists tightened as he glowered at his younger sibling. "Remus? Explain."

Remus beamed at his older brother as if there was nothing tense at all in the moment. "Ah, Stefan. How are you? I brought a few guests to see the king."

"I see that. I trust you can control your escorts?"

"Actually, they belong to Miss Ella, here. She's my secret lover."

Ella flushed crimson and buried her face in her palm. "Would you knock it off with that? Pleased to meet you, Chancellor, sir."

The Chancellor studied Ella, and then light dawned in his eyes. "Ah, yes. Rory's little friend. Quite the entrance you're making, young lady." He studied his brother with a wary expression, and then sighed. "Well, it's not as if I'm going to stop you. Come on in." He held open the grand double doors that stretched two stories high, shooting the guards a look of apology. "I hope you know what you're doing, Remus."

Remus kept Ella on his arm with a grin. "Oh, Stefan. I rarely know what I'm doing, only that it'll be an adventure. Won't you join us?"

Ella's stomach was in knots as she walked with the two important men, rethinking her plan and wondering if it was foolish. She wanted to be heard. She longed for the Lupine and their problems to be seen. But with every step she took, she wondered if they would be viewed as the victims they were in it all, or if they would always be seen as society's menace.

The fine ruby draperies made sweat break out on the nape of her neck. The intricately woven tapestries that hung along the grand hallway told stories of a lineage she knew she had no business being near. Still, she had to try. If after today the king still couldn't give his blessing, she would have to accept it and walk away from Henry for good.

An endless string of panic flowed through her until they stopped in front of a short line of three women who were waiting their turn to greet the king and the beloved Prince Henry. They were decked out in the latest fashions, their dresses low-cut, tight and meant to draw Henry's eye. The women shrieked at the sight of the wolves, and one even ran away, forfeiting her spot as next in line.

The Chancellor ran his hand over his face. He looked much like Remus, only aged with a bit of gray brushing his temples. There were also a few lines of worry around his eyes from being second-in-command of a kingdom. He had a seriousness to him, juxtaposing Remus' constantly cool demeanor. "If I haven't told you before, dear brother, you sure do know how to make an entrance."

"Wait until you see the surprise I have planned for your birthday. At least this way people get a good story." When the Chancellor didn't appear amused, Remus rolled his eyes. "It was her idea, not mine, though I fully support it. Any secret lover of mine can do as she pleases. I'm an utter slave to her whims."

"I'm too nervous for your jokes right now," Ella admitted, her hand brushing over her churning stomach. She took a deep breath to center herself, closing her eyes as Remus kissed her temple.

He let his lips rest there while he spoke quietly to her. "You look smashing, Miss Ella. And remember, you're the only one Henry wants to see."

Ella ran her hands down her flannel, making sure it

wasn't wrinkling at the edges as she stood straighter. "Better?"

He kissed her nose. "Best."

The Chancellor adjusted the red sash he wore across his tailored black suit, stepping forward as the next girl moved into the courtroom. "Rory and Cordray are in the ballroom. After the women are dismissed, they're free to drown their sorrows in as much of the king's wine as they please."

"She won't be dismissed," Remus assured his brother.

"You'll be lucky if you're both not locked up after this."

Ella's voice was quiet but she had to know. "Has Henry chosen anyone yet?"

"No, and not for lack of options. Some even came prepared with songs and skits and other such talents to show off for him. It's been quite the eventful day for him. He's been given quite a few gifts as well."

Ella patted her pockets with wide eyes, glancing ahead at the woman who was next, noting her smug smile as she fingered a brightly-wrapped package. "I don't have anything for him! I didn't think this through."

Remus wrapped his arms around her, bringing her chin up so he could gaze lovingly into her eyes. "There's not a thing he wants more than you. Remember that."

Ella stiffened when the door opened to usher in the only other woman in the line, leaving her to be announced next. She pressed her forehead to Remus' chest, listening to his whispered instructions for her to breathe through the panic and center herself. "Quick now, send out your Sight. I want you to look into the ballroom and see how many concealed weapons you can find."

"What?"

"You can offer the king's son more than just your heart. You can give him protection like no one else. The ballroom is through the courtroom. Quick now, send out your Sight."

Ella did as she was guided. She sent her Sight on a mission, seeking out anything that might be dangerous. The sea of beautiful dresses and sleek suits set her mind whirling, but she reined it in, knowing she didn't have much time. Her eyes touched on a string quartet, their bows commanding the hundreds of dancers in the gold-bedecked ballroom.

The dancing was formal and filled with men picking off the women who were coming down from feeling rejected after so much buildup. She saw Rory and Cordray, grinning as they waltzed together next to Adam and Belle, who looked at each other as if there was no one else in the enormous ballroom.

Ella had never searched out a specific item before, but once she visualized a dagger, her brain skipped all over the ballroom, seeing through coat pockets and purses, dinging on twenty-seven concealed daggers in less than a minute.

"We shouldn't be here," Ella said as she brought

herself back to the people in front of her. "I need to tell the guards about the threat."

"What's going on, Remus? What's she talking about?"

"First things first." Remus turned Ella as the double doors opened. "I don't think you should keep your prince waiting any longer."

The king stood as the wolves made their way into the courtroom first. "Who let the Lupine into the castle? Guards!"

The three wolves froze, and Ella could hear their internal debate on whether or not they should fight back to avoid being detained. "Wait! Your majesty, they're with me." Ella forgot her fear when four guards moved in toward her puppies. She stood firmly in the center of the three and held up her hands. "They came because they need your help."

The king scowled at the Chancellor and Remus. "What's the meaning of this?"

Remus moved to stand next to Ella. "Hear her out, your majesty."

The king held up his hand to pause the guards, meeting Ella's eyes with a regal glare that made her want to shrink away. "I'm listening. Do not make me regret it."

42

ALWAYS AND ONLY YOU

Ella had a speech all prepared, but the facts tumbled out from her faster than she'd planned. She was worried that her wolves would be taken before she could get the whole story out. "They're being abducted by Davin Industrial! They were taken out of their home in the woods and injected with something against their wills that muted their Pulses for a few days. Then they had trackers placed under their skin that I'm not skilled enough to remove without hurting them. We don't know why this happened, but we know you didn't authorize experimentation on the Lupine."

The king moved off the throne, and it was only then that Ella realized Henry wasn't there. "Slow down. You're accusing Davin Industrial of experimenting on the Lupine? Do you have proof?"

"I mean, they're right here. You can check them for trackers."

The king looked too much like his son when he cocked his head to the side, studying her with a narrowed eye. He wore a beige suit with his gold crown, the blond hair giving way to wisps of white around his temples. He was just as tall as Henry, making Ella feel small when he approached, holding his hands up to the guards. "How do I know you didn't put them in there? Accusing Davin Industrial of animal experimentation is serious."

Ella placed her hand on Connor's head, who stood straighter at her touch. "I have their word. They told me everything. They're scared of what's swimming around in their veins now. They have no idea what they were injected with. They need your help before other members of the Lupine are abducted."

He shot Remus a withering look. "Very funny. You can't hear them speak."

Ella straightened, her temper flaring. "Do you have any idea how hard it was for me to even get here tonight? I don't care if you think this is all some big joke. I can hear them."

The king entertained her sass. "Okay, how?"

"By listening! Something you should've been doing long before my magic showed up on the scene." The wolves gathered around her, resting their noses on her shoes and Remus' to show whose side they were on.

Remus chuckled, but then covered his mouth with a

cough. "She's not wrong, your majesty. I've been tutoring her. She has amazing abilities that I'd be happy to talk to you about when your guards aren't here."

The king crossed his arms over his chest, sizing up the woman before him. "My guards aren't the ones running the gossip magazines. Show me what you're so certain of."

Remus shook his head, and Ella raised her chin defiantly. "I won't be the one who's experimented on next. I'm taking a big risk, telling you all of this. I was told you were powerful, that you're a good man who can help people who need it. Well, here they are, survivors who deserve to be heard."

"Surely you know the Lupines aren't citizens who are privy to my help."

Ella lowered her chin, grief flooding her at his edict. "I know that you've been entrusted to look after all the living beings in Avondale. I don't see why that wouldn't extend to those who can't speak for themselves. I would think they'd need a compassionate king more than anyone else." She shook her head slowly, hoping she hadn't read the king all wrong. "Don't break my heart and tell me you're the kind of ruler who only cares about people if they can vote for him."

The king ran his hand over his face. "You have no proof."

Ella banded her arms around her stomach and leaned in, lowering her voice in hopes it wouldn't carry to the guards. Too many men in uniform lined the walls, waiting for the king's signal to fight the Lupines. "Do you trust Remus?"

"Of course. He understands magic better than anyone I've ever known."

Remus placed his hand on her back, lending support and giving her the green light to confess the secret she'd kept so tight to the vest.

Ella's muscles tightened. "I can See things that others can't, and I can Hear things no one understands. But this isn't about me. This is about them. They want the trackers out, and they deserve to know what they were injected with. I can only give them a voice. You can actually help them. Please, your majesty. They were your subjects before they were cursed. They didn't ask for this." She swallowed hard. "All they're asking is for you to see them again, instead of forgetting that your people still need you, even when they're too broken to speak."

The king stepped back, touching his chin while he studied the wolves. "Alright. You have my ear. Guards, you're dismissed. See that my son is kept out of the courtroom. He doesn't need to be involved in whatever this is."

Ella swallowed hard at mention of Henry but said nothing about her unquenchable longing to see him. There were more important things at stake than securing herself a boyfriend.

The king waited until it was just Ella, Remus, the Chancellor and the wolves before he got down on one knee and waved Guadalupe forward. "Remus, do you take responsibility for them if they attack in my castle?"

Remus nodded, but Ella held out her hand in front of him as if to offer herself up as a shield for her tutor. "No, he doesn't. I do. This was my idea, not his."

Remus softened. "Only because I wasn't brave enough to stand up for my convictions. Your majesty, I've been studying the Lupine for quite some time now. I've seen Ella's gifts, and I trusted her judgment enough to help her get the Lupine into the palace to see you. If she says Davin Industrial is experimenting on them, it's an allegation I'd take seriously."

The Chancellor touched his forehead, his worry palpable. "Do you know how many people on the council have a vested interested in Davin Industrial? It's the Baron's company, for crying out loud."

Remus rolled his eyes. "I've got no qualms being the one to point the finger. Every councilmember who's on the board of that company is vocal about their vote to register and force the pill upon Lethals. The Lupine were their first patients. If they'll do something like this to them, it's only a matter of time before Lethals are next. And after them, people like Ella, who would never harm a soul, but who have mutations to their magic that might scare the public."

The king kept his eyes on Guadalupe, who sat obediently in front of the king without twitching as King Hubert stroked her fur. "What are you getting at?"

Ella knelt down behind Guadalupe and ran her fingers through the thick fur on her back. "We're saying they're moving on without you. They're experimenting on the Lupine because they were confident you'd vote their way to make the pill available to be manufactured outside the government."

"Child, I haven't talked to anyone about my vote. I only just cast it an hour ago. The Chancellor read us the verdict tonight that the right to manufacture the pill wouldn't be granted to anyone but the government until we can draw up terms on the bill we can agree are fair."

She wanted to hug Henry for helping shoot down a bill that could be dangerous in the wrong hands. The need to comfort Cordray welled up in her, but she tried to focus on the matter at-hand.

Ella met the king's eyes with a warning. "The people who put trackers in the Lupine and experimented on them are dangerous. Either they were certain you'd vote their way, or they didn't care if you did."

The king's hand stilled on Guadalupe, his gaze hardening as he considered the many implications of her statement. "You seem to have big opinions. I don't run my country on opinions, though."

"Good. Run them on facts. These three will submit to being tested so we can find out what they were injected with. They want your people to take their trackers out."

The king shook his head, his jaw tight. "You realize you're asking me to get involved in something the government has no grounds to stick its nose into? Putting trackers in the Lupine was voted down, but there's no punishment set in place for those who do."

"Then make one. You know this is wrong!" Ella noted the ruby signet ring on his finger and shook her head. "Look, I don't care if the government gets involved. I'm not asking the council. I'm asking you. I know you have a veterinary degree."

The king drew a long breath, held it in his lungs while he considered her petition, and then released it. "Alright. As a private citizen only, yes, I can help you."

Ella's eyes swept shut as gratitude welled up in her. How she wanted someone fair and measured as him to be her father-in-law. Relief washed through her, making her feel lighter. "Thank you. You have no idea how scared they are."

The king held up his hand. "In exchange for my help, you'll tell me more about how you came to hear them speak. I'm not willing to let my questions go unanswered."

Dread filled Ella's throat but she consented, nodding to the king. "If you can be discreet, then sure."

The king stood after scratching under Guadalupe's chin, noting with a small smile that she moved to stand next to him, positioning herself as his loyal pet. "Very well. Tonight is not the night for this, though. I trust you can keep them somewhere safe until... Let's say Wednesday? Remus, I can come to your house to examine them, if you wish."

Remus stuck his hand out to the king, beaming that their plan hadn't ended in an arrest. "That would be splendid. Now, if you don't mind, Ella's going to see to tightening up your security. She can see through handbags and pockets, and found quite a few concealed weapons out in the ballroom."

The king's eyebrows shot up. "What?"

Remus' hand on Ella's shoulder stabilized them both. "Happy to help," Ella said, her chin lowering. "And I know you've made your decision about me, but I'd still like to see him, if that's alright."

"Who?"

She started wringing her fingers, her nerves building, now that she had something she truly desired for herself at stake. "I didn't know about the photo. I'm not trying to swindle him, I swear. We were happy together. I only wanted to be good for him."

The king looked curiously to Remus, and then light dawned in his eyes. "Ah, you're the girl from the photos. I'm not sure why you think I should have a say in who Remus dates. It's none of my business." He smirked down at Guadalupe, who was standing at his side as if she was his loyal guard dog.

Ella went pale and began stammering, so Remus jumped in. "If I may, Royal Watch got it wrong."

The king waved his hand. "Remus, honestly. She's a little young for you, but why you would ever think I would stand in your way is beyond me. Go enjoy the ball."

Ella's nerves got the better of her, and her Hearing went out without her telling it to. Just beyond the courtroom doors, she Heard the one voice she'd been aching for.

Henry's tone was growing on desperate with a touch of irritability to it. "It's midnight, yeah? Then there aren't anymore women coming? That's all of them?"

"Yes, your majesty."

Ella Saw him turn away, and a desperate cry started in the balls of her feet and rose up in her throat, breaking the laws of physics as it ripped out of her. "Henry, wait!"

She ignored the others in the courtroom, Seeing his flinch at her Voice that seem to come from nowhere. She knew she couldn't be heard through the walls when the music from the ballroom was wafting into the corridor. It was her magic, sending her Voice out to surpass human limitations.

Henry's head whipped around. "Ella?"

"In the courtroom!"

Remus shook her back to the present. "What was that? Your eyes went completely white!"

"What? They did? Are they normal now?"

The king stepped back. "Remus, who is this woman?"

When Henry muscled his way past his guards and burst into the courtroom, he let out a cry of relief. "You came for me!"

Ella shook herself free from Remus and ran to Henry, throwing her arms around his neck. She held on tight while he lifted her toes off the floor and turned in a circle. "Of course I came. I'm sorry I'm so late. Lady Tremaine knocked me out with a crowbar and locked me in the closet."

"She'll be hanged for harming you. Tell me you're real. Tell me I didn't suffer through that parade of women who weren't you all for nothing. Tell me you're truly here, and that you're truly mine."

Ella waited until he set her feet back down on the polished marble floor. She cupped his face, taking in his handsome features coupled with the modest gold grown. "I was yours from the start, but you know it's not up to me. And really, it's not up to you." She turned to the king, who she realized was gaping at them. She buried her face in the home she'd made of Henry's chest. "I love you, Henry. Always and only you."

"I love you, and this night isn't ending until we're together." He gripped her hand, and the two trotted over to the king, standing before him like two teenagers asking for permission to borrow the fancy car.

The king stared at his son in confusion. "Henry?"

"The whole point of this night was for me to find someone to spend my life with. Well, I found her. Dad, this is Ella. This is the one I want to be with."

The king took two steps back and held up his finger. "No. No, no."

Ella's hope crumbled in her chest but she didn't release Henry's hand. Part of her couldn't let him go this time. They'd been apart for too long after having been through just plain too much. "Please, your majesty. Get to know me. I can be good for Henry." She scrambled for reasons to be accepted as an option for the king's son. "I have my own home, my own job, so I wouldn't be living off of Henry. I have a spotless record. Aside from bringing wolves into your palace, I've never done a thing to upset your rule."

Remus stood tall at her side. "See reason, your majesty. Ella would be a fantastic asset. Your son would never be safer. Ella can spot concealed weapons, which would keep Henry away from anything dangerous. She can hear whispered plots against the throne. She's already used her gifts to keep several councilmembers from harm."

Henry's hand tightened around Ella's. "I love her, Dad. It's Ella or no one."

The king's brows puckered in confusion as he stepped back, pointing at Ella with a look of concern. "You're not her." Then he pulled his phone from his pocket. "*This* woman. This is the one whose picture I had taken off of Royal Watch." He thumbed through his phone and pulled up a picture of Drizella licking Henry's ear through his angry expression, which could quite easily be misconstrued as a smolder. "You told me you were in love with a woman named Ella, and this came across my press secretary's feed. I assumed Ella was short for Drizella." He pointed at Ella again. "This? This is who you were talking about?"

Henry looked up at the ceiling and let out a cry of relief. "I didn't understand how you could possibly loathe her that much without even meeting her."

The king shook his head, wiping his hand over his face. "Oh, Son. I didn't have to meet Drizella to know she wasn't for you. I stand by my choice that the girl in the picture is not welcome in our family. There are so many nude photos of her on the internet, and most of them are her posing with a picture of you. It's enough to turn any father's stomach."

Henry's smile couldn't be contained as he bobbed on the balls of his feet like a boy on Christmas morning. "Drizella is Ella's stepsister. She's horrid. This is Ella, Dad. This is the woman I've been seeing in secret."

The king's hand flew over his chest, his eyes flicking between the two who were still joined at the hand. "Well done on the secret part. I had no idea. I didn't think secrets were possible in our position, so I guess she can be trusted not to blather our private life to the press."

"Of course, your majesty," Ella offered with a slight bow.

The king's eyes flicked to Remus, who held up his hands before the king could get his entire question out. "And you two aren't..."

Remus shook his head, grinning at the misunderstanding. "Ella's my student. The picture was taken entirely out of context."

Henry thumbed Ella's knuckles, his eyes pleading like

a desperate man. "Please, Dad. You have to see how happy I am with Ella, and how miserable life has been without her for the past couple weeks."

"You two split up?"

Henry shook his head in two jerky movements. "Only because she wouldn't be with me if you were determined not to give your blessing, which you told me you would never do when you thought she was Drizella."

The king let out a slow chuckle, covering his mouth. "I'm sorry, it's just... I honestly thought you were lovesick for this Drizella woman. I always hoped for you to be swept off your feet someday, but I never imagined it would be her. She's vile, and her mother is even worse." He waved his hand to excuse himself, and then inclined his head to Ella. "Forgive me. I shouldn't speak ill of your stepmother."

Ella was too stunned to do anything but gape at the king. "You don't disapprove, then?"

The king shook his head, a smile still toying with his lips. "Any woman who can come in and command me in my own throne room for such an unselfish cause has what it takes to stand next to you, Henry."

Elation welled up in Ella, and before she knew what she was doing, she flung her arms around the king's shoulders, hugging him as she choked back a sob of relief. "Thank you!"

The king fumbled, but finally encircled the woman in

his arms. "Will you be good to my son? Will you uphold all that is pure and true in Avondale?"

"Yes, your majesty. I promise."

He gave her a squeeze and then released her, gazing down on her with unconcealed affection. "Then you have my blessing." His eyes shifted to his son, posturing with importance. "You'll find a way to make it work with someone whose Pulse is so very controversial?"

"It'll work," Henry assured them both. "We'll make it work." Then he turned to the woman who always kept him waiting. "Please, Ella. Promise me we can make this work."

Ella looked up into the blue eyes that had charmed her from the start, knowing that no matter what, she wouldn't find love like his anywhere else. "Yes, Henry. If it won't push you and your father apart, then yes. We can be together."

Henry didn't wait for decorum or privacy. He gathered Ella in his arms and kissed her without permitting another moment to pass them by.

Her stomach fluttered and the unsettled bits of her heart finally slid into place, making her feel as if she belonged with the man of her many hopeful dreams. Her hands curved around the nape of his neck, playing with the strands of hair as if they had all the time in the world to toy with each other.

"Always and only you," Henry whispered, holding her

too tight to ever let her go. He'd lost her too many times to take chances.

Ella kissed his smile once more, melting them both with softness only they could bring out in each other. "Always and only you."

43

HAPPILY EVER AFTER

$\mathcal{H}$enry didn't wait a moment to announce that he was off the market. He brought a blushing Ella into the ballroom, dancing with his one and only choice in front of the entire guestlist, most of whom were appalled that the prince had chosen a girl brazen enough to wear jeans and a flannel to a royal ball.

Rory, Cordray, Remus, Adam and Belle were the few who watched with rapture as Henry and Ella shared their first public dance and their first on-camera kiss. In true Henry fashion, the prince could only restrain himself for so long. After one song, he dropped down onto one knee, pulling out his mother's ring that had been burning a hole in his pocket for two weeks. "Always and only me?" he begged, hope and adoration shining in his eyes.

Ella's vision clouded over with tears, but she made sure

to keep the sight of him before her clear as she nodded. "Yes, Henry. Always and only you."

"What? No!" Drizella screamed, and launched herself with venom toward Ella, furious at the scene. The music screeched to a stop. "Do you even know who she is? She's no one! She's our servant!"

With a click of Henry's fingers, Drizella was whisked away and put outside for the duration of the royal ball, which was quickly becoming Prince Henry's impromptu engagement party.

When Drizella let loose that Ella had been their servant, the jealous stares melted into looks of compassion. Softened eyes were painted with the whimsy of a bedtime story as they all witnessed the rapture in Prince Henry's gaze. That the prince had chosen a servant for his bride won over the hearts of many. It made his charm a thing that transcended harsh opinion, as was his way.

Lady Tremaine wasted no time at all pulling aside one of the reporters and letting loose all of Ella's secrets to the press, putting the spin on it that Ella was dangerous, since she could send out her Pulse. "She can hear government secrets, you know, with her being able to hear through walls. She's a danger to the throne, which is probably why the king is sanctioning this union. Best keep the enemy close, if you know what I mean."

It was Rory who raised her voice, her face pink with anger as she took the focus of the camera from Lady

Tremaine. "This woman is horrible! She gave her own daughter a black eye. She locked the soon-to-be-princess in a broom closet. Even on the day her daughter gets engaged, she can't say a kind word." Rory squared her shoulders to the camera. "Embrace your new princess as I have, as the king has."

Lady Tremaine would not be overshadowed, not even by the Chancellor's daughter. "As Remus Johnstone has? She's thrown herself at any number of powerful men. Why, she even tempted the Baron to try and get ahead. Unfortunately for her, the Baron only has eyes for me. So sad that she would stoop to seducing her stepmother's boyfriend. Can you imagine?" Lady Tremaine countered with a simpering smile. "That'll be all." Then she turned on her heel and snapped her fingers at Anastasia, who was still gaping at Ella with no words, only incoherent stammering.

Henry encouraged the string quartet to play, drowning out Lady Tremaine as she moved on to the next reporter, and the next, spreading her tales of controversy. He turned and cupped Ella's face, making sure to draw her eyes from the growing whispers. "This means nothing. There's only you and only me here tonight. Lady Tremaine isn't part of this moment."

Ella swallowed hard and finally nodded. "Always and only you," she promised.

When the double doors opened, it was the king

himself whose presence made the ballroom fall still with silence. Then everyone bowed in reverence to the crown. King Hubert stretched his hand out, not toward Ella, but with a menace to a person behind her. "Guards, arrest the Baron!"

With wide eyes and a wet nose, the Baron took a step back from the crowd, his arms raised in surrender. "Your majesty, I can't imagine what problem there might be."

"It took me all of five whole minutes to extract the tracker your company injected in the Lupine."

"Tracker?" The Baron's bony hand flew up over his heart as he scrambled to assemble a viable excuse. "Surely you can't think I would do such a thing. I've served the council faithfully for years. And even if I had, there's no law against it. They're merely animals." He snapped his fingers at the nearest accomplice. "Herchon, grab my things. I'll discuss this with you in private, your majesty, once you've calmed enough to see reason."

The king's arm raised, and the guards lining the walls closed in. They didn't require an explanation, only their king's command. "I would never approve of something so inhumane. How we treat the least of us proves our true character, and now I know the depths of yours. There may not be a law against it, but I will see that there is." He held up a tiny silver object for all to see. "The serial number matches tracking devices that were registered to your company. The Lupine were once our kinsmen but you've treated them like cattle. This crime rests on your head, and I'll make sure the work of your bloody hands is exposed for the entire kingdom to see."

When the Baron began to argue, Henry piped in with a booming voice that commanded everyone's attention. "The Baron tried to purchase my future bride for unseemly purposes. He put his hands on her, and her stepmother entertained the offer just to make a few bucks. If he can't be charged for his crimes against the Lupine, I'll see he's tried for molesting my future wife."

Henry's arm was tight around Ella, ensuring that she witnessed justice being played out for her.

The king stiffened, his nostrils flaring as he turned to Ella. "Is this true?"

She clung to Henry and nodded, cringing that her worst moments were being laid bare for the kingdom to dissect, but grateful for the vindication all the same. Cameras flashed, capturing her cheek buried in the meat of Henry's shoulder, and the fiercely protective look on the prince's face.

The king's voice boomed through the ballroom. "Take the Baron away! No woman in my kingdom will fear for her safety from a councilmember."

Not a minute later, the Baron was cuffed and led out of the ballroom, leaving Lady Tremaine with her mouth wide open as she was escorted out of the palace.

The ballroom was silent until Adam spoke up. "And I thought my parties were controversial. Well done, Henry."

Slowly, Henry's grip on Ella loosened, and a tired smile

soothed the worry that wrinkled the corners of his eyes. "You know how I love a good spectacle." Then he rubbed Ella's back, leaning his chin to her forehead so he could inhale the scent of her hair to center himself. "Are you alright, blue eyes?"

Ella cuddled into his warmth, which had always done its best to shield her from life's cold cruelties. "After tonight? Yes, Henry. I think I just might be."

THE SUBJECTS SLOWLY BEGAN TO RISE. MURMURS splintered out as the king broke his anger to greet his guests with polite handshakes and nods, keeping Guadalupe close at his heels. The music picked back up, and a few couples began dancing.

Rory rubbed her temples. "At what point do we pull the fire alarm so Henry and Ella can have a moment alone? This is far too much controversy in their first hour of being publicly together."

Cordray glanced at the two, who were holding each other, ignoring the questions the reporters shouted at them. "She looks too happy to be bothered by scandal. Smart girl."

Adam and Belle moved to stand beside them. "They look so sweet together," Belle mused with a wistful smile on her face.

Adam shook his head, narrowing his eyes. "Why can't

we get married yet? I swear, if Henry gets married before me..."

"We'll get married soon enough. I'm just glad I got to see it all. Look how much they love each other. It's like no one else in the world exists." When a few cameras turned to snap photos of Adam and Belle, she buried her face into his sternum, hiding in the shelter his body provided.

Adam smirked at her shyness and tucked his finger under her chin, drawing up her face so he could brush a light kiss to her lips, giving them yet another picture-perfect pose. "Can't let Henry upstage us."

Belle squeezed Adam's side, relishing in his slight squirm at her tickle.

Rory watched her two best friends fawn over the women who'd captured their hearts. "You and Henry are such saps now. I love it."

Ella and Henry gazed at each other, reveling in the freedom that came with some serious limitations. Every moment would be photographed and scrutinized. Each brush of their hands would be gossiped about. Still, even in the throng of party-goers, Ella and Henry saw only each other.

"Tell me a story, Henry," she said quietly, her arms looping over his shoulders so she could tease the hair at the nape of his neck.

Henry led them in a slow sway to the violins that encouraged romance and happily-ever-afters. His lips brushed against her ear, sending the thrill of a shiver through her body. "Once upon a time..."

The End.
Love the book?
Leave a review.

44

UGLY GIRL

Enjoy a free preview of *Ugly Girl*, book one in a 14-part fantasy romance series with creatures based in French folklore.

JUDAH'S LAUGH WAS MUSIC TO MY EARS AS HE HIGH-FIVED me, our pool sticks clanking together. "That was an awesome shot. We should've bet more," he said, eyeing the pile of twenties on the ledge that were weighted by a cube of chalk.

The atmosphere in the noisy bar was just starting to hit its sweet spot, with the blaring music enticing the college crowd to remember everything that was good about being young and away from home. We frequently came here after I finished a soccer game, yet somehow there were always a couple guys drunk enough to challenge us, even though we were undefeated at pool.

"Is it mean to take their money like this?" I asked, tilting my head at my best friend's dark curly hair that was slightly sticking up in the back. Neither of us looked in the mirror all that often, but relied on each other to either comb out the quirks, or decide if they should be left to add to our slightly off-center personalities.

Judah guffawed. "Don't you dare start with that pesky conscience tonight, Rosie Avalon. They were sober-ish when we started playing." Judah scrutinized the pool table, and I could practically feel him bisecting right angles and saying nonsense words like "hypotenuse" in his head. Gotta love him. He took his shot and sank the ball, beaming that we were still on top of our game of round robin. We laughed as we did our obnoxious Cabbage Patch dance, the brown curls of my ponytail swishing in time with my pool stick. The guys on my soccer team chuckled at our usual antics, but a few people on the fringes gave us weird looks.

Me. They gave *me* weird looks. Not that I could blame them. I had scoliosis, which resulted in a pretty sizeable hump on my back. Pair that with my lazy left eye, and I was ripe for receiving at least one grimace a day. One of my stellar nicknames in high school had been Baby Got Too Much Back. The other one was Crater Face, due to the painful acne that never went away. Judah was my other half because he'd never once looked at me like I was the ugly girl, and I'd never teased him about being super into Star Trek, spending his entire life at the top of the curve, or being Jewish. (I mean, come on, people. It's the twenty-first century already. You'd think the anti-Semitic comments would've died out before we were born, but there were always a few jaggoffs whose mission in life was to derail the evolution of the species.) I'd learned to accept the girl in the mirror and not hold back my personality. Just because I wasn't a blonde cheerleader didn't mean I was about to sit on the sidelines and sulk my whole life.

I was the starting striker for the Blue Hornets. The cheerleaders could have the blondes, for all I cared. I'd found my people long ago, and they didn't need me to be prom queen. Their main concern was if I could score, which I had no trouble proving game after game.

"Don't feel like foreplay tonight?" I asked, taking in our opponents' frowns of frustration. Our competition was droopy-eyed from their newly minted legal drinking-aged licenses, and not amused at our dance.

Judah tapped his watch, which also served as his day planner. "You've got to study for finals still."

I felt eyes on me, but I tried to ignore it. I pretended I didn't mind being talked about. It was the pointing that did me in. I rolled my hunched shoulders back as best I could, but no matter how straight I stood, I was still a little stooped. I did my best to push out the world and focus on the game. "Double or nothing if I make this shot blind." Maybe I was showing off just a little. I was in a great mood after the shutout, flying high off the adrenaline that kissed my forehead on the soccer field.

One of our challengers who was four beers into his night leaned against the table. "Not a chance. I've seen you pull that trick before. I still don't know how you do it."

"Magic," I teased, wiggling my fingers as I lined up my shot. I paused to play with the locket on the thin gold chain around my neck. When my Aunt Lane had given it to me, she'd warned me to never take it off – it was my good luck charm. My luck tended to run freezing and scalding, but I placated her all the same.

Judah and I put them out of their misery quickly, since Judah was annoyingly right, and I did have to get home to cram for finals. It wasn't truly over until we finished off the chorus of Queen's "We are the Champions", which we nailed because we sang it at least once a week in this very bar after just such a victory. Our pool winnings kept our grocery budget firmly at a notch above ramen noodles, so we came here as often as we could.

I tried not to pay much attention to our goalkeeper, Kyle, who was arguing with his girlfriend, but they were hard to ignore. It was an hour after a victory, so their fight was right on schedule. Last time their clash was over him kissing her too hard, and smearing her Barbie pink lipstick. That had been one long night.

"I saw you looking at that skank!" Melanie's voice was shrill, which was the only tone I'd ever heard on the girl. I idly wondered what it would sound like if she ever whispered.

Kyle's indignation was so faked, *I* didn't even buy it. "Who? Women come to our games sometimes, Mel. They're half the population. I wasn't looking at anyone in particular. Just playing the game."

"Three times you laughed at a joke that girl told after the match. You think I didn't see it?"

Kyle scrunched his nose. "Who, Rosie? She's my teammate. Jeez." I was the only girl on the soccer team.

Melanie huffed, her arms akimbo. "I don't care if you joke with the ugly girl. It's the one in the halter top who you couldn't stop grinning at that I have a problem with."

My movements stilled as I leaned on my pool stick. Judah hadn't heard, because he was still being an obnoxious winner, dancing as he counted our take. It was just me who could stand in my defense, only I never wanted to in these situations. Melanie was right. I'd gone through many painful chiropractic treatments to try and straighten my hump, but scoliosis wasn't one of those things that went away with a simple crack of a spine. No matter how many times I went to the dermatologist, a heavy smattering of acne covered my cheeks, chin and forehead. I knew no guy ever looked my way, and over the years, I'd become okay with it. It helped me find out who my true friends were, and who not to waste my time around. Still, Melanie's words punched me in the gut. I wanted to believe the best in humanity, but sometimes it was a struggle.

Kyle's genuine displeasure at Melanie's slam made me stand a little taller, though he didn't say, "No, Rosie's not ugly," but rather, "Hey, she's my friend, and you need to cool it with that kinda talk."

I swallowed down the bad spot on an otherwise awesome night, working up a grin for Judah, who'd finally come down from his gloating. "You ready to go, Ro?" Judah asked, tucking our winnings into his pocket.

I put on my best fake smile and pounded my fist in the air. "I'm super way pumped to study!"

The crowd was thickening, hitting the point in the night where, if you hadn't already secured a chair, you were nursing your beer standing up for the rest of the evening. I held onto Judah's hand so we didn't get separated as we weaved through the college students who'd come to celebrate the end (or near end) of the semester.

I was starting to feel claustrophobic right as someone bumped into me from behind, knocking my hand out of Judah's. The bulky body bumped me forward into a woman, who turned to scowl, and then reared back with the infamous grimace when she saw what I looked like.

I held up my hands like claws and hissed, as if I was a hag who was about to put a hex on her, cursing her into decades of unending slumber. If I was going to be gawked at like I was hideous, I wanted to really earn the part.

Judah snorted a laugh at the girl's horrified expression.

He gripped my hand tighter so we didn't get separated as we slipped through the crowd, finally making our way out onto the cracked sidewalk. The neon from the bar's sign lit Judah's smile just enough for his levity to migrate to me. "Did you see her face? I thought she was going to pee herself. I love when you do that. And if I didn't say so in there, good game."

I bowed under the streetlight to my adoring fan, grinning as I righted myself. The smell of exhaust and semi-fresh air was a welcome reprieve from the peanut shells and bottom-shelf beer I'd been breathing in all night.

Judah did a doubletake, his brows furrowing in confusion as if I was wearing a weird hat or something. He took three steps back, and then two forward to squint at me, pushing his Buddy Holly glasses further up on his nose. "Rosie, your face! Did you... Are you wearing makeup or something?"

My nose crinkled. "Huh? Why would you even ask me that? I don't even own any makeup. You know that."

For the first time in his life, Judah pointed at my face in distaste. "Your acne is gone. Like, you were normal just a minute ago, but now your skin is all... I dunno. You don't look like you."

"Who do I look like, then?" I challenged, hurt that he would point at me like the circus freak I often felt like.

"You look like your Aunt Lane! I mean, the similarities were always there, but now..."

My hand went to my throat to play with my necklace. I

often did that when I wanted to soothe myself after being looked at like I wasn't pretty in a world where things like pretty mattered a little too much. My fingers touched the naked skin of my neck above my blue jersey, fumbling around for the chain that should've been there, but suddenly wasn't.

As if trying to pat down a fire, I felt all over my collar and my shirt, a panic rising up in me at losing the one precious thing I owned. "Oh, no! Judah, where is it? My necklace is gone!" I blinked rapidly as my left eye started to twitch while I searched around me for the sentimental treasure.

Judah frowned and turned on his phone to use as a flashlight, searching the concrete from where we stood all the way back to the bar. "I'm not seeing it. You sure you didn't take it off?"

I threw my hands in the air after shaking out my shirt and still coming up empty. "In all the years you've known me, have you ever seen me without that necklace? I never take it off! Lane made me promise to keep it on forever. Oh, she's going to flip." My vision started to swim, making the cars passing by look blurry, and then unnervingly detailed, disorienting me enough to take a step back. Rapid blinking made things clearer, but still didn't reveal my necklace anywhere in sight.

"I can't picture Lane getting pissed that you lost something. I can't picture her mad at you, period. It's an honest mistake, Ro. We'll come back in the morning and check the lost and found. It's probably on the floor in there. Chain was bound to break one of these days."

I groaned at the thought of people squashing the locket that had belonged to my long-deceased mother. My aunt had taken the locket from my mother's meager belongings and passed it down to me. "It's the only thing of my mother's that I have! Judah, we have to find it."

"Alright, alright. Don't worry. I'll help you."

My left eye started to itch as if there were phantom spiders running all over it, so I ran my index finger across my eyelid. I grimaced when I felt heat radiating out in a circle around that whole section of my face. I started blinking rapidly to clear away the foreign sensation, willing myself not to lose my cool and smack myself in the head to make the tingling stop.

When my gaze fell on Judah after my vision finally focused, he jumped back in horror. "Gah! What's wrong with your eye?"

It was the hurt that had never come from him until this moment. All the other kids in school had blanched at my lazy left eye, but Judah never cared that I looked different. Now he was acting like the woman who'd cringed in the bar when she'd gotten a good look at me. To have him comment on my wonky eye in the same minute he was acting all horrified by the rest of my face was a double whammy that made me take a step back. Anger welled up inside of me and spewed itself all over my best friend. "Are you just now noticing that I look like this? What's your deal, Judah?"

He seemed to remember himself and cleared the gap between us, hands raised. "I don't mean it like that. Your skin is totally as clear as a baby's, and your eyes are pointing in the same direction! It's freaking me out! How are you doing that?"

I felt my face and, sure enough, my skin was devoid of pockmarks. There wasn't even any of the scarring I'd acquired from acne gone rogue throughout the years. "Wha... Are you serious?" My optometrist swore up and down that my vision hadn't been affected by my lazy eye, but I began to notice that even though it was nighttime, I was able to see a little clearer – the edges of everything were a bit crisper. "Judah?" My voice came out in a pinched bleat of panic.

"I'm sure there's a totally logical explanation. Maybe it's a trick of the moonlight?" he suggested, though I could tell he didn't believe his conjecture.

I shook my head, feeling all turned around and borderline emotional. "A lazy eye doesn't just fix itself in a blink!"

"Okay, let's go home where there's actual light. Then we can see what we're dealing with. Maybe I'm wrong."

"Are you ever wrong?" I asked, incredulous.

"No," Judah replied apologetically. It was true. Judah was always at the top of the curve in school, but was blessed with the grace not to lord it over the dummies like me who were barely hanging on. His shoulders deflated when he took in the effect his unfiltered words had on me. "Come here. I freaked you out with my pointing. I wasn't thinking. I'm sorry."

Judah held out his arms, and I didn't hesitate to crash into them, resting my trepidation on his shoulder in hopes it would evaporate there. "Don't point at me like that anymore," I said quietly, letting him know that he was my safe place, and taking that away would be a devastation I wouldn't recover from. "Everyone else can, but you? You're my..." I fished around for the right word, but landed on shtick. "You're my pimp daddy."

Judah snorted into my hair. "You're totally right. I'm sorry, hot mama. Are you okay?"

"I lost my necklace, so no. Everything else can take a backseat to that. My acne is really gone? I saw myself in the mirror after the soccer match, and I was still me."

"Not a trace of it, Ro. And your left eye is pointing straight now. It wasn't that way when we were playing pool in there just a few minutes ago."

I was about to crack a lame joke to ease the seriousness, but a sudden ache in my back forced me to roll my shoulders through our hug. A gust of air thrust out of me when it felt like something suddenly shoved me from inside my spine. The push held enough of a punch to catch me off-guard, changing the most basic things about my appearance, and freaking me out when I was already on the brink. "Oof!"

Judah scrambled to hold onto me as my legs gave out. I whimpered pathetically when my back decided to be a total wuss and start spasming. "Hey, what's wrong? What's happening?"

"My back hurts! Oh, man! Super way painful. Give me a second." I tried to stand on my own, but my spine was in full-on contortion mode. Judah held me, despite my protest and my torso bending away as it tried to center itself.

A terrifying crack sounded, rippling down my spine. Judah and I cried out in alarm as one voice, but he held me until I was finally able to find my footing. I slowly stood with a bit more stability, rolling a kink from my shoulders.

Judah hopped back with alarm clear on his face. He lifted his finger to point, but remembered himself and lowered it. Instead I followed his eyeline and patted my shoulders in fear.

The noise from the college kids passing by blurred into the background when my fingers reached over my shoulder and landed on... nothing. I pulled in a deeper breath than I'd ever managed before, my lungs expanding with extra room that came from standing up straight.

Only I'd never stood up straight before.

"My hump," I whispered, amazed and terrified. My mouth fell open when I realized that I was seeing the world from a vantage point of about two inches higher than usual, due to not being stooped anymore.

Judah shook his head, his hand over his mouth. "Rosie, your hump is gone!" He looked like he was about to say something else, but the newfound air that dragged inside of me was pushed out in a forceful gust.

Something heavy pulled at my chest, making the whole area feel bruised and unsteady. Discomfort mutated to pain as I moved my arms over my chest. I'd always had a flat chest, with no breasts to brag about. That, I'd been grateful for, though. Having immobile A-cups meant you could run faster on the field without being bogged down by weighty body parts.

My mouth fell open as dread colored my cheeks. Beneath my banded arms, I could feel my chest growing at an alarming rate. The whole area ached so bad I had to bite down on my lower lip to keep from screaming. Inches and inches expanded faster than I could conceal them, my skin stretching grotesquely as the elasticity of my sports bra was tested to its limits.

And then both straps snapped.

Never in all of our years as friends who'd seen each other through puberty had Judah ever glanced at my chest. He gawked like a teenager with no thought of social propriety as I scrambled to hide my spontaneous breasts. "Did those just... Are your..." He couldn't say the word "boobs" to me, which was good, because I might've imploded on the spot from mortification if he did.

"I'm going to go look for my necklace!" I shouted, horrified and utterly drenched in confusion. I worked the tattered remains of my bra over my hips and discarded the sad fabric in the nearest garbage can, flummoxed and a little terrified that I was morphing into something... not me.

I didn't wait for him, but barreled back into the bar, holding my bosom in place with my arms crossed. Goose-bumps were covering my arms, and tears of angst threat-ened to spill out of me. My shoulders and my chest felt like someone had taken a baseball bat to them, but the terror at the suddenness of it all hurt far worse. I pulled out some cash in my haste to find my necklace, and slapped it on the bar top. I rarely drank more than a beer or two, but my back ached, and my chest felt like the skin might tear at any moment. Frankly, I was surprised it hadn't. I slammed the shot in hopes it would be my pain reliever.

I'd never cried in a bar before, and was firm that tonight wouldn't break that trend. I didn't know what was going on with my body, so I decided I would deal with all of that later when I had a mirror and, I dunno, a sedative or something. My nerves were on the brink of a total breakdown.

My necklace. I have to find it and get out of here.

I renewed my focus, determined that I wasn't leaving until I had the locket around my neck once more. I was great at finding things. I was always the kid who had the most Easter eggs in my basket. I'd never lost my car keys. Not once. I was a human GPS who could find true North blindfolded. I followed my gut, and it led me to whatever I needed to find. It was how I landed so many flawless shots. My gut told my pool stick where to aim, and I never had a problem. I inhaled the stench of beer that stank like it had been soaked into the walls, warning my gut that it was go time. Judah came in a few minutes later, shaken but ready to be helpful in my quest to find my locket and get the crap out of there.

Three hours later, the bar was closing and we were being pushed out on to the street with a promise that the owner would call if they found anything.

Judah didn't say a word, but kept his arm around me as we walked, my eyes on my shoes and my hands blackened from running them over every inch of that disgusting, sticky floor. I had one family heirloom. One. My Aunt Lane salvaged one thing off my mother's body before it had been cremated. The locket was gone now, and though I had no memory of my mother, the fragile connection I had to my roots was gone with it.

Read *Ugly Girl* today!